Harry Dolan graduated from Colgat
philosophy and studied fiction-writin
He earned a master's degree in philos
Carolina at Chapel Hill and worked fo as a freelance editor.

Dolan, who grew up in Rome, New York, now lives in Ann Arbor, Michigan, with his partner, Linda Randolph. He is the author of *Bad Things Happen*.

Praise for Harry Dolan:

'A riveting crime novel . . . Relentless pacing, a wry sense of humor, and an engaging protagonist add up to another winner for Dolan'
Publishers Weekly

'Dolan mixes his pitches with an ace's judgment...The rare crime novel with something for everyone who reads crime fiction'
Kirkus

'A wonderfully moody and atmospheric story reminiscent of the masters of the noir mysteries. Tightly plotted, sophisticated, and engrossing, this is a winner'
Nelson DeMille

'You better believe he has a gift for storytelling . . . the narrative comes with startling developments and nicely tricky reversals. There's also something appealingly offbeat about the wry, dry tone of its humour . . .'
New York Times Book Review

'If I say that the novel is as well plotted as Agatha Christie at her best, I don't mean to make it sound old-fashioned; it's not. Even more than Christie, this novel reminded me of Patricia Highsmith. There's some lovely writi endless
fun – a nove od crime
fi

Also by Harry Dolan

Bad Things Happen

VERY BAD MEN

HARRY DOLAN

EBURY PRESS

3 5 7 9 10 8 6 4 2

Published in 2012 by Ebury Press, an imprint of Ebury Publishing
A Random House Group Company

First published in 2011 in the US by Amy Einhorn Books,
an imprint of G.P. Putnam's Sons, Penguin Group (USA) Inc.

The Random House Group Limited Reg. No. 954009

Addresses for companies within the Random House Group can be found at:
www.randomhouse.co.uk

A CIP catalogue record for this book is available from the British Library

The Random House Group Limited supports The Forest Stewardship Council
(FSC®), the leading international forest certification organisation. Our books
carrying the FSC label are printed on FSC® certified paper. FSC is the only forest
certification scheme endorsed by the leading environmental organisations,
including Greenpeace. Our paper procurement policy can be found at:
www.randomhouse.co.uk/environment

Printed and bound by CPI Group (UK) Ltd, Croydon, CR0 4YY

ISBN 9780091933128

To buy books by your favourite authors and register for offers visit
www.randomhouse.co.uk

To my mother and father

There's a necklace in my office, a string of glass beads. It hangs over the arm of my desk lamp, and any little movement can set it swaying. The beads are a middle shade of blue, the color of an evening sky, and when the light plays over them they look cool and bright and alive.

I'll tell you where they came from. Elizabeth was wearing them the first time we kissed. It happened here in the office on a winter night, six stories up over Main Street in Ann Arbor. Elizabeth is a detective, and that night she'd been called out to the scene of a car accident: crushed metal and broken glass, and other crushed and broken things. Three fatalities, one of them a child. The kind of accident you don't want to see, the kind you hope you can forget.

She saw it, and afterward she wanted to get as far away from it as she could. She came to me. I was working late and I heard the hallway door open, heard her footsteps cross the emptiness of the outer office, and then she was standing in my doorway. She's tall, and the long overcoat she wore only emphasized her height. The coat had snowflakes melting on the shoulders. It was open, and the blouse she had on underneath was unbuttoned at the neck. The fingers of her right hand worried over the blue beads at her throat. That was her only movement; the rest of her stood still.

I knew her well enough to know something was wrong. Her face was pale, and her hair—black and shiny as a raven's wing—fell loose around it. I got up from my desk and went to her, and her stillness as I approached made me leery of touching her. I started to lay a palm on her shoulder, then drew it back.

Snow fell lazily outside my office window. We stood together for a long while, and I didn't ask her anything. I waited for her to tell me, and she did. She told me all of it, everything she had seen. The words poured out of her in a relentless stream. Her fingers on the glass beads counted off each terrible detail.

When she was done, she turned her face away from me. Shyly. Almost awkwardly. And awkwardly I stepped back and, not knowing what else to do, offered to pour her a drink from the bottle of Scotch I keep in the deep drawer of the desk.

She didn't want a drink.

I watched her shed her overcoat and fold it over the back of a chair. Watched her close the distance between us, her eyes steady on mine. She kept them open when she kissed me; they were the same blue as the glass beads. The first kiss was slow and lingering and deliberate. We both knew what it was: an act of defiance. It's human nature. We look on death and we rebel; we want to prove to ourselves that we're alive.

These thoughts passed through my mind, but I didn't have time to dwell on them. The second kiss was harder and more eager. I felt her hands move over my shoulders to the back of my neck, felt her fingers twist into my hair. She pressed herself against me and we held on to each other, and I could feel the heat of her, the vitality, the coiled energy of her body.

THERE'S A LIMIT to how much of this memory I intend to share, and I think we've reached it. The rest is hers and mine and no one else's. But that's where the necklace came from, the one I keep in my office. Elizabeth left it behind that night.

I'm telling you this for a reason. It has to do with motives.

If you took that necklace to a jeweler, he'd say it wasn't worth anything. The beads are only glass, and they're held together by a string. And on some level I know that's true.

But I also know that if a thief tried to take those beads away from me, I'd do everything in my power to stop him. I wouldn't hesitate to kill him, if that's what it took.

THIS STORY I have to tell—it's not about a necklace. But it is about the motives people have for killing one another. That's a subject I know something about, not least because I'm an editor and people send me stories about killers all the time. My name is David Loogan. Most of the manuscripts that come to me are awful, but some of them have promise. I find the best ones and polish them up and publish them in a mystery magazine called *Gray Streets.*

Maybe it's not surprising, then, that my part in this story begins with a manuscript.

The facts are simple enough. I found it on a Wednesday evening in mid-July, in the hallway outside my office. That's not unusual. Local authors leave manuscripts out there more often than you'd think.

This one was different, though. It came in a plain, unmarked envelope and amounted to fewer than ten pages. It was the story of three murders, two already committed, one yet to come. And it wasn't fiction.

There was no signature or byline. The man who wrote the story didn't want to give himself away. He had typed it on a computer and printed it out in a copy shop. Of course, I didn't know that at the time. Elizabeth discovered it later.

When I turned the manuscript over to her, I had an outside hope that it might yield some useful piece of physical evidence. Crime labs can do wonders now with hairs and fibers, with DNA. I thought there might be fingerprints on the pages, other than my own. But when she sent the manuscript to the lab, it was a dead end. It rendered up no secrets—nothing to tell her who wrote it or what his motives were.

If you want to know the answers to those questions, we'll have to go back. Back before that day in mid-July. We'll have to put aside the usual rules, because this is a story that doesn't want to follow them. It has its own ideas. Although it's mine, and Elizabeth's too, it doesn't really begin with us. It begins in northern Michigan, in the city of Sault Sainte Marie. It begins in a hotel room.

It begins with a notebook.

CHAPTER 1

The notebook is a simple thing, but elegant. Lined pages bound with thread between soft black covers. Small enough to fit in a pocket. Vincent van Gogh made sketches in a notebook like this. Ernest Hemingway jotted lines of terse dialogue in Parisian cafés.

Anthony Lark uses his to make a list.

Three names, in rich black ink. *Henry Kormoran. Sutton Bell. Terry Dawtrey.* The letters flow gracefully. The pen is a Waterman, an heirloom from Lark's father.

Kormoran and Bell should be relatively easy. Both of them live in Ann Arbor—Kormoran in an apartment, Bell in a modest house with a wife and daughter. The wife and daughter complicate things, but on the whole Lark is unconcerned. He can manage Kormoran and Bell.

Dawtrey is another story. He's serving a thirty-year sentence at Kinross Prison, twenty miles south of Sault Sainte Marie.

LARK LEFT his notebook on the hotel bed and padded barefoot to the ice machine down the hall. He caught ice chips in a plastic bag, just a handful, enough to soothe his brow. The headaches had been coming more frequently.

He had been fine this afternoon when he drove past the gates of Kinross Prison. He didn't know what he expected to see, maybe something like a fortress. Tall buildings of stone. Ramparts and buttresses. Lofty walls with turrets for the guards.

The reality was less impressive. There were a few broad buildings of homely tan brick. The sun cast the shadows of the guardtowers across the yard. Two high chain-link fences, topped with razor wire, surrounded everything.

Lark had been raised in a working-class neighborhood in Dearborn, on the outskirts of Detroit. Take away the towers and the fences, and he might have been looking at his old high school.

Still, the fences and towers would be enough to keep him from Terry Dawtrey. In theory, he could make a go of it, if a dozen things went his way. He could acquire a high-powered rifle. He could find some cover in the flat, featureless land that surrounded the prison. Dawtrey could walk out to the front gate with a target painted on his chest.

Lark pondered the problem in his hotel room, lying against the pillows with the ice pressed to his forehead. There was another alternative. He could find some pretext for a visit to Dawtrey. He could walk through the gate, submit to a search. They would lead him to a room with bland cinder-block walls. A common room with lots of tables, full of convicts' wives and their restless children. He would sit at a table across from Dawtrey. There would be no glass between them, not like in the movies. He would have no weapon, but he would only need something sharp—a stem broken off from a pair of eyeglasses. It could be done.

But there would be no going out again past the guards. It would be a one-way trip.

A hard problem. He needed to consider it some more. He pressed the power button on the television remote and flipped through the channels. Cop shows, infomercials, cable news. He wasn't really looking for the woman, but he found her on CNN. Sometimes it happened that way. She was at a podium with a crowd around her. Young people holding up signs. She had as much of a tan as you could get, living in the state of Michigan. She had hair like black silk and wore it in a short, stylish cut.

He had the sound muted, so he didn't hear what she was saying, but it hardly mattered. She smiled, and the people applauded and waved their signs. The smile was wondrous. Without it, she could seem stern, aloof.

With it, she was joyous and mischievous at the same time. He remembered something he'd heard once: That smile alone should be worth ten points at the polls.

Watching her helped. The ice helped too. It cooled the ache behind his brow. He was tempted to check out in the morning and drive south to Ann Arbor. That was what most people would do. Take the easier way. Deal with Kormoran and Bell. Save Dawtrey for last. Put off confronting the problem. But that's not the way he was raised.

Always do the hardest thing first, his father used to say.

THE NEXT NIGHT, Anthony Lark found himself in a town called Brimley on the shore of Whitefish Bay, sixteen miles southwest of Sault Sainte Marie. He ate dinner at the Cozy Inn, a restaurant that catered to tourists. He sat at a table in a corner and kept his eyes on an old man who had settled in on a stool at the bar.

Lark knew there were Chippewa Indians in Brimley. They ran the Bay Mills Casino, the area's main attraction. The old man at the bar looked like he had Chippewa blood. He had a weathered face marked with deep vertical lines, the kind of face you might find carved into the side of a cliff. He had a compact frame and limbs that might once have been sturdy and thick—before time diminished them.

Lark knew the man's name. He had found it in the Brimley telephone directory. He had written it in his notebook with his Waterman pen.

The man lived in a cabin not far from the shore of Lake Superior. A wooden shanty, really, one of a score of cabins scattered in the woods, with a warren of unpaved lanes running between them. It would be a pleasant place to live now, in the summer, in the dense shade of old birch trees. In the winter, Lark thought, it would be hell.

He had spent an hour in the cabin around midday; he had found a key under a wooden bucket on the porch. The old man had been away at work. A drawer full of pay stubs told the tale: he had a job at the casino, probably on the cleaning crew. His wages were pitiful.

The cabin had a cramped living room, a small kitchen, a smaller bath. No bedroom, just a fold-out sofa bed. A bare minimum of possessions. The medicine cabinet over the bathroom sink held a straight razor, a toothbrush, toothpaste. The furnishings of the living room included a TV set with rabbit ears and a wall calendar illustrated with watercolor sparrows. Lark leafed through the pages. Someone had written the letter "T" on every other Saturday.

A framed photograph hung next to the calendar: a school picture of a boy fourteen or fifteen years old.

A ringing telephone startled Lark as he studied the photo. He followed the sound to the kitchen, where a battered beige phone sat on the counter beside a primitive-looking answering machine. The tape in the machine began to turn, the old man's outgoing message. Then a beep and a woman's voice, rough with cigarette smoke.

"Charlie, are you there?" she said. A pause. "Maybe I'll see you at the Cozy later."

When the old man got home from work, Lark was sitting in his Chevy a little distance down the lane. He watched the man step down from the cab of a pickup and trudge to the cabin door. He might have done it then, might have simply followed the man inside, but it seemed too abrupt somehow. And it was still daylight. Better to do it after dark.

Lark drove to the Cozy Inn and had a leisurely dinner—fish caught from the bay, french fries, coleslaw. He had brought a newspaper with him from Sault Sainte Marie, and after the waitress cleared his plate away he started reading the front page. She brought him the bill and he gave her a sizable tip and after that she left him alone.

The old man came in at eight and took up his position at the bar. He drank shots of Irish whiskey and mugs of beer. By ten o'clock most of the tourists had left and the locals began to fill the place with raucous voices and laughter. At eleven a woman came in wearing a leather skirt and a knitted blouse. Hair dyed black. Fifty-five years old, Lark thought, hoping to pass for forty.

"There you are, Charlie," she said to the old man.

"Madelyn, you vixen," he said, patting the stool beside him.

As Lark watched them from the corner—Madelyn producing a cigarette from a beaded purse, Charlie lighting it with a Zippo—he wished that he were done. He should have taken care of things at the cabin. He felt a headache coming on and took a pill (*Imitrex*) from a small tin that once held breath mints. He didn't expect the pill to work. He could feel the pain creeping into the space behind his eyes, curling and twisting like the smoke of Madelyn's cigarette.

A voice in his mind said, *The headaches are a symptom.* His doctor's voice. It was something his doctor had told him again and again.

The trouble started near midnight. Lark had a beer in front of him that he'd been nursing for an hour. He watched a crowd of young people heading for the exit. Clean-cut, well-dressed—dealers from the casino, if he had to guess. The last of them held the door for a brawny man heading in.

That one's not a dealer, Lark thought. *A laborer or a fisherman maybe.*

Madelyn knew him. She got up and met him halfway across the room.

"Kyle, my love," she said carelessly.

He was a younger man, maybe forty—the age she was pretending to be. He wore denim work clothes and heavy canvas boots. She led him to the bar, ordered him a drink. She chattered away at him, her hands brushing his collar or resting on his arm. She had the nervous energy of a woman caught where she shouldn't be.

The old man, Charlie, sat forgotten beside her, his face souring as the minutes passed. The other patrons at the bar seemed to lean away from the three of them, as if they sensed what was going to happen.

Lark watched it from his corner table. Charlie putting a hand on the back of Madelyn's neck. A proprietary gesture. Madelyn turning to shoot him a look. Kyle, hunched over his glass, doing his best to ignore what was happening, until he couldn't ignore it any longer.

Kyle got to his feet, and Charlie followed. Madelyn made a halfhearted effort to get between them, but Kyle pushed her gently aside.

Lark knew that the quickest way to win a fight was to break the other guy's nose. A broken nose puts a man down, takes all the struggle out of him.

Charlie knew it too. He made a fist of his right hand and jabbed at the bigger man's face.

Kyle saw it coming and ducked down to catch the punch on his forehead.

The bones of the hand are delicate, the bones of the skull less so. Charlie drew his fist back with a cry. Kyle shook his head to clear it, then stepped forward casually and scuffed a work boot over the wooden floorboards, sweeping the old man's legs out from under him. Charlie landed on his backside and on his wounded hand, howling and curling up on the floor.

Kyle reached behind him for his glass, drained it, and headed for the door, beckoning for Madelyn to follow. She glared at him and growled, "Damn it, Kyle," but she went with him after only the briefest of glances at the old man.

Lark left the bar a few minutes later. By then some of the locals had helped Charlie up onto his stool and wrapped a handkerchief around his knuckles and set him up with another beer.

DARK UNDER THE BIRCH TREES. Lark found the cabin again, drove past it, and parked at the side of the lane. He cut the Chevy's engine and waited. A tire iron lay on the seat beside him.

Charlie's pickup truck appeared at one in the morning, rolling to a stop on the lawn. The old man stumbled up the stone-paved walk and went inside. Lark got out of his car with the tire iron, crossed to the porch, and retrieved the key from underneath the wooden bucket.

The door squeaked on its hinges when he opened it, but not enough to catch the old man's attention. In fact, when Lark stepped into the cabin, the old man was nowhere to be seen. A table lamp cast its glow over the sofa and the television. Over a pair of worn shoes abandoned on the carpet.

Lark saw the lamp reflected in the dark glass of the window behind the sofa and quickly crossed the room to draw the curtains. As he stood by the window he heard the rush of water running, and without thinking he vaulted the sofa and pressed himself against the wall beside the bathroom door.

With the tire iron raised in his right hand, he waited for the door to open. A minute passed, then two. From his earlier visit he knew that the window in the bathroom was a frosted square too small for a man to climb through. Charlie must be waiting on the other side of the door.

Lark said, "You may as well come out. How did you know I was here?"

A brief delay, and then the old man's voice came through. "You stomp around like an elephant. Who are you? A friend of Scudder's?"

"I don't know who that is."

"Kyle Scudder. You're one of his pals?"

"No, but I saw what he did to you at the bar. You should have your hand looked at. I can help you."

"Are you a doctor?"

"I know some first aid."

"I don't need your help. You clear out, before I call the cops."

"The phone's out here."

"I've got a cell."

Lark looked around at the ragged sofa, the threadbare carpet, the worn-out shoes.

"I don't think so," he said.

He could hear faint sounds through the door. The old man's breathing. The medicine cabinet being opened, then softly closed.

"All right, I'm coming out."

Lark lowered the tire iron and stepped in front of the door, pivoting so that his right shoulder faced it. He braced his feet, waited for the knob to turn, and hit the door with everything he had.

CHAPTER 2

The razor won't do you any good," Lark said.

"Fuck you."

The old man sat on the floor where he had fallen, his back against the vanity of the sink, the straight razor from the medicine cabinet clutched in his left hand. His right hand, still wrapped in a handkerchief, came up to wipe the blood that ran over his upper lip.

"Your nose is broken," Lark said.

"I've had it broken before," said the old man, his speech distorted only a little, like someone talking through thick glass.

"Ice might help."

"Fuck you."

"Leave the razor and come out," said Lark, "and I'll get you some ice."

He backed out of the doorway and watched as the old man laid the razor on the floor and pulled himself up the vanity and to his feet. The man swatted away the hand Lark offered and made his way to the sofa, where he fell back against the cushions and pressed the heel of his left hand gingerly against his nostrils.

Lark kept an eye on him from the kitchen. He laid the tire iron on the seat of a kitchen chair and took an ice tray from the freezer, a pair of dish towels from a drawer. He piled it all on the chair and carried the chair into the living room.

He bundled some ice cubes in a towel and the old man accepted them without a word, laying the bundle against the side of his nose. Lark filled the second towel and pressed it against his own forehead.

"What's wrong with you?" the old man asked.

"I get headaches."

The old man's laugh sounded half like a groan. "That's a damn shame."

"It's a symptom," Lark said absently, and then a thought occurred to him. He had settled into the chair with the tire iron across his lap, but now he rose and put the iron and the towel on the floor and dug his notebook from his pocket.

He found the page he wanted and held it a foot away from the old man's eyes. "Tell me what you see," he said.

Twisted strands of iron-gray hair hung over the old man's brow. His eyes squinted. "That's my name."

"Is there anything odd about it?"

"What do you mean?"

"Is it moving?"

"What are you talking about?"

"What color would you say it is?"

"Is this a joke? It's written in black."

Lark turned the notebook around and read the name. *Charlie Dawtrey.* "Yes, the ink is black. I know that. Intellectually. But the words seem red to me. They don't seem red to you?"

The old man's eyelids fluttered. "God in heaven."

"They don't ripple, like they're floating on water? They don't expand and contract, like they're breathing?"

"God in heaven. I'm talking to a crazy man."

"I'm not crazy," Lark said, turning back a page. "What about these names?"

He watched the old man's eyes move down the list. *Henry Kormoran. Sutton Bell. Terry Dawtrey.*

"That's my son. My son and two of his no-good friends."

"But you don't see the letters breathing?"

"Is this about my son?"

Lark closed the notebook and slipped it into his pocket. "Are you close to your son?"

"Not for a long time."

"If something happened to you, would it matter to him?"

"What's this about?"

"Would he mourn, if you were gone?"

"What do you want here?"

A dull ache wound itself in a figure eight behind Lark's brow. He returned to the chair and reached for the towel-wrapped ice.

"I want you to answer my question," he said. "I think if you were gone, it would affect him. He would mourn your passing."

The old man sat forward slowly. His ice pack lay neglected on the sofa cushion beside him. His nose had stopped bleeding.

He said, "Mister, if you think you can get to my son by hurting me, you've gone off the rails. No one's going to care much when I'm gone, least of all Terry."

"You haven't kept in touch with him?"

"He's been in prison the last sixteen years. I gave up on him, and he gave up on me, a long time back."

"You never go to see him?"

"Not anymore. So why don't you clear out now, and take whatever grudge you've got with you."

"I don't have a grudge."

"You're wasting your time."

"I don't think so. You have a sparrow calendar."

The old man brushed iron-gray hair out of his eyes. "What?"

"There's providence in the fall of a sparrow. I'm pretty sure that's in the Bible."

"Oh Lord, you've gone crazy again."

"I'm not crazy. That line about the sparrow—it means we're all part of a bigger plan. You shouldn't be afraid of playing your part. You shouldn't lie to get out of it."

"I haven't lied to you."

The towel was damp against Lark's brow. He felt a drop of icy water roll along the bridge of his nose and onto his cheek.

"You have a sparrow calendar," he said again. "Every other Saturday is marked with a 'T.' Short for 'Terry.' You're still close to him. You visit him at the prison every other Saturday."

The old man didn't try to deny it. He flexed the fingers of his swollen right hand. His eyes settled on Lark's.

"You don't look good. How's your head?"

Lark shrugged the question away.

"Maybe it's trying to tell you something," the old man said.

The pain traced its figure eight. The ice helped, but not enough.

"The headaches are just a symptom," said Lark. "I'll have them until I deal with the underlying problem."

"Is that what you're doing? You imagine killing me is going to solve all your problems?"

"It's all I can think of."

The old man shook his head sadly. "Look, mister, you don't want to do this."

"The truth is, I don't. If there were another way, I'd try it. But they've got fences at the prison, and towers. This is the only way I can get at him."

The old man's eyes fell shut and a jagged breath escaped him. When he spoke, his voice was a whisper.

"The men in that prison are animals. Terry's been in there sixteen years. Do you think there's anything you can do to him that hasn't been done? Do you think you're going to make him suffer, by killing me?"

Lark drew the towel away from his brow, dropped it to the floor. A cube of ice skipped quietly over the carpet.

"It doesn't matter if he suffers," Lark said. "The point is, they're going to let him out. That's how it works, isn't it? Just for a few hours."

The tire iron lay at Lark's feet. He bent to pick it up.

"I can't get through the fences, or past the towers. But I think they'll let him out. He'll be at your funeral."

CHAPTER 3

Doesn't matter how you get there, Lark's father used to say. *Just so long as you get there.*

Thomas Lark spent thirty years building Mustangs at the Dearborn Assembly Plant on the Rouge River. After the first few months the job lost all its appeal, but he clung to it anyway, because he only wanted a few modest things—a wife and a family and maybe a fishing boat—and it didn't matter how he got them as long as he got them.

So he stayed on, weathering layoffs and buyouts, and he found a wife—Helen, a kindergarten teacher. They had a son, Anthony. And Thomas Lark bought four boats over the years, starting with a small aluminum skiff, ending with a twenty-four-foot fiberglass runabout. His three decades on the assembly line earned him two years of retirement before a valve in his heart gave out and he collapsed on a dock one fine spring morning an hour before sunrise.

Helen Lark, who had spent her days teaching children their letters and numbers, never complained about the equation of her husband's life: thirty years in exchange for two. When Anthony Lark wept at his father's funeral, she drew him close and did her best to comfort him. Then she took him by the shoulders and said, "Promise me you'll use the time you're given."

He thought of her on the morning after his encounter with Charlie Dawtrey, and though he would have liked to sleep the day away he decided it wouldn't be right. He had a few days, at least, until Dawtrey's funeral, but there were preparations he needed to make.

He took a long drive south through mild June heat, crossing over the

Mackinac Bridge around midmorning—Lake Michigan on his right, Lake Huron on his left. He kept on driving, first to the town of Grayling on the Au Sable River, then west to Traverse City. At a sporting-goods store on Front Street he bought a Remington hunting rifle, a scope, and a box of 30-06 cartridges. He ate lunch in a park by the water and watched the sailboats out on the bay.

He drove back to Grayling in the afternoon and got on I-75 heading north. When he saw an exit that looked like it wouldn't lead much of anywhere, he got off the interstate and drifted along until he found an unpaved road that took him through bramble fields and past an abandoned grain silo.

Three miles after the silo, he pulled over to the side of the road and got the rifle out of the trunk. He mounted the scope, loaded the magazine, and fired into a stand of trees thirty yards from the roadside. The first shot chipped bark from a sickly looking ash and shocked a pair of crows into the sky—a reckless flutter of black wings against the blue. He took a few more practice shots, returned the rifle to the trunk, and drove back to I-75.

The next day he made some calls from his hotel room and found the funeral home handling the arrangements for Charlie Dawtrey. A mass would be held at Saint Joseph's in Sault Sainte Marie. The burial would be directly after at a local cemetery. The date for the funeral was July eighth, still a week and a half away. He took some encouragement from that. The family would need time to arrange to have Terry Dawtrey attend.

The days passed slowly, but Lark didn't mind. Sometimes in the evenings he flipped through the channels and managed to find the woman with the wondrous smile. He watched her with the sound down and his headaches stayed away from him.

If he couldn't find her, he could always read. He had some paperback novels with him—Dennis Lehane and Michael Connelly—and several copies of a mystery magazine called *Gray Streets.*

He had an affinity for crime stories because the language tended to be simple, the sentence structure straightforward. The words stayed put on the page—not like the names he had written in his notebook, which still seemed to float and breathe in a way that made him uncomfortable.

There was a term for his condition; his doctor had told him all about it. *Synesthesia.* A confusion of the senses. A rare affliction that manifested itself differently in different people. Some experienced sounds as having color. Some associated textures with emotions. In Lark's case, written words were endowed with color and movement.

Ornate language tended to unsettle him. Passages from nineteenth-century novels might glow like hot coals or squirm like heaps of snakes. In fact, he tried not to read anything written before the First World War. Hemingway made a good cutoff point. Hemingway's sentences were a nice deep blue, and they mostly held still, like stalks of wheat on a windless day.

Novels from the 1950s and '60s were generally safe. Kurt Vonnegut wrote comfortable blue-green prose that moved patiently, like a slow upward escalator. Joseph Heller was a different story. Heller's characters rarely came out and said anything: instead they "cried heatedly," they "declared jubilantly," they "whispered cautioningly." All those adverbs made it impossible for Lark to get through *Catch-22*. For Lark, adverbs buzzed like static on a television screen or swarmed like marching ants.

Mystery novels rarely gave him any trouble. A wisecracking first-person narrative flowed reassuringly, a stream of cool green letters. So mysteries and newspaper stories occupied Lark's days as he waited for the funeral of Charlie Dawtrey.

Dawtrey's death was all over the papers. The early stories hinted at progress. The sheriff of Chippewa County believed there could soon be a break in the case. Then a headline announced that an arrest had been made: Kyle Scudder.

The development caught Lark off guard, though he told himself he should have anticipated it. Scudder had been in a fight with Charlie Dawtrey on the night of the old man's death. He had knocked Dawtrey to the floor in front of a barroom full of witnesses.

In the days after he read the headline, Lark filled several pages of his notebook, writing a summary of his encounter with Charlie Dawtrey. He thought at first that he should go into reasons and motives, but when he did, the sentences were black (not a good black) and bristly and grainy. They trembled on the page until he scratched through them and decided he would stick to the facts.

It crossed his mind that he could send his account to Kyle Scudder's lawyer and spare an innocent man from being put on trial for murder. But in the big scheme of things it seemed unimportant. He didn't feel any responsibility toward Scudder.

There's no justice in the world, his father used to say.

But Lark felt strongly that he needed to lay claim to the death of Charlie Dawtrey. *We all need to own our actions,* he thought. *Otherwise no one will ever know us.* That bit of wisdom never came from his father. It was something his doctor was fond of saying.

We all want to be known. We all want to be seen for who we really are.

THE SUN GLOWED on the copper spire of Saint Joseph's Church. The bell in the tower struck ten and Anthony Lark listened from his Chevy in the lot across the street. He could see the vestibule standing open, a pair of heavy oaken doors swung wide.

Dozens of mourners had already gone inside, far more than Lark had anticipated. He had thought of Charlie Dawtrey as a man with a single son, but now he supposed there must be other children, a whole extended family. Lark watched them ascend the granite steps of the church.

The woman from the Cozy Inn—Madelyn—arrived late. She had a teenaged boy with her, the one whose photograph hung on the wall of Dawtrey's cottage.

Lark saw them pass inside, and then he watched a sheriff's cruiser draw up in front of the granite steps. A stocky deputy with curly hair stepped out on the driver's side and walked around the front of the car, looking up and down the street. A second deputy—younger, slimmer—opened the rear passenger door and hauled out Terry Dawtrey.

Dawtrey wore a gray suit that hung loosely on him, no tie. His dark hair was shaved down to stubble. His hands were clasped in front of him. A glint of sunlight caught the circlet of a handcuff on his wrist.

Shackles on his ankles too. He hobbled sideways up the steps, one deputy close at his elbow, the other watching the street. When the three had disappeared into the vestibule, Lark started his car and rolled out of the lot heading west.

WHITELEAF CEMETERY LAY at the foot of a hill studded with pines. Lark walked among the trees carrying his rifle in a rolled-up blanket. He had left his car a quarter mile back, on the side of a road that bordered the cemetery. He thought it would be all right. He had spotted another car parked nearby, a rusty Camaro half on the gravel and half in the weeds by the roadside.

Lark found the spot he had picked out the day before, a smooth piece of ground in the shade of a white pine that offered a vantage on the cemetery below.

The better part of an hour passed before the first cars arrived. Lark observed them from the ridge of the hill, where he sat with the rifle lying across his knees. As he waited for the sheriff's cruiser, he had the sudden panicked thought that he had made a mistake. Maybe the deputies wouldn't bring Terry Dawtrey here, maybe the service at the church was all that he would get.

Lark watched the pallbearers gather at the rear of the hearse. A black-suited funeral director arranged them on either side and they drew out the casket. Still no sign of the cruiser, and Lark thought seriously about lighting out for his car. He could find the cruiser on its route back to Kinross Prison and run it off the road. It might not be too late.

The priest from Saint Joseph's stood at the graveside, a small group of mourners around him. Madelyn stood a little apart, in a dark blouse and a long skirt. The boy from the photograph leaned against her.

The pallbearers delivered the casket. The priest opened his Bible. And the sheriff's cruiser, at last, rumbled slowly over the gravel of the parking lot.

By the time Terry Dawtrey shuffled across the cemetery lawn, flanked by a deputy on either side, Lark had positioned himself under the boughs of the white pine. He lay on his stomach, the butt of the rifle at his shoulder, elbows and toes nestled in soft bowls of pine needles. Through the scope he followed Dawtrey's progress across the lawn, but the stocky deputy obscured his shot.

Lark rested his rifle on the ground. The deputies led Dawtrey to the far side of the grave, away from the other mourners. The priest began to speak, but his words came to Lark only indistinctly. Lark let his gaze wander over the lines of headstones. Only a few looked as if they had been tended. A plastic vase stood before one of them, filled with roses and fern.

Lark's eyes trailed along the lines of stones and then jumped to the cemetery fence: pillars of cast concrete set at intervals with black iron bars running between them.

Part of the fence cut across the slope of the hill beneath him, and someone had tied a strip of yellow cloth to one of the bars. The ends fluttered in a mild wind.

The priest kept things brief, and when Lark focused again on the ceremony the funeral director was working his discreet magic, pressing a button to lower the casket into the grave.

Some of the mourners went forward to reach into a mound of earth and cast handfuls of it onto the casket. Madelyn and the boy were among them. When the crowd began to disperse, the deputies led Terry Dawtrey to the mound so he could repeat the ritual, digging into the earth with his two cuffed hands, letting it drift through his fingers like dark rain.

Afterward, Terry Dawtrey huddled together with the two deputies. A moment later they separated. Lark brought the rifle to his shoulder and watched Dawtrey begin to walk along a path leading away from the remnants of the crowd, with the slim deputy following at a respectful distance. The stocky deputy went to have a word with the priest.

Lark peered through the scope and saw Dawtrey's scuffed black shoes and the chains of the shackles skittering along the path. The scope trailed up and the crosshairs passed over Dawtrey's laced fingers and the silver rings of the handcuffs. It trailed farther until the circle framed his face. Eyes intense, searching.

Lark pulled back from the scope and took in the larger scene: Dawtrey hobbling toward the grave with the vase of roses in front of it, each step bringing him closer to Lark's position. The slim deputy now several yards behind.

He looked again through the scope, at Dawtrey's bowed head, at the weary set of his shoulders. He put the crosshairs on Dawtrey's chest, a patch of white shirt between the lapels of the jacket. His finger tensed on the trigger.

A sharp series of pops broke the quiet—rapid like machine-gun fire. Lark jerked back from the scope and looked to his left to find the source of the sound. Sparks flashed in the distance, shooting up from the gravel of the cemetery parking lot. A pair of boys, laughing, danced back from the sparks. Cutoff jeans and tennis shoes. Open shirts revealing skinny, tanned torsos. Sixteen years old, seventeen at the outside. One of them set the flame of a lighter to a fuse and tossed something onto the gravel, and another series of pops lit up the air.

Lark turned back to the scene on the cemetery lawn in time to see Terry Dawtrey squatting by the vase of roses, plucking something from the grass. Then the fingers of Dawtrey's right hand touched each of his ankles in turn, and the shackles fell away onto the path. He shot up like a sprinter out of the block—no sign of hunched shoulders or weariness now. He touched right hand to left wrist, left hand to right wrist, and the circles of the handcuffs dropped into the grass. His arms pumped and he made straight for the strip of yellow cloth tied to the fence.

Lark put his eye to the scope of the rifle, wobbled the crosshairs to Dawtrey's chest, and squeezed the trigger. Nothing happened. He drew back from the scope and shook the rifle as if that might solve the problem. Divided his attention now between the rifle and the scene below. Dawtrey closing on the fence. The two boys in cutoffs climbing onto bicycles and making their escape. Scattered mourners looking from Dawtrey to the parking lot and back. The stocky deputy pushing the priest aside, jogging past the mourners.

The thin deputy tearing along the path after Dawtrey, drawing his pistol from the holster on his belt.

Lark worked the bolt of the rifle and the useless cartridge flipped through the air and landed soft in the pine needles. Down below, Terry Dawtrey reached the fence and leapt up to catch the high horizontal bar with two hands. The slim deputy shouted for him to stop.

Dawtrey scrambled over the fence, landing awkwardly and pitching sideways into the slope of the hill. Clawing the wild grass to regain his feet. The deputy behind him, shouting through the fence.

The butt of the rifle against Lark's shoulder and the crosshairs on the open collar of Dawtrey's white shirt. As Lark began to squeeze the trigger, Dawtrey's chin tipped upward and a red-black spot appeared in the hollow at the base of his throat.

The sound of the gunshot reached Lark and he squeezed reflexively and the rifle fired just as Dawtrey dropped to his knees on the slope. The bullet passed harmless over his shoulder. Lark let the rifle touch the ground and looked down at the slim deputy standing with his pistol between the bars of the fence. Smoke rising from the muzzle. Lark could hear the deputy's curse traveling up the hillside, could see the man's face turn away in an ugly grimace. Could see him jam the pistol angrily into his holster.

Dawtrey lay moveless in the grass, the top of his stubbled head no more than twenty yards down the slope. Lark, on knees and elbows, retreated from the ridge of the hill, dragging the rifle with him. A babel of voices below. The stocky deputy shouting orders.

Lark stayed low until he was well back from the ridge. Then he wrapped the rifle in the blanket and started walking back to his car.

THAT EVENING the shooting led the news. The notorious Terry Dawtrey gunned down by a sheriff's deputy in the course of an attempt to escape. Lark watched the coverage from his hotel bed. A bag of melting ice forgotten, his headache only a distant rumor.

The woman with the wondrous smile turned up on one of the stations. A reporter called to her from a crowd, asked for her reaction to Dawtrey's death. But she shook her head somberly and gave no comment.

At midnight Lark switched off the television and reached for his notebook. He found an empty page and used his Waterman pen to sketch an outline of the day's events—because we all need to own our actions.

Around one o'clock the notebook tipped forward onto his chest. He blinked out of a doze and turned onto his side, found the pen where it had rolled onto the bedspread. He paged back through the notebook until he came to his list: *Henry Kormoran. Sutton Bell. Terry Dawtrey.* The red letters breathed on the page. Kormoran and Bell were living in Ann Arbor. Lark would let himself sleep late in the morning, and then he would drive down and find them.

After a moment's hesitation he drew a line through Dawtrey's name. He felt entitled, even though things hadn't gone exactly as planned.

He had wanted the man dead, and the man was dead. It didn't matter how you got there, just so long as you got there.

CHAPTER 4

Here's what I remember about that day. Wednesday, July fifteenth. The day the manuscript came to me.

I was in my office at *Gray Streets,* editing a story. My cell phone hummed at six-thirty in the evening, creeping along the surface of my desk. I left it alone for a moment, searched for a particular page, and wrote a sentence in the margin. Then I picked up the phone and saw Elizabeth's name on the display. I flipped it open.

"Lizzie," I said. "How would you spell 'wrassling'?"

The question didn't faze her. "Like 'wrestling,' only with an a."

"I tried that, but it didn't look right. Now I've got it with two s's."

She thought it over. "That's vulgar," she said. "And colloquial."

I swiveled my chair, propped my feet on the windowsill, and said in my most serious tone, "What are you wearing?"

I knew the answer. I'd seen her that morning when she left the house. She had on slacks the color of her raven hair, and a simple white blouse. And a necklace of glass beads—a mate to the one draped over the arm of my desk lamp, but in green rather than blue. Glass-bead necklaces are the only jewelry she ever wears. Her daughter makes them.

Elizabeth chuckled at my question. "This isn't that kind of call, David. I wanted to let you know I'll be late tonight. Business."

"Not the book thieves again."

"Not them. Worse. A body in an apartment on Linden Street. Looks like it's been there a while."

"Homicide?"

"Strangled with a cord, is what I hear. Carter's already there. I don't know how long I'll be."

"I'll wait up."

"You don't have to."

"I will anyway. Be careful."

We said good-bye and I closed the phone, but it buzzed again before I could put it down.

I opened it. "I'm not here."

"I can see your feet in the window," Bridget Shellcross said. "Why don't you come down. I've ordered two gimlets."

"You're the boss."

I closed the window and gathered the pages of the story I'd been working on, sliding them into a folder.

On my way through the outer office I passed a stack of envelopes on the reception desk. Manuscripts from hopeful authors. I left them there. In the hall I turned to lock the door and my gaze fell briefly on the black letters on the pebbled glass: GRAY STREETS. DAVID LOOGAN, EDITOR.

I nearly missed the envelope in the hall, propped beside the door frame. It looked like just another manuscript. I picked it up and tucked it under my arm with the folder.

Down the stairs, five flights, through the lobby, out onto the street, and the sea of humanity was like something from a Third World capital.

Every July, over the course of four days, half a million people pass through the streets of downtown Ann Arbor. They look like tourists in a foreign city, and like tourists they're here mostly to eat and shop. Hamburgers and pizza, kabobs and funnel cakes. Sculptures and paintings and handmade jewelry. The Ann Arbor Art Fair. Half a million people, and most of them seemed to be milling around between me and Bridget Shellcross, who had somehow secured a table across the street in front of Café Felix.

When I reached her she rose and kissed me on the cheek. She had to stand on tiptoe to manage it. Bridget is something over five feet tall, and the something is roughly the thickness of a blade of grass. She wears her brown hair short and artfully disheveled, and though she tends to dress in black, today it was an ivory-colored blouse and a burgundy skirt.

Bridget is a mystery writer, and a few months back she became the publisher of *Gray Streets* after buying the magazine from the widow of the previous owner. She lets me run things as I see fit. About the only time I see her is when we get together for a drink.

I dropped my envelope and folder on the table and we sat, and I asked her how she would spell "wrassling."

A sip from her vodka gimlet—there was another in front of me, but I didn't touch it—and she said, "I'd need to know the context."

I opened the folder and handed her the story I'd been editing. "Page six, in the margin," I said. She found it and read it silently. I knew it by heart.

The phone rang and when I answered it a voice told me to hold the line, and I held it like a Cuban fisherman wrassling a marlin.

She laughed, but not so much that she was in danger of spilling her drink.

"This is Fletcher's new story?" she asked me.

"Yes. He thinks he's the next Raymond Chandler. Leans heavily on the similes, so I figured one more wouldn't hurt."

Bridget flipped through the pages. "You've done a lot of tinkering with this."

"I have a theory about editing. You can do anything you want with a manuscript, you can rewrite it line by line, as long as your handwriting is very small and very neat. If the pages look tidy, the author'll go along."

"That's your theory?"

"It helps if the publisher backs you up."

"Don't drag me into this."

I took the pages back from her. "You think Fletcher will object?"

"I imagine he'll scream bloody murder, but I've never met the man. Do what you want. If he doesn't like it, he can send it to *Ellery Queen*. See how far he gets with them."

The waitress from Café Felix had been waiting for a break in our conversation. Now she asked me if there was a problem with my vodka gimlet.

"It's fine," I told her. "But it seems to have lost its way." I slid it over in front of Bridget, who surrendered her empty glass.

"David'll have Scotch," she said. "Neat."

I shook my head no. "David'll have lemonade."

The waitress left, and by the time she came back the crowd in the street had thinned a little—people drifting south to listen to a band playing covers of Bob Dylan songs. An overlong harmonica solo turned out to be the opening of "All Along the Watchtower."

Bridget caught me staring across the street. "What's the matter?" she asked.

I drank some lemonade. "There he is again."

"Who?"

"Do you see him? He's wearing sunglasses and a safari hat."

She frowned. "David, they're all wearing sunglasses and safari hats."

"He's standing under the awning of the gift shop there, holding a bottle of water."

"They're all holding bottles of water."

I waited for her to follow my gaze and pick him out. He looked about thirty years old, with wide shoulders, a short neck, a lean jaw. He stood with his head slightly bowed, the way tall people do sometimes when they don't want you to notice they're tall. But he was no more than average height. He wore a plaid shirt and cargo pants.

"What do you make of him?" I said to Bridget.

"Well," she said, "he has no fashion sense."

"Notice how he looks around, taking things in. But he's not looking over here."

She decided to humor me. "That's suspicious."

"I've seen him before. Earlier today, outside Starbucks. I think he's been following me."

"He's probably here for the Art Fair."

"I don't like the look of him. Do you have a gun?"

Her handbag, on the table, was roughly the size of a pack of cigarettes.

"Where would I put it?" she said.

"All I've got is a Swiss Army knife. I'd rather have a gun."

"I don't think you'll need to shoot him."

"If I had a gun, I could let him see it and maybe he'd go away. If I let him see I've got a pocketknife, I don't know what that gets me. Maybe a merit badge."

"He looks harmless, David."

"They all look harmless. I don't like the cargo pants. Too many places to conceal a weapon. I'd like to go over there and make him empty out his pockets."

"I think you should stay put and drink your lemonade."

I nodded toward the entrance of Café Felix. "If he starts to come over here, you should duck inside."

"We'll both duck inside. But he's not going to come over here."

"I've got the knife. I think I could hit his femoral artery. He'd bleed out in about a minute. Does that sound right?"

"I'd rather not find out."

Bridget was wearing sunglasses like everyone else—hers were rimless and black—but now she took them off and graced me with a look of concern.

I smiled to let her know that I wasn't really going to get into a knife fight in the middle of the Ann Arbor Art Fair. I wasn't going to cut anyone's femoral artery. And she relaxed, because David Loogan says some wild things now and then but he's reliable. And the sun was shining and the sky was blue, and she was right to think I'd been kidding. Mostly.

I took another look at the man in the plaid shirt and cargo pants. He was still under the awning, looking south toward the band playing Dylan. I brushed my fingers over my pocket to reassure myself the knife was there. And I revised my estimate. It wouldn't take a minute for him to bleed out. Maybe thirty seconds.

BRIDGET AND I moved on to other subjects. She asked after Elizabeth, who had been investigating a ring of book thieves: high school kids who'd been shoplifting textbooks from the university store and selling them to a used bookshop. The key question was whether the bookshop owner was in on the scheme or whether he was merely stupid and careless—and it wasn't really a question, because one of the kids had already flipped on him. But all that was on hold, I told Bridget, because right now Elizabeth was looking into a murder on Linden Street.

After a while Bridget's latest squeeze stopped by, an ethereal woman with blond hair who lives off a trust fund and plays the lute in darkened coffeehouses on Saturday nights. Her name is Ariel or Amber, and I may be wrong about the lute. It may be a cittern.

Eventually the two of them slipped off for dinner at Palio, but I stayed behind. The band had run through many of the more familiar Dylan songs and had started in on "Things Have Changed." The unfashionable fellow across the street was still keeping me company. I noticed something now that I hadn't seen before. He had a bandage wrapped around his left hand.

I polished off my second lemonade and picked up the envelope I'd brought down from the hallway. Nine by twelve, no writing on the outside, sealed with a strip of tape. I hauled out my knife and unfolded a blade, and if the fellow in the plaid shirt was intimidated he didn't let it show. One slice along the flap and the knife went back in my pocket.

I drew out the thin manuscript—eight or ten pages clipped together. I read the first line and it turned out that Dylan was right. Things had changed.

When I looked up, my companion was staring at me from across the street. And though he'd been loitering under the awning all this time, now he turned on his heel and headed south at a rapid clip.

I jumped up from the table, nearly colliding with an older couple who'd been waiting for me to leave. The wife was fanning herself with an Art Fair brochure, and the husband was hefting a stone garden ornament, a jaunty-looking duck, which he thumped down on the table to claim it.

By the time I gathered up the envelope and the pages and my folder, I'd lost sight of my peculiar companion. I moved into the middle of the street, into the sea of tourists—all of them wearing sunglasses, half of them wearing safari hats. I bounced on my toes to get a better view. Facing south, I could see the stage where the band was playing on the eastern side of the street, and beyond it a line of food vendors. On the western side was a long row of artists' booths—open tents of white canvas. Down the center were two solid lanes of people, one traveling away from me, the other approaching.

I spotted a patch of plaid half a block away, but it was gone the next instant. I started off at a run, slipping between a pair of college kids in basketball jerseys, aiming for a landmark I had chosen: a gangly sculpture of a figure in bronze. But before long I got stuck behind a woman pushing a baby in a stroller, and by the time I reached the sculpture there was no plaid in sight.

I pressed on, due south, past ceramic tiles and photographs of wildlife. I came to a booth selling Celtic jewelry and caught a glimpse of plaid turning a corner and disappearing behind a wall of white canvas. When I rounded the corner he was there, close enough for me to clap my hand on his plaid shoulder and spin him around. He tripped on the curb and fell backward onto the sidewalk. The safari hat went flying, his sunglasses were askew, and I could see he was wearing khakis, not cargo pants. There was no bandage around his hand. It was the wrong man.

He said, "What the hell?" and waved me away angrily when I tried to help him up. He went after his hat, ignoring my apologies. I wandered back into the street. I thought about heading farther south, but I realized the man I was looking for could be anywhere now—down an alley, onto another street, into any one of a score of shops or restaurants.

I decided to go back to the office. I had the folder and the envelope and the pages rolled into a tube in my left hand, and I unrolled them as I walked and brought the thin manuscript to the top. I flipped to a page in the middle and scanned the lines of type, catching random words: *pushed, broken, table lamp, headache.* It was all a jumble, but it didn't matter. The opening line was enough; the rest was just detail.

I turned back to the beginning and read it again, a simple declarative sentence:

I killed Henry Kormoran in his apartment on Linden Street.

CHAPTER 5

The apartment had a steel-gray door with the number (*105*) on a plate above the peephole. The first thing Elizabeth Waishkey saw when she passed through was a chair overturned in the kitchen. Then a steak knife and drops of blood on the linoleum.

The disorder continued in the living room, where a cheap coffee table was listing on three legs. The fourth was halfway across the room, lying on the carpet in front of the gas fireplace. A yellowed photograph lay nearby, its top corners torn away.

The glass front of the fireplace sparkled with reflected light. A flat-screen television was tuned to CNN with the sound muted.

A lamp shade rested on the cushions of a sofa. Elizabeth looked around for the lamp. Down a narrow hallway off the living room she found the broken remnants of a bulb. Two doorways at the end of the hall, and from one of them came a flash of light.

She called out to Carter Shan to let him know she was there.

From the doorway, she could see Shan standing at the foot of the victim's bed, framing a shot with a digital camera. His brow furrowed beneath his brush-cut hair and he pressed the button. The flash brightened the room.

There was a wallet on the night table by the bed. Inside, Elizabeth found a driver's license that bore a picture of a man with a plain, pleasant face and eyes that twinkled for the camera. Henry Kormoran in life.

She couldn't see his face now. His body lay prone across the narrow bed. He had on a Harley-Davidson T-shirt and sweatpants. White socks with a hole in one heel. There was a bald spot at the crown of his head, and a single fly buzzing around the circle of pale scalp.

The smell had been faint in the hallway, but now it was strong. Rank and sweet, the smell of decay. It would have been even worse if not for the air-conditioning. A hot day outside, but in here the air was cool.

The lamp that Elizabeth had been looking for was lying on the bed beside the body. Its cord was wrapped around Kormoran's neck.

Shan stepped around the bed to frame another shot. "You saw the mess out there," he said.

"I saw."

"Looks like the fight started in the kitchen. The blood on the floor, I don't think it's his. I don't see any cuts on him."

"You think he grabbed the steak knife to defend himself."

Shan nodded his agreement. "And nicked his attacker. Then they move into the living room. One of them tackles the other, they crash into the coffee table, knock over the lamp. Kormoran breaks loose, runs down the hall."

"His attacker throws the lamp at him. That's when the bulb breaks."

"Kormoran reaches the bedroom, but there's no way to lock the door. The killer pushes it in. He's got the lamp. He hits Kormoran with it—there's dried blood in Kormoran's hair. Then he wraps the cord around Kormoran's neck and strangles him."

The flash from the camera lit up the room.

"You called Eakins?" Elizabeth said.

"She's on her way." Lillian Eakins, the medical examiner.

A last look at Kormoran's license and Elizabeth put it back in the wallet.

"How long do you think he's been here?"

Detective Carter Shan leaned in to frame a close-up of the neck. He was a slim, serious-looking man, medium height, tie clipped to his shirt, sleeves rolled up to his elbows.

"More than a day," he said, "but less than two."

"What are you basing that on?"

"Eyes are cloudy. Rigor has come and gone. Hands and face are just starting to swell. Flies on him, but no visible larvae."

"That's all very scientific."

He lowered the camera and smiled faintly. "Also, his sister talked to him almost exactly forty-eight hours ago. Around six on Monday. She arranged to meet him yesterday for lunch but he never showed. She tried calling him and got no answer, so she came here today and convinced the apartment manager to let her in. She's the one who found the body."

"What's she like?"

"She's a looker—I think she got all the best DNA in the Kormoran family. A little cold. I didn't see any tears. I got her name and number. Told her she'd need to make a statement."

Elizabeth nodded. "Good. Are you finished here?"

"Yeah. Why?"

"I could use some better air."

She watched Shan tuck the camera into a pouch on his belt and the two of them walked down the hall to the living room. She breathed deep and looked around. Noticed something she had missed before: four small strips of masking tape on the wall above the fireplace.

She dropped to one knee to study the photograph on the floor. A young Henry Kormoran, nine or ten years old, posing with his ball and glove. A man with an easy smile standing beside him, probably his father. She had the odd feeling that she had seen this image before today, that she should recognize the name "Henry Kormoran."

There were four strips of tape on the wall. Two of them had held up this photograph.

"Where's the other picture?" Elizabeth said aloud.

Shan had already gone looking for it. She saw him pull something from between the cushions of the sofa. She got to her feet and looked at it over his shoulder.

It was a five-by-seven print, a reproduction of a painting in oil. A portrait of a woman in her twenties. Dark eyes, tanned skin, long black hair parted in the middle.

"Oh," she said, drawing the word out.

"Who is she?" Shan asked.

"You don't know?"

"Give me a hint."

"She's older now. Wears her hair shorter. She's not smiling here, but if she were, you'd see a whole lot of white teeth."

"Give me another hint."

Elizabeth nodded toward the silent television. A pair of talking heads shared the screen.

"Stay tuned to CNN and you're bound to see her," Elizabeth said. "She's been getting lots of coverage lately."

"Callie Spencer?"

"Callie Spencer. The next junior senator from the state of Michigan. If you believe the polls."

Shan laid the picture on the sofa cushion. "What does she have to do with Kormoran?"

"You could say he helped launch her political career."

THE SKY WAS STILL LIGHT as Elizabeth drove to City Hall. Carter Shan had stayed behind at Kormoran's apartment, looking after the scene until Lillian Eakins came to collect the body.

Elizabeth took a roundabout route, avoiding the streets closed off for the Art Fair. She checked her cell phone as she drove, saw a message from David, but decided it could wait. She called Owen McCaleb, chief of the Ann Arbor police, to let him know she was on her way. He and some of the other detectives from the Investigations Division had already begun to build the file on Henry Kormoran.

That's what a murder investigation comes down to—details in a file, the shaping of a narrative. At City Hall, details were already being gathered: old news articles pulled from the Internet, faxed case files from the authorities in Chippewa County.

They told the story of Henry Kormoran. Elizabeth didn't know every detail, but she had heard it before. It was the story of a seventeen-year-old bank robbery.

On a dreary October morning, five men drove up to the Great Lakes Bank in Sault Sainte Marie in a black SUV. The driver waited outside. The other four went in, gloves and ski masks, duffel bags to hold the loot. Floyd Lambeau, Sutton Bell, Terry Dawtrey, Henry Kormoran. Lambeau was the leader; he had a double-barreled shotgun. The others carried handguns.

They were looking for a big score. It wasn't enough to empty the cash drawers. They wanted what was in the vault. Money from the casinos.

They went in fast and loud, got the customers and tellers down on the floor. Dawtrey, following Lambeau's orders, dragged the bank manager back to open the vault. But it took longer than anyone expected.

Kormoran was watching the doors, and he saw someone coming. His job was to make sure no one entered; if anyone did, he was supposed to force them down to the floor with the others. But he wasn't expecting what he saw: a cop in a gray uniform. Harlan Spencer—the sheriff of Chippewa County.

Spencer's wife had been nagging him to open a certificate of deposit. This was the morning he'd decided to get it done. He parked his unmarked cruiser across the street and saw the driver of the SUV watching him. Something about the driver's demeanor put Spencer on guard. As he approached the vehicle his hand strayed unconsciously to his service weapon, a nine-millimeter Glock.

Before he reached the SUV, it sped away. The driver was never found. He was the only one of the five who got away.

Henry Kormoran panicked. He had the crazy thought that if he ran fast enough he could catch up to the SUV. He left his gun on the floor of the bank vestibule and stepped out into the bleak daylight with his hands raised. Spencer had his Glock drawn now and ordered Kormoran onto the ground.

Kormoran turned and ran. His raised hands saved him. Spencer was reluctant to shoot an unarmed man in the back. Instead he returned to his cruiser, started it up, jacked it out into the middle of the street with its lights flashing, and called for backup on his radio.

Floyd Lambeau was the next one out of the bank, holding his shotgun one-handed and dragging a teller with him, his forearm tight across her throat. He looked up and down the street as if he expected to see the black SUV tear around the corner at any moment. When it didn't, he headed for the nearest car, a compact Ford whose driver couldn't move forward because of the sheriff's cruiser but couldn't move back because of the cars behind him.

Standing behind the driver's door of the cruiser, Spencer called out to Lambeau, telling him to drop the gun. At the same moment, the teller got hold of Lambeau's thumb and bent it back. He howled and she twisted away from him, and when he brought the barrel of the shotgun up, Spencer shot him in the heart with the Glock.

By the time Terry Dawtrey and Sutton Bell came out, Spencer had moved the teller and the driver of the Ford out of the open and into a shop down the block. Lambeau's body lay in the street. Back at his cruiser, shielding himself behind the driver's door, Spencer heard the wail of sirens in the distance. He wondered if help would reach him in time. It seemed unlikely.

And here was Terry Dawtrey, with a revolver pressed against the temple of the bank manager. And Sutton Bell standing behind them, a black duffel bag weighing at his left side.

Spencer told them calmly that they'd come to the end of the line. Dawtrey laughed and said they would take the cruiser. He would blast the bank manager if Spencer didn't turn over the keys.

Spencer told him it wasn't going to happen. Dawtrey repeated his demands as if he were speaking to a slow child. He drew back the hammer of the revolver, and Spencer, his Glock steady, willed the bank manager to make a move. But the manager was made of less stern stuff than the teller. His eyes pleaded and Spencer knew he wasn't going to be any use.

A shot rang out, louder than the sirens. The bank manager pitched forward and Terry Dawtrey was on his knees, left hand pressed against his thigh, blood seeping through the faded denim of his jeans. It took a second for Spencer to understand what had happened: Sutton Bell, realizing that things had gotten out of control, had turned his gun on Dawtrey. Now Bell held his arms up to surrender. His revolver, still smoking, tumbled from his fingers and fell to the ground. Spencer came out from behind the door of the cruiser, and the bank manager ran toward him, obscuring his view of Dawtrey. Spencer pushed the manager aside and saw the muzzle of Dawtrey's gun.

Dawtrey's first bullet sliced through the sleeve of Spencer's uniform. The second struck his left shoulder and turned him around. The third slammed into his spine.

There were three more shots, but none of them found their target. The recoil sent them high, and by then Harlan Spencer lay sprawled in the street. He stayed conscious long enough to feel the hands of one of his deputies turning him over gently onto his back. Long enough to see another deputy tackle Terry Dawtrey as Dawtrey reached for Sutton Bell's revolver. Long enough to know that he couldn't feel any sensation in his arms or his legs.

It took months of therapy for Spencer to regain the use of his right arm and hand. His left arm never came back fully. His legs never came back at all.

His daughter, twenty-three, dropped out of law school at the University of Michigan to help take care of him, then returned to graduate at the top of her class. Callie Spencer spent seven years in the Washtenaw County prosecutor's office, handling the worst domestic violence cases. When she decided to run for the Michigan House of Representatives, she had an unbeatable résumé: advocate for battered women and abused children, daughter of a hero cop.

She served two terms in the Michigan House and a third was hers if she wanted it, but then the venerable John Casterbridge announced his retirement from the United States Senate. And after a tough primary, it looked as if Callie Spencer was on track to replace him.

Elizabeth parked at City Hall and walked around to the front steps. As soon as she passed into the lobby she saw a figure rising from a bench. Dressed in white linen, as if he'd just stepped off a sailboat.

"David," she said.

His copper hair was curly in the summer heat. He wore the hint of a grin, but there was something grave about him too. "I know you'd rather I didn't come here," he said.

She didn't deny it. "Is everything all right?"

"Did you get my message?"

"I haven't had time to listen to it."

He picked up an envelope from the bench. "There's something you ought to read."

"Can it wait?" she said. "I really need to get upstairs."

He already had the envelope open. He handed her a manuscript.

"Read the first line," he said.

She started to say, "David—" but then she saw the words on the page.

I killed Henry Kormoran in his apartment on Linden Street.

"David, where did you get this?"

"I'll tell you," he said, "but you'd better read the last line too."

She flipped to the end.

Sutton Bell is next.

CHAPTER 6

Over the last two decades, fields of houses have grown up around the edges of Ann Arbor, filling in the white spaces on the map. Their streets are laid out in straight lines and arcs, and the houses follow a few simple models, with small variations in color and architectural detail.

The Bells lived in a place with white vinyl siding and an ornament over the garage door that looked like the keystone of an arch. When Elizabeth arrived, the patrol car she'd requested was already parked out front. One of the two uniformed officers stepped out to greet her—a brawny kid named Fielder.

"All quiet?" she asked him.

"Yup," he said. "Bell's not home. Or his wife. His daughter's in there with the nanny. She's a trip, the nanny. Tried to read my palm."

The nanny turned out to be a bejeweled woman with wispy hair. She met Elizabeth at the door and led her back to a family room where an eight-year-old girl sat on the floor drawing with colored markers on a pad of newsprint.

The girl looked up at Elizabeth and grinned shyly. The perfect specimen of a happy child: tow-headed, blue-eyed, angelic.

Elizabeth waved to her, wiggling her fingers, and the girl returned the wave and went back to her drawing.

"I'm not sensing any danger," the nanny said in a low voice.

Elizabeth answered in the same tone. "Is that right?"

The nanny led her to a corner away from the girl.

"I don't want to teach you your business, dear," the nanny said, "but usually I have strong intuitions, and I'm not picking up anything."

"Do you know where Mr. Bell is right now?"

"I'm afraid I don't. I tried to reach him when that young man, Mr. Findley—"

"Officer Fielder."

"—when he told me you were concerned for Sutton's safety. I tried Sutton at work, but they said he left early. At five."

"Where does Mr. Bell work?" Elizabeth asked.

"At a clinic in town," the nanny said. "He's a nurse practitioner. That's why I'm not worried. He's a healer now." She paused to emphasize her point. "He's had violence in his life, but that was in his past. His future is peaceful."

"What about his wife?" Elizabeth asked.

"Rosalie's future is peaceful too. They're intertwined, you see."

"I meant, where does she work?"

The nanny's eyes twinkled as if the misunderstanding amused her. "She sells cosmetics at Macy's at the mall. They close at nine, so I expect her home any minute."

"Does she have a cell phone?"

"They both have them, but they're not shackled to them. I think that's healthy—"

Elizabeth interrupted her. "Could you give me their numbers?"

The woman put a gentle hand on Elizabeth's shoulder. "I can if you like, dear, but I've already left messages for both of them. You can spend your energy trying to find them, but if you'll just wait I think they'll come to you."

In a rattle of jewelry, the nanny headed off to get the numbers. Elizabeth drifted over to the girl, who was working intently on her drawing. Jagged pine trees in green. A house with a peaked roof. A smiling man holding something that could have been a lollipop or a flower or a microphone.

Elizabeth thought the man must be Sutton Bell, but before she could ask she heard the sound of the front door opening and closing. Then raised voices and footsteps approaching. The nanny trailed after a well-dressed woman with fine clear skin.

"Now, Rosalie—" the nanny said.

"What's going on?" said Rosalie Bell to Elizabeth. "Is Sutton all right?"

An edge of panic in her voice. Elizabeth stepped close and spoke to her calmly.

"I need to find him. Do you know where he is?"

"He's working tonight."

"I tried him at work—" the nanny began, but Elizabeth raised a hand to quiet her.

"I understand he left the clinic early," Elizabeth said.

Rosalie Bell shook her head impatiently. "I'm not talking about the clinic. He had a gig at the Art Fair tonight."

A jingling of bracelets as the nanny touched her fingers to her chin. "Oh, of course."

Elizabeth ignored her and focused on Rosalie Bell. "Maybe you could fill me in. I thought your husband was a nurse practitioner."

"That's his day job," the woman said. "But he's also in a band called the Chrome Horsemen. They play covers of Bob Dylan songs."

ANTHONY LARK HELD a glass of ice against his forehead. Condensation ran down the surface of the glass and into the gauze wrapped around his left hand. He drew a breath, and most of what he took in was smoke.

A cardboard coaster on the bar in front of him bore a logo like a billiard ball: the number eight within a white circle, with a larger circle of black around it. The Eightball Saloon. Music played upstairs, in a club called the Blind Pig. Loud music with a thumping rhythm that was starting to find its way to a spot behind Lark's eyes.

From his seat at the end of the bar, Lark could survey the room. Two pool tables dominated the space, green rectangles illuminated by a smoky haze of yellow light. The light came from fixtures hung on long chains suspended from the ceiling. Both tables were in use, but Lark had his eyes on the closer one, where four men in their thirties were playing doubles. They wore jeans and T-shirts. One of them was clean-shaven, but the others sported varying degrees of stubble.

The clean-shaven one was Sutton Bell.

An hour ago they had finished their set, broken down their equipment, and hauled it to a van in a parking structure nearby. Lark had thought they might go their separate ways, but they had stayed together and he had followed them here, to this dive on First Street, safely out of range of the tourists at the Art Fair.

And now Bell leaned over the table to shoot the seven in the corner, and the others hooted when the ball sank into the pocket. They drank beer from longneck bottles.

Lark set his glass on the coaster and tried to get the attention of the bartender, a twentysomething guy with a pierced eyebrow. But he was at the other end of the bar putting a cosmopolitan down in front of a woman who looked like she could be a lawyer or a real estate agent.

She was nicely put together in a charcoal gray skirt that probably came with a matching blazer, but she wasn't wearing the blazer. She was wearing a tailored silk blouse with pearl buttons—three of them undone. Wavy brown hair with blond highlights. Smooth forehead, pert nose, alluring mouth.

She was on her second cosmopolitan now and once in a while she turned to look around the room—with particular attention to Bell and his friends. Maybe she knew them, Lark thought, or maybe she had seen them play and thought it might be fun to hook up with a musician.

The bartender took Lark's glass and brought it back filled with rum and Coke. Reaching for his wallet, Lark felt a sharp pain in his hand. It had started to swell beneath the gauze.

Things had gone less than smoothly at Henry Kormoran's apartment. Lark had gone there in the daylight and Kormoran had opened the door for him readily enough. But nothing's ever easy—something his father used to say—and though he had brought along the tire iron, it was nothing like the old man, Charlie Dawtrey. Kormoran had managed to knock the iron out of Lark's hand and then had come up with a steak knife, and after that there had been broken furniture and the lamp and the cord. A close thing right down to the end.

Lark sipped his Coke and held the glass against his cheek. The air in the Eightball Saloon was warm and the smoke stung his eyes.

Sutton Bell came up to the bar for another round of longnecks, and Lark turned away reflexively. He had ditched his safari hat and sunglasses in favor of a baseball cap from a shop on Liberty Street. But he had taken off the cap in order to cool his brow, and without it he felt exposed. He told himself he shouldn't worry. Sutton Bell wasn't going to be around to identify him.

Lark had no tire iron tonight, but he had what he needed in the pockets of his cargo pants. A sap made from a woolen sock and a bag of marbles. A six-inch chef's knife in a cardboard sleeve. They would do the job.

He wiped his forearm across his brow and it came away slick with sweat. He picked up his cap from the bar and put it on, pulling the bill low on his forehead. He wished Bell would leave—soon, and alone.

Sometime later there was a loud crack of billiard balls—Lark felt it in the space behind his eyes—and a cheer went up. One of Bell's friends had sunk the eight ball on the break.

The woman in the silk blouse rose from her place at the bar and walked past Lark, heading for a dim hallway in the back. The restrooms were there, and a door that opened into an alley. A minute later, Sutton Bell said his good-byes, over protests from his friends, and followed the same route. Lark wondered if the two of them had prearranged their exit, if the woman was waiting for Bell even now in the alley.

He slid off his stool and walked down the hallway, hit the metal bar on the exit door with his hip. Outside, the clean air braced him. The door closed, dulling the rhythm of the music within. He saw Bell framed at the end of the alley, saw the top of Bell's head as the man looked up at the sky.

Lark took the knife from one of the deep pockets on the legs of his pants and slipped it into his back pocket, within easy reach. He did the same with his homemade sap.

In the lot behind the bar, Bell's steps were light and careless. Lark followed him. He knew where they were going. Bell's car wasn't parked in the lot; it was on the street two blocks away. Lark's Chevy was on the same street.

By the time Sutton Bell reached the sidewalk, he was whistling. Lark recognized the tune: the harmonica lead-in to "All Along the Watchtower."

They came to the end of a block and Bell crossed, tennis shoes scuffing over the surface of the street. Lark picked up his pace and began to close the distance between them. Cars passed, heading east into downtown. Leaves rustled in the night wind.

When only ten feet remained between them, the whistling cut off suddenly and Bell turned, walking backward for a few steps. He stopped beneath a maple tree.

"I don't have what you need, my friend."

His voice was pleasant. It drew Lark up short.

"What do you think I need?" he asked warily.

"Smack, coke, whatever it is, I don't have it." Bell showed his empty hands. "I'm not holding. And I don't have any money either. So there's nothing I can do for you."

Lark narrowed his eyes. "I don't want your money."

"That's good, because I don't have any. I'll give you some advice though. Go home and get some rest."

Taking a step forward, Lark could feel the weight of the sap in his pocket.

"That's your advice?"

Bell's nod was almost imperceptible. "I saw you in the bar. You looked like hell. You don't look any better out here. I think you're running a fever."

"It's a hot night."

"It's not the heat that's making you sweat, my friend. I've seen it before."

Lark flexed the fingers of his left hand, felt the sharp pain there. He raised the hand for Bell to see. "I cut myself the other day," he said. "I think it may be infected."

Bell frowned and moved closer. "You should have it checked out. There's an Urgent Care on South Industrial Drive. You know where that is?"

"I could find it if I had to."

"They can clean it for you and give you antibiotics. A ten-day course of Keflex ought to do it."

"Keflex," Lark said. He almost took out his notebook to write it down. Bell was very close now, almost within reach. Lark pictured what he needed to do. Draw out the sap. Lunge forward and aim for Bell's temple. One solid blow could bring him down. If not, then a second. Then drop the sap and bring out the knife. Drag the blade across Bell's throat.

"You can go right now," Bell said, and it took Lark a moment to realize he was talking about the Urgent Care. "They're open all night. But you should take a cab. It's too far to walk." He had a wallet open in his hands. He held out some bills. "That should be enough."

Lark reached for the bills with his bandaged left hand.

"You said you didn't have any money."

"That's all I've got," said Bell. "If you don't get there tonight, go tomorrow. I work there. I'll take care of you myself. The name is Bell."

Lark stuffed the bills in his shirt pocket, just to have them out of the way.

"I know your name," he said. "I've got it on my list." For a wild moment he wanted to take out his notebook and show Bell the page. Ask him if he could see the red letters breathing.

"What are you talking about?" Bell said. "Do I know you?"

As he reached for the sap in his back pocket, Lark said, "Let me ask you: Do you ever think about Harlan Spencer?"

That got Bell's attention. "Who are you?"

"Do you think about Callie Spencer?"

"I don't know what you're up to—"

"Do you have her portrait on your wall?" He could feel the wool of the sap between his fingers, could hear the marbles clicking together. "Do you watch her on the news?"

"You're starting to scare me, pal." It was *pal* now, not *my friend*.

"You don't have to be scared. I'll make it quick."

In the shadows under the maple tree, Lark pulled the sap free of his pocket and raised it high. Bell's wallet dropped to the sidewalk as his arms came up defensively. The sap descended, struck his left hand, drove it into his temple. Put him down on one knee. He fell backward as Lark raised the sap again.

The only sound from Bell was a soft groan, but the street was suddenly alive with noise. Clipped footsteps and a woman's voice shouting, "Hey! Stop!"

Lark turned without thinking and saw the woman from the bar—silk blouse, dark skirt. Still far off, but she started to run now.

As he turned back to Bell, he felt a hard blow to the hollow behind his right knee. He toppled over and when his bandaged hand hit the sidewalk it felt as if it had been driven through with a dagger.

When Lark gathered himself to rise, Sutton Bell kicked again at his leg, but it was a weak gesture. Bell was still on the ground, clutching his temple. Lark got to his feet, but the sap was gone, off in the grass somewhere. He had the knife in his pocket but his left hand was on fire and the woman was close. She was reaching into her handbag. If she came out with a gun or a can of Mace, things could go bad fast.

Bell was on hands and knees now and Lark drove his shoe into the man's ribs, sending him rolling into the grass. Without looking back Lark stalked off down the sidewalk and had his keys out before he got to his car. Cranked the engine, left the lights off, tore into the street. Saw the woman crouching over Bell as he passed. He rounded the corner with the tires squealing.

After a few blocks he slowed and turned on his lights. And after a few blocks more he had to pull over for several minutes on a residential street, because the ache behind his eyes had begun to twist itself into a hangman's knot.

CHAPTER 7

Sutton Bell looked boyish, with his long dark hair and lanky frame. He had a bruise on his temple and a brace on his left hand, and they had him sitting up on a gurney in an exam room in the ER of the University Hospital. To Elizabeth he looked like a kid who had fallen off his bike.

He was alert and cheery, but his wife watched over him protectively from her perch on the edge of the gurney.

"Can this wait?" she said to Elizabeth.

"It's better if it doesn't."

News of the assault had come to Elizabeth while she was still at the Bell house. Rosalie Bell insisted on driving straight to the hospital, leaving her daughter with the nanny. Elizabeth took a detour; she knew the doctors would need time to work, so she drove by the Eightball Saloon first and talked to the bartender and Bell's friends. They told her about a woman who had witnessed the attack. Silk blouse, gray skirt, heels. She had lingered until the ambulance came, and had followed it in her car.

Elizabeth had looked for her in the ER waiting room, but hadn't seen her.

Now, in the exam room with Bell and his wife, Elizabeth felt like an intruder. It was plain that Bell's wife wished she had stayed away.

"He has a concussion," Rosalie Bell said.

Sutton Bell spoke up. "It's a mild concussion."

"You don't know that," said Rosalie Bell. For Elizabeth's benefit, she added, "The doctor said we have to be cautious. Sometimes all the symptoms don't appear right away."

"The hand took the brunt of it," Sutton Bell said mildly. "Fractures to the middle phalanges of the index and second fingers. I should be worried about playing the guitar again."

Rosalie Bell shook her head. "He plays terrible guitar," she said. "He only ever bothered to learn three chords."

"That's true," he said. "Fortunately I have a beautiful singing voice."

"You have a singing voice that sounds like Bob Dylan's," she countered. Then, to Elizabeth: "Couldn't you talk to him tomorrow?"

Bell laid his good hand on his wife's knee. "I'll talk now. The concussion's not serious. If it were, I couldn't say 'fractures to the middle phalanges' without slurring the words." He nodded to Elizabeth. "Ask me whatever you want to ask."

She sat in the room's only chair and took out her notebook. Started with a request for a description of his assailant, then stepped back and had him lead her through the events of the evening, from his band's performance at the Art Fair to his encounter with the man who had attacked him.

She had him repeat as much of their conversation as he could remember, especially the part about Callie Spencer.

"It didn't make sense," Bell said. "He wanted to know if I ever thought about her. If I had her picture on my wall."

Elizabeth jotted this down without comment, but Bell was watching her closely.

"That means something to you," he said.

No harm in telling him the truth. "Henry Kormoran was found dead in his apartment earlier today. He had a picture of Callie Spencer in his living room."

She could see it was news to him. He looked down at the brace on his hand.

"You think the man who attacked me killed Kormoran."

"It looks that way."

His eyes came up. "Why?"

"I'm hoping you might be able to shed some light on that. Have you talked to Kormoran recently?"

"I haven't had anything to do with him for seventeen years."

"What about Terry Dawtrey?"

A confused expression passed over Bell's face. "Terry Dawtrey's dead. I read it in the paper. You think that's connected to what happened tonight?"

Elizabeth shrugged. "Let's say the possibility intrigues me."

"The paper said Dawtrey tried to escape and got shot by a sheriff's deputy. How could that be connected to this?"

"I'm not sure yet. Let me ask you something else. Did the man who attacked you seem familiar? Is it possible you'd seen him before?"

"I saw him at the bar. And maybe at the Art Fair."

"What about seventeen years ago, at the Great Lakes Bank in Sault Sainte Marie?"

More confusion. "I don't follow. You think he might have been at the bank? A customer?"

"Or a robber."

Bell let out a short breath that might have been a laugh. "Floyd Lambeau's dead. Dawtrey's dead. And you just told me Kormoran's dead. That leaves me, and I didn't slug myself tonight."

"You're forgetting someone," Elizabeth said. "The getaway driver."

He stared thoughtfully across the room. "You think it was Jimbo?"

"Was that his name? I don't remember that from the reports I've read."

"It wouldn't be in the reports," said Bell. "It's just my little joke. I never knew any of their names, not at the time. Except for Floyd. Everybody knew Floyd. But he thought it would be better if the rest of us didn't know each other's names."

"That must have made things awkward. You had to meet with the others beforehand, to plan the robbery. How did you refer to each other?"

"Floyd gave us nicknames. He used to call me Sunshine. Dawtrey was Moonbeam; Kormoran was Rainbow. We only met the driver once before the day of the robbery. He wasn't in on the planning. So he never got a nickname. But I thought of him as Jimbo."

"Why?"

"Probably because it rhymed with Lambeau and Rainbow. I never called him that to his face. I don't think I exchanged two words with him."

"And in the years since then, you've never seen him again?"

"No."

"Do you think it could have been him tonight?"

"If you hadn't suggested it, it would never have occurred to me."

Elizabeth rose from her chair. "Is that a no?"

"I don't know. We're talking about someone I saw seventeen years ago. He'd be around thirty-seven now. The guy from tonight—I'd say he's younger than that, but I can't be sure. Both of them were white. Not tall, not short. Average. I don't know. Do you really think it could have been him?"

"It's something we have to consider."

Sutton Bell looked up at the ceiling. He asked a question of no one in particular.

"Why would Jimbo want to kill me?"

His wife took hold of his good hand. Elizabeth said nothing.

Bell went on in a mystified tone. "He's the one who drove off that morning. Saved his own neck. Left us all stranded there. If anything, I should want to kill him."

THE ER WAITING ROOM at University Hospital is an orderly place, at least on a Wednesday night in July. No shouting, no frantic motion. When Elizabeth finished with Bell and his wife and went out past the reception desk, she heard a tired-looking man complaining to an administrator about his insurance coverage. She saw a pair of EMTs wheeling in a gray-haired woman on a gurney. She saw Carter Shan come through the sliding doors behind the EMTs.

"The chief sent me to check up on you," he said.

"Is that right?"

"Actually, I volunteered. How's Bell?"

"He seems all right. It looks like they'll keep him a while, for observation."

"When he leaves, he might want to try a different exit. There's a news crew outside."

"Lovely."

Shan started to ask what she had learned from Bell, but Elizabeth was only half-listening. She had spotted a woman sitting at the end of a row of chairs, in the shadow of a tall artificial fern. She wore a white silk blouse and a gray skirt. She matched the description of the woman from the Eightball Saloon.

Shan had noticed her too. "What's she doing here?" he asked.

Elizabeth answered automatically. "She followed the ambulance that brought Bell in."

"Does she know him?"

"I don't know, but she saw his attacker. We need to question her."

"She witnessed the assault on Bell?" Shan said. "She's a busy little thing, isn't she?"

Something in his tone made Elizabeth frown. "What are you talking about?"

He raised his hand in a wave, and the woman waved back.

"She was at Kormoran's apartment," he said. "She's the one who found the body."

They watched the woman rise under the shadow of the fern.

"That's Henry Kormoran's sister."

CHAPTER 8

The woman in the silk blouse had a dusting of freckles across the bridge of her nose. She had tried to cover them with a layer of foundation, but they had managed to fight their way through. Elizabeth estimated her age at twenty-five.

"I'm afraid I lied to you," the woman said, looking at Shan.

"That's unusual," said Elizabeth.

"Is it? People never lie to you?"

"They lie all the time," Shan said. "What they don't do is admit it. It's disappointing."

"I shouldn't have done it. I apologize."

Elizabeth traced a finger along one of the plastic leaves of the fern. "It's disappointing because Detective Shan here would much rather catch you in a lie. If you're just going to admit it, there's no challenge. You could at least make him work for it. What you should have done is let us take you back to the station, put you in a room alone—"

"Under glaring lights—" added Shan.

"In a chair that wobbles, because we've filed down one of the legs. And once you're there, we'd let you wait. For an hour—"

"Maybe two."

"And then Detective Shan would come in and slap a thick folder down on the table. And just when you're prepared to admit everything, he'd find an excuse to leave—"

"I usually pretend I forgot to bring a pen," Shan confided.

"That's a classic move," said Elizabeth. "And by the time he gets back with a pen, you're so anxious that you blurt out a confession before he even sits down, because you're afraid he's going to leave again." She paused, shaking her head. "And it could have been like that, you would have made his night, but you had to come out and admit that you lied."

The woman in the silk blouse looked back and forth between them, a faint smile on her lips. "I'm almost sorry I missed all that," she said.

"It's a lost opportunity now," said Elizabeth. "What did you lie about?"

"I'm not really Henry Kormoran's sister."

"Who are you?" Shan asked her.

She reached into her handbag and passed Shan a business card.

Elizabeth glimpsed her name, LUCY NAVARRO, and the title of the paper she worked for—*The National Current.*

"A member of the press," Shan said.

"The rest of what I told you was true," said Lucy Navarro. "I arranged to meet Henry Kormoran for lunch yesterday, but he never showed. So I went to his apartment tonight. I told the manager I was his sister so he'd let me in."

"Why did you want to meet Kormoran?" asked Elizabeth.

"Isn't it obvious? Callie Spencer's running for the Senate. Terry Dawtrey gets shot down at his father's funeral. Kormoran's connected to both of them by a seventeen-year-old bank robbery. There's a story there somewhere."

"Is that why you went looking for Sutton Bell? Because he's part of the story too?"

"I've tried to contact Bell before," Lucy Navarro said. "After what happened to Kormoran, I figured I'd better track him down."

"How did you find him?"

"I Googled him. Saw that his band was playing at the Art Fair. I got there too late to hear them, but they're musicians, right? I figured they'd go for a drink after. The Eightball Saloon was the third place I tried. I wanted to talk to Bell alone, so I waited at the bar. I slipped off to the ladies' room while he was playing pool, and naturally that's when he decided to leave."

"So you followed him," Elizabeth said. "Did you get a look at his attacker?"

"I saw him in the bar, but the lighting wasn't the best. He had a bandage on his hand. He wore a baseball cap."

"What color were his eyes?"

"I've no idea."

"What about his hair?"

It had been dark rather than light, the woman thought. Her description of the suspect's car turned out to be similarly vague. A sedan. Gray or green, or maybe blue. American rather than foreign. She hadn't seen the license plate.

When Elizabeth ran out of questions, Lucy Navarro had some of her own.

"Do you think he's the same man who killed Henry Kormoran?" she wanted to know. "He would almost have to be, wouldn't he?"

Elizabeth agreed, but she said, "I really can't comment."

"The bandaged hand tends to connect him with Kormoran, doesn't it? There was a knife and blood at Kormoran's apartment."

"I can't comment on that either."

"Will you be interviewing Callie Spencer about this case?"

Elizabeth turned to Shan. "Now that's a good question—"

He nodded. "It's a shame we can't comment."

ANTHONY LARK PRESSED a cardboard cup against his brow. The ice inside had melted but the soda was still cool, and the cool helped to loosen the knot behind his eyes.

His car idled in the hospital parking lot. Through the windshield he could see the sliding glass doors of the emergency room, the bright lights within.

The doors opened and a woman walked through. Even at a distance he recognized her as the woman from the bar, the one who had come running after Sutton Bell.

Two people came out with her: a tall woman with black hair pulled back in a ponytail, and a slim Asian man in a tie and shirtsleeves. They looked like cops, Lark thought. They acted like cops too, waving away the reporter and the cameraman who approached them from a news van parked by the curb.

He lowered the cup and rested it on his knee. His hand ached beneath the bandage. Antibiotics. That's what he needed. Keflex. Sutton Bell had told him so. They would have it right there, in the hospital, but he couldn't go in. He couldn't go to a doctor's office or a clinic either. They'd be watching for him.

He would wait a day or two. Maybe the hand would get better on its own. If not, he'd figure something out. For now, he would have to lie low. He had been overconfident with Bell. He should never have written that line: *Sutton Bell is next.* That was tempting fate. He should never have left the manuscript outside the *Gray Streets* office—though to be fair to himself, he had left it after hours. He didn't think anyone would find it before the morning, after Bell was already dead.

We all want to be known. To be seen for who we really are. But he had been too eager.

He could still get to Sutton Bell. They would watch the man now—at his home, at his work. But for how long? Lark could afford to wait. Things would be harder, but it could still be done.

It was all for the sake of Callie Spencer, the woman with the wondrous smile.

He needed rest, a good night's sleep. He put the car into gear and drove slowly out of the parking lot and into the street.

CHAPTER 9

In the heat of summer, the front door of the Waishkey house swells in the frame; it takes a solid push to open it. The sound of its opening woke me after midnight. I heard Elizabeth extracting her key from the lock, wedging the door back into the frame.

I heard her unclip the holstered pistol from her belt. Her footsteps crossing the tiled foyer to the threshold of the living room. She came in and laid the pistol and her bag on the coffee table and sat in the chair across from mine.

"David, I thought we agreed you wouldn't wait up."

"That's not the way I remember it," I said.

She turned to look at the sofa where her daughter was sleeping. Sarah Waishkey—tall, slender, sixteen years old—lay curled on her side in denim shorts and a loose white T-shirt. She wore a braided leather band around her right ankle. Her long black hair fell across her forehead onto her pillow, and her hands rested palm-to-palm beneath her cheek. I'd seen the pose before. She slept like a girl in a Renaissance painting.

"She should be in bed," Elizabeth said in a hushed voice.

"I tried to tell her she shouldn't wait up. She didn't go along."

"Imagine that."

"She's strong-willed."

The girl is not my daughter, just as Elizabeth is not my wife and her house is not my house. But it's a near thing. It's close. It's *almost*.

A great many things about my life are almost.

One night a long time ago, I got into a fight with a very bad man on the top level of a parking garage. He died, and I was almost convicted of murder. Last year, Elizabeth and I got tangled up with another very bad man in the woods of Marshall Park, and I almost got her killed, and almost died myself.

These days I spend most of my nights in her bed. I eat at her table. I'm teaching her daughter how to drive. And though her house is not mine, it almost is. I come and go as I like. I pay half the mortgage every month. I keep a toothbrush and a change of clothes in the *Gray Streets* office, and on nights when I work late I sometimes sleep there, on a sofa in the storage room. But apart from that, everything I have is here, in this house.

I try to keep my distance from her work. Her colleagues in the police department have accepted our relationship—almost. But they'd rather not be reminded of me. Crime in the city of Ann Arbor is Elizabeth's business, not mine. Technically I shouldn't ask her about cases, and she shouldn't tell me.

Tonight, as Elizabeth sat back in the chair across from me, as her daughter slept a few feet away, I almost kept my curiosity in check.

"What did you find out about the man in the plaid shirt and the safari hat?"

Elizabeth touched the string of glass beads at her throat before she answered me.

"He wore a different hat when he assaulted Sutton Bell tonight," she said.

"That's devious."

She gave me the details of the attack on Bell. It didn't sound like she held out much hope of finding the man in plaid.

"We could've had his fingerprints," she said, "but the Eightball Saloon has what must be the most efficient bartender in town. He wiped down the bar after Mr. Plaid left, and sent his glass to the kitchen to be washed."

"Maybe he left his prints on the manuscript I gave you," I suggested.

"Maybe." She didn't think so. I didn't either.

"I pieced together a description from Bell and some of the other witnesses," she told me, "but I don't know what it'll be worth. We'll work up a composite."

I picked up a sketch pad from the coffee table, found the right page, and passed it to her. The page held a pencil sketch of the man I had seen at the Art Fair—hat and sunglasses and all.

"Sarah did this?" she asked me.

I nodded. "I only saw him from across the street. She did a good job with what I could give her. The basics are there: the length of his jaw, the shape of his mouth."

"It should help."

Elizabeth put the sketch pad back on the table and picked up a sheaf of papers lying there—a copy of the man in plaid's manuscript. I'd made it that evening, before I turned the original over to her. I'd done my best to preserve any evidence the pages might contain, even though I'd already handled them. I figured running them through a photocopier would be a bad idea, so instead I used a digital camera to snap a picture of each page, then loaded the images onto my office computer and printed them out. I thought I was entitled; the manuscript had been left at *Gray Streets,* after all.

It hadn't been left there by chance.

I understood it as soon as I read the first line. *I killed Henry Kormoran* . . . I knew that name. I knew a little something about the Great Lakes Bank robbery.

A few months back, I read a newspaper article about Callie Spencer and got curious about her history. I did some research on the robbery and found the details intriguing—especially the part about the fifth robber, the one who never got caught. I kept turning the scenario over in my mind, and eventually I used it as a springboard for a short story.

I published the story under a pseudonym in *Gray Streets*. The man in plaid must have read it there. I had to assume that was what brought him to the hallway outside my office door.

So I thought I was entitled to a copy of his manuscript. I don't know if Elizabeth agreed with me, but she returned the pages to the coffee table without comment. She had her own copy. I could see it poking out of a pocket of her handbag.

"Have you read it?" I asked her.

"Not all the way through."

I'd read the thing twice while I waited for her to come home. I didn't like it either time.

"You should read it," I said, "and we'll talk about it after."

She shot me a half-amused look. "Will we?"

"I've been thinking. If you're going up north I think I should go with you."

Her amusement turned to puzzlement. "Why would I go up north?"

"You'll see, once you've read it," I said, and then I added the words I'd been rehearsing while I waited. "I don't want you to go alone. I know how things are, with budget cuts in the department. They might be tempted to send just one person. I assume they'll keep an eye on Sutton Bell, and that'll take a lot of manpower. So if they send you up north, I'll go with you."

"David, what are you talking about?" She reached for her copy of the manuscript. "What's in here?" she said. "Why would they send me up north?"

I glanced at the sketch on the coffee table.

"Because the man in plaid has been there," I told her. "Part of his story is set there—in Sault Sainte Marie. The opening pages are about Henry Kormoran, and the last line is about Sutton Bell, but the middle . . . the middle is all about Terry Dawtrey."

CHAPTER 10

The drive from Ann Arbor to Sault Sainte Marie is three hundred forty miles. Take Route 23 and I-75 and you can make it in a little over five hours, not counting stops. As you travel north beyond Flint and Saginaw, the urban gives way to the rural, and fields and trees come to dominate the landscape. Off behind those trees are sparkling lakes you won't see from the highway. There are cabins on the shore, places where city dwellers go to escape the heat of the Michigan summer.

When you approach the tip of the state's Lower Peninsula you find tourist towns that want to sell you stuffed moose dolls and T-shirts silk-screened with images of black bears. Every other shop boasts gourmet fudge. The Mackinac Bridge is a tourist attraction in itself—five miles of steel and cables passing over the straits that join Lake Michigan to Lake Huron.

On the other side lies the Upper Peninsula and fifty more miles of I-75 before you reach Sault Sainte Marie on the border with Canada. Elizabeth and I arrived in the evening on Thursday and drove out to the edge of the Saint Mary's River. We watched the light fade over the rough water before doubling back to check in to our hotel.

We'd made a late start. It had taken Owen McCaleb a while to make up his mind to send Elizabeth north. Then we had to pack the car and make arrangements for Sarah to stay with Bridget Shellcross. We didn't get on the road until midafternoon.

On Friday morning we rose early and drove to the Chippewa County Sheriff's office, a tan brick building on Court Street. The sheriff met us in the lobby. Walter Delacorte: six feet tall with broad shoulders and a stomach that bulged without quite seeming fat. He put on a pair of amber-lensed sunglasses and walked us down the block to a diner with a CALLIE SPENCER FOR SENATE sign in the window.

"You've come a terrible long way," he said, "and you at least deserve a good breakfast. I'd hate to see you leave disappointed."

The smell of bacon and strong coffee hit us as soon as we stepped inside. A waitress led us past a long counter to a booth in the back, away from the other customers. We made small talk over omelets, Delacorte inquiring about our drive and my line of work. He turned out to be a fan of crime fiction. Only after the waitress cleared our plates away did he and Elizabeth get down to business.

"I understand why you've come," said Delacorte, "but I'm not sure I can help you. I've got my doubts about whether the man you're looking for was ever in Sault Sainte Marie."

"Did you read the manuscript I sent you?" she asked him, unfolding a copy on the table. The man in plaid's manifesto. She had faxed Delacorte the pages before we left Ann Arbor.

"I've read it," he said. "It makes a good yarn, and I can see why you thought you should pass it along. But I'm not convinced. Put yourself in my shoes."

He tapped the pages with a thick finger. "Whoever wrote this claims to have murdered Charlie Dawtrey. But I've got a man in custody for that—fella named Kyle Scudder. He got into a fight with Dawtrey. That's a fact. It happened at the Cozy Inn over in Brimley. And a few hours later Dawtrey got beaten to death. There's no mystery about what happened."

Delacorte leaned back and rolled his broad shoulders. His gray uniform fit him well; it seemed to have been tailored to accommodate his stomach. He had eyes of a lighter gray, and black hair streaked with silver.

"As for Terry Dawtrey," he said, "that's no mystery either. They let him out of prison for his father's funeral and he made a run for it. One of my deputies had to shoot him. I wish to hell it hadn't happened, but there it is. It doesn't need explaining. Now you come along with this story that's supposed to have been written by a man who was at the cemetery that day." The sheriff's finger tapped the manuscript again. "He claims to have been on the hill with a rifle. Says he fired a shot at Dawtrey and missed. But nobody I've talked to saw him there. He's a phantom. So what am I supposed to do with this information? You might just as well tell me that my car runs because there are gremlins turning the wheels."

Elizabeth nodded toward the manuscript. "If he wasn't there, then how do you explain this?"

"It's a piece of creative writing."

"It's pretty detailed."

Delacorte's eyes looked kindly. "I agree, it's not bad. But there's really nothing there you couldn't pick up from the news coverage."

"The man who wrote this described how he killed Henry Kormoran," Elizabeth said. "And he didn't get it from the news, because he wrote it before Kormoran's body was discovered."

"Then it sounds like he killed Kormoran. That's for you to work out, down there in Ann Arbor. And I'm responsible for the Dawtreys up here."

"He also made a threat against Sutton Bell on the last page. And Bell was later attacked. Bell, Kormoran, and Terry Dawtrey were all involved in the Great Lakes Bank robbery. Doesn't it make sense to assume these cases are related?"

The sheriff ran his tongue over his front teeth thoughtfully.

"I don't doubt that they're related," he said. "Maybe you've got a copycat on your hands down there. Maybe he heard about Dawtrey getting shot and decided it was a wonderful thing. Maybe he thought someone should take out Kormoran and Bell too—and figured he was just the man to do it. But that wasn't enough for him. He wanted to take credit for the Dawtreys too. So he wrote up this story."

"So it's fiction?"

"As far as the Dawtreys are concerned. I've got no reason to think otherwise. The evidence just isn't there."

The waitress came by to refill our coffee. Delacorte loaded his with sugar and cream.

"Could we talk about the evidence, then?" Elizabeth asked him.

He stirred his cup. "You've come all this way. We can talk about anything you like."

Elizabeth smoothed back a lock of her hair and said, "I'm curious about Kyle Scudder, the man you think killed Charlie Dawtrey. You said they got into a fight. What started it?"

"The usual," Delacorte said. "They got into it over a woman. Gal named Madelyn Turner. She and Dawtrey were married for a while, years ago. They've got a son, around fifteen years old. The boy stayed with her after the marriage ended."

"Why did it end?"

"You'd be better off asking why it started. Charlie Dawtrey was already pushing sixty when he met Madelyn; she would've been forty or so. He was never any prize. Worked at lousy jobs all his life. But Madelyn was considered a beauty in her day. She went through a string of men. Some of them wealthy, successful.

"She lasted about three years with Dawtrey, then took up with a fella named Alden Turner and stayed with him seven years before he passed away."

Delacorte drank some coffee before continuing. "I don't think Dawtrey ever really got over her. They stayed in touch—they had the son together. Kyle Scudder started seeing her a few months ago. I suspect he didn't realize the difference in their ages. Madelyn's in her mid-fifties now, but she tries not to look it. Scudder is forty-two. They met when she hired him to do some landscaping at her house. He fell for her. Got to be jealous of her spending time with Charlie Dawtrey. He caught them together at the Cozy Inn that night. The fight started when Charlie put a hand on Madelyn in a way Kyle Scudder didn't like."

"What does Scudder have to say?" Elizabeth asked. "Does he admit to killing Dawtrey?"

"He denies it. Says he was with Madelyn at her place all night."

"What does she say?"

"Depends on when you ask her. At first she said Scudder followed her home from the Cozy but she didn't let him in—because she was angry about the way he'd treated Charlie. Then she changed her story. Said she and Scudder spent the night together."

I broke in then. "Why the change?"

Delacorte looked me over as if he had forgotten I was there. It was a cool, efficient look, intended to remind me that I was out of place: a civilian sitting in on a meeting where technically I didn't belong. Delacorte had allowed me to be here as a courtesy to Elizabeth.

He smiled briefly to let me know he would indulge me by answering my question.

"Mr. Loogan," he said, "if I understood why women do the things they do, I'd have a better job than the one I've got. If I had to guess, I'd say Madelyn told the truth the first time. But once she thought about how much trouble Scudder was in, she decided to cover for him."

"What about witnesses?" Elizabeth asked him.

"Charlie Dawtrey lived alone in a cabin in the woods. No close neighbors. No one heard or saw anything."

"Murder weapon?"

"We didn't find it at the scene. Coroner said it was probably a metal pipe or a tire iron." Delacorte's lips made another brief smile and he laid his hand atop the manuscript. "I know how much that pleases you, since it matches what's written here. But I have to tell you that our coroner likes to talk to the press. Whoever wrote this could have gotten the tire iron idea from the newspaper."

"And I imagine you're going to tell me Kyle Scudder owned a tire iron."

The smile came back, and this time it held a hint of self-satisfaction.

"Everyone owns a tire iron, right? We got a search warrant for his truck and his house. Funny thing is, we didn't find a tire iron. He says he had one, but he lost it. The story is, he stopped to help a lady with a flat a few weeks ago. He thinks he might have tossed it in her trunk by mistake. He never got the lady's name, of course."

"You think he's lying," Elizabeth said.

"I think he had time to dispose of the tire iron. Charlie Dawtrey's body wasn't found until late the next day. His son went over to see him. Madelyn's boy—Nick. Rode his bike over. They were supposed to go fishing."

Elizabeth leaned forward and I watched her in profile. She gazed at Delacorte as if she were trying to read his thoughts.

Finally she said, "You're not worried that you're making a mistake—that Kyle Scudder might be innocent?"

"I just don't see it," Delacorte said. "But it's really not my call. I've turned everything over to the county prosecutor. I'll pass your story along to him, but he believes we've got a solid case."

Elizabeth drew a long breath and I could tell she had decided to let the matter rest.

"Let's talk about Terry Dawtrey," she said.

Delacorte nodded his consent.

"He was serving a thirty-year sentence," Elizabeth said. "Does it seem strange to you that they would let him out, even for a few hours?"

"The warden at Kinross made that decision, but I can't say it surprises me. A man's father dies, you try to make allowances."

"But Dawtrey was a high-profile prisoner. He went away for shooting Harlan Spencer, and now Callie Spencer's running for the Senate."

Delacorte sipped coffee before he answered. "The way I heard it, the warden ran the idea past Harlan Spencer, and he didn't object. That doesn't surprise me either. I used to work for Harlan, when he was sheriff. I couldn't say if he's forgiven Dawtrey, but I know he's made his peace with what happened."

"Two of your deputies picked up Terry Dawtrey down at Kinross and drove him to the church, and to the cemetery."

"That's standard procedure. I assigned Sam Tillman and Paul Rhiner to handle Dawtrey. They had escorted prisoners before—without incident."

"What went wrong this time?"

The sheriff looked around the diner, and I thought he meant to summon the waitress for more coffee, but he was making sure no one was close enough to overhear.

"This is between us," he said.

"Of course," said Elizabeth.

"Tillman and Rhiner are suspended right now, and the whole thing is under review. What I tell you can't go any further."

"I understand," she said.

He gave me a warning look and I gave it right back to him. I think he decided I was harmless.

"The fact is, they screwed up," he said. "Terry Dawtrey behaved himself at the church service. When they got to the cemetery, Tillman and Rhiner let down their guard a little. They should have stayed right at Dawtrey's side the whole time, but they didn't. Tillman is a member of the congregation at Saint Joseph's. He stopped to chat with the priest at the graveside. Rhiner let Dawtrey wander off. Dawtrey told him he wanted to visit his grandmother's grave. Rhiner followed him, but at a distance. They had Dawtrey in shackles. Where was he going to go?"

"But Dawtrey managed to free himself from the shackles," said Elizabeth.

"He had help. Someone left a vase of roses in front of his grandmother's headstone, with a handcuff key in the grass beside it."

I pointed to the manuscript. "That detail is in here."

"It was in the newspaper too," said Delacorte. "We're not sure where the key came from. Access to handcuff keys is supposed to be restricted, but I've seen them for sale on eBay." For my benefit he added, "Handcuff locks are pretty much universal. They all open with the same kind of key."

The waitress came around again with coffee, and Delacorte did his thing with the cream and sugar.

"What about the roses?" I asked him. "Did you try to trace them?"

"A rose is a rose. We couldn't tie them to a particular shop. No prints on the vase."

He raised his brows as if inviting me to ask him something else. When I didn't, he turned back to Elizabeth and continued where he had left off.

"Once Dawtrey had the shackles off, he made a run for the cemetery fence. Rhiner ordered him to stop. Dawtrey climbed the fence and would have gotten away if Rhiner hadn't shot him. Someone had left a car for him on the other side of the cemetery hill. An old Camaro that belonged to a kid who delivered pizzas. It'd been stolen the night before. The kid left it running outside an apartment building while he made a delivery, and when he came out it was gone."

"Any leads on who stole the car?" Elizabeth asked.

"No one saw anything, naturally," said Delacorte. "And the car had been wiped clean of prints. We found the keys above the visor, some cash in the glove box, and a change of clothes and shoes in the trunk."

"That's some reasonably sophisticated planning," she said.

"Yup. And then there was the diversion. Two boys on bikes who set off fireworks in the cemetery parking lot. They drew attention away from Dawtrey at just the right moment, so he could unlock the cuffs."

"You haven't been able to identify them?"

He hesitated, looking down into his coffee cup. "You need to understand the situation. My deputies had their hands full. Rhiner hated having to shoot Dawtrey. After he'd done it, he climbed over the fence and tried to perform CPR. Tillman had a crowd of mourners to deal with. He got on the radio and called for backup. Neither of them had time to chase after a pair of teenagers on bikes."

"And none of the mourners could help you identify these kids?"

Delacorte looked up from his coffee and sighed.

"I don't know how to say this without offending you, Detective Waishkey."

"Just go ahead and say it."

"We've got a bay near here called Waishkey. It's named after a Chippewa chief. Are you part Chippewa, Detective?"

"Waishkey is my ex-husband's name."

"That's not an answer to my question," Delacorte said, "but I don't mind. Charlie Dawtrey was half Chippewa. His son Terry was a quarter. I'd wager that everyone at the funeral had some Chippewa blood. I deal with Chippewa people all the time, and most days they're as cooperative as anybody else. But in this case a white deputy shot a Chippewa man—never mind that he was a prisoner trying to escape. That makes people angry. And then the sheriff comes to them asking for help tracking down a couple of Chippewa kids? Nobody at that cemetery was willing to tell me anything."

"So no one told you they saw a man with a rifle on the hill?"

"No."

"And no one said they heard an extra shot, apart from the one Rhiner fired at Dawtrey?"

The sheriff's face took on a pained expression. "You ask around, you'll hear all kinds of talk about extra shots. Some people confused the sound of the fireworks for the sound of gunfire, and some people would just like to stir up trouble. There are rumors that Rhiner emptied his clip into Dawtrey. But I can tell you there was only one shot fired that day."

"So neither of your deputies heard a second shot?" Elizabeth said. "It might have sounded like an echo." She gestured toward the manuscript. "According to this, the man with the rifle pulled his trigger just as he heard the sound of Rhiner's shot."

"That cemetery is surrounded by hills on three sides. Anybody who thinks they heard an echo probably did." Delacorte patted the table with his open palm—a sign to let us know he was ready to wrap things up. "We could go back and forth about this, but I've got business to attend to and you've got better things to do with your time."

He reached for his wallet and started counting out bills. I did the same. The waitress had left the tab midway between us.

"Long as you're here," Delacorte said, "you owe it to yourselves to see the Soo Locks. Busiest locks in the world: ten thousand ships go through every year. And if you get a chance to cross over to the Canadian side, I recommend the train tour through the Agawa Canyon. Can't beat the scenery."

He slid out of the booth and got to his feet.

"Far as this other thing goes, it's like I said. There's no question about what happened to Terry Dawtrey. He tried to run and he got shot. Your man on the hill and his rifle—I don't need them. I can make sense of what happened without them. Sometimes the simplest explanation is the true one. There wasn't any man on the hill."

CHAPTER 11

Outside the diner Walter Delacorte slipped on his sunglasses and walked us back to our car. The last we saw of him he was strolling along Court Street. As soon as we got in the car Elizabeth said two words. "Rod Steiger."

It took me a second, but I understood. *"In the Heat of the Night,"* I said.

"He played the chief of police. That's who Delacorte reminds me of. Rod Steiger, only with more charm and less integrity."

She started the car and pulled out into the street.

"He reminds me of William of Occam," I said.

"What was he in?"

"The Middle Ages. He was an English philosopher."

After the briefest pause, she said, "Occam's razor."

I nodded. "Occam's razor. You should never multiply entities beyond necessity. So if you can explain what happened without positing a rifleman on the hill—"

"—then there was no rifleman."

"Exactly. Sheriff Delacorte just gave us a lecture on metaphysics."

"Then I guess our trip to Sault Sainte Marie wasn't entirely wasted."

"I think we've still got time to see the locks."

She lowered the driver's window and the wind caught her hair.

"I hate to disappoint you, David. But I don't think we're going to make it to the locks."

. . .

WE SPENT THE NEXT hour and a half taking in the sights of Sault Sainte Marie. Our first stop: the office of Arthur Sutherland, Kyle Scudder's attorney. Elizabeth gave Sutherland a composite sketch of the man in plaid and a copy of the manuscript describing Charlie Dawtrey's death. And though he interrupted her five or six times—because his phone kept ringing and he kept answering it—by the end of the meeting she had convinced him that he might actually have an innocent client on his hands.

Next we drove by Deputy Rhiner's house, a tidy place with a granite birdbath in the front yard. There was a Buick parked in the driveway beneath a walnut tree, but no one answered to our knock. Elizabeth left her card in the mailbox beside the front door.

We had about the same luck with Deputy Tillman, who lived in a wood-frame house on the west side of town, between the interstate and the railroad tracks. A dog barked at us from the side yard as we climbed onto the porch. The woman who came to the door looked frazzled. She had a baby on her hip and a toddler clutching the hem of her skirt. Both were girls, both had ribbons in their hair. Looking past them, we could see a third girl inside, maybe around six. She was running in circles and singing along with a song from a CD of children's music.

The woman—Tillman's wife—had no patience for Elizabeth's questions. She told us her husband was out and she wasn't sure what time he'd be back. Then she took the card Elizabeth offered and closed the door on us.

We made it to Whiteleaf Cemetery around midday. Drove through the open gate and left the car in the only shaded space in the lot. It took us a few minutes to find Charlie Dawtrey's headstone. We strolled along the path where Terry Dawtrey had walked and found a stone engraved with the name AGNES DAWTREY—his grandmother's grave, the one he had told the deputy he wanted to visit.

The vase of roses had been taken away, but this was where Terry Dawtrey had knelt in the grass and picked up the handcuff key. Then he had made a run for the fence.

We could see where he had ended up. There was a patch of ground on the other side of the fence edged with remnants of police tape. On a bar of the fence, someone had knotted a strip of yellow cloth, which looked to have been torn from a bath towel.

"That's a marker," Elizabeth said.

She took a sheet of paper from her pocket and unfolded it—a map printed from the Internet. It showed the cemetery and the surrounding roads.

"The roses showed Dawtrey where to find the key," she said, "and that strip of cloth told him where to run." She glanced down at the map. "If he ran in a straight line and over the hill, he would have come out on Portage Road. That's where the stolen Camaro would have been waiting for him."

I stood with Agnes Dawtrey's grave at my back and started walking toward the section of fence marked with the yellow cloth. Elizabeth walked along beside me.

"In the manuscript, the man in plaid says Dawtrey was running toward his position on the hill," I said. "He would have been up there under one of those pines with his rifle."

As we neared the fence Elizabeth took my arm to stop me. "He fired one shot down at Dawtrey and missed," she said.

It wasn't a question, but I answered her anyway. "That's right."

She pointed at the ground ahead of us, where a hunk of turf had been torn up and then replaced.

"Someone dug up his bullet."

THE WIND MADE RIPPLES in the wild grass on the slope of the hill. From the ridge above, I looked down at the crime-scene tape snaking through the grass.

"This is the spot," I said.

Elizabeth stood close beside me. We had walked the long way, out through the cemetery gate, around the fence, and up to this point on the hill.

A white pine, and needles thick on the ground underneath—just like the setting the man in plaid described. If you were to lie on your stomach under the pine, you could see everything down below, and no one would see you unless they were looking very carefully for you.

Elizabeth knelt and ran her palm over the needle-covered ground. She said, "According to the manuscript, the rifle jammed the first time, and he had to clear the round from the chamber. It landed in the pine needles. The rifle fired on the second try, and the shell casing would have ejected and wound up in the needles too. He doesn't say that he picked anything up afterward."

"No," I said.

I got down there with her and we searched the ground. We didn't find anything.

"Maybe he picked up the round and the casing," she said. "That's what a pro would have done. He might have thought it wasn't worth mentioning in the manuscript."

"Do you think he's a pro?"

She shook her head. "He acts like someone who's making it up as he goes."

"If he didn't take the round and the casing, someone else did. Delacorte, or one of his deputies."

"We don't know that."

"But we think it, don't we?"

She didn't say anything for a while. We were back on our feet, looking down at the wind-blown grass.

"It's possible the deputies never knew anyone was up here," she said eventually. "The rifle shot could have been mistaken for an echo. The bullet missed Dawtrey and buried itself in the ground. But once I faxed the manuscript to Delacorte, he would have come here to look things over."

"He could have dug up the bullet," I said, "and collected the round and the casing."

"It's possible."

"But what's the point? Why the cover-up?"

"I'm not sure. Maybe Delacorte just wants to put this all behind him. It's bad enough his deputies had to shoot a prisoner. If he admits there was a rifleman on the hill, that makes things worse. It raises questions he can't answer."

Her voice trailed off as if she'd been distracted by something below. I followed her gaze and saw a car passing in through the cemetery gate.

It looked familiar. Beside me, Elizabeth said, "Is that Paul Rhiner's Buick?"

The car came to a stop and the driver's door opened. The man who got out had on blue jeans and an untucked shirt. He went over to our car and looked through the windows, then started off across the cemetery lawn toward Charlie Dawtrey's grave.

"What's he doing?" I said.

"He's checking up on us."

Rhiner—if that's who it was—paused near Charlie Dawtrey's headstone and turned in a slow circle.

"He couldn't have followed us here, could he?" I asked Elizabeth.

"I doubt it," she said. "Delacorte probably sent him."

"You didn't tell Delacorte we were coming here."

"He didn't need to be told. I've got questions about Terry Dawtrey's death. Of course I'm going to come here."

Rhiner finally looked up. He stood staring at us, with a hand raised to shield his eyes from the sun.

"Should we head down?" I said.

"Let him come up."

It looked like he might. He started walking toward the gate, as though he intended to go around the fence and up the hill. But as he reached the parking lot another car drove in: a yellow Volkswagen Beetle. He gave it a wide berth, but the driver, a young woman, got out and began to follow him.

"Who's this now?" I said.

Elizabeth answered in a low voice. "A nuisance."

Down below, Rhiner and the woman had a conversation we couldn't hear. Before long, Rhiner turned his back on her and got into his car. We heard the engine come to life and watched the tires roll over the gravel. When the Buick got to the road Rhiner punched the gas and roared away.

Elizabeth pulled me back from the ridge and bent to scoop up a handful of pine needles. Before I could ask her why, she said, "Let's go."

WE TOOK THE LONG ROUTE again down the hill and around the fence. We found the woman waiting for us, leaning against her car. She seemed to have dressed to blend in with the locals: denim and twill and sturdy canvas boots.

Elizabeth made introductions. "David, this is Lucy Navarro. Lucy—David Loogan."

We said our hellos.

"Lucy's a reporter," said Elizabeth. "She's with the *New York Times*."

The woman flashed a grin and shook her head. "The *National Current*."

"Really?" Elizabeth said mischievously. "Are you positive?"

"Just about. Is there any chance you might tell me what you were doing up on the hill?"

Elizabeth had taken my arm as we crossed the parking lot, and now she rested her head on my shoulder and said, "David, she wants to know what we were doing on the hill."

I plucked a pine needle from her hair. "Missed one," I said.

Lucy Navarro ignored our playacting and soldiered on. "Paul Rhiner just left. Did he come here to meet with you?"

Elizabeth turned to look toward the road. "Is that who that was?"

"Rhiner's the one who shot Terry Dawtrey. Are there any new developments in that case? Anything that might shed light on the murder of Henry Kormoran or the attack on Sutton Bell?"

"She asks good questions, doesn't she?" Elizabeth said to me.

"And such a lot of them," I said.

"Maybe you'd care to answer one," said Lucy Navarro.

"I would," Elizabeth said, "but we're running late. David, what time is the train?"

I glanced at my watch. "If we leave now, we should make it."

"What train?"

Just before we turned to head back to our car, Elizabeth leaned in toward Lucy Navarro and said, "I shouldn't tell you this, but if you cross the border into Canada, there's a train you can ride through the Agawa Canyon. Off the record, just between us, I hear the view is spectacular."

CHAPTER 12

The fastest way to Brimley would have been via I-75 and Route 28. Elizabeth took a more scenic route, driving through the wooded countryside on county roads, picking up West Six Mile Road and following it through Brimley State Park. Lucy Navarro trailed along behind us in her yellow Beetle.

We drove south through what passed for the center of town and turned west on an unpaved lane that took us out to a converted farmhouse with a thick square chimney and a long sloping roof. We turned into the driveway; Lucy drove on past.

Elizabeth had phoned ahead and Madelyn Turner greeted the two of us at the door and ushered us into a front room dominated by a fireplace built of fieldstones and topped with an oakwood mantel.

She offered us a seat on a leather sofa and brought us lemonade, but before she could sit down a boy of about fifteen drifted in from another part of the house. Five foot six, black-haired and freckled. She introduced him as her son, Nick, and whispered something in his ear, and he went out again. A moment later a door clapped shut, and I could see, through one of the room's broad windows, that he had gone into the side yard.

His mother settled into an armchair and said, "I don't want Nick to hear us talking. He took it hard, what happened to his father, and then to Terry. It's more than a boy should have to bear."

Elizabeth leaned forward, elbows on her knees. "I understand he's the one who found his father's body."

"I wish I hadn't let him go over there alone," said Madelyn Turner. "But he loved Charlie. I couldn't have stopped him from going if I tried. That boy rides everywhere on his bike, and Charlie only lived two, three miles away."

"How did you and Charlie Dawtrey meet?"

Madelyn reached for a pack of cigarettes on a side table, then thought better of it.

"It happened after the bank robbery," she said, "when they put Terry on trial. Charlie went to the courthouse every day, and when they took a break at noon he would go out and sit on a bench in a park nearby. I had a job then at a boutique in Sault Sainte Marie, and I used to eat lunch in the park when the weather was nice. One day we struck up a conversation, and then it became something more."

"I understand he was quite a bit older than you were," Elizabeth said.

"I've always been attracted to older men," said Madelyn. "They generally have much more to offer. I had some fine times when I was young, and they usually involved a man who was older than I was. If I had a mind to, I could tell you stories, my dear."

It wasn't hard to believe. Her dark hair showed some gray at the roots, but her eyes were lively. She had strong cheekbones. Her jawline had gone soft, but not too soft. The clothes she wore—knitted blouse, knee-length skirt—fitted her too snugly, but their snugness hinted at the figure she must have had when she was younger.

"Now Charlie was a lovely man, and very sad," she said. "Worried for his son, of course. In the beginning, I felt sorry for him. I wanted to save him. But I needed something from him too. I was a widow. Charlie and I helped each other."

"But you didn't stay together," said Elizabeth.

"No. When they sent Terry to prison, it broke Charlie's heart. I thought I could change things by giving him another child. After Nick came along, I kept waiting for Charlie to be happy. But some wounds don't heal."

Madelyn gazed off through the window. Out in the yard, I could see her son playing on an old tire that hung by a rope from the bough of an elm tree.

"Charlie and I divorced, and I got married again—to Alden Turner, who helped raise Nick and left us this house. But Charlie was always part of his son's life, especially after Alden passed away."

"And was he part of your life too?" Elizabeth asked.

"Charlie and I would get together from time to time for a drink and a laugh. He had mellowed over the years. He could be good company when he wanted to be."

"Is that what happened the night Charlie died—you got together for a drink?"

"That's right."

"But Kyle Scudder didn't approve."

Madelyn pursed her lips. "Kyle has a jealous streak, and a bad temper. He didn't understand about Charlie. And Charlie didn't help things. He never liked Kyle. He thought Kyle was too possessive."

"I spoke to Sheriff Delacorte this morning," Elizabeth said. "He told me you changed your story about what happened that night. First you said Kyle followed you home but didn't stay, then you said he spent the night here."

A dark look passed over Madelyn's face. "When I found out about Charlie—" Her voice broke and she started again. "Nick called me when he found the body, and I went there and I saw . . . It's not something I'll forget. It was hours later when the sheriff asked about Kyle, and I'd had time for a few drinks. I was angry with Kyle about the way he'd treated Charlie at the Cozy Inn. I wasn't thinking straight. But the truth is Kyle stayed here all night. He couldn't be the one who killed Charlie."

"He might be the one who goes to prison for it," Elizabeth said.

"I can't believe that. The truth will come out. Justice will be done. It has to be."

"What makes you so sure?"

"Kyle's innocent. I have to think that's what matters most. Don't you?"

"I'd like to," Elizabeth said, reaching into her bag beside her on the sofa. "And as a matter of fact, I believe he's innocent." She drew out a copy of Sarah's sketch of the man in plaid. "Have you ever seen this man?"

I didn't hear Madelyn Turner's answer. She crossed to a desk in a corner of the room, looking for her reading glasses. Out in the yard Nick Dawtrey was standing by the tire swing. He seemed to be staring in at me. I picked up my glass of lemonade and excused myself, saying I needed to stretch my legs.

Passing through the entry hall to the kitchen, I found a screen door that opened onto a patio. I circled around to the side yard and walked toward the elm tree. Nick swayed on his toes, one arm wrapped through the center of the tire. He wore a shirt that hung loosely on him and blue jeans torn at the knees.

As I approached him, I could see Lucy Navarro in the distance. She stood next to her Beetle on the roadside by the end of the long driveway. There was a dog out there with her, part spaniel and part something else—a ragged-looking thing, brown and white. The dog yapped playfully, its tail wagging. Lucy was feeding it scraps from a fast-food wrapper. I watched her tear off a chunk of hamburger bun and toss it in the air, watched the dog leap up to catch it.

Nick Dawtrey was watching too. "Do you know her?" he said.

Across the distance, I could hear Lucy laugh. The dog danced for her on its hind legs.

"Not really," I said. "Whose dog is that?"

"He's a stray," said Nick. "I've seen him around."

Lucy ran out of scraps and spread the wrapper in the grass by the road. She got a bottle of water from the car and poured some into the shallow bowl formed by the wrapper so that the dog could drink.

Beside me, Nick let go of the tire swing and it swayed back and forth like a pendulum.

"Are you a cop?" he asked.

He hadn't said much in the house and I thought he'd be shy. But he seemed self-assured.

"I'm an editor," I told him.

"Your wife a cop?" He meant Elizabeth. I saw no reason to correct him.

"Yes."

"She from here?"

"She's from Ann Arbor."

"I mean originally. Is she Ojibwa?"

I wasn't sure I'd understood him. "Did you say Chippewa?"

"Ojibwa. Only a white man would say Chippewa."

"I don't know if she's Ojibwa or not."

That earned me a disappointed stare. "Maybe you should find out, sport."

"Probably," I said.

Out by the roadside, Lucy was pouring the dog another drink of water. I turned away from them to focus on Nick.

"I'm sorry about what happened to your father," I told him.

He made a sour face. "Everybody says that. What do you know about it?"

"I know he was murdered."

"You prolly think Kyle did it."

That *prolly* was the first thing he'd said that sounded like a fifteen-year-old.

"Actually, I don't."

"What about your wife?"

"She doesn't think so either," I said. "She wants to find out what really happened."

That brought a laugh. Knowing, bitter. "No," he said. "She doesn't."

"What's that supposed to mean?"

"She's a cop. Cops look out for each other."

The tire swing spun slowly in the air.

"You think the cops murdered your father?"

"Course they did. Why you look so surprised, sport?"

"I don't think cops generally go around murdering people."

"That's something else only a white man would say." His voice made *something* into *sometheen*.

"You have freckles," I said.

I could see that it confused him.

"So what?" he said.

"So you're as white as I am. You can knock off the Indian routine. Why would the cops kill your father?"

"Think about it. They kill him. Terry comes to the funeral. They kill Terry."

"Terry tried to escape."

A shrug. "If he didn't, they would've found some other excuse."

"You think they planned to kill him all along?"

He looked at me as if I'd disappointed him.

"Terry shot a cop," he said. "Put him in a wheelchair."

"That was seventeen years ago."

"You think the other cops forget something like that?" *Sometheen.* "You ever met the sheriff—Delacorte?"

"I've met him."

"You think he's sorry Terry tried to run? You think he's working hard to find out how that happened? You want some roses, sport?"

My turn to be confused. "What?"

Nick pointed toward the house, where a cluster of rosebushes grew not far from the patio. I'd walked past them without noticing.

"I'll cut you some roses," he said. "You can give them to your wife. You want some fern to go with them, I'll give you that too." He pointed toward a line of trees. "It grows wild in the woods."

I thought about Terry Dawtrey and the handcuff key someone had left for him on the cemetery lawn. With a vase of roses to mark the spot.

"Did the sheriff come by here to talk to you and your mother?"

"Sure he did."

"Did you offer him roses?"

Nick Dawtrey grinned. "You catch on quick for a white man. I offered. He didn't want any. Tell you what else, I rode over to Sault Sainte Marie last week. Sheriff's office is on Court Street. I spent an hour riding around the block, over and over."

I understood what he meant when I saw his bike leaning against the side of the house. Two strips of yellow cloth hung from the handlebars like streamers. Just like the strip of cloth someone had tied to the fence at Whiteleaf Cemetery.

He was telling me he had ridden that bike in circles around Delacorte's office.

"And I know he saw me," he added, "because he came outside. I did everything but hand him a confession. He doesn't want to know. He's happy with the way things turned out."

CHAPTER 13

"Where'd you get the vase?" Elizabeth asked.

She was soaking in the tub in our hotel room, white clouds of foam floating on the surface of the water. A trio of candles on the counter cast a golden light over the room. Nick Dawtrey's roses and some wild fern stood in a glass vase on the edge of the tub.

"The desk clerk gave it to me," I said. "She also gave me the bubble bath. They've got a basket of it behind the desk, in case you forget to bring your own."

I was sitting on the tile floor, leaning against the tub. The fingers of my left hand skimmed through the white clouds.

Earlier, we had stopped for dinner in Brimley at the Cozy Inn—a chance to question waitresses. One of them thought the sketch we showed her looked familiar. The man in plaid might have been in the bar on the night Kyle Scudder and Charlie Dawtrey had their fight. But if he was, he paid with cash, not credit. We weren't going to find him that way.

Madelyn Turner hadn't recognized the sketch. Neither had Nick.

I took the wheel on the drive back to Sault Sainte Marie. Elizabeth made phone calls. She talked for a while with Sarah and checked in with Owen McCaleb. The department had people watching Sutton Bell's home and workplace, but so far there had been no sign of the man in plaid.

Elizabeth tried calling Sam Tillman, but the deputy's wife said he still wasn't home. There was no answer at Paul Rhiner's house.

Now I watched the candlelight play over the ceiling and felt the warmth of the water on my fingertips. I heard Elizabeth say: "If they don't want to talk to me, I can't make them. I don't have the authority up here to question anyone. I was pressing my luck today with Madelyn Turner. If Walter Delacorte wanted to shut me down, he'd have every right."

"But there's something rotten about Delacorte," I said. "He's not even trying to find out what really happened at Whiteleaf Cemetery. It's like Nick said: He doesn't want to know."

"I could make an issue of that, but I can guess what would happen. They'd arrest Nick for conspiring to help Terry Dawtrey escape. And they'd make him rat out his friends—the kids who lit the firecrackers, and probably helped him steal the getaway car. Would you want that?"

"No."

"Neither would I."

Her knee came up out of the water, just beneath my hand. I trailed my palm down the smooth skin of her calf.

"I don't think he'd rat anybody out," I said.

She closed her eyes. "You like him."

"What's not to like? If I were in a tough spot, I'd want a brother like Nick Dawtrey." I came to her ankle and started back up again. "So what are we going to do?"

"Nothing. If Delacorte's hiding something, he's going to keep hiding it. McCaleb wants me back home tomorrow."

"But there are other people you could talk to—people who were at Charlie Dawtrey's funeral."

"I could. And maybe someone got a glimpse of the man in plaid up on the hill. But that won't help me find him."

I watched her in silence—the way the strands of her black hair moved with the water.

After a time I said, "Are you part Ojibwa?"

Her smile came first, then her eyes opened. "Where'd you pick up that word?"

"From Nick. He wanted to know if you were from around here."

"I was born in Bay Mills, a few miles from his mother's house."

"You should have shown me. I'd like to see where you grew up."

She tipped her chin from side to side in the water. "There's nothing there anymore. Just an overgrown field. They tore the house down a long time ago."

The muscles of her calf felt tense beneath my fingers.

"You still haven't answered my question," I said. "You didn't answer when Delacorte asked either."

She drew a long breath and let it out. "My father was named Parish. His ancestors came from England. My mother was Ojibwa."

"How come you never told me that?"

"I wasn't sure how you'd react."

"What do you mean?"

Mischief in her blue eyes. "I was afraid you'd think I was some sort of exotic creature. You wouldn't know how to behave."

She sat up slowly, braced her palms on the rim of the tub, got her feet under her, and stood—in what seemed like a single smooth motion. I stood at the same time, admiring her in the candlelight, and though I kept my eyes on hers I was aware of the water and the foam flowing down between her breasts and along her stomach and over her thighs. I trailed my fingers over her collarbone until they came to the hollow of her throat.

"You should have told me," I said. "It wouldn't have made a difference. I already thought you were an exotic creature."

A GOOD WHILE LATER I woke in the dark under the thin covering of a hotel sheet. Elizabeth lay beside me, her hair spread over both our pillows. Sometimes she sleeps on her stomach, with her head turned to the side. And though I didn't expect her to spontaneously stop breathing—not really—I put my hand on her back between her shoulder blades to make sure. I felt a gentle rise and fall.

I slipped out of bed and made my way toward the bathroom, following the faint glow of candlelight. Closing the door, I ran water in the sink and drank some from my cupped hands. My clothes lay scattered on the tiled floor. I put them on, blew out the candles, and went out again.

I found a key card on the bureau and took it with me out into the hallway. The carpet felt rough against my socked feet. A low hum led me to an alcove with an ice maker and vending machines. Nothing there to my liking. I wanted fruit. An orange would be perfect.

I took the stairs down to the first floor and passed through the lobby to the dining room. A television mounted on the wall played a cable news show at low volume. On the long buffet counter stood a lone pot of coffee, a pitcher of ice water, and a bowl of apples.

"Mr. Loogan," a voice said.

Lucy Navarro had on the same twill shirt she had worn earlier. It came down to her thighs, which were bare. I had to look twice to make sure she had gym shorts on underneath.

She said, "I see you've managed to get all the pine needles out of your hair."

I picked up an apple. "I didn't know you were staying here."

"It's the only hotel that suits my purpose. Pour me some water, will you?"

I filled two Styrofoam cups from the pitcher and brought them to a nearby table. She sat across from me with her back to the television.

"Did you ever talk to Paul Rhiner?" she asked me.

I took a bite of my apple and shook my head no.

"He wouldn't talk to me either. And Sam Tillman's wife slammed the door before I could finish a sentence. What do you think they're hiding?"

I studied the apple and said nothing.

She went on, undeterred. "I didn't get anywhere with Madelyn Turner either. Apparently someone told her I work for a cheap tabloid."

"Huh."

"She wouldn't let me near the boy, of course. You were with him in the yard for a while. What did you talk about?"

"Baseball."

There's a look you sometimes see in the eyes of intelligent people when you lie to them and they know it's a lie but there are no hard feelings because, in the first place, it's a playful lie and, in the second place, they never expected you to tell them the truth. Just then, Lucy Navarro had that look.

"I don't think you talked about baseball," she said.

"Isn't that what fifteen-year-old boys talk about?"

"Maybe twenty years ago. Today it would be video games. You didn't ask me what my purpose was."

"Pardon?"

"I told you this hotel's the only one that suits my purpose. You didn't ask what it was."

I set the apple down on the table. "What's your purpose, Lucy?"

"I'm trying to cultivate you as a source. How am I doing?"

She bit her lip like an ingénue. Her hair, with its blond highlights, fell carelessly around her face. She looked young. I remembered watching her by the roadside at Nick Dawtrey's house—the way she laughed when the stray dog danced for her. There'd been something appealing about her energy, her delight in that unguarded moment. She had that same energy now, though it was subdued, under control. She had turned serious.

I asked her, "Where are you from—California?"

"L.A.," she said. "How'd you know?"

"Lucky guess. Your legs are tanned, and you're not afraid to show them off. You project an air of confidence even though you don't really know what you're doing. How long have you been a reporter?"

"Not so long."

"They didn't train you much."

She smiled. "Does it show?"

"Usually if you want to cultivate someone as a source, you don't come out and tell him you want to cultivate him as a source. Why did the *Current* send you to Michigan?"

"To cover Callie Spencer."

"Have they given up on stories about Elvis and space aliens?"

"The *National Current* is a serious newspaper."

"I like the way you say that with a straight face."

Her eyes twinkled. "I've practiced."

"Is the *Current* looking to wreck Callie Spencer's political career?"

Lucy shrugged. "I imagine they wouldn't mind, if it sold papers. But I intend to follow the story, wherever it leads. No more, no less."

A hint of professional pride had crept into her voice.

"Where do you think it's leading?" I asked her.

"Right now—back to Terry Dawtrey. Did you know his grandmother died a few years ago? Back then, the warden at Kinross Prison wouldn't let him out for the funeral. This time he did."

"Maybe the warden has mellowed," I suggested.

"Maybe this time somebody wanted Dawtrey out," Lucy said. "How much do you know about the Great Lakes Bank robbery?"

"I know the gist."

She started ticking off bank robbers on her fingers. "The man who planned the thing—Floyd Lambeau—he died. The driver got away. Of the three who were caught, Dawtrey got by far the most prison time. Kormoran served just six years, Bell less than three."

"That makes sense, doesn't it?" I said. "Dawtrey's the one who shot Harlan Spencer."

"That's true, but the others got off pretty lightly. Dawtrey spent all that time in prison and then, when he seemed to catch a break—when they let him out for his father's funeral—he wound up dead. It makes me wonder if everything is as it seems. What really happened to Terry Dawtrey? Did someone orchestrate his release? Did someone plan his death? These are questions I'd like to ask Detective Waishkey, if I thought she'd answer them."

I showed her my empty palms. "I'm not going to answer them either."

"Come on, Loogan," she said. "Give me something. What were you doing today on the hill above Whiteleaf Cemetery?"

I listened to the murmur of the television and said nothing.

"What about Sheriff Delacorte?" she asked me. "You and Detective Waishkey met with him this morning. What did he tell you?"

I pressed a thumbnail into the side of my Styrofoam cup.

"Is he happy about Detective Waishkey coming up here, asking questions? Did he try to warn her off the case?"

This was a new idea. It made me frown. "Nobody tried to warn her off the case," I said.

She tipped her head to the side, curious. "Are you telling me the truth?"

"Why would I lie?"

The sound of the television receded and I watched Lucy Navarro reach into the pocket of her shirt and bring out a folded tissue.

"They put us on the same floor," she said. "I'm in room 305. I have to walk past your room to get to the elevator. Earlier tonight I found something in the hallway outside my door. Do you want to guess what it was?"

I picked up my apple, took a bite. Waited.

"A bullet," she said. "Nine-millimeter, I think."

She laid the tissue on the table and unfolded it. There were two bullets inside.

"I found one outside your door too," she said. "Are you sure no one's trying to warn you off the case?"

CHAPTER 14

The magazines in the waiting room had mailing labels on the covers, with the same name on each label: DR. MATTHEW KENNEALLY.

Anthony Lark held a copy of *U.S. News* in his lap. His left hand felt okay as long as he kept it still. If he flexed his fingers, the pain was like a steel wire being drawn through his flesh.

He had a clean bandage on it, white gauze secured with tape. He had showered and shaved and was wearing a fresh blue button-down shirt and slacks.

He glanced at the receptionist, saw her talking on the phone behind the sliding glass panel. He had no appointment, but she had promised she would try to get Dr. Kenneally to see him. She couldn't interrupt the doctor during a session, but his current session would be over in a few minutes.

So Lark waited in the dark-paneled room. Seven chairs—but only one other patient: a mousy woman trying to hide behind a copy of *Entertainment Weekly*.

The air in the room felt thick and warm. Lark thought he had a fever, because of the infection in his hand. He needed antibiotics. Dr. Kenneally could write prescriptions; he had given Lark the pills he used to combat his headaches. The police knew about Lark's hand; his injury had been reported in the news. So he couldn't go to just any doctor. It came down to a matter of trust. So here Lark was, trusting that Dr. Kenneally wouldn't turn him over to the police.

Lark waited. The receptionist was still on the phone. The magazine in his lap concealed his left hand. He looked down at the white label, at the letters of Dr. Kenneally's name. They troubled him.

The letters in "Matthew" were a cool tan like the wood of a healthy tree after you've peeled away the bark, but the letters of "Kenneally" were a dark brown that verged on black. The letters of "Kenneally" divided themselves into tiny dots that skittered over one another like swarming insects. "Kenneally" ended in "ly"; it wasn't an adverb, but it was *like* an adverb. And adverbs made Lark uneasy, because they *swarmed.*

He turned the magazine over to hide the mailing label. What if he had made a mistake? Maybe the receptionist had seen his hand. Or maybe she had noticed him trying to hide it, and that had been enough to arouse her suspicions. Suppose she had already consulted Dr. Kenneally and he had told her to call the police. She had been on the phone a long time. Now, as he watched her, she turned and stared directly back at him.

He bent the magazine around to peek at the mailing label. The letters of "Kenneally" had spread apart into a million tiny fragments, jagged bits of black that leapt and jittered. Lark jumped to his feet and the magazine dropped to the floor. He stepped quickly past the reception window and reached for the knob of the hallway door. Without thinking he turned it with his left hand and the steel wire sliced through him.

He heard the receptionist calling his name, but he didn't look back. He clamped down on the pain in his hand and ran—along the hall, down the stairs. He slowed only when he hit the open air, his breath sawing through his lungs. Beads of sweat poured out of his scalp as he stalked across the parking lot to his Chevy.

LARK STOPPED FOR GAS at a Marathon station near the north campus of the University of Michigan. He worked the pump with his right hand and kept his left down at his side, the long sleeve of his shirt covering most of the bandage.

He had driven from Dr. Kenneally's office to a shopping center nearby, where he had parked and let the car's air-conditioning cool him. He had closed his eyes to rest for a moment and had opened them to find that nearly two hours had passed.

Now, with his tank full, he drove south to a neighborhood of willows and oaks and green lawns that sloped up to stately white houses. The Spencer house stood taller than the others. The horseshoe driveway was paved with cobblestones and bordered by a low hedge. Lark saw a white van in the driveway. He knew what it meant. The van had a wheelchair lift. Harlan Spencer used it when he traveled, as he often did, appearing with his daughter on the campaign trail.

Finding the van here meant that Spencer was home. Callie Spencer might be here too. There was a guesthouse in back of the main one, where she often stayed—Lark had read about it in a magazine.

He circled the block and when he came around again he saw a car parked behind the van in the driveway. A woman stood by the driver's door. Her hair shone silky black in the sun, and for a second he thought it was Callie Spencer. But Callie had short hair; it scarcely reached the base of her neck. This woman had pinned up her hair so that it only seemed short. She was taller, her skin not as tanned.

He slowed the car. He recognized her. She walked toward the front door of the house, and he remembered when he had seen her: the night he went after Sutton Bell. She was one of the cops from the hospital.

CHAPTER 15

The door opened to Elizabeth's knock. The woman who opened it had white hair and a lined, handsome face. She introduced herself as Ruth Spencer, wife of Harlan, mother of Callie, and led Elizabeth upstairs to her husband's studio.

The air in the house felt cool, though the temperature outside stood in the nineties. Elizabeth already missed the milder weather of Sault Sainte Marie. A sprinkling of rain had fallen that morning as she and David began the drive south. With a stop for lunch they made it in seven hours, the temperature rising as they drove.

The trip north had raised more questions than it answered, and Owen McCaleb had made it plain that she was needed here. "We can't worry about the Dawtreys," he'd told her. "We need to focus on Kormoran and Bell."

As a first step, she had called Harlan Spencer, who had agreed to meet with her. She had dropped David at home, staying long enough for a shower and a change of clothes. Now she followed Ruth Spencer up to a large room with tall windows facing west.

A row of canvases lined the eastern side of the studio, each one propped against the wall. There were landscapes and still-life paintings of flowers. Some realistic, almost photographic; others so rough that they bordered on abstract. An orange sunset in a deep blue sky. The vivid yellow petals of a daffodil.

A table occupied the center of the room, cluttered with brushes and tubes of oil paint. An easel stood next to it, holding an unfinished canvas.

Harlan Spencer dropped his brush into a porcelain cup, wiped his hand on an apron that lay in his lap, and motored his wheelchair across the room to greet Elizabeth.

"You'll forgive me," he said. "I've been traveling for a week. I miss the paint when I go for more than a few days without it. Would you rather talk downstairs, or out in the garden?"

"Not at all," Elizabeth said. "Right here will be fine."

Ruth Spencer brought a straight-back chair in from another room and then went out again. Harlan Spencer rolled his wheelchair to the table, where a tray of iced tea sat amid the paint tubes and brushes. As he poured two glasses, Elizabeth saw a canvas she hadn't noticed before. While the others rested on the floor, this one hung in a wooden frame on the northern wall. The image was familiar: a portrait of Callie Spencer in her twenties.

"That's one of my early works," Harlan Spencer said.

Elizabeth sat and accepted the glass he offered her. "You started painting after—" She left the thought unfinished.

"Yes," he said. "After. I never had any interest in art as a young man, and if anyone had told me I should be a painter I would have laughed. But a bullet in the spine makes you reconsider things."

He had a deep, resonant voice, the voice of the sheriff he had been, not the artist he had become. He sat straight in the chair, his broad shoulders held stiff. His open collar revealed a sinewy neck, and the muscles of his right arm were prominently defined. His other arm rested on the arm of the chair, supported by a brace so that his fingers could work the chair's controls. His legs, beneath the fabric of his pants, were long and wasted thin. His brow was deeply lined and his fringe of gray hair had been shaved close to his scalp.

"It became clear early on that my legs were never going to carry me again," he told Elizabeth. "My right arm and hand were weak, but the physical therapists had high hopes for them, and they thought I might regain some function in my left hand too. My wife sat by my bed and made a list of occupations for a one-armed man. Not a long list. But 'painter' was on it."

He sipped from his iced tea and held the glass balanced on the arm of his chair.

"I've learned since that some determined souls get by with even less than I've got. If their fingers don't work, they hold the brush in their teeth. But back then, looking over the list we made, it occurred to me that one hand would be enough to hold a gun to my temple. I might have done it if I hadn't had my wife and daughter with me."

Elizabeth looked up at the portrait. The expression was one of determination: steady eyes, lowered chin, lips together in a firm line.

"I understand your daughter dropped out of school to help with your recovery," she said.

"Callie moved back to Sault Sainte Marie to be with us. I told her she shouldn't, but she wouldn't listen. We set up a studio in her mother's sewing room, and in the afternoons Callie would sit for hours and I would try to paint her. I knew nothing about mixing color or brushwork. I learned everything by trial and error. We made a deal that if I could paint a portrait that satisfied her, she would go back to law school."

He nodded toward the painting. "After months of failures I managed one success. So she moved back down here. Eventually her mother and I followed, so we could be close to her."

Elizabeth spotted a newspaper among the clutter on the table. The story of Henry Kormoran's murder occupied the front page.

"You've been reading up on my case," she said to Spencer.

"Old habits," he said.

"The paper didn't mention this, but Kormoran had a small print of Callie's portrait in his apartment."

"That's interesting."

"Where could he have gotten it?"

"I had an exhibition a few years ago," Spencer said. "That painting was part of it, and the gallery made reproductions to sell. The company that printed them did another run this year, after Callie declared her candidacy for the Senate. You can find them in card shops now."

"Can you think of any reason why Kormoran would have had one?"

Spencer stared up at the painting, considering his reply. "I think in a strange way he felt connected to my daughter. He wrote me a letter once, telling me how sorry he was for his part in the Great Lakes robbery. This was after his release from prison. Kormoran was a sad case. He came from a good family, and when he got into trouble they were ashamed of him. They got him a lawyer who made a plea deal, and after he served his time they didn't want anything to do with him. I think he believed that getting involved in that robbery was the worst thing he had ever done. It wrecked his life and poisoned his relationships. But he saw Callie's success as a sort of silver lining. It was one thing he could point to that his actions hadn't ruined. It's pitiful sometimes, the things we cling to."

His eyes came back to Elizabeth.

"You feel sorry for him," she said.

"I feel sorry for all of them. Kormoran, Bell, even Dawtrey. They were kids and they got caught up in something not of their own making."

"They were twenty-year-olds. Don't you think they should have known better?"

Spencer set his iced tea on the table beside him.

"They were taken in by a con man," he said. "Floyd Lambeau fooled a lot of people—and some of them didn't have the excuse of being twenty. The man could talk. He gave lectures on Native American history all over the country. I understand the University of Michigan once offered him a tenure-track job. He turned them down. His résumé said he had degrees from Princeton and Berkeley, but when they looked into that—after the Great Lakes Bank, after I shot him—it turned out he'd never been to either one. Never attended any university at all."

Sunlight from the window gleamed on Spencer's scalp and made shadows on his brow. "Lambeau was forty-eight at the time of the robbery, and he'd been scamming people all his life. College students were his favorite targets: smart, idealistic kids. They'd come to his lectures and stay afterward to talk. He'd collect them and meet with them in little discussion groups. Salons. Most of them were white and privileged, and he'd play on their sense of guilt. In Floyd Lambeau's version of history, Europeans were always the villains. As for the victims, well, he didn't mind changing it up. Sometimes it was the Indians being exploited—Lambeau claimed to be Chippewa. Other times it was endangered species, or the environment.

"But there was always some cause Lambeau claimed to be fighting for, some movement or charity that needed support. It all sounded legitimate to the kids in his salons, and when they put up their money the checks were made out to leagues and foundations. But the money ended up in Lambeau's pocket."

Spencer paused to worry his thumb over a spot of dried paint on the arm of his chair. Then he resumed his story.

"He could have gone on like that indefinitely, I think. He had a nice racket going, and no one suspected anything. But there were limits to how much he could take in with his fake charities, and he was looking for a bigger payoff. And the money was only part of it. I think Lambeau couldn't help but push things. It must have amused him, manipulating these college kids. How far could he get them to go?

"When he recruited Kormoran, Bell, and Dawtrey for the Great Lakes Bank job, he appealed to their sense of justice. He said he needed the money for a noble cause. There was a case in the news at the time—a pair of Chippewa brothers named Rosebear who had been arrested for murder. They were accused of raping and killing a white woman in Dayton, Ohio. There was a witness who claimed to have seen them leaving the woman's house in a hurry that day, and their fingerprints were all over inside, and one of them had left DNA behind in the victim's bedsheets.

"It looked like a strong case—except for the fact that the Rosebear brothers had a legitimate reason for being in the house. They were working for the victim, refinishing her basement. As for the DNA, one of the brothers said he was having a relationship with the woman, a completely consensual affair. And as for the witness, he was an employee of the woman's husband, who happened to be a prominent businessman with political connections. Some people suspected that he had found out about his wife's affair, killed her in a rage, and paid one of his employees to put the blame on the Rosebear brothers.

"That version of the story was probably true, and it was the version that Kormoran, Bell, and Dawtrey heard from Floyd Lambeau. The Rosebear brothers were facing the death penalty. They couldn't begin to afford a proper legal defense. It would take far more money than Lambeau could hope to raise through donations. Desperate measures were called for. Lambeau promised that every penny from the Great Lakes robbery would go to help those two brothers. It was a lie, of course: He never intended to give the money away. But Kormoran and the others believed him.

"Lambeau filled their heads with grand ideas. They thought they were going to save the lives of innocent men. But when the robbery went wrong, it was as if his spell had been broken. Henry Kormoran realized it early; he dropped his gun and ran. They found him a couple miles away, trying to hitch a ride. Terry Dawtrey held on to his gun. He was tougher than the others; he came from a working-class background. I think that's one reason Lambeau chose him.

"But I shot Lambeau, and then Dawtrey came out with the bank manager as a hostage. Sutton Bell had a choice to make. He realized, too late, that the whole thing was crazy. He made the right call, shooting Dawtrey in the leg. Things might have gone much worse if he hadn't."

"Bell seems to have come out of this in good shape," Elizabeth said. "He's got a wife and a daughter. A respectable job. I've talked to him. He's a likable man."

Spencer nodded. "I've talked to him too. I think he's created the kind of life he might have had if he'd never met Floyd Lambeau. If things had gone differently, the others might have done the same. Even Dawtrey."

"That's a very forgiving attitude," said Elizabeth.

Spencer looked at her from under his lined brow. "I hated Terry Dawtrey for a long time," he said. "In the beginning it might even have done me some good. I saw a lot of hopeless days, and the hate gave me something to hold on to. But sooner or later you have to let it go."

He went quiet, looking away at the clutter of tubes and brushes on the table.

"I've spoken to Walter Delacorte," Elizabeth said. "He told me the warden at Kinross consulted you before letting Dawtrey out for his father's funeral."

"That's true. I thought it would be petty to object." He turned his head back to her. "I gather you had a bit of a dustup with Walt."

"I wouldn't call it that."

"A professional disagreement, then. You believe the man who murdered

Kormoran spent some time in Sault Sainte Marie. You believe he killed Dawtrey's father, and tried to kill Dawtrey too."

"I have reason to think so."

"Walter Delacorte was first on the scene after Dawtrey shot me," Spencer said. "I wouldn't be alive today if not for him. I can tell you his heart's in the right place. He can be stubborn though, and if he starts down a certain road you can have a hell of a time getting him to turn back. But I'd rather not get involved in any differences you may have with him."

"I understand."

"That said, I'd like to help you if I can. Kormoran's murder and the attack on Bell—you think they're related to the Great Lakes robbery?"

"Yes," said Elizabeth. "The killer might have had something to do with what happened back then." She reached into her bag and brought out two drawings: the pencil sketch Sarah had made, and a computer-generated composite. She laid them down on the table.

"Sutton Bell didn't recognize him," she said, "but I'm hoping you might."

Spencer brushed the composite aside. He picked up the pencil sketch and studied it. "This is good work. Police sketch artists are a dying breed. I didn't think Ann Arbor had one."

"We don't. My daughter drew that."

"She has talent. But I'm afraid I don't know who he is."

"Picture him younger. Could he have been one of the college students Floyd Lambeau collected?"

He returned the drawing to the table and said, "I suppose it's possible."

"Could he have been the fifth robber—the getaway driver?"

The lines on Spencer's brow deepened. "Now that's something that never would have occurred to me, if you hadn't mentioned it."

"Bell said the same thing."

"I only got a glimpse of the driver's face that day, and after everything that happened I was never really able to recall him."

Elizabeth ran her fingers over the margin of the drawing.

"What do you think happened to him?" she asked.

"Who can say?"

"Do you think he was like the others—a good kid steered down the wrong path by Floyd Lambeau?"

"Probably."

"So maybe he turned out like Bell, with a good job and a family."

Spencer brought his hand up to rub his chin. "I wonder. It's not so simple, with the driver. You know why, I suppose."

Elizabeth knew. The driver was the only one to get away from the Great Lakes robbery—but he didn't get away clean. He sped off in the black SUV that morning, tearing south and west through the streets of Sault Sainte Marie toward I-75. But Spencer used the radio in his cruiser to put out a BOLO on the SUV, and when the driver approached the interstate he found the way blocked. A young officer with the Sault police had parked his patrol car at the bottom of the entrance ramp.

The driver of the SUV didn't stop.

He struck the rear fender of the patrol car and barreled past, up the ramp and away. The impact sent the patrol car spinning and tumbling over an embankment. The officer—a recent recruit named Scott White—died before help could reach him. The crash had snapped his neck.

"They found the black SUV the next day," Spencer said, "abandoned at the side of a lonely road near a town called Dafter, less than ten miles south of Sault Sainte Marie. It'd been wiped down and vacuumed clean. The driver must have had help from someone. He was never seen again. I wonder sometimes if he remembers Scott White. I imagine he does. He'll never be prosecuted for the bank robbery—the statute of limitations ran out years ago. But he still has White's murder hanging over him. There's no statute of limitations on that."

Spencer rested his hand on the arm of his chair. "Maybe he got back on the right path and made a life for himself. If he did, it seems unlikely he'd have a reason to come after Kormoran and the others at this late date."

"I think you're right," said Elizabeth, pointing to the drawing. "This probably isn't him."

"Who is it, then? And what's his motive?"

"He had words with Sutton Bell, before he assaulted him. He asked if Bell ever thought about you or Callie. Asked if Bell watched Callie on TV, if he had her portrait."

"You said Henry Kormoran had her portrait in his apartment."

"Right. I believe Kormoran's killer saw it there. It's interesting that he would mention the portrait to Bell. There's an implied message there: *You have no right to even look at Callie's picture.* The man we're looking for may think of himself as Callie's protector."

"But Kormoran posed no danger to Callie," Spencer observed. "Neither does Bell. Do you think this man's delusional?"

"If he is, that gives us something to go on," Elizabeth said. "If he feels a connection to Callie, he may have tried to contact her at some point."

A spark of understanding lit up Spencer's eyes. "You want to talk to her."

"Yes."

"She's in Lansing tonight. She and Jay have an apartment there." Jay would be Jay Casterbridge, Callie Spencer's husband. "She's coming to Ann Arbor tomorrow. We're hosting a small get-together here."

"I've left messages for her," Elizabeth said. "She hasn't returned my calls."

"She's very busy, but I'm sure she'll want to cooperate in any way she can."

Elizabeth looked at Spencer steadily and didn't say anything.

"Did that sound unconvincing?" he asked her.

"A little."

His mouth lengthened into a smile. "It sounded very unconvincing to me—like something the father of a politician would say. We both know that Callie's first instinct will be to keep her distance from you. She won't want her name and the words 'murder investigation' spoken in the same breath."

"Tell her I understand that," Elizabeth said. "But I need to talk to her."

"I'll do what I can."

HARLAN SPENCER OFFERED to show Elizabeth out; he had an elevator that opened into a room off his studio. She thanked him and told him she could find her own way, and when she left him she heard the hum of his motorized chair rolling back to his canvas and his paint.

She paused on the landing halfway down the stairs and through the tall window saw Ruth Spencer working in her garden. Descending the remaining steps, Elizabeth crossed through the entry hall. She went out the front door and drew it shut behind her.

She spotted the basket right away: round, made of wire mesh, brimming over with ripe tomatoes. It rested on the hood of her car. She walked over and lifted it up, intending to take it around to the back of the house so she could thank Ruth Spencer for the gift.

Then she saw the note: a sheet of paper folded in half beneath the blade of the windshield wiper. As she reached for it, Ruth Spencer appeared at the corner of the house, peeling off her gardening gloves. Elizabeth held the basket up, calling out her thanks, and the other woman waved and said, "You're quite welcome. It's nothing, really."

Elizabeth returned the basket to the hood of the car and unfolded the note, expecting to find some pleasantries written there. Instead she saw seven words in black ink, the letters ragged and coarse, as if they had been scratched onto the paper with the point of a blade.

LET ME HAVE BELL AND I'M DONE.

CHAPTER 16

The sign glowed in red neon, but to Lark the letters and numbers were a soft, cool blue:

OPEN 24 HOURS

The letters shimmered in the night air. Lark stared at them across an expanse of parking lot. The air blew warm through the open window of his car. Sweat dripped down through Lark's hair and along his temple.

His notebook lay on the seat beside him, open to the page he had torn out. The note he left for the lady cop had been an impulse. But he wanted to make it clear he wasn't some crazy person who intended to go on killing. Dawtrey was dead, and Kormoran too, and Bell would be the last. Lark wanted that understood.

We all want to be known.

After leaving the note, he had slept the afternoon away. The apartment where he was staying was a quiet place with thick walls.

He had rented it at the beginning, when he first made his plans. He knew he might need to stay in Ann Arbor for a while. He couldn't be sure how long Kormoran and Bell would take. *Hope for better, plan for worse,* his father used to say.

An apartment would be safer than a hotel, he thought. The one he chose was off State Street, a skip and a jump from I-94. The complex catered mostly to graduate students; he had gotten a cheap rate for the month of July.

He had crashed through the long afternoon and into the evening, on a mattress laid on the floor in the bedroom. He woke around ten and took some aspirin, washed down with water from the tap. He believed the aspirin might be keeping his fever in check, and it helped a little with the pain in his hand.

He thought the hand was getting worse. The wound seeped. When he changed the bandage he noticed a yellow stain in the gauze.

Quit stalling, he told himself. *If you let this go on, you'll miss your chance. If the fever runs higher, you won't be good for anything. You know what you need to do.*

So he had driven here, and now he saw the sign in the distance. The cool blue letters called to him.

OPEN 24 HOURS

He picked up his baseball cap from the seat beside him and put it on. The rifle he had used at Whiteleaf Cemetery was in the trunk. He turned off the engine and pulled the key from the ignition.

ELIZABETH PARKED HER CAR next to Carter Shan's and stepped out into the warm night. Shan popped the lock on his passenger door so she could slide in next to him.

"How come you get all the excitement?" he said.

Through the windshield she could see the entrance to the Urgent Care clinic where Sutton Bell worked. A neon sign glowed in the window.

OPEN 24 HOURS

"Bell's inside?" she asked.

Shan nodded. "Ron's in there with him." Ron Wintergreen was a fellow detective from the Investigations Division. "Let's see the note."

Elizabeth took a photocopy from her pocket and passed it to him.

LET ME HAVE BELL AND I'M DONE.

"He sounds almost reasonable," said Shan. "Like he's trying to bargain with us. I suppose it's wrong of me to wish we could make the deal. I've had about enough of this. I'd like to get home."

Shan had an ex-wife who lived outside Detroit, and a son he only got to see on weekends. Elizabeth knew he resented anything that kept him from spending time with the boy.

He passed the photocopy back to her and she slipped it into her pocket. After finding the note this afternoon, she had talked to the neighbors up and down the Spencers' street. One of them—a schoolteacher in her forties—said she had seen a man on the sidewalk, but hadn't paid him any mind. Ruth Spencer said the note had already been in place when she left the basket of tomatoes on Elizabeth's car.

From the Spencer house, Elizabeth had gone to City Hall to make her report to Owen McCaleb. The note had been sent to the county lab, though she didn't think it would do any good. So far, the man in plaid had left no fingerprints behind.

By the time she left City Hall, the downtown streets were beginning to return to normal. The Art Fair had ended and most of the vendors had packed up their booths. She drove home for a late dinner with Sarah and David, and now she sat with Shan watching the entrance of Bell's clinic.

As they watched, the door opened and an ancient-looking man came out, leading an equally ancient woman who hobbled along with a cane in either hand.

"Has it been like this all night?" Elizabeth asked Shan.

"Like this, but less lively."

"He's not going to come here. Not tonight. It won't be so easy. The whole thing is probably pointless—"

"Maybe not," Shan said. "Look behind us, one row back, two cars to the left."

Elizabeth folded down the visor on the passenger side. There was a mirror mounted there, and she adjusted it until she could see the car Shan had described. A figure sat behind the steering wheel—wearing a baseball cap, his face hidden in shadow.

"How long has he been there?" she asked.

"A few minutes. I thought he might go shopping, but he's just been sitting there." The parking lot served both the clinic and a grocery store.

The figure in the mirror stirred, and the car door opened. The dome light came on, but the bill of the cap obscured the man's face.

"Let's see what he's up to," Elizabeth said.

She got out of the car before Shan could respond, and began walking as if she were heading to the grocery store. The man in the baseball cap went to the trunk of his car and opened it. Elizabeth cut to her right and approached him along the row of cars.

"Police," she said. "Keep your hands where I can see them." She had her nine-millimeter out of the holster and down at her side.

"What did I do?" said the man in the cap. He was bent over the open trunk.

"Hands where I can see them," she repeated.

He was going to try to flee—either in the car or on foot. She could see it. He slammed the trunk and stepped toward the driver's door, but Shan stood there blocking it. The man in the cap pivoted and took off west across the lot.

He kept to a straight line along the row for twenty yards, then dodged south behind a parked van. Elizabeth chased after him, passing through the narrow channel between the van and a dented Honda, then cutting west again, coming up fast on the street—Industrial Drive—busy with traffic.

The man in the cap charged on, his footfalls muted in the heavy air. Elizabeth had begun to close on him when she heard Shan come up beside her, breathing in a steady rhythm. The man in the cap came to the strip of grass that separated the parking lot from the street and he didn't break stride. A squeal of brakes as a pickup swerved to avoid him and at the last moment he spun around and lost his balance. Then they were on him—she and Shan. They caught him and hauled him back, threw him sprawling facedown onto the grass.

Elizabeth holstered her pistol and planted her knee on the small of his back, and Shan got a handcuff around one of his wrists and yanked the other from underneath him.

"Take it easy," said the man in the cap.

Shan closed the cuff around the other wrist. "Is it him?"

Elizabeth pried apart the man's curled fingers. No bandage on either hand. No wound. She grabbed the baseball cap and tossed it aside.

"It's not him."

Shan pulled the man's wallet from his hip pocket. "Who is he, then?"

She cursed softly and got to her feet.

"He's a sheriff's deputy from Sault Sainte Marie," she said. "His name is Paul Rhiner."

SIX MILES AWAY, in the city of Ypsilanti, Anthony Lark pushed a shopping cart through a near-deserted parking lot. His rifle lay in the basket of the cart, the barrel facing forward and down, the stock resting near his right hand.

Automatic doors swished open to admit him.

The baseball cap shaded his eyes against the lights as he rolled the cart all the way to the back of the store. He came to a counter with a sign above it that said DROP OFF. The letters were a pleasant pale green.

Behind the counter, a heavyset woman in a white coat counted out pills in a plastic tray.

"Thank God you're open," Lark said.

The woman stared down at the pills and answered him in a bored voice. "Twenty-four hours a day. What can I do for you?"

"I need Keflex," he said. "I have an infection."

Finally she looked up. "Can I see your prescription?"

He pulled the rifle from the cart one-handed.

"I don't have a prescription."

CHAPTER 17

Shan drove Paul Rhiner to City Hall and sat him at a table in the break room of the Investigations Division. Elizabeth joined them a few minutes later, after having a look at the deputy's car.

When she sat down next to Rhiner, she could smell beer on his breath.

"I've never understood it before," he said.

"What's that?" she asked him.

"You know how sometimes you'll be looking for a guy—maybe somebody called in a complaint, or there's a warrant out for him. And when you find him, as soon as he sees you he starts running. So you chase him down, and when you've got him on the ground he always says the same thing: 'I didn't do anything.' And you have to ask him, 'Why did you run, then?' And it's always the same answer: 'Because you chased me.'"

Shan had taken off the cuffs and poured Rhiner a mug of coffee. Rhiner sat with his elbows braced on either side of the mug.

"I always laughed at guys like that," he said. "But this time it's true. I didn't do anything, and I only ran because you chased me."

"How much have you had to drink, Paul?" Elizabeth asked him.

Rhiner rubbed his temple. "I think you know the answer to that."

"Why don't you tell me."

"If you searched my car, you know."

She had found a pint of Jim Beam on the passenger seat, a third of it spent. Five empty beer cans on the floor in the back, another seven unopened in a cooler in the trunk.

"How long has this been going on, Paul? I saw you yesterday at Whiteleaf Cemetery up north. Were you drunk then?"

"I wouldn't say drunk."

"Did you come to the cemetery to talk? Why didn't you stay?"

"That reporter was there," Rhiner said. "She started asking questions. It got to be annoying."

"Last night, someone left a bullet outside the door of her hotel room."

"You think I did that?"

Elizabeth reached into her bag and brought out a nine-millimeter pistol. She had found it, loaded, on the seat of Rhiner's car beside the Jim Beam.

"The bullet was a nine-millimeter," she said. "Somebody left one outside my door too."

The pistol was unloaded now. She laid it on the table.

"I didn't leave any bullet outside your door," Rhiner said. "What would be the point?"

Elizabeth leaned back from the table. "It could be seen as a warning that I should stop looking into what happened to Terry Dawtrey."

"Did it work? Are you going to stop?"

She folded her arms and said nothing.

"Of course not," said Rhiner. "It's a gimmick out of a bad movie. No one would expect a threat like that to work, not if they had any common sense."

"They might if they were drunk," Shan suggested.

"I haven't been that drunk."

Rhiner kept his eyes focused on Elizabeth. She thought he was telling the truth.

"What were you doing at the clinic, Paul?" she asked.

"You must have found the answer to that too. It was underneath the gun."

She dug into her bag again, pulling out several folded pages. A copy of the manuscript written by the man in plaid. She tossed it onto the table.

"I faxed this to Walter Delacorte two days ago," she said. "Did he give you a copy?"

Rhiner looked as if the idea amused him. He shook his head.

"Where'd you get it, then?" she asked him.

"I may be suspended, but I still have friends in the sheriff's department."

The deputy's eyes shifted to the coffee mug in front of him. He picked it up with two hands, put it down again.

"Is he for real, this kook who says he beat Charlie Dawtrey to death?" Rhiner asked.

"He's real," said Shan.

"And he came to the funeral to kill Terry Dawtrey? He was on the hill with a rifle?"

"He fired a shot," Elizabeth said. "Did you hear it?"

Rhiner stared into the coffee. When he spoke, his voice was subdued.

"That's one of the things I've been trying to figure out. I had my own shot ringing in my ears. The bullet I put into Terry Dawtrey—that was the first time I ever had to shoot anybody."

"So you came down here to find the rifleman from the funeral?"

The barest of nods. "I thought he might come after Bell at the clinic. I guess you had the same idea."

"What would you have done if he had shown up there?" Elizabeth asked. "Would you have shot him?"

"No."

She glanced at the pistol on the table. "You see how it looks, don't you? You're suspended. You shouldn't even be carrying a gun."

"It's not my service weapon—they took that after I shot Dawtrey. But it's legal."

"I don't care if it's legal," she said. "I want to know why you had it with you outside the clinic."

Rhiner used the back of his hand to slide the coffee mug away from him. "I could use a drink," he said.

"That's the only drink you're going to get."

A long breath escaped from Rhiner's lips. The break room lights left his face in shadows. He spread his fingers, bone thin, over the scarred surface of the table.

He said, "I never wanted to kill him. Terry Dawtrey. I meant to hit him in the leg. Lousy shot." His voice hollow, as if he were speaking from a long way off. "He was alive when I got to him. I turned him over in the grass and put my hand on his heart. Felt it beating. My shot went through his neck. His eyes were open wide and he made a clicking sound in his throat. I realized he couldn't breathe."

Rhiner's fingers bore down on the table. He seemed to be trying to keep them from trembling. "I did what you're supposed to do," he said. "I tipped his head back a little, pinched his nostrils shut, and breathed into his mouth. But the bullet had passed through his windpipe. The air I sent into him whistled right back out. I covered the wound with my hand and kept trying until the paramedics came, but it didn't do him any good."

He ran a palm over the thinning hair of his scalp. "I've dropped ten pounds since then," he said. "I haven't slept more than three hours a night. I keep seeing his face. His eyes were open the whole time."

Rhiner looked at Elizabeth and Shan. Jabbed a thin finger at the man in plaid's manuscript.

"Walt Delacorte told me this is all made up," he said. "But you believe it's true, don't you?"

"Yes," Elizabeth said.

"The man who wrote this, he's real. I need to find him."

"You're not going to gain anything by killing him."

Rhiner swallowed. Closed his eyes. "I don't want to kill him. I never want to kill anyone again. I don't think I could stand it. I need to talk to him. The gun was just supposed to be a threat to make him talk. He's the one who made this happen. He had to have a reason. I need to know." A tremor at his temple, a vein pulsing beneath the skin. "Nothing's going to be right until I know."

CHIEF OWEN MCCALEB'S office was one floor above the break room. McCaleb sat on a corner of his desk, a wiry man of fifty-five wearing a gray jogging suit. The heels of his running shoes drummed against the front of the desk as Elizabeth and Shan filled him in about Paul Rhiner.

"Do we have grounds to hold him?" he asked when they finished.

"There's the obvious," Shan offered. "He was outside Bell's clinic with a loaded pistol."

McCaleb turned to Elizabeth. "Do we think he represents a threat to Bell?"

She stood by the window with her arms crossed. "I think he's telling the truth. Shooting Dawtrey got to him. He thinks finding the man in plaid will help him make sense of it. He doesn't care about Bell."

"What about the bullet outside your hotel room in Sault Sainte Marie?" McCaleb asked. "You think Rhiner had anything to do with that?"

She shook her head. "I don't see it."

"All right. Let him sleep it off tonight, and send him home in the morning. I'll call Sheriff Delacorte and ask him to keep an eye on him."

Shan pointed to Rhiner's gun, which was lying on the desktop.

"What about that?" he said.

"Does he have a permit for it?" asked McCaleb.

"He does," said Elizabeth. "I checked."

McCaleb went behind the desk, unlocked the center drawer, and laid the gun inside.

"Tell him we misplaced it. If we find it, we'll send it to him."

"That's not the only gun registered in his name," Elizabeth said. "He could be back in a couple days with a fresh one."

"Make sure he realizes we're giving him a break this time, and we don't want to see him here again." McCaleb shut the drawer and locked it. "We've got other things to worry about," he said. "I just heard from the chief of police in Ypsilanti. It looks like your man in plaid has been on the move. A little while ago someone matching his description held up a pharmacy. With a hunting rifle."

CHAPTER 18

Harlan Spencer's studio had too many windows for my taste.

The room spanned the width of the house, and the western wall was mostly glass: six tall windows in a row, with curtains of deep red linen thrown back to let in the twilight. The eastern wall held another six, of a more modest size.

It was Sunday evening. I had on my best gray suit over a white dress shirt and no tie—a concession to the warm weather. On my lapel I wore a campaign button that read CALLIE SPENCER, A NEW BEGINNING.

I'd heard from Elizabeth about her visit with Harlan Spencer the day before. The portrait of Callie Spencer that she'd told me about remained on the north end of the room, and on the east were other paintings, propped against the wall below the windows. Spencer's easel had been removed, along with the table that held his paints and brushes, and chairs had been brought in and arranged in groups of three and four. A bar had been set up along the south wall.

Around thirty people occupied the room—the high end of an Ann Arbor cocktail crowd. The mayor was there, with his wife, and I could pick out at least three professors from the law school. The owner of a seafood restaurant on Main was trying to make conversation with a woman who ran an art gallery on Liberty, but she was ignoring him; she had her eyes on Spencer's canvases.

Harlan Spencer himself sat in his motorized chair in the center of the room, with his wife in a leather club chair on his left. On his right sat a silver-haired man with a long nose and deep-set eyes—Senator John Casterbridge.

The senator was well into his seventies. He came from a wealthy family: Casterbridge Realty owned rental properties all over the state. But as a young man he had enlisted in the army and served two tours of duty in Vietnam, flying medevac helicopters for the First Cavalry Division.

He had spent forty years of his life in government, most of them in the Senate, where he was known as an advocate for veterans. He sat on the Intelligence and Armed Services committees and had been a confidant of presidents. People said he was privy to most of Washington's secrets, but he wasn't telling. He had never written a memoir and rarely gave interviews.

I'd never met him before, but I thought he looked worn out. His face seemed drawn and his suit fitted him loosely. I could see veins standing out on the backs of his hands where they lay folded over his stomach. His legs stretched out in front of him, one thin ankle crossed over the other.

A younger version of the senator hovered near the bar, holding a tumbler of Scotch. Jay Casterbridge had inherited some of his father's looks. He had the Casterbridge nose, and a thick head of dark hair that would turn silver when the time came. His face was fuller, and he carried more weight than his father did, though no one would have called him heavy.

I watched him working on the Scotch and talking with a woman in a red dress who was the dean of something or other at the university. I thought he looked a little wistful, as if he might have preferred to take his drink off someplace where they could be alone.

I'd read a profile of Jay Casterbridge in a magazine, and I knew that at one time he'd been expected to follow his father into politics. Every few years there'd be a rumor that he intended to run for Congress, but it never went beyond a rumor. He was a partner in a law firm in Lansing, but his primary occupation was running Casterbridge Realty. The closest he'd come to exhibiting any political ambition was when he married Callie Spencer.

Callie Spencer was the cause of my concern about the windows. She was standing in front of one of the tall ones now. With the lights on inside and darkness falling outside, I could see her silhouette reflected in the checkerboard panes of glass. Someone looking up from the street would be able to see her clearly. The man in plaid could be down there with his rifle. He could fire a shot and the only warning would be the tinkling of shattered glass.

Part of me wanted to go over there and drag Callie Spencer to the floor before it happened.

I stayed where I was, watching her. She wore a white dress belted in black at the waist; it left her arms bare, and quite a lot of her legs. I'd seen her making the rounds, chatting with her guests. She tended to draw people in close, and at some point she would reach out and rest her hand on a shoulder, a small gesture of familiarity.

Now she was talking to Amelia Copeland, a gray-haired woman who had a foundation that gave money to community theaters and public radio stations. The two of them stood apart from the other guests.

The woman took Callie by the elbow. I moved closer to hear what she was saying.

"My dear, it's quite hopeless. You ought to give it up."

"I think I'll hang on a little longer, Amelia. At least until the fall."

"But it's impossible. You're far too young."

Callie smiled politely. Her left hand held a neglected glass of red wine.

"We'll have to let the voters decide about that," she said.

"But don't you see, it's not up to them," said Amelia Copeland. "It's a matter of law. I'm surprised no one's told you. I can only assume they want to spare your feelings."

"Well, that's nice of them."

"But it's in the Constitution. You're not old enough to be a senator. You have to be thirty-five."

Callie's smile grew a little broader. "Are you sure about that?"

"Quite sure, my dear."

"Because if that were true, someone should have said something before now."

Amelia Copeland nodded once. "My point exactly. Look into it. You'll see I'm right."

Callie made her move then, hand on shoulder. She dialed the smile up to full strength.

"I don't doubt you for a moment, Amelia," she said.

The older woman basked in the light of the smile before drifting off in the direction of the bar. Callie Spencer, alone for a moment, raised her wineglass to her lips.

I let her drink and then stepped closer and asked, "Are you always so politic?"

She turned to face me. "It seems that way."

"If I remember, it's the president who has to be thirty-five. A senator can get away with being thirty."

"If I remember, I'm thirty-nine. But I didn't have the heart to tell her. Amelia gets melancholy when she's had too much wine."

I offered her a hand. "I'm David Loogan."

She clasped it briefly. "Of course you are."

"I wonder if you could do me a favor."

She lifted her eyebrows. "What would that be?"

"Step away from this window. You're too exposed. It's making me nervous."

Something in her posture changed. She seemed to relax, as if a puzzle that had been troubling her had been explained.

"I wondered what you were doing," she said. "You've been watching over me." She turned to look out the window. "Did you see someone down there?"

"If he's down there, you won't see him," I said. "He could be across the street, hidden beneath the canopy of one of those trees."

"Which one? That maple there, or the elm?"

"I'm not joking."

Her brown eyes appraised me. "No. But you're worried over nothing. This is my parents' house. I'm safe here."

"Anyone could get in here. I could've walked in with a gun and no one would have been the wiser."

"I'm glad you didn't," she said. "A gun would have ruined the lines of your suit."

"Have it your way," I told her. "But if we're staying here, you should let me be the one standing in front of the window."

She stood silent for a few seconds, rolling the stem of her wineglass between her fingers, and I realized for the first time that she was smaller in person than she appeared on television. I put her height at five-six, and two inches of that came from her heels.

She said, "I was misinformed about you, Mr. Loogan."

"How so?"

"I was advised to stay away from you—because I had nothing to gain from being associated with you. And now you've practically volunteered to take a bullet for me. Would you excuse me for a moment?"

"Sure."

She went over to the north end of the room and spoke to a man lingering by the doorway. I hadn't noticed him before. He had a plain face and a strip of bald scalp bordered on either side by hair the color of straw. He looked at least fifty, and wider at the hips than at the shoulders. The suit he wore seemed a decade out of date.

He listened to what she had to say, glanced in my direction, and went out through the doorway. Callie Spencer walked back to me, her heels clicking along the hardwood floor.

"That's Alan Beckett," she explained. "He used to work as an adviser for the senator and now he does the same for me. He's the one who vets the invitation lists for gatherings like this—and makes sure no one comes who wants to shoot me. I've asked him to send someone to see if anyone's loitering across the street."

"What changed your mind?"

"Nothing really. I'm sure no one's there. But now we can talk without you fearing for my life. What shall we talk about?"

"I don't know," I said. "Politics?"

"You don't strike me as a man who takes politics seriously."

"Why do you say that?"

"Because you're the only one here wearing one of these." She tapped the button on my lapel. CALLIE SPENCER, A NEW BEGINNING.

I said, "Maybe it's all the rest of these people who don't take politics seriously."

She let out an easy, natural laugh. "We pass those buttons out to the true believers," she said, "to college kids who need something they can pin to their backpacks to show how idealistic they are. I expect to see them at campaign rallies, but not at cocktail parties."

"Maybe I like the message."

"Maybe you think it's empty," she said. "You wouldn't be the only one."

"No, it's really quite clever," I said. "It solves a tough problem. How many terms has John Casterbridge served in the Senate—four?"

"Five."

"Five. And you're running as his successor. You want people to think they're voting him another term. But you can't come out and say that. 'Callie Spencer, More of the Same'—that's not going to inspire anyone. And you can't afford to be seen as criticizing the senator in any way—no matter what changes you plan to make once you're in office. And you'll want to make changes because, just for starters, the auto industry's been bleeding away for years and unemployment is higher in Michigan than anywhere else in the country. 'A New Beginning' is just vague enough to work. It implies that things are going to get better, without actually admitting that there was anything wrong with them before."

"You forgot to mention how well it fits on a bumper sticker," she said dryly. "You're not saying anything I haven't thought myself. 'A New Beginning' is the least of it. Look at my website sometime. You'll see I'm in favor of greater fairness in the tax code, reasonable spending cuts, sensible gun control, responsible health care reform, and sustainable environmental policies. Sometimes when I'm giving a speech, I worry I might float away on all the lofty generalities."

"What's the point, then?" I asked her. "Why would you want to run for office?"

She looked around as though she meant to make sure no one was close enough to hear us.

"Someone has to," she said mildly.

"Is that supposed to be a serious answer?"

"Someone's going to be the next senator from Michigan," she said. "I think I could do a passable job. There are other people who could do it—but they wouldn't do better than I would, and some of them would do much worse. If I can prevent someone worse from getting into office, that's half the battle. Ask John Casterbridge. If you could get him to talk, he'd tell you that what he's most proud of are the things he's opposed. From the big ideas that sounded good but would have been disastrous in practice, to the small idiocies that never saw the light of day because he quietly blocked them. I don't make any grand promises, but if I'm elected I'll try not to do any harm. And I might manage to do some good. Voters who expect more than that are kidding themselves."

Her brown eyes were steady on me till the end. Now they waited for my reaction.

"That's not bad," I said. "You should put that into a speech."

She graced me with a smile that grew slowly, like the sun rising over water.

"I wouldn't dare," she said. "And if you repeat it, I'll have to deny I ever said it." Her manner changed then. She'd been letting me see something real, but now she put it away and locked it down.

She said, "I'm glad you could come tonight. I wish we could talk more, but I have to pay attention to my other guests." She reached reflexively to touch my shoulder, and before I could say anything she moved on.

When she had gone I looked around and spotted Elizabeth talking to Harlan Spencer. She was in the chair John Casterbridge had occupied only a few minutes before. The senator was nowhere to be seen.

At the bar I picked up two tumblers of club soda. I held on to one and the other went on the low table beside Elizabeth's chair. I lingered for a moment, listening to Harlan Spencer tell a story from his youth in Sault Sainte Marie, then bent down beside Elizabeth and told her I was heading out to get some air.

The sounds of the party faded as I descended to the first floor. I passed one of the caterers in the entryway; she held the door for me as I went out.

Too warm outside for a jacket. I took mine off and folded it over my arm. Strolled along the curve of the horseshoe driveway. The street was quiet. I walked around to the back of the house, past a fenced-in garden. A broad path of flagstones ended in a ramp that led up to a whitewashed gazebo. In the diffused light from the house I saw someone there, leaning against the railing—John Casterbridge.

He waited until I set foot on the ramp and then spoke, his voice quiet but commanding.

"Did they send you down to spy on me?"

"No one sent me," I said.

"Because if that son of mine wants to police my morals, he can damn well come down and do it himself."

I stepped into the gazebo through an archway of hanging vines.

"I'm just out for a walk," I said.

"That makes you a sensible man," said the senator. He looked at the glass I was carrying. "What have you got there?"

"Club soda."

Distaste turned down the corners of his mouth. "Pour it out. I picked this up from one of the caterers." He moved aside to reveal a bottle of Jameson whiskey standing on the railing. "We'd better drink it before someone takes it away from us. Do you smoke?"

"I never have."

"Just as well," he said, bringing up a cigar he'd been holding discreetly at his side. "I've only got one. I gave up cigarettes thirty years ago, but I never lost the taste for good tobacco."

I draped my jacket over the railing and pitched the club soda out onto the lawn. The senator filled my tumbler from his bottle. He brought a shotglass out of his pocket and filled that as well.

"Money or connections?" he said.

"Pardon?"

"Usually if you get invited to a shindig like this, it means you've got either money or connections. So which is it?"

"Not money," I said. "I guess it must be connections—to the Ann Arbor police."

"You're here with that policewoman. Whaley."

"Waishkey."

"To talk to Callie about the lunatic who's running around killing people. How's that for slick?"

"I'm not sure what you mean."

"My daughter-in-law is a smooth operator," said John Casterbridge. "She doesn't want to be associated with a murder investigation, but she knows she'll have to talk to the police at some point. So she'll do it now, on the weekend, when no one's paying attention to the news. She'll do it here, rather than at City Hall, where there might be cameras waiting for her. She'll get it over with, and by tomorrow it'll be old news. That's slick, wouldn't you say?"

"Sure."

"Probably Beckett's idea. But Callie ran with it—she learns fast. She'll do all right for herself. The press likes her."

He sipped from his shotglass. "You like her," he said. "I saw you talking to her."

"We discussed politics. She's an impressive woman."

"You want to tread carefully there, son. She's taken."

He delivered the remark gently, almost affectionately, without a hint of anger. I wasn't sure what to make of it. I could read nothing in his eyes.

"I think you've got the wrong idea," I said.

"It might be good for her to let her hair down and live a little. God knows, we all should live a little. But you need to be careful."

"I think—"

He raised his glass suddenly to silence me. I heard footsteps on the flagstone path.

"Here comes the vice squad," he said.

I recognized the outlines of the man coming up the path. Narrow shoulders, broad hips. Alan Beckett.

Casterbridge laid his cigar on the railing between us. I shifted a little to hide the bottle of whiskey. Beckett came up the ramp and into the gazebo, shaking his head wearily from side to side. "Senator, we've talked about this."

Casterbridge said nothing and took a drink of whiskey.

Beckett reached calmly for the shotglass. The senator let him have it.

"Who gave this to you?" Beckett asked.

"Don't be a bore, Al."

"Who?"

"I'm capable of getting my own drinks."

Beckett glanced at me. I swirled the whiskey in my tumbler. He didn't try to take it.

Instead, he offered me a courtly nod. "Mr. Loogan, you'll be pleased to know we've searched up and down the block. We found no one hiding in a bush, or behind a tree. No one with a rifle—or a weapon of any kind. We found an insurance salesman walking a schnauzer, but he had no criminal record, not even a parking ticket. In short, all quiet. Nothing to report."

I listened to his speech without reacting. He seemed disappointed and turned back to John Casterbridge.

"Senator, I think it's time to call it a night. I'll have your car waiting."

"I'll be along when I'm ready."

I thought Beckett might bow, but he only nodded again.

"Of course."

He poured out the dregs of the senator's shotglass and reached for the cigar on the railing. I snatched it up first.

"This belongs to me," I said.

He smoothed his palm along his scalp and squinted at me. In the end, he decided to let it go, but the decision cost him. I watched him turn away and retreat along the path in the dark.

I passed the senator his cigar and he settled it between his teeth. He dug in his pocket for a box of matches and fired it up, drawing smoke in a series of short puffs and letting it out in a long stream that twisted in the night air.

"What was that about?" I asked him.

He drew on the cigar again before he answered. "The horses have all run off and Al's in charge of the barn door."

"I don't follow."

"Some people think I should live forever." He shrugged. "What was that guff about searching in the bushes?"

"I expressed a concern for your daughter-in-law's safety. I guess Al didn't like it."

The senator held his cigar up to admire it. I thought he would say something more to me about treading carefully, but he seemed to have forgotten all that.

He tapped the ash from his cigar and it drifted to the floor of the gazebo.

"Nothing's going to happen to Callie," he said. "Her father'll see to that. Don't underestimate Harlan Spencer. The man can't walk but he still goes to the shooting range. He's deadly with a Glock, even now. Keeps one in that chair of his, tucked out of sight. No harm's going to come to Callie Spencer in her father's house."

He took a last draw from the cigar and extinguished the remnant under the sole of his shoe. He came out with another shotglass from somewhere and set it carefully atop the railing. Then he winked at me, reached for the whiskey, and unscrewed the cap.

"Nice work, holding on to the bottle," he said.

CHAPTER 19

By the time I saw the senator to his car, the temperature had fallen a few degrees and the stars were out. His driver was a young guy who moved with military efficiency; he held the door and the senator got in with a smooth, practiced grace. I watched the car travel down the drive and away.

The other guests had departed and the caterers were cleaning up, under the direction of Ruth Spencer. I climbed the stairs to the studio and found Elizabeth talking with Callie Spencer. Jay Casterbridge sat beside his wife, and Harlan Spencer looked on from his wheelchair. Alan Beckett lounged in a club chair nearby. I stopped just inside the room, leaning against the door frame.

Elizabeth had her long hair braided and pinned up. She wore a string of beads around her neck: black glass smooth as pearls. One of Sarah's creations. Her black dress was cut modestly in the front, but deeper in the back to reveal her shoulder blades.

She had brought along sketches of the man in plaid and a copy of his manuscript. Callie Spencer examined the sketches and passed them to her husband.

"I don't recognize him," she said to Elizabeth. "I've read the news stories, and my father told me about your theory. You think this man may feel some connection with me."

"That's right," said Elizabeth. "He may have tried to contact you. Have you received any unusual correspondence lately? A letter or an e-mail that didn't sound quite right?"

"People send me odd letters fairly often," said Callie. "The really strange ones go in a special file, along with the ones that are angry or threatening. Alan can get you those, if you like." She turned to Beckett and he nodded his agreement.

"Yes, I'll want to see them," Elizabeth said. "But if this man has written to you, I don't think the letters would be threatening—at least they wouldn't threaten you. They might express anger over what happened to your father years ago—anger directed at Terry Dawtrey or Henry Kormoran or Sutton Bell."

"I don't recall any like that."

"It's possible that if this man wrote to you, his letters might not contain threats at all. They might sound ordinary. He's killed two people, and tried to kill two more, but he spoke to Sutton Bell before attacking him, and Bell thought he seemed rational. If you got a letter from him, it might look like any other letter from a constituent. He might write to you about some issue that's important to him."

Callie's brow furrowed. "I've served two terms in the state legislature. I've received hundreds of letters from constituents. Thousands. I don't see how they could help you."

"But you keep them, right? You file them away."

"Yes. But I can't have you going through those files. And even if I could, what good would it do? You've just said his letter might look ordinary."

Elizabeth picked up the manuscript from her lap. "Not exactly."

"What does that mean?"

"Look, what I'm going to tell you is confidential," Elizabeth said. "It hasn't been reported in the press. I have to ask you not to repeat it."

"All right," said Callie.

Elizabeth looked around to Jay Casterbridge and the others, and they all nodded.

"This is a communication we've received from the killer," she said, holding up the manuscript. "It's his own account of his crimes. It's unsigned, and he's careful not to give anything away about himself—"

Callie interrupted. "But you think there's something in there that could lead you to him."

"It's not what's in here," Elizabeth said. "It's what's missing."

"What do you mean? What's missing?"

"Adverbs."

I'D READ THROUGH the man in plaid's manifesto five or six times, but it was Sarah who made the discovery about the adverbs. Elizabeth and I heard about it that morning.

Sunday morning at the Waishkey house means sleeping late. It means an excessively large breakfast. Sarah does most of the cooking, but once in a while I manage something simple. Scrambled eggs or French toast. Or, in this case, pancakes.

I had butter melting in a skillet, and sausage links in a separate pan. Sarah sat at the table, slicing bits of apple into the pancake batter. Elizabeth was telling us about the man in plaid, who had robbed a pharmacy with a rifle the night before.

"That doesn't sound right," Sarah said.

"That's what happened," said Elizabeth.

"It's a violation of the basic principles."

"Basic principles?"

"The basic principles for robbing a store," Sarah said. "We talked about this once. You don't use a rifle, you use a handgun, because you can hide it until you need it. You keep the element of surprise. When you're ready, you pull out the gun and wave it in the cashier's face."

"I don't remember this conversation," Elizabeth said.

"You want him frightened, and you don't want to give him time to think. You use simple commands: *Open the register. Give me the cash.* You want an edge in your voice. If you sound calm, he might not take you seriously."

Elizabeth tilted her head. "When did we talk about this, exactly?"

"Middle school," Sarah said. "You were helping me write an essay. It was supposed to be 'How to Make a Pie,' but we strayed a little from the topic." She finished slicing the apple and passed me the bowl of batter. "When he gives you the money, you need a free hand to take it. That's another reason to use a handgun instead of a rifle."

"Middle school?"

"Seventh-grade English class. I got a B. I could have had an A, if only you knew how to make a pie. So why would this guy use a rifle? Is it because he's crazy?"

I poured some batter into the skillet. Elizabeth was leaning against the counter beside me.

"I'm not sure it makes sense to call him crazy," she said. "There's a logic to what he does. He used a rifle at Whiteleaf Cemetery because it was the only thing that would serve if he wanted to kill Terry Dawtrey from a distance. When he needed to hold up a pharmacy, he used the rifle again, because he already had it. Maybe a handgun would have been better, but the rifle worked well enough."

The sausage sizzled in the pan and I turned down the heat. Elizabeth continued. "Holding up a pharmacy isn't the same as holding up a convenience store. You can't expect to get in and out as fast. Yelling at a pharmacist, waving a gun in her face—that's not going to help. You want to attract as little attention as possible.

"The man in plaid put his rifle in a shopping cart and rolled it through the store without anyone noticing. He asked for two things: an antibiotic called Keflex and a painkiller called Imitrex, which is used to treat headaches. The pharmacist gave him both and he put the rifle back in the cart and rolled it out again. No one got a look at his car. There were video cameras in the store, but they shot him from above, and the baseball cap he wore concealed his face.

"If he's crazy, it doesn't seem to be doing him any harm. It's not going to help me catch him. I don't know what will."

"You'll catch him," Sarah said. "He'll give himself away. He already has. It's in his manuscript."

"When did you read his manuscript?" Elizabeth asked, frowning.

Sarah shrugged. "The other day. You must have left a copy lying around."

"No, I didn't," Elizabeth said, looking at me. I focused on the work at hand, flipping the pancake in the skillet.

"Does it matter?" asked Sarah.

"Technically, it does," Elizabeth said. "But we'll let that pass. I didn't find anything in his manuscript that hints at his identity. What did you see that gives him away?"

"It's not what I saw. It's what I didn't see."

"ADVERBS," ELIZABETH SAID to Callie Spencer. "He doesn't use them. There's not one in the entire manuscript."

Callie gave her a wry look. "Are you serious? You want to search my files for letters from constituents that don't have any adverbs?"

"I know it's unusual."

"It's absurd. Even if I could set aside the privacy issues—and I can't—a lot of people keep things brief when they're writing to their representatives. If they only write a few lines, they're probably not going to use any adverbs."

"The man we're looking for goes out of his way not to use them," Elizabeth said. "He writes 'in a rough manner' instead of 'roughly.' 'Without much sound' instead of 'quietly.' If you got a letter from him, it would stand out."

From the doorway I thought I could see a change in Callie Spencer's expression—she seemed to waver. Harlan Spencer must have seen it too.

"You'd have to be very discreet," he said to Elizabeth.

"Naturally," she said.

"Maybe you should consider it," Spencer said to his daughter.

Callie glanced at Jay Casterbridge, who tapped an empty glass on his knee.

"Do what you think is right," he said.

She looked around at Alan Beckett. He slouched in his club chair with his chin resting on the knuckles of one hand.

"It would have to be done just so," he said. "If word got out, it could look awful."

Callie turned to face Elizabeth again. Spine straight, chin raised. It was a transformation I had seen before. She put away her doubts, locked them down.

"No," she said. "Never mind how it looks. The people who write to me have to be able to trust that I'm not going to turn their letters over to the police without cause. I can't have you knocking on people's doors and questioning them because they wrote a letter with an odd turn of phrase."

She got to her feet. Elizabeth did the same, gathering the manuscript and the sketches of the man in plaid.

"I'm sorry," Callie Spencer said. "I wish I could be of more help. I'll make sure you have access to our threat file. But that's the best I can do. There have to be limits."

CHAPTER 20

Some nights I have the kind of dreams that make you sit up suddenly awake, casting around to get your bearings in the dark. The kind that make you wonder if that window you're seeing has always been there, in precisely that place, if it was open when you went to sleep, if that patch of grainy black is a doorway, and if there's someone waiting in the hallway outside it.

They're not nightmares, not exactly. Though I have those too. Every few months I have one where I'm running through an old house full of stairs and twisted corridors. There are men with guns chasing me—though I've never once in real life been chased by a man with a gun. Sometimes in the dream I have a gun myself, but when I pull the trigger nothing happens. And sometimes the gun fires and the bullets find their marks, but the men keep coming.

But I'm not talking about nightmares. The dreams I have most often are what I call clearing dreams: I'm in a clearing in the woods at night, stars and moon suspended over the bare branches of the encircling trees. Usually I have a friend with me, and we're digging a grave.

Something I have done in real life.

The friend has dark hair and pale skin. He and I trade off with the shovel. When he's working I stay close to him, sitting on the edge of the grave with my feet dangling. When I'm working he rests nearby with his back against the smooth bark of a beech tree. I try to keep my eyes on him, but as we dig, the wall of the grave obscures my line of sight. As the grave grows deep, I see something pale at the bottom and I set the shovel aside. I crouch down and brush the earth away with my fingertips to reveal my friend's face: brow smooth, eyes closed, mouth in a peaceful line.

When I climb out and look to the beech tree he's always gone.

I had a clearing dream that night after the party at the Spencer house. I came awake in the dark, and the doorway of Elizabeth's bedroom was a black rectangle like the mouth of a grave. I sat up and let my heart settle into a slow rhythm and let the black shape resolve itself into a doorway again.

I tried to go back to sleep, but twenty minutes later I found myself dressing in a polo shirt and jeans, gathering my wallet, cell phone, and keys. I knelt beside the bed and put my palm against Elizabeth's back to feel the rise and fall. Her eyes opened.

"Where are you going?"

"Office," I said. "Can't sleep."

"Dream?"

"Yes."

"Come back."

As if I might not. "Okay."

Our shorthand conversation done, she closed her eyes again.

On my way down I passed Sarah's room, and through the half-open door glimpsed dusky sheets and raven hair in the light that came up from a streetlamp. Downstairs I tried to close the front door as quietly as I could.

I walked out to my car and drove off, east toward downtown. Came at last to a stoplight flashing red and went north on Main. Not much traffic on the streets, but even now there were students on the sidewalks. Somewhere a bar had let out. A group of frat boys crossed Main in the middle of a block, loud and careless. One of them tripped and set the others laughing. I slowed to let them pass.

Café Felix was dark. I drove around behind the *Gray Streets* building and parked near the service entrance: a steel door beneath a yellow bulb in a metal cage. Often as not, someone leaves the door propped open with a brick. I found it that way now.

The elevator took me to the sixth floor. A chime sounded my arrival and the doors rumbled open. Under the lights of the hallway I walked past an accounting office and a documentary production company and came to *Gray Streets*. I had my key in the lock before I noticed anything amiss.

Someone had cut a neat square from the pebbled glass of the door.

Thoughts occurred to me. The square was big enough to reach through and turn the dead bolt. Whoever cut it could still be inside. The sound of the elevator would have given them warning.

I lingered in the hallway and pictured the dresser at home where I had picked up my wallet, phone, and keys. My Swiss Army knife had been there with them, but I didn't remember taking it, and when I patted my pocket it wasn't there.

Leaving the door ajar, I drew my key from the lock and spent a moment thinking about the sensible thing to do. The prudent thing. I decided I should leave, go back down to the car. Call someone. No need to take chances.

I let another moment pass before I eased the door open and stepped into the outer office. Prudence has never been my strong suit. I pocketed my keys and flipped the light switch. Fluorescents flickered on. No one leapt at me.

The reception desk looked undisturbed. The door to the inner office was closed. Likewise the door to the storage room. I stood quiet for several seconds, listening.

Nothing.

The door to the inner office has a lock, but I rarely engage it. The knob turned and I went in, flipping on the lights. A coatrack on my right, empty except for a dusty black fedora. Filing cabinets, bookshelves. Gray gunmetal desk. Papers on the desk, neatly arranged. Maybe a little more neatly than I had left them.

I went around behind the desk and opened the left-hand drawer. It has a false bottom with a compartment underneath; I had hidden a spare copy of the man in plaid's manuscript there. I cleared away the pens and the stapler and lifted out the bottom. The compartment was empty.

Slipping off my shoes, I padded to the outer office and stood for a few seconds listening at the door of the storage room. Heard nothing. I went back and slipped my shoes on again and walked past the reception desk to the photocopier. It was powered off. I lifted the document feeder slowly and laid my palm on the glass. It felt warm.

I picked up the phone on the reception desk, touched nine-one-one on the keypad, and waited.

"My name is David Loogan," I said. "I've had a break-in at my office." I recited the address, then listened for a moment with my eyes on the storage-room door.

"Thank you," I said. "I'll come down to the lobby to let the officers in."

I replaced the receiver and picked up a ream of paper from beside the copier. With the paper under my arm I walked out into the hallway, pulling the door shut behind me. Down the hall to the elevator. Pushed the button. The doors rumbled open. Seconds later they rumbled closed. Seconds after that I was back outside the door of *Gray Streets,* pressed against the wall to the left of the door frame, with the ream of paper held two-handed over my right shoulder.

Before long I heard sounds from inside: the door of the storage room opening and closing, soft footsteps crossing the carpet. Then a delay, probably a detour into the inner office. Finally more footsteps, coming closer. The doorknob being turned. I watched the door sweep inward, shifted my weight to my left foot, and swung the ream of paper around.

She had good reflexes. Lucy Navarro. Better than mine.

She ducked her head and brought her right arm up to ward off the paper. I tried to check my swing, not enough, and the corner of the ream struck the pebbled glass of the door, sending shards across the carpet. Sending the door crashing into the wall.

Lucy stepped back, both arms up now, covering her face.

"Jesus, Loogan!"

I tossed the paper on the floor. The door bounced off the wall and a long, jagged chunk of glass dropped out of the frame, like an icicle falling from an eave.

"Jesus," she said again.

I took hold of her forearms and drew them away from her face. She had her eyes closed tight. She tried to pull away from me.

"Hold still," I said.

I plucked a speck of glass from her hair and another from a spot just below the lower lid of her left eye. I moved her face gently from side to side, searching for more.

Finally I said, "Open your eyes."

She opened them and blinked several times. Stared back at me, pupils huge, green irises. I didn't see any glass.

"You're all right," I said.

I let go of her and walked past the reception desk, heading for the inner office. At the doorway I turned and saw her standing on the same spot, blinking. She wore a pale yellow summer dress with sandals, a handbag slung over her left shoulder.

"Come on," I said.

I settled in behind the desk, opened the left-hand drawer, lifted the false bottom. My copy of the man in plaid's manuscript was back in place. By the time I closed the drawer, Lucy had taken a seat in the guest chair across from me. She dropped her bag on the floor.

"Let's have it," I said.

"Have what?"

"You know what I mean. The manuscript."

She pointed at the desk. "I put it back."

"You made a copy."

"I didn't have time."

"I checked the copier. The glass is still warm."

"The glass is warm. You're a trip, Loogan. What are you doing here this late?"

"I come here sometimes when I can't sleep."

"How come you can't sleep?"

"I get to thinking about all the troubles in the world. Are you going to give me the copy you made, or do I have to call the police?"

"I thought you already called them."

I rolled my eyes at her.

"So that was all an act?" she said. "Did you know it was me hiding in the storage room?"

"If I'd known it was you, I wouldn't have tried to slug you with five hundred sheets of recycled bond. Hand over the manuscript, Lucy."

"I told you, I never made a copy. I turned the machine on, but it was still warming up when I heard you get off the elevator. I barely had time to kill the power and duck into the storage room."

I almost let it go. I think it was the yellow dress. It made me want to give her the benefit of the doubt. What can you say about a woman who wears a yellow dress to break into an office at night? How bad can her intentions be?

Still, I was reasonably certain she wasn't telling the truth. Not that it bothered me. Not really. I watched her sitting there, bent slightly forward, the palm of her right hand open in her lap, her left hand rubbing her shoulder. Lips curled in a smile. Innocent eyes looking back at me. It was like being lied to by a basket of kittens.

I shook my head. "You made a copy and it's either in your bag or somewhere under that dress. I'd frisk you myself, but I like to think I'm a gentleman. I'll leave it to the police."

I reached casually for the phone and laid the receiver on the desktop so we could both hear the dial tone. I pressed the nine. She tried to stare me down, but when I pressed the first one, she picked up her bag and took out several sheets of paper rolled into a cylinder.

She tossed them on the desk. I flattened the pages and left them facedown between us. She returned the receiver to its place.

"All right," I said. "Let's hear it."

"Hear what?"

"Only a handful of people know about this manuscript. How did you find out about it?"

"I can't compromise my sources, Loogan. Journalistic ethics."

"Yes, I can see you've got journalistic ethics. It's a shame you don't have the regular kind." I reached again for the phone.

She put her hand on the receiver. "Arthur Sutherland," she said. "Kyle Scudder's lawyer in Sault Sainte Marie. I went to see him. He had a copy of the manuscript on his desk. He hid it away before I could read any more than the first line—but the first line is a real hook. 'I killed Henry Kormoran.' I knew I needed to see the rest."

She tossed her shoulders carelessly. "Kormoran was killed here in town, so I assumed the killer must have sent his confession directly to the Ann Arbor police. I knew Detective Waishkey wouldn't tell me anything, so I spent some time hanging around the watch commander's desk at City Hall. Listening to gossip. Do you know who the cops talk about around the watch commander's desk, Loogan?"

"Who?"

"You and Detective Waishkey. They said you came there to see her the night Kormoran's body was discovered. And you had an envelope with you."

I laid a hand over the pages on my desk. "How much of this did you read?"

"Enough to understand why you took your trip to Sault Sainte Marie, and what you and Detective Waishkey were doing on the hill at Whiteleaf Cemetery. Do you think this is true? He was there with his rifle? He took a shot at Terry Dawtrey?"

I gave her a blank look and said nothing.

"Stop being so cagey, Loogan. You and I can help each other. There's something going on here. Something bigger than a nut with a rifle on a hill. What do you think of Callie Spencer?"

"What do I think of her?"

"You went to her party tonight," Lucy said.

"How do you know about that?"

"Gossip, Loogan. So what did you think? Did you talk to her?"

"For a few minutes."

"What was your impression?"

"She's a politician. She wants to get elected."

"Does she want it bad enough to send a nut with a rifle to kill Terry Dawtrey? Bad enough to send him after Henry Kormoran and Sutton Bell?"

I studied her face. Her pale green eyes gazed back at me. "You're not serious," I said.

"Why not?"

"It doesn't make sense. Why would she want them dead?"

"To get them out of the way."

"They were never in the way," I said. "Dawtrey was in prison. Kormoran and Bell were leading unremarkable lives. They were a footnote in Callie Spencer's story: the men who robbed the Great Lakes Bank and put her father in a wheelchair."

"But what if they were a threat to her?" Lucy asked.

I studied her some more. Sat back and put my feet up on the desk.

"What do you know?" I said.

"That's better, Loogan. You're starting to take me seriously. Tell me something. If you tried to contact Callie Spencer, would she take your call?"

"Why?"

"Because she won't take mine. I'm starting to feel desperate. If I tell you what I know about Terry Dawtrey, will you try to get me a meeting with her?"

I gave her my best hard stare. "What do you know about Dawtrey?"

"You'll call her?"

"I doubt it'll do any good."

"But you'll try?"

"Yes. Tell me about Dawtrey."

She turned her face away from me and her voice went quiet. "I think I got him killed."

CHAPTER 21

She told me the story haltingly at first, her eyes wandering from the file cabinets to the bookshelves to the window. But soon she became animated, getting up from the chair and pacing the room.

"I talked to Dawtrey this spring," she told me, "a few weeks before he died. Right around the time Callie Spencer won her party's primary. The *Current* wanted a story about the Great Lakes Bank robbery—it was the most sensational part of Spencer's history. Solid tabloid material. They had sent reporters to interview Dawtrey before, but no one ever got in. He didn't want to talk. At least that's what the people at the prison said."

She didn't let that stop her. She pretended she was his cousin and they let her see him. The visitation room at Kinross was a dreary place, she said. Crowded and noisy. She found Dawtrey sitting off in a corner. The first thing she noticed was that he had bruising around his left eye and a cut just above his eyebrow.

"What happened to you?" she asked him.

He started to bring a hand up to his face, then stopped and put it back on the table.

"Nothing happened," he said.

"You can tell me," she said. "I'm a reporter."

His eyes came to life. He almost smiled. "No kidding," he said. "And I thought you were my cousin."

"If someone beat you up, I can help you," she said.

He really did smile then. "What you gonna do, cuz? Print it in the paper? Guy in prison got beat up—that's not news."

She started to answer but he interrupted her. "What're you after? You wanna hear my hit?"

"Your hit?"

"The Great Lakes Bank. It's the only song I ever sing. That what you're here for?"

She told him it was.

"What's the angle?" he said.

She said nothing, unsure how to answer him.

"Callie Spencer?" he prompted. "That why you're here?"

"Yes. She's running for Senate." Lucy felt clumsy, stating the obvious. But Dawtrey made her nervous.

"I heard about that, cuz," he said. "You wanna make her look good, talking to the bad man who shot her father?"

"I want to hear whatever you want to tell me," she said.

Dawtrey fell silent, rubbing at the base of his neck. "The morning of the robbery," he said at last, "we all met at the hotel where Floyd Lambeau was staying. He had a minibar in his room. I had a drink before we got in the SUV. A shot of whiskey to calm my nerves."

"That's what you want to tell me—that you were drinking?" Lucy said. "Do you think that helps explain what happened that day?"

"No. But some of the stories back then said I was drunk. It takes more than a little whiskey to get me drunk. I want to set the record straight."

Lucy thought she saw a touch of mischief in his eyes, but she said, "All right. What else?"

"Floyd was a piss-poor bank robber," said Dawtrey. "He should have thought more about what could go wrong. About escape routes. You don't think about banks having more than one exit, but they do. I found out later that the Great Lakes Bank had a door in the back that opened into an alley. We never thought to look for it at the time. Floyd went out the front, where the sheriff was waiting. So did I. That's one thing I regret."

"Do you regret shooting Harlan Spencer?" she asked him.

He looked around the visitation room. "It put me in here."

"So you would have made a different choice, if you had it to do over?"

"Is that your angle?" he said, his voice sharp. "You want me to say how sorry I am?"

"I don't have an angle—"

"You can say whatever you want. Say I'm sorry as hell. I'm sorry the SUV drove off. Sorry that Floyd was lying dead in the street. That Sutton Bell shot me in the goddamn leg. You can say I'm sorry I didn't make a different choice, with my blood running out of me and Spencer's gun aimed at my face. Say I wish I took more time to reflect on my decision."

Dawtrey's voice had risen, and one of the guards came over to tell him to calm down. The guard put a thick-fingered hand on his arm and Dawtrey seemed to wilt. He bowed his head and didn't lift it again until the guard went away.

Lucy pitched her voice low. "Is it the guards?" she asked him. "Are they the ones who beat you up?"

Dawtrey squared his shoulders and his smile came back. He shook his head at her.

"You're cute, cuz," he said. "What paper you from?"

"The *National Current*," she told him.

"Why didn't you say so?" he said, laughing. "If I knew that, I coulda give you something juicy. Tell you about the time I slept with Callie Spencer. You looking for a good story, all you got to do is ask."

"I'm only looking for the truth," she said.

"You sure that's not the truth?" Dawtrey said. "You know everybody Callie Spencer ever slept with?"

"Okay. When did you sleep with her?"

"You fill in the details any way you want. I'm just giving you the idea."

"That's not an idea I can use," Lucy said. "What else have you got? Something real."

He glanced around, leaned closer to her. "I got something real. But I don't think you'll use it."

"Try me."

"Floyd Lambeau," he said.

Lucy raised her brows. "Lambeau slept with Callie Spencer?"

"You got a one-track mind, cuz," Dawtrey said, laughing. "She woulda been awful young for him. But Floyd and I did see her once, in Sault Sainte Marie."

That got Lucy's attention. "When?" she asked.

"A month before the robbery. We went there to take a look at the bank."

"And?"

"And Floyd pointed her out to me. *That's the daughter of the sheriff of Chippewa County,* he said. *At least, that's what the sheriff thinks.*"

Dawtrey rolled his shoulders back and waited.

"So . . . what?" Lucy said to him. "You're telling me Harlan Spencer isn't Callie's real father?"

"Better than that, cuz," he said with a sly grin. "You think about it."

She thought about it, and it dawned on her. "Lambeau?" she said.

Dawtrey winked at her. "Puts a whole different spin on Callie Spencer, doesn't it? It's one thing if she's the daughter of the cop who shot the bank robber. It's another if she's the daughter of the robber. That won't get her in the Senate, will it?"

Lucy shook her head slowly. "I can't print this."

"I told you you wouldn't."

"I'd need proof. Otherwise it's hearsay."

"Go get some proof, then."

"It would have to be DNA," she said. "How am I going to get DNA?"

Dawtrey gave her a disappointed look. "You make me sad, cuz. I tell you just about the best story I got, and all you do is complain."

"It's not like I can ask Callie Spencer to give me a blood sample. I don't even know if you're being straight with me." Lucy gazed at the ceiling of the visitation room, her thoughts racing. Suddenly she looked back at Dawtrey. "Wait a minute, what did you say? This is *just about* the best story you've got?"

His sly grin returned. "You heard that, huh?"

"I heard it," she said. "If this is just about the best, what have you got that's better?"

He made a clicking noise with his tongue. "You're not ready for that, cuz."

Naturally it was right then that the guards announced that visitation was over. Dawtrey stood up out of his chair.

Lucy stood too. "What the hell have you got?"

"I like you, cuz," Dawtrey said. "You come back, we'll talk again."

"Tell me."

"One thing at a time," he said. "You print what I told you and—"

"And what?"

"And then we'll see. Maybe I give you the driver."

BY THE TIME Lucy finished her story, she had stopped pacing. She stood by the window in her pale yellow dress, looking at me expectantly.

"The driver?" I said. "He was talking about the fifth robber, the one who got away? Do you think he was putting you on?"

"I don't know."

"It doesn't make sense," I said. "If he knew the identity of the fifth robber, why would he keep it secret all these years?"

"I don't know that either," Lucy said. "I never got a chance to talk to him again."

"What about Dawtrey's story about Callie Spencer? You didn't print it."

I watched her shoulders shrug beneath the straps of her dress. "Even the *National Current* has standards."

"Could it be true?" I asked her. "Could Floyd Lambeau be her father?"

"Dawtrey's not the only one who thinks so," she said. "I found an obscure website that mentions the idea, with pictures that are supposed to show the family resemblance."

"Do they?"

"They do if you want them to. Otherwise no. As far as I can tell, the website went up during Callie's first campaign for the Michigan House of Representatives. But the idea never caught on. No respectable news outlet would touch the story."

"But you looked into it."

She spread her hands in a noncommittal gesture. "It could be true. Floyd Lambeau and Ruth Spencer were about the same age. He's known to have given lectures in Sault Sainte Marie. You can place him there around the time Callie Spencer must have been conceived."

"Which proves nothing."

"Right," she said. "So Lambeau may or may not have been Callie Spencer's father. But what I know for sure is that Dawtrey told me he was—and a few weeks later, Dawtrey wound up dead."

I shook my head. "I have a hard time believing Callie Spencer had anything to do with that. How would she even know you talked to Dawtrey?"

"There were other people in the room. Visitors, prisoners. Guards."

"So someone overheard you? And then what?"

"And then it got back to Harlan Spencer. You think he doesn't have connections at Kinross Prison?"

I shot her a skeptical look. "So he told his daughter and she arranged to send a nut with a rifle to kill Terry Dawtrey at Whiteleaf Cemetery?"

"Maybe Spencer never told her. Maybe he arranged it himself."

"You're forgetting something," I said. "The nut with the rifle didn't kill Dawtrey. One of the deputies did—Paul Rhiner. Did Spencer arrange that too? Did he arrange for Terry Dawtrey to try to escape?"

"I still have some details I need to work out."

"You have nothing but details you need to work out."

Lucy came away from the window and sat down across from me again.

"First things first," she said. "I need to talk to Callie Spencer. You'll call her for me?

"I'll call her. Don't expect much."

She pointed to the manuscript on the desk. "What about this? What's it going to take for me to walk out of here with a copy?"

"I can't let you do that."

"The *Current* would pay."

"Not interested."

"No. You've got ethics, and not the journalistic kind. Maybe you could answer a couple of questions for me, then."

"You don't quit, do you?"

"Two questions, Loogan. First, the man who wrote this—why did he send it to you? It would be more natural to send it to the police, or to the newspaper. Why send it to the editor of a mystery magazine?"

I could have told her my theory—that the man in plaid had been drawn to *Gray Streets* because of a story I'd written, a story based on the Great Lakes robbery. But I didn't feel like explaining it all to her.

"Maybe he's a fan of mysteries," I said with a shrug. "What's your second question?"

She smoothed an errant lock of hair from her brow. "Who would want to break into your office?"

"You mean, apart from you?"

"Apart from me."

"I don't know. Why?"

"Because somebody did. I came here tonight with every intention of breaking in, but I didn't have to. Someone else cut that square of glass out of your door."

CHAPTER 22

The knock on Anthony Lark's door came at noon on Monday.

Perched on a stool by the kitchen counter—one of the few pieces of furniture that came with the apartment—he listened to the sound. A soft tapping, not the loud thump that a cop's fist would make.

He swallowed a mouthful of orange juice and refilled his glass. Whoever was tapping gave up and went away.

Lark had taken a tablet of Keflex on Saturday night. He had taken two more on Sunday and another this morning. His fever had broken. The wound on his left hand seemed less swollen, but was still painful to the touch.

The orange juice was good, better than anything Lark could remember tasting in a long time. He thought about going out to get something to eat. It would be too risky to sit in a restaurant and order a meal, but he toyed with the idea just the same. He wanted a steak. And a beer to wash it down.

He would settle for take-out Chinese. He knew a place nearby. As he looked around for his keys, the tapping started again. Soft. Persistent.

He shuffled to the door. Through the peephole he could see a woman's face. Brown-skinned: Indian, or Pakistani. Young, slightly exotic, with fine cheekbones and black hair that came to her shoulders.

He watched her raise her hand to tap again on the door. Her dark eyes stared at him, as if she could see him through the peephole. He waited for her to leave.

When she brought her hand up yet again, he opened the door.

She stepped back as if he had startled her. "Here you are after all," she said.

He heard a trace of an accent. Not Indian. British.

"I was getting dressed," he told her.

"Sorry to be a bother. We haven't met. I live 'cross the hall."

She offered her hand. Long, delicate fingers, no polish on the nails. He clasped it for a polite interval and let it go.

"I wonder," she said, "have you seen a cat?"

"A cat?"

"He's a faded calico, gray and orange." The woman took a stack of flyers from under her arm and handed one to Lark.

"His name is Roscoe," she said. "I had a friend visiting at the weekend." She stressed the second syllable: week-*end*. "She left the patio door open and Roscoe got out. He's not used to being outside."

Lark made a show of studying the picture on the flyer. "Have you looked out by the Dumpsters? I've seen cats there before."

"I've tried there," the woman said.

He offered the flyer back to her. "Sorry I can't help."

"Hold on to it, would you?" she said. "My number's there. In case you see him."

"Sure," he said.

She lingered in the doorway. "You're new here, aren't you? Just moved in?"

"That's right," Lark said.

"Where from?"

"Ohio." A safe answer. No one cares about Ohio.

"Toledo?" she asked. "That's the only place I've visited in Ohio."

Lark tried to make sense of her. The questions were friendly and she seemed genuinely interested in him. She was making eye contact, but she was also stealing glances past him into the apartment.

"Not Toledo," he said. "Cincinnati."

She looked past him again and he realized what she was doing. She wanted to see if he had her cat.

"Where are my manners?" he said. "Would you like to come in?" Without waiting for an answer he stepped back from the door and into the kitchen. He put the flyer on the countertop.

"Something to drink?" he said. "I've got orange juice."

She hesitated in the doorway and then made up her mind. "That would be lovely."

He filled a glass from the cupboard, one of a set he'd bought at a Salvation Army store. She came in and stood on the other side of the counter in his living room, looking around at his bare possessions. He had a small television set; a milk crate filled with books and magazines.

"I'm still waiting for my furniture to be delivered," he said, sliding her glass across the counter.

She turned back to him and laid down her flyers. "Are you at the university?"

"No."

"What do you do?"

"Claims processing," he said, "for an insurance company." It was the last job he'd held.

"That sounds interesting. Do you enjoy it?" She asked the question carelessly, looking down the narrow hall that led to the bathroom and his bedroom. He could tell she wanted to go down there, to reassure herself that he wasn't holding her cat prisoner. He watched her thinking about how to manage it.

"I like it well enough," he said. "And it pays the bills."

She frowned. "What's that?"

"Claims processing."

"Oh," she said. "Right." Her eyes lighted on the orange juice. He could see her making a decision.

She picked up the glass and drank. Orange juice dribbled down the front of her blouse. It seemed almost like an accident.

"Look what I've done," she said, wiping her chin with the back of her hand. "Do you mind if I use your bathroom?"

"Down the hall," he said helpfully. She was already heading that way.

She passed out of his line of sight and he heard the door of the bathroom close, water running. He waited in the kitchen, decided to let her take her time. Let her look in the bedroom; there was nothing to see. A mattress, some clothes. The apartment of an untidy man, but not a dangerous one. Not a stealer of cats.

There was nothing to alarm her, he thought. His rifle was in the trunk of his car. And though he had no mirror handy he believed he looked passable. He had showered and washed his hair. He had on clean clothes. A drawing of him had been in the newspaper, but she might not have seen it. She was probably a student. How many students read the newspaper?

In any case, the drawing resembled him only vaguely. Among other things, it showed him with a hat and two days' stubble, and now he was hatless and clean-shaven. He didn't think she had recognized him. If she thought he was a killer, she would never have come in.

So she didn't think he was a killer. She thought he was someone who might have taken her cat. When she realized he hadn't, she would go back to her apartment and he could forget about her.

He heard footsteps and looked up to see her emerging from the hall, dabbing at her blouse with one of his towels.

"Everything all right?" he said.

She smiled shyly and nodded. "I should get out of your hair. I've troubled you enough."

"Not at all."

Folding the towel, she set it on the counter. Lark thought she would leave. Not yet.

"Maybe you need to get to work," she said.

It took an effort to keep his expression friendly. Why was she still here?

"It's such a nice day," he said. "I called in sick."

"Are you?"

He considered idly how he might kill her. He still had the chef's knife he'd bought to use on Sutton Bell. It was in a drawer close by.

"Am I what?" he asked.

"Sick," she said. "I noticed your hand. What happened?"

Both his hands rested lightly on the counter. He looked down at the left one, wrapped in its gauze. Maybe she recognized him after all. His wound had been reported in the paper.

The drawer with the chef's knife was within reach. He could picture the dark wooden handle. Out of the corner of his eye Lark saw the flyer she had given him. LOST CAT. The letters glowed like hot coals.

"It's not as bad as it looks," he said. "I had an accident. Slicing apples. I sliced my palm instead."

"Did it hurt?"

He gazed at her across the counter. She stood like his reflected image, her brown hands resting on the folded towel. On the back of one of them he saw two thin, curved lines. Cat scratches, a few days old.

"I didn't feel it," he said. "Not at first."

She's still suspicious, he thought. *She wants to see underneath the gauze.*

He brought his left hand up and contemplated the palm. "It's funny how that works sometimes, isn't it? You don't even feel it."

Casually, as if the idea had just occurred to him, as if it were a natural thing to do, he peeled the tape from the gauze with the fingers of his right hand. He unwound the bandage and let it fall in a heap on the countertop.

He made sure she saw the back of his hand—smooth and unmarked—and then showed her the palm. The cut was short and straight and looked nothing like a cat scratch.

She made a sympathetic face when she saw it. "That looks painful."

"It's getting better," he said.

The shy smile returned and she seemed to decide, finally, that he was harmless. He thought for a moment that she would want to stay and talk some more.

Instead, she picked up her flyers—all but the one she had given him.

"Nice to meet you," she said.

He nodded. "Same here."

"You've got my number," she said, "if you see Roscoe."

It might have been his imagination, but something in the tone of her voice made him think she might not mind him calling even if he didn't see Roscoe.

"I've got it," he said.

She went to the door and he went with her. Watched her cross the hall to her apartment.

Back in the kitchen he wrapped the gauze around his hand again. He opened the drawer and brushed his fingers over the handle of the knife.

He could go across the hall right now and knock, and she would answer. It would be easy.

The letters on the flyer—LOST CAT—had settled into a smooth blue-green, gently bobbing like a boat tied at a dock.

Lark remembered being hungry and thought about take-out Chinese. He closed the drawer, found his keys, and went out.

CHAPTER 23

I talked to Lucy Navarro again on Monday night, but before that I heard from Nick Dawtrey and the senator had his accident.

I'd left my card with Nick and told him to call me if he got the urge to ride his bike in circles around the Chippewa County sheriff's office again. I had filled him in about the man in plaid, but I knew he didn't want to let go of the idea that the cops were somehow behind his father's death, and that they had deliberately murdered his half brother Terry. I'd asked him to be patient, to wait and see what Elizabeth could find out.

He reached me on my cell phone at the *Gray Streets* office. His voice had the same tone I remembered, older than his fifteen years.

"I've been watching the sheriff, sport," he said.

"Hello, Nick."

"Walter Delacorte—he went shopping today. Bought paint and rollers. You think that means anything?"

"Probably not."

I waited for him to tell me what he thought it meant, but he had already moved on.

"I heard Paul Rhiner came down your way, tried to shoot somebody else."

"He didn't try to shoot anyone," I said.

"I heard the Ann Arbor cops hauled him in, but then they let him go."

"Elizabeth talked to him," I said. "She thinks he's genuinely sorry about having to shoot Terry. She thinks it's eating away at him. He told her he only meant to wound your brother, not kill him."

"And she believed him? What'd I tell you, sport? Your wife's a cop. She's gonna side with the other cops."

"That's not the way it is, Nick—"

"He's back up here now. Rhiner. Got back yesterday and hasn't left his house. He lives alone, but somebody brought him sacks of food and bottles of booze. Left them on his porch. I'm not sure who."

"You shouldn't be spying on Rhiner. Or Delacorte. This isn't a game—"

"Don't worry 'bout me, sport. Nobody saw me."

"You need to stop."

I heard his breath over the line. "I'll stop as soon as you can tell me what really happened to my father and Terry. You find anything out yet?" His voice made it *anytheen.*

I stood by my office window and thought about my conversation with Lucy Navarro. About her meeting with Terry Dawtrey and what Terry had told her about Callie Spencer. I could tell Nick about it, but it would only feed his suspicions.

He listened to my silence and said, "That's what I thought."

"Things take time," I said.

His laugh sounded bitter. "No kidding. Maybe you tell that to Kyle Scudder. They still think he killed my father. My mother, she went to Sault Sainte Marie today, talked to Kyle's lawyer. Lawyer talked to the prosecutor, but the prosecutor says he won't drop the charges. Kyle's lawyer filed a motion to dismiss, but he says it'll take time. Everything takes time."

"It does."

"My mother spent all afternoon on the phone, calling everybody she can think of. I don't know what she expects to do. Maybe have a protest march or something."

"Maybe that'll help."

"You're killing me, sport." *Killeen.*

"Listen," I said. "You need to let your mother and the lawyer handle things. And stay away from the cops in Sault Sainte Marie."

"If I don't keep watch on the cops, who's gonna find out the truth? You really think your wife's gonna do it?"

"Yes."

The line went quiet for a few seconds, but then I heard his voice.

"Tell her to hurry up."

AFTER I GOT OFF the phone with Nick, I spent an hour updating the *Gray Streets* subscription list. The magazine was supposed to have a secretary to deal with things like that, but the old one had left in the spring and I hadn't replaced her yet.

Around five-thirty a couple of the magazine's interns wandered through. At one time all the interns were students from the university's English department, but lately I've been branching out. One of them was a computer science major. Another studied history and wanted to be a playwright. I sent them each off with an armload of manuscripts from the slush pile. Maybe one of them would find a gem. Probably not.

By the time they left, the glazier I'd hired to replace the broken glass in the hallway door had finished the job. I wrote him a check for a sum that made me think I'd chosen the wrong line of work, and he packed his tools and went away.

When I left *Gray Streets,* I stopped at Whole Foods and picked up grilled shrimp and red peppers and zucchini. I had them warming in the oven when Elizabeth got home. She and I were on our own; Sarah had gone to a friend's for dinner.

We ate in the backyard, lounging in Adirondack chairs, watching the low clouds turn golden in the western sky. Afterward, we got out the clippers and trimmed a wisteria vine that had begun to send tendrils over the fence and into the neighbor's yard. From there we went at the hedges on either side of the house, and soon the ground was strewn with branches that would need to be bagged and hauled to the curb.

I went to the garage to look for bags, and when I returned Elizabeth had her cell phone to her ear. She said something I didn't catch, and then, "I'm leaving now."

I watched her close the phone. "Work?" I said.

"Traffic accident."

"And they need you there? How bad is it?"

"It's not a question of how bad, it's a question of who."

SENATOR JOHN CASTERBRIDGE sat on the grass beneath an oak tree. Legs crossed, forearms resting on his knees. His car, a Mercury Grand Marquis, rested askew in the street nearby. Third Street, near the intersection with Jefferson.

Elizabeth parked half a block away. She cut the engine, left the windows rolled down. Without turning to me she said, "Technically, you ought to stay here."

She got out and I trailed behind her. In the center of the intersection sat a patrol car with its lights whirling silently. As she approached it, a uniformed cop stepped over to meet her. A young guy named Fielder.

They spent a few minutes going over what had happened. The senator had been driving south on Third. Another driver—a twenty-year-old in a Jeep—had been heading east on Jefferson. The intersection was a four-way stop. The senator had entered it first, but the Jeep had run through a moment later, striking the rear fender of the senator's Mercury and spinning the car a hundred and eighty degrees.

We could see the Jeep a little way up Jefferson, two wheels in the street and the other two up over the curb.

"We've got witnesses," Fielder said, indicating a young couple who stood nearby. The woman rocked a stroller back and forth, trying to entertain a toddler with curly red hair.

"Family out for a walk," Fielder said. "The husband wasn't paying attention, but the wife says she saw the senator's car come to a stop before entering the intersection. Says the kid in the Jeep barreled on through."

"Anyone hurt?" asked Elizabeth.

"The driver of the Jeep had some abrasions from his air bag. EMTs took him to the hospital. The senator refused to be looked at. Says he's fine. He seems all right—physically."

Elizabeth lifted her eyebrows, waiting for Fielder to explain.

"He wants to be on his way," Fielder said. "Says he's on an errand. A matter of life and death. I tried to find out more, but he says it's top secret and I don't need to know."

"Do you think he's been drinking?" Elizabeth asked.

Fielder shook his head. "I didn't smell anything on him. But something's not right. Dispatch is trying to get in touch with his son."

Elizabeth looked off at the senator sitting in the grass. The leaves of the oak tree fluttered in the air above him.

"All right," she said. "I'll talk to him."

I stayed by the patrol car with Fielder while Elizabeth crossed the street and joined the senator beneath the oak. He got up when she approached. He seemed steady enough on his feet.

The sky had dulled to blue and black. The whirling lights of the patrol car lent an air of unreality to the scene. A few people came out onto their porches. The couple with the stroller seemed to grow impatient, and Fielder went over to talk to them.

After a time, Elizabeth returned, her footsteps sharp in the calm of the night. The senator had returned to his seat on the grass.

"How is he?" I asked.

She sighed. "He gave me the same story he gave Fielder. He's on an errand. When I pressed him for details, he said he needs to get to his wife."

The statement hung in the air between us. We both knew what was wrong with it. The senator didn't have a wife; she had passed away years ago.

"He needs help," Elizabeth said. "I have to see if anyone's gotten through to his son yet."

She waved at Fielder and started walking toward him. I circled the front end of the patrol car and drifted across the street toward the oak, hands in pockets, taking in the scenery.

When I reached the senator's spot, I joined him on the grass. The sleeves of his cream-colored dress shirt were rolled up to his elbows. The legs of his trousers rose to reveal his ankles. He had on penny loafers, no socks.

"Is it your turn next?" he said. "Did they send you here to question me?"

I gazed up at the sky of leaves and branches. "I'm just out for a walk," I said. "It was either this or stay home and do yard work."

"You're a sensible man. It's a good night for a walk."

"Could be cooler."

He leaned back on his arms. In the light from a streetlamp I could see the veins standing out on his wrists.

"I never minded the heat," he said. "Have you been behaving yourself?"

I plucked at a blade of grass. "More or less."

"I understand you phoned my daughter-in-law."

That was true. I had called Callie Spencer earlier that day, because I had promised Lucy I would. Callie had surprised me by agreeing to Lucy's request for an interview.

The senator regarded me sternly. "You need to be careful," he said. "She's taken."

"I know."

"Temptation," he said. "We're all tempted."

I listened to the rustling of the leaves. The senator had gone silent, though he looked as if he had more to say on the subject of temptation. Something had distracted him. I saw him staring past my shoulder, strands of silver hair falling over his forehead, his eyes suddenly keen.

I turned and saw a Lexus drawing up to the curb on the other side of Third Street. The driver's door opened, and Alan Beckett hauled himself up from behind the wheel. He wore a suit of the same vintage as the one he'd worn the night before, and he tugged at his collar as he crossed the street. He moved ponderously. The air seemed to drag on him.

He stepped onto the curb and drew out a handkerchief to mop the sweat from his scalp.

"Senator," he said. "This won't do."

"Al is an endomorph," John Casterbridge said to me, as if we were still alone. "It's in his genes. He can't be blamed, really."

"Senator—"

"That's why he lumbers like a walrus, like a creature not meant to go on land."

Beckett ignored the insult. "We've been over this, Senator. You have a driver. If you want to go somewhere, he takes you."

"Al thinks I need to be carted around like freight."

"He takes you," Beckett said, "and no one runs any stop signs, and no one gets hurt."

I broke in. "The senator didn't run the stop sign. The other guy did."

The words rolled off Beckett. He continued as if I hadn't spoken. "And we avoid scenes like this, with police and onlookers and the attendant embarrassment for your family."

Casterbridge looked up at Beckett. Anger tensed his shoulders.

"I don't care to hear you talk about my family, Al."

"Not to mention your constituents," Beckett said. "What do you think they're going to make of this . . . this episode?"

The senator smiled grimly at that. "Don't worry about my constituents. They'll survive this, the darlings. It may bruise their tender sensibilities, but they'll endure. Bless their black, flabby little hearts."

"That's enough," said Beckett, wagging his head back and forth in disgust. "I'm going to talk to the police now, see if you're free to go. Maybe it's best you stay here."

The senator waved him off. "Do what you need to, Al."

Beckett scowled at me before he left us. I watched him lope away toward the intersection, where Elizabeth and Fielder were waiting.

He seemed to take the tension with him. John Casterbridge tipped his head back, filled his lungs with air. Let it drain slowly out.

"I shouldn't have said that about Al," he told me. "He doesn't move like a walrus. A walrus is a graceful creature, one of the good Lord's marvels."

His palm skimmed the grass. "He's not as bad as he seems. He comes from good stock. Grew up in Battle Creek. His father was a tradesman. Salt of the earth."

Having said his piece about Alan Beckett, he rooted in a pocket of his trousers and produced the stub of a cigar and a box of matches. Soon he had the tip of the cigar glowing, and as he shook out the flame of the match the action jarred my memory. I reached into my own pocket and came out with a small metal cylinder.

The senator saw it and set the stub between his teeth to free his hands. I passed him the cylinder and watched him unscrew the cap on the end. He tipped the cigar out and read the label on the band.

"Not bad," he said. "Where did you get this?"

It had been a gift from the owner of the shop that prints *Gray Streets*. The last time I delivered an issue, he was celebrating the birth of a grandson.

"I got it from a friend," I said. "I'd like you to have it."

He tipped it back into the cylinder, nodding his thanks. He put the cylinder in his pocket. "For later," he said.

After that, we sat in silence. I watched the neighbors chatting with one another on their porches, Beckett talking to Elizabeth in the blue and red light of the patrol car. John Casterbridge finished off the stub of his cigar and tapped out the remnant against the sole of his shoe. The scent of the smoke lingered sweet in the air.

A hint of it remained when Beckett came back to us. His conversation with Elizabeth seemed to have mellowed him.

"Come on, Senator," he said in a voice that was almost gentle. "We're going."

I got up from the ground and offered Casterbridge a hand, but he rose on his own.

"What did they say about my car?" he asked Beckett.

"Don't worry about it. I'll arrange to have it towed."

Casterbridge folded his arms. "I need that car, Al. I have an errand."

Beckett stepped down from the curb and into the street. "I'm driving you home, Senator. Whatever else you need to do can wait until morning."

"My errand can't wait. It's urgent."

I thought Beckett might get angry, but he only rubbed his scalp wearily and said, "I don't have time for this. It's late. We'll talk about it on the way."

Casterbridge wavered, letting his arms fall to his sides. I watched him take a step toward the street.

"I've got a car, Senator," I said. "I'd be happy to drive you wherever you need to go."

He looked back at me and then at Beckett, who waited silently in the street. The senator's eyes were shadowed. His indecision played itself out in small gestures: scratching at his elbow, plucking at his sleeve.

When he made up his mind he answered me quietly, with one of the saddest smiles I had ever seen.

"You head home, son. It's no good. The place I need to go is a long way off."

A REPORTER AND A CAMERAMAN arrived at the intersection of Third and Jefferson around two minutes after the senator slipped away. Elizabeth gave them no comment. They didn't bother with me.

Back at the house we found Sarah lying on the sofa watching the same reporter on the ten o'clock news. She wanted to hear all about what had happened, and while Elizabeth stayed behind to tell her, I went upstairs.

I found a note on the dresser in the bedroom. Sarah's handwriting. *Lucy Navarro called. I gave her your cell. Any relation to E. L. Navarro?*

I powered up my cell phone, and before I could wonder who E. L. Navarro was, it began to vibrate. I flipped it open. She didn't give me a chance to say hello.

"Loogan, you're a magician."

"How's it going, Lucy?"

"I heard from Callie Spencer. That's how it's going. She agreed to meet with me. She said you had called and persuaded her."

"I have a way with people."

"What did you say to her?"

"I told her the truth. Told her you had the crackpot idea that Floyd Lambeau was her father."

"That's all it took?"

"That's all. If she agreed to meet you, she probably thinks she can convince you otherwise."

"We'll see. I've got the meeting, that's the important thing. Tomorrow at two at the Spencer house. I'm letting you know, just in case."

"What do you mean?"

A hazy silence. Then: "You know what I mean, Loogan."

I knew. Because something in her voice had changed. It sounded grave.

I remembered her theory about the Spencers—that they might have hired the man in plaid. That they might have arranged to have Terry Dawtrey killed.

"Come on," I said. "You think you're going to ask the wrong question and—what?—the Spencers are going to make you disappear?"

"I can't rule it out," she said.

"Actually, I think you can."

"We'll see. I'll call you after, let you know how it goes. If you don't hear from me, well, you do what you think is right. If I disappear, maybe you can find me."

Her voice had turned careless and light, but I thought I could still hear an undertone of gravity in it.

"If you can't find me," she said, "I wouldn't mind being avenged."

CHAPTER 24

All men by nature desire to know. Aristotle said that in his *Metaphysics*. I picked it up in a college course on philosophy twenty years ago, the same course where I learned the meaning of Occam's razor and a few other semi-useful bits of wisdom.

All men by nature desire to know. It explains why parents snoop through their children's diaries, why people slow down to gawk at accidents on the highway, and why I went with Lucy Navarro to her meeting with Callie Spencer.

And even though I didn't really believe Lucy was in danger, that was part of it too. I remembered the bullets that someone had left outside our hotel rooms in Sault Sainte Marie.

I picked Lucy up at a quarter to two, and we arrived at the Spencer house right on schedule. We found Callie strolling in the sunlight on the lawn near the curved driveway; her parents were out for the afternoon, and her husband had driven back to Lansing.

She took us on a tour of the house, through her father's studio and her mother's garden. As we wandered over the back lawn toward the guest cottage, she chatted about a proposal coming up for a vote in the Michigan House of Representatives, a law that would extend health coverage for children living in poverty. A reminder of the good she was doing in the state legislature, and a hint of what she might do in the Senate.

Vines crept up the brown brick walls of the cottage, and a midsize silver Ford was parked on a gravel drive beside it. Ornamental grass grew along the path to the front door. The door opened into a large, high-ceilinged room. Stainless-steel appliances in the kitchen on the right, boxy leather sofas in the sitting area on the left.

Callie Spencer led us past the sofas to a glass-topped desk beside a window that faced the main house. She waved us into a pair of upholstered chairs. Our tour was over.

She set her eyes on Lucy Navarro and said, "You want to talk about Floyd Lambeau."

Lucy laid her sunglasses on the edge of the desk and drew a notepad from her bag.

"That's right."

"I can save you time," said Callie. "You want to know if Lambeau's my father. He's not. It's an old charge, made years ago by a nasty political opponent. There's nothing to it."

"I didn't hear it from one of your political opponents," said Lucy. "I heard it from Terry Dawtrey, who claimed he got it from Lambeau himself."

Callie sat down in a swivel chair behind the desk. "That's a new twist," she said, "but it doesn't change things. The story's not true. There's a reason no paper has ever printed it."

I watched her lean back in the chair, a lawyer confident of her case.

She said, "Floyd Lambeau's blood type was AB. You can find it in his autopsy report. It's a matter of public record. My blood is type O. That's public too. I did a campaign for the Red Cross once, encouraging other type Os to donate. Lambeau's not my father because a type AB can't be the father of a type O. It's impossible. A type O has to inherit the O gene from both parents. A type AB doesn't have an O gene to pass on."

Lucy made notes on her pad. Sitting beside her, I could see the page clearly. When I read what she'd written, my estimation of her rose by several points.

"I'm glad you agreed to talk to me," she said to Callie. "If I had turned in this story, I would have looked foolish."

Does she think I haven't read Lambeau's autopsy report? the notes on the pad said. *Does she think I never looked up her blood type?*

"Maybe you'd be willing to clear up a few other things for me," she said to Callie Spencer.

Sorry I wasn't entirely straight with you, Loogan, the notes said. *Forgive me?*

Callie nodded her agreement, and Lucy went on. "I spoke to Terry Dawtrey in prison this spring. He claimed to know the identity of the fifth robber—the driver in the Great Lakes Bank robbery. Does that surprise you?"

Callie looked skeptical. "Who did he say it was?"

"He didn't get around to telling me. He dropped some hints, though. I'm working on following them up."

"Sounds like he was trying to string you along."

"So you weren't aware that he had made that claim?"

Callie's shoulders rose and fell. "How would I be?"

"Is that a no?" Lucy asked.

"That's a no."

"Does it strike you as odd that your father was never able to identify the fifth robber?"

That brought a hint of a frown to Callie's face. "I'm not sure I understand you."

"Your father saw the driver outside the bank," Lucy said, "but he could never give a description of the man."

I thought I heard an edge of impatience in Callie's reply.

"My father was shot in the spine that day," she said. "He underwent hours of surgery. I think he can be forgiven for a lapse of memory."

"I didn't mean to be critical." Lucy shrugged the topic away. "Did you ever meet Floyd Lambeau?"

Callie swiveled her chair sideways, laid a palm on the glass of the desk. "He gave a lecture at the University of Michigan once, while I was at the law school. I attended the lecture." She lifted her fingers from the glass. "I've talked about that before. There's no story there."

"You never met Lambeau on any other occasion?" Lucy asked.

"No."

"So if someone told me they saw you two together, that would be a lie?"

"Did Terry Dawtrey tell you that?"

Lucy shook her head. "Henry Kormoran told me."

The answer surprised me, and I thought it must have surprised Callie too. But she said, "Then Henry Kormoran was lying. Or mistaken."

Lucy closed her notepad and laid it on the desk beside her sunglasses.

"Don't you want to know when and where Kormoran said he had seen you with Lambeau?"

"You're obviously eager to tell me," said Callie.

"The 'when' is intriguing: a few weeks before the Great Lakes robbery. The 'where' is even better—would you care to guess?"

"No."

Lucy turned to me. "What about you, Loogan?"

I thought of one obvious possibility. "At the Great Lakes Bank?"

"Good guess," said Lucy. "Kormoran told me he drove Lambeau to Sault Sainte Marie to check out the bank. I think you'd call it 'casing the joint.' They parked in front of a bakery across the street and watched the bank entrance for a few minutes. Then Lambeau sent Kormoran into the bakery to get him some coffee. When he came out, Lambeau was gone.

"Kormoran waited in the car. He saw Lambeau walk out of the bank a few minutes later, accompanied by a young woman. They stood talking on the sidewalk and then they parted. She backed away from Lambeau, smiled at him, and went on her way. When Lambeau returned to the car, Kormoran asked who the woman was.

"Lambeau wouldn't tell him. 'You don't need to get too curious about her,' he said. But Kormoran never forgot her, and years later when he saw you on television he made the connection. You were the woman from the bank. He told me he was sure of it, because he remembered the woman had a gorgeous smile."

Callie Spencer withdrew her hand from the desktop. In the sunlight I could see her fingerprints on the glass.

"That's a good story," she said in a soft voice. "Far better than the one where Lambeau is my father. A person can't choose who her father is. But if I helped Lambeau case the Great Lakes Bank, that would certainly make a good headline."

"So you're denying it?" Lucy asked.

Callie stood up and gazed through the window toward the main house. The sunlight made her face pale.

"Yes," she said, turning back to Lucy. "But don't let that stop you from printing it. If I were you, I'd include the line about my gorgeous smile. That's a nice detail. It really sells it. You'll want to bury my denial in the last paragraph, and see if you can find a picture of me from back then. One where I'm smiling."

She walked around the desk, her heels clacking against the hardwood floor, and though she didn't tell us to clear out, I understood that was the message. Lucy understood too. She picked up her bag and her notepad and we followed Callie outside. One shallow step took us down to the path with the ornamental grass beside it, and there Lucy turned back.

"I'm sorry," she said. "I forgot my sunglasses."

She went in to retrieve them, leaving me alone with Callie on the path. Callie looked down at the stones beneath our feet, and I couldn't tell what she was thinking. I was thinking about the portrait her father had painted, the one on the wall of his studio. Callie Spencer in her twenties, solemn and determined, her lips together in a line.

I said, "She's not going to find a picture of you from back then where you're smiling."

Callie looked up from the stones. "Probably not. I didn't do a lot of smiling then. Crooked teeth. My parents' insurance didn't cover braces. I never got them until I was twenty-seven—four years after the Great Lakes robbery."

"So if Henry Kormoran really saw you smile back then—"

"He wouldn't have called it gorgeous."

I nodded toward the cottage door. Lucy had left it half open.

"You could tell her that," I said.

Callie Spencer's scowl was like the darkness under clouds.

"I've already lectured her on blood types. Am I supposed to put her in touch with my orthodontist? She can write what she wants. It's such an absurd story, I have to think people will see through it."

I thought it might be wise to change the subject.

"How's the senator?" I asked. "I saw him last night."

Wrong question. The clouds got darker.

"He's fine," she said curtly. "Why's your friend taking so long?"

She mounted the step and pushed open the door. "Miss Navarro?" she called. Following behind her I saw Lucy turn from the desk and hurry toward us, her sunglasses held at her side.

"Sorry," she said.

Callie ushered her out silently, and the silence lasted through the long walk back to the main house. She stood by the crescent drive until Lucy and I were in the car and away.

When we reached the tree-lined street I turned to Lucy. "What did you do?"

"I don't know what you're talking about, Loogan."

"You didn't forget your sunglasses."

She twirled the glasses around by the stem. "Sure I did."

"You didn't need that long to find them. What were you up to in there?"

Suddenly she looked very pleased with herself. "Do you think I was up to something?"

"If I had to guess, I'd say you were either searching—though I don't know what for—or planting a bug. Which was it?"

"Neither one."

"What were you doing, then?"

"Absolutely nothing."

I gave her a disapproving look and didn't say anything.

"I swear to you," Lucy said. "I went in, picked up my glasses, and stood by the desk waiting for someone to call me."

"Why?"

"So Callie Spencer would think I was up to something."

CHAPTER 25

"She doesn't know what she's doing," I said to Elizabeth that night.

We had the news on with the sound turned down to a mumble. I sat on the end of the sofa and she lay with her feet in my lap. She had spent most of her day staking out the clinic where Sutton Bell worked. No sign of the man in plaid.

"Lucy's clever, but not as clever as she thinks she is," I said. "All she knows about being a reporter is what she's seen in movies and read in books. She thinks if she acts like a character in a story would, she'll be all right."

Elizabeth shut her eyes and smiled faintly. "Does she remind you of anyone?"

THE SPENCER HOUSE occupied a corner lot on Arlington Boulevard, at the intersection with Bedford Road. When Lucy and I drove away that afternoon, we headed south, rolling gently downhill. I intended to drop her at her hotel and spend a couple of hours at *Gray Streets*. She had other ideas.

"Hang a right, Loogan."

"What for?"

"Are you in a hurry to get somewhere?"

I hung a right, then two more, and we circled around again to Bedford Road and parked in the shade by the curb. From there we could see the Spencer house with its sloping lawn, and the guesthouse farther back. We could see the glimmer of Callie Spencer's silver Ford.

I powered the windows down and shut off the engine, and Lucy explained why she wanted Callie to think she was up to something.

"I want to know who she talks to, but I don't have any way of bugging her cottage. Despite what you might think, the *Current* doesn't give its reporters eavesdropping equipment. So I had to improvise. If she thinks I planted a bug—"

"—she won't make any calls from the cottage," I said. "But what's to stop her from walking over to the main house and using the phone there?"

Lucy tapped her sunglasses against her thigh. "If I've played this right, she won't take the chance. I've been in the main house too."

A dozen objections occurred to me. "She must have a cell phone—" I began.

"Maybe," Lucy said. "But a little paranoia goes a long way. If she thinks her landline's bugged, she might wonder how secure her cell phone is. I'm hoping she'll get in her car and drive somewhere—talk to somebody in person. If she does, I can follow her."

"What if there's no one she needs to talk to?"

"No. I've given her some things to think about. She'll want to talk it over with . . . somebody."

The pause before the final word made me suspect she had a particular somebody in mind.

"You think she knows the fifth bank robber," I said. "You think she's going to lead you to him."

She didn't answer. I watched her fold her glasses and tuck one of the stems into the collar of her shirt.

I said, "You told her Terry Dawtrey dropped hints about the identity of the fifth robber—hints that you were following up."

"That was a bluff. I wanted to give her something to worry about."

"And that stuff about Henry Kormoran seeing her at the Great Lakes Bank with Floyd Lambeau—was that a bluff too?"

"No. That's what Kormoran told me."

"The way I heard it, you never got to talk to Kormoran. He died before you could meet with him."

She stared out through the windshield, avoiding my gaze.

"I may have given Detective Waishkey that impression," she said.

We watched a squirrel stand up on the curb, hesitate, then bound across the street.

"How many times did you talk to Kormoran?" I asked.

"Just once," she said. "In the spring."

"And you think he was killed because of what he told you about Callie Spencer?"

"I think it's possible."

"How would anyone know what Kormoran told you?"

"I brought it up with Dawtrey when I visited him in prison. He couldn't confirm it, by the way. He and Lambeau saw Callie in Sault Sainte Marie, but as far as Dawtrey knew, she had nothing to do with the Great Lakes robbery."

The squirrel leapt onto the trunk of a maple and vanished into a veil of green.

"Let me see if I can summarize this brilliant theory of yours," I said. "Terry Dawtrey told you he knew the identity of the fifth robber, and you told him about Kormoran's claim that Callie Spencer helped Lambeau case the Great Lakes Bank. Someone overheard all this in the visitation room at Kinross Prison and passed it along to the Spencers. And they arranged to have Dawtrey and Kormoran killed. Is that about right?"

"That's right."

I looked off toward the cottage and the silver car. "And now that you've planted the idea in Callie's head that her house is bugged, you want to sit here and see if she leaves for a secret rendezvous with the elusive fifth man from the Great Lakes robbery."

Lucy slipped out of her shoes and put her feet up on the dash.

"You make it sound far-fetched," she said.

"We stayed there for an hour," I told Elizabeth. "Callie didn't go anywhere, and no one came to see her. When I'd had enough, I drove Lucy to her hotel. She never went inside, just climbed into that yellow Beetle of hers and headed back toward the Spencers'."

Elizabeth reached for the remote and clicked off the television. She lay silent for a few minutes, fiddling with the glass beads of her necklace, the way she does when she's thinking.

"It's all talk," she said after a while. "Dawtrey said this, Kormoran said that. They could have been lying to Lucy. She could be lying to you. I'd settle for one piece of physical evidence. If Callie Spencer and Floyd Lambeau cased the Great Lakes Bank together, there would be videotape from the surveillance cameras. If I had that tape, I'd have something."

"I asked Lucy about that," I said. "There's no tape of Lambeau casing the bank, alone or with anyone else. She thinks it must have been destroyed—part of a cover-up."

"Of course she does. But it might never have been collected. Or if it was, there might have been no reason to keep it. Lambeau died. He never stood trial." Elizabeth got up and raked her hands through her tangled hair. "It's all talk," she said. "Speculation."

Later on, after we had gone to bed, I lay awake and listened to night sounds. A moth fluttering against the window screen. The rhythm of Elizabeth's breathing. I thought she had fallen asleep, but she stirred and reached for the pad she keeps on her nightstand. It's a habit she picked up from me, a writer's habit. Ideas need to be caught on paper.

I heard her pen working, faint as sand shifting in the wind.

When it stopped I asked her, "What is it?"

"Probably nothing," she said. "But if Kormoran believed he had seen Callie Spencer with Lambeau at the Great Lakes Bank, that could explain why he had a copy of her portrait in his apartment. He might have needed it to remind himself of what she looked like back then."

THE NEXT MORNING I picked up bagels and orange juice and drove back to Bedford Road. I found Lucy Navarro's yellow Beetle parked in the same spot where she and I had been the day before. Lucy was sitting in the shade nearby, on a low stone wall that marked the edge of someone's front yard.

She waved to me and I walked over and sat down, offering her a bottle of orange juice, putting the sack of bagels between us. She'd changed clothes since the last time I'd seen her.

"I wondered if you'd stay here all night," I said.

"I took a break," she said. "Got some sleep at the hotel. But I've been back here since seven-thirty."

It was close to ten now. I looked off at the Spencers' guest cottage in the distance. Callie Spencer's silver Ford was in the drive.

"Anything happening?" I asked.

"Nothing," Lucy said. "Callie went to the main house last night for dinner, then back to the cottage around nine o'clock. Since then she hasn't been anywhere, as far as I know. I'm glad I haven't had to chase after her, though. I've been dealing with my own situation here."

I started to ask her what she meant, but she gestured at a spot in the grass between the wall and the sidewalk, not far from our feet. There was an oval shape there that I'd mistaken for a stone. It was the brown shell of a turtle. When I looked more carefully I could see its head, the dark points of its eyes. I could see its mouth moving; it was chewing on a leaf of clover.

"He's been here all morning," Lucy said. "He keeps wandering out into the street. I'm afraid he'll get run over."

As if on cue, the turtle made a break toward the curb. He wasn't big—maybe six inches from head to tail—but he moved pretty fast. He crossed the sidewalk and stopped midway through the strip of grass on the other side.

Lucy looked on tensely, ready to go after him.

"I've pulled him out of the street seven or eight times already," she said. "I don't know what he'll do if I have to leave."

I watched him skitter through the grass and over the curb. Lucy jumped up to retrieve him.

"Maybe you should carry him to the other side," I said, "if that's where he wants to go."

"I tried that," she said, holding the turtle two-handed. "If you take him over there, he wants to come back this way. There's no pleasing him."

A car rolled by in the street. Lucy deposited the turtle in the grass close to the stone wall and sat down again.

"And before you ask, I tried putting him on the other side of the wall," she said. "He wouldn't stay." She pointed past me toward a break in the wall where a driveway ran between two small pillars of stone. "He went all the way around and came back out. He's determined. I'm worried about him."

I couldn't think of anything to say to that, so I twisted the cap off my orange juice and took a drink. The day was getting warm, but it felt nice there in the shade. The turtle stayed put in the grass. He had withdrawn into his shell.

A boy rode by on a bicycle on the other side of the street. Lucy opened the bag between us and picked at a bagel. After a while she said, "You think I'm nutty."

"No," I said.

"You do. Because of the turtle. I'm not nutty, Loogan. I'm not one of those people who can't bring themselves to swat a fly, or who feel guilty if they step on a worm. I don't even mind much if something happens to a frog. But a turtle deserves some consideration."

I twisted the cap back onto my orange juice. "I'm not denying it," I said.

"You think I'm nutty."

I set the bottle on the wall between us. "Let me ask you this. What's your policy on spiders? You find a spider in the house, what do you do?"

"I hate spiders," she said, a little too quickly. "If I see a spider, I crush him with a rolled-up newspaper."

I watched the pale green of her eyes and waited. She didn't blink.

"I don't believe you," I said.

She looked away and popped a bit of bagel in her mouth, chewing it slowly. She rolled another bit between her fingers. "All right," she said. "It depends. If he looks nasty I might crush him. But if he looks nice enough I'll try to coax him onto a scrap of paper, take him outside. Let him loose in the garden."

She was grinning, and I felt myself doing the same. I didn't say anything. She reached over and punched my arm.

Before long, the turtle poked his head out of his shell and stirred himself into motion. He made it across the sidewalk, but Lucy got ahead of him and intercepted him at the curb. I got to my feet as she brought him back. "Let me try," I said.

She passed him to me and I carried him one-handed over the fence and across a well-tended lawn. There were shrubs and hedges planted around a white Victorian house, and none of it looked very inviting. But when I walked farther back I found a small artificial pond surrounded by fieldstones and flat pieces of slate. Lily pads floated on the surface of the water. A small frog hid in the shadow of a hyacinth.

I saw a patch of clover growing by the stone border of the pond and set the turtle down there. After a minute his head came out of his shell and his dark eyes looked up at me.

"Stay," I told him.

I backed off ten feet or so and waited there to see if he would follow. Over by the house a landscaper was pruning an ornamental pear tree. He stopped to watch me and I offered him a friendly nod. When I looked back, the turtle had climbed onto a piece of slate. I took that as a victory.

I walked back across the lawn and joined Lucy by the wall. When I told her about the pond, she was happy but skeptical.

"He still might come back," she said.

"I don't think so," I said. "We came to an understanding."

I LEFT HER THERE and headed downtown, and by the time I got to the office it was close to eleven. The elevator took me up to the sixth-floor hallway, and as I approached the door to *Gray Streets,* I noticed a package there, on the floor beside the door frame. Not an envelope this time. It was a long, thin paper bag with the end twisted tight.

My mind works in funny ways, and the first thought that came to me was *pipe bomb*. It had roughly the right shape. But the bag was the kind they give you at a liquor store and the diameter tapered off at the twisted end like the neck of a bottle. I took a chance and opened it and found a bottle of Scotch—Macallan, single malt.

I brought it in and stood it on the corner of my desk. There was no note to indicate where it came from. I sat and pondered it for a while, then found my cell phone and called Bridget Shellcross.

She sounded sleepy when she answered. "Hello, David."

"Hi, Bridget. Did you leave a bottle of Scotch outside my door?"

I heard whispering on the other end of the line, and a soft, airy giggle—the kind that might have come from an ethereal woman who played the lute.

Bridget made a shushing noise and said, "Lord knows I've thought of it, David. It would be more economical than buying it for you one glass at a time. Are you at the office?"

"Yes. I found the bottle when I came in."

"Well, as long as they didn't throw it through the window you're ahead of the game."

I nudged the bottle with my fingertip. "Sorry to bother you."

"No bother. Should I be worried?"

"I don't see why."

"Maybe you've got an admirer."

"Maybe I do."

I closed the phone. The bottle might have come from the senator, I thought. Or from Callie Spencer, though I suspected her feelings for me didn't run toward admiration.

I reached for a manuscript I'd been editing, a story about a corrupt detective searching for an heiress. I went through seven pages, jotting notes in the margins, before my phone began to buzz along the desktop.

I glanced at the screen and flipped it open. "Hello, Nick."

"Hey, sport. Remember how you told me to stop spying on the cops in Sault Sainte Marie?" When he said *told,* it came out *toll.*

"I remember."

"I didn't stop," he said. "Want to hear the latest?"

I put my feet up on the desk. "Sure."

"You know how Paul Rhiner's been holed up in his house? I figured out who's been bringing him food and booze. The sheriff. Delacorte. What does that tell you?"

He didn't need me to answer. It was obvious: Walter Delacorte wanted Rhiner to stay put, and didn't mind if he stayed drunk.

"What else?" I asked.

"The other deputy, Sam Tillman? He's been fighting with his wife. Last two nights, he's been sleeping on the couch."

"Nick, listen to me. You shouldn't be looking through Tillman's windows at night. You'll get yourself shot."

He dismissed my concern with a click of his tongue against his teeth. "I haven't told you the best part," he said. "Rhiner's been staying in, right? But that changed this morning. This morning he came out, hauled a bunch of trash to the curb. Lots of empty liquor bottles. Then half an hour ago I saw him again. He locked up the house and got in his car. He was carrying something in a folded newspaper. Don't know what. He's gone now. What about that?"

He didn't give me time to answer. "I think the sheriff's gone too," he said. "His car's not at home, or at his office either."

I shifted the phone from one ear to the other. "All right, Nick. I'm glad you told me. But you need to let it rest now—"

"It's always the same with you, sport. Is that the only song you know?" His impatience crackled over the line. "How's your wife? Is she the one who sprung Kyle Scudder?"

I brought my feet down off the desk. "What are you talking about?"

"You don't know anything, do you?" Nick said. "They let Kyle go. Guess they figured out he didn't kill my father. They cut him loose last night. All charges dropped. I thought maybe your wife had something to do with it."

Elizabeth had said nothing about it.

"Maybe it was the protest your mother organized," I said.

"No. That never happened."

"Either way, it's over. You can lay off. Leave the cops alone."

"My father's still dead, sport. So's Terry. And nobody seems to care much. You and me, we got different ideas of 'over.'"

I started to tell him again that he needed to let it rest, but the line was empty. Dialing him back, I got his voice mail: *Leave a message and maybe I call you.* I figured I could try to argue with him, but it would be like talking to a wall, or a fifteen-year-old. I told him to be careful.

I went back to the manuscript, but before long I got another call, this time on my office phone.

"Gray Streets."

"May I speak to Mr. David Loogan, please?" A woman's voice.

"This is," I said.

"Ah, Mr. Loogan. I've been reading your magazine and I have to tell you I find it enchanting."

"Enchanting?"

"I'm particularly enamored of a story called—what was it now? Oh yes—'Killer in the Sun.' Delightful. Simply the tops."

She sounded slightly manic, and there seemed to be a rush of wind in the background. I envisioned her racing along in a convertible, with one hand on the wheel and the other holding a phone to her ear.

"I'm sorry. Did you say 'the tops'?"

She carried on as if she hadn't heard me. "I have to say I've become smitten with *Gray Streets,* and I simply must find a way to lend it my support."

"I'd be happy to sell you a subscription, ma'am."

Her laugh was high and delicate like crystal. "A subscription? Oh, Mr. Loogan, I believe I can do better than that."

"You'll have to forgive me," I said. "I didn't catch your name."

"I suppose I didn't offer it. This is Amelia Copeland."

Amelia Copeland, from the party Sunday night. The woman who told Callie Spencer she was too young to run for the Senate. The one who headed a foundation that supported the arts.

She gets melancholy when she drinks too much wine, Callie had said. I could only assume she had sobered up. The transformation was remarkable.

"Now, Mr. Loogan," she said, "we simply must get together and discuss things. I'm in a rush at the moment, but why don't you call my assistant and set up a luncheon appointment for next week." She rattled off a number. "You will, won't you?"

"I will."

"Delightful. Ta-ta."

Before I could ask her if she had really said *Ta-ta,* she rang off. I dropped the handset into the cradle and tried to go back to my editing, but I had a hard time concentrating. I assumed Callie had brought *Gray Streets* to Amelia Copeland's attention. I wondered if she had done it before or after the visit Lucy and I had paid her. I wondered what her motive might be. I wondered if I should call her and ask. Then I took a break from wondering, locked the office, and went across the street for a sandwich at Café Felix.

I was back at my desk half an hour later. I hunkered down and made it through eight more pages. By then the detective had found the heiress at a hotel in Los Angeles and let her know that he was professionally obliged to take her back to her father in Chicago—but also that he wasn't a stickler about his professional obligations and maybe they could work something out. They were in the middle of some rather steamy negotiations when my desk phone rang again.

"Gray Streets."

"Mr. Loogan, this is Alan Beckett."

I almost didn't believe him. His voice seemed light, cheery. I'd only ever heard him sound sarcastic or annoyed.

"What can I do for you?" I said.

"There's something I'd like to discuss."

"What's on your mind?"

"Better if we talk in person. I can be at your office in five minutes."

"All right. Sure."

I hung up the phone and retrieved my pencil. Scratched out a couple of unnecessary adjectives. Then I reached for my cell and dialed Lucy Navarro.

She answered on the second ring. "Hey, Loogan."

"Are you still on Bedford Road?" I said.

"Still here."

"Has the turtle come round again?"

"I haven't seen him. What's up?"

"I'm not sure. Have you heard of Alan Beckett? He's Callie Spencer's adviser."

Her laugh had an odd, sharp quality. "I'm familiar with him," she said.

"He's on his way to see me. He sounds pleasant. Personable. Makes me think I'm going to wind up in a ditch somewhere."

I listened as she let out a long breath. "I thought this might happen," she said. "I talked to him earlier, after you left here. I think I disappointed him. Now he'll go to work on you."

"What does he want?"

"You'll see. Try to resist if you can. And keep a tight grip on your soul."

CHAPTER 26

I met Alan Beckett at the hallway door, and he bounced in with an exaggerated vigor. He had forgone his usual decade-old suit in favor of blue jeans, a gaudy Hawaiian shirt, and a shapeless white sports coat. He wore tennis shoes. As he went past the receptionist's desk in the outer office he turned in a surprisingly graceful circle, taking in the space.

"Memories," he said. "I had an office like this once, years ago, Mr. Loogan. I wonder if you can guess what my business was back then."

"I'm not going to guess."

"No? Just as well. I was a political candidate. Does that surprise you?"

"Nothing surprises me today." I gestured toward the inner office. "Why don't you have a seat."

I stood by the door and let him pass through. He was carrying a book under his arm, and he laid it carelessly on the edge of the desk as he sat down in the guest chair. The book was a hardcover with the dust jacket gone. I couldn't see the title.

"I was a candidate for city council," he said. "Never mind where. I ran my entire campaign out of an office much like this one."

"Did you win?"

He smiled indulgently. "That's what people always want to know. Not what goals I hoped to achieve, or what issues I wanted to address." He shrugged. "No, I didn't win, Mr. Loogan."

I took my seat. "What issues did you want to address?"

"I had one issue. I wanted to fix the zoning laws." He tilted his head. "That doesn't sound very idealistic, does it? But I'll tell you, they make a difference. Get the zoning right and you get businesses coming in. That brings in smart, skilled people. Broadens your tax base. That pays for police, firefighters, schools, parks—things the smart people need to raise their families. Get the zoning wrong and it runs the other way. All those smart people go somewhere else."

"Why do you think you lost?"

"My opponent was a family man. He had a fine thick head of hair. He appeared in television commercials with his sleeves rolled up, out among the common people, talking to them very earnestly. Of course you never heard what he said, you only heard the music and the announcer's voice."

Beckett let out a huff of air and added, "He's still a city councilman. I've advised a U.S. senator, and I hope to advise another." He nodded toward the bottle of Macallan on my desk. "I see you got my gift."

"I got it," I said warily. "I don't know what the occasion is."

"Call it a peace offering. You and I have gotten off on the wrong foot."

He rubbed his thumb over his chin. "It's my fault," he said. "I feel a certain responsibility for the senator. I have to be careful about who gets close to him, and what their intentions are."

"I've chatted with him twice," I said. "I like him. I don't have any intentions."

"He likes you too. That may be why I've been unfriendly toward you. I don't mind admitting it. I had to spend years gaining his trust, but he took a liking to you right away. I felt a little envious."

He sounded subdued, almost humble. The effect was disarming.

"How's the senator doing?" I asked him.

"He's fine. What you saw the other night—well, he has his bad days." Beckett dismissed the subject with a raised hand. "The senator's not the reason I came here."

"What's the reason, then?"

"I thought you might be willing to do me a favor."

I felt myself smile. "Is that right?"

"I'd like you to talk to Lucy Navarro," he said. "Get her to drop all this nonsense about Terry Dawtrey and Henry Kormoran—this ridiculous claim that Callie helped Floyd Lambeau case the Great Lakes Bank."

"And why would I do that?"

"Do you believe the claim is true, Mr. Loogan?"

"No."

"Do you think any purpose is served when politicians are subjected to baseless charges in the press?"

"If the charge is baseless, the problem solves itself, doesn't it? As you said, the claim is ridiculous. Even if the *National Current* prints it, no sensible person is going to believe it."

"If there's one thing I've found," Beckett said, "it's that the world is full of people without any sense. If the *Current* prints that claim, it's bound to find traction with a certain segment of the population."

"That's a problem for you. But I don't think pushing Lucy to drop her story is the solution." I picked up a pencil from the desk. Pointed it at him. "You realize that's just what she expects, don't you? She already thinks the Spencers may have had a hand in killing Dawtrey and Kormoran. If you try to buy her silence now, it'll only make you look guilty in her eyes."

Beckett's lips came together in a pained expression. "I think it goes without saying that Callie Spencer had nothing to do with the deaths of Terry Dawtrey and Henry Kormoran. And I don't know where you got the idea that I wish to buy Lucy Navarro's silence."

"You're not offering her anything in exchange for dropping her story?"

"Of course not. That would be completely improper."

"And you're not offering me anything for convincing her to drop it?"

"I'm asking it as a favor."

I sat back from the desk and studied him. His cheeks were pink as a baby's. The garish colors of his shirt made him look like a buffoon. But his eyes held a keen intelligence.

"You're good," I said. "I don't see how anybody ever beat you, no matter how fine a head of hair he had."

"I'm sure I don't understand you," he said.

"I got a call from Amelia Copeland today. Am I supposed to believe you didn't put her up to that?"

He smiled. "Amelia is a lovely woman. A dear friend of the Spencers and the Casterbridges and, I'm pleased to say, of mine. But no one 'puts her up' to things."

"So it's a coincidence that she called to tell me how enchanted she is with *Gray Streets,* and that she wants to lend the magazine her support?"

"I'm not surprised you heard from her. She's always been a fan of mysteries. Her library at home has shelves full of Agatha Christie and Patricia Highsmith. She could do you a good turn, if she wanted to. That foundation of hers has more money than God."

"She wants to get together next week. Why do I get the feeling that the meeting could go well or badly, depending on whether or not I help you convince Lucy Navarro to drop her story?"

"I think you're being overly suspicious. I don't have any control over who Amelia gives her money to."

"You have no interest in the matter, then? You won't care if I decline her offer?"

Beckett plucked at a thread on his sports coat. "It's nothing to me, one way or the other. But I should think a man in your position would welcome Amelia's generosity."

I steepled my fingers under my chin. "And what's my position?"

"You're in the business of publishing short stories, in a world where hardly anyone reads them anymore. How are your circulation numbers, compared to a year ago?"

"I think they may be up a little."

"I believe they're down, and more than a little. You're being kept afloat by Bridget Shellcross. She's an author, I gather. Writes books about an art dealer who solves crimes with her cat."

"You've been misinformed."

"Have I?"

"It's her dog."

"I don't see how it would matter. Are you on good terms with Ms. Shellcross?"

"We get along."

"How long do you think she's going to keep putting money into the magazine?"

"We haven't discussed it."

He dropped his voice a bit. "How old are you, Mr. Loogan?"

"That's getting a little personal, isn't it, Al?"

"You're thirty-nine. Your annual salary is unconscionably low." He named a figure, like a carnival worker guessing my weight. It was close enough that the difference didn't matter. "And for that," he said, "you're expected to carry this operation on your shoulders."

"When you put it that way," I said, "it does sound unconscionable." I aimed my steepled fingers at him. "Let me ask you something. Lucy Navarro doesn't have a magazine that needs funding. So what did you offer her?"

"I've offered her nothing," he said. "Just as I've offered you nothing."

"Naturally. It's all Amelia Copeland's doing. She waves her wand and my pumpkin turns into a carriage, my mice into horses." I stared at him. "How long do you think you're going to be able to keep a lid on this scandal surrounding Callie Spencer?"

"There is no scandal surrounding Callie Spencer," Beckett said.

"She decides to run for the Senate, and suddenly the Great Lakes Bank robbers—including the man who shot her father—start dying. If that's not a scandal, it's getting awfully close."

"None of that has anything to do with Callie."

"No, how could it?" I said. "Callie's golden. People like her. The press likes her. They're willing not to ask too many questions. But there's still a killer on the loose. He's after Sutton Bell. He tried once and failed. What if he succeeds the next time? Is everyone still going to say, 'Well, this can't have anything to do with Callie Spencer'?" I watched for some reaction, but Beckett seemed entirely at ease. "And then there's the fifth robber, the driver. He's a wild card, isn't he? I'm wondering when he'll turn up. Aren't you?"

That earned me a puzzled look. "The driver has managed to stay hidden for seventeen years," Beckett said. "Why would he show himself now? I don't think that's anything to worry about."

"I think you are worried about him. Otherwise you wouldn't have broken into my office."

The puzzlement faded from Beckett's features, but only for a second. Then it came back strong and deliberate. His pink brow furrowed. "You invited me into your office," he said.

"I'm talking about the last time you were here."

"I've never been here before today."

"You were here over the weekend," I said. "Someone cut a square of glass out of the door." I waited a beat. "The senator told me two things about you the other night. He said you came from Battle Creek and your father was a tradesman. I'm an overly suspicious man, so I ran a Google search on 'Battle Creek' and your last name. One of the results was Beckett Glass. Your father was a glazier."

"That's true," he said with a shrug, "and I can understand why it would arouse your suspicions. But why would I break into your office?"

"Because all men by nature desire to know."

"I beg your pardon?"

"It's a quote from Aristotle. You broke in because there was something you wanted to know. It all goes back to last Wednesday."

"I don't understand," he said.

"Last Wednesday someone tried to kill Sutton Bell," I said. "But before he did, he left a manuscript outside my door. It was a description of his crimes—how he beat Charlie Dawtrey to death and tried to shoot Terry Dawtrey, how he strangled Henry Kormoran."

"Would this be the manuscript Detective Waishkey brought with her on Sunday night?"

"That's right."

"But Sunday night was the first time I heard about it."

"I don't think so," I said. "Elizabeth faxed a copy to Walter Delacorte in Sault Sainte Marie last Thursday. Delacorte sent it on to Harlan Spencer, his old boss from seventeen years ago. Spencer told Callie about it, and Callie told you."

"You're making a lot of assumptions."

"I'm really only making one—that all you people talk to each other. Elizabeth wanted Delacorte to take the manuscript seriously, so she had to tell him where it came from, and he would have passed that information along. So you knew it had been left at my door. But you didn't know why. If the killer wanted it to go to the police, he could have sent it to them directly. If he was looking for notoriety, he could have sent it to the *Ann Arbor News,* or one of the Detroit TV stations."

"So you think I broke in here to find out why the killer delivered his manuscript to *Gray Streets.*"

"Not quite. I think you found the answer to that without breaking in. It's not hard to figure out. Something attracted the killer to *Gray Streets*. We know he's fixated on the Great Lakes Bank robbery. *Gray Streets* published a story about a bank robbery earlier this year—'Only Paper' by Peter Fletcher. It's based, very loosely, on the Great Lakes robbery. It's told from the point of view of the driver, and it's the story of his revenge on the other robbers. The details don't matter. What's important is that it's on our website. Anyone looking for a connection between *Gray Streets* and the Great Lakes robbery could have found it. Just like you found it."

"So you say."

"So I say. You found it and you got curious about the author, Peter Fletcher. The bio note that accompanies the story says he's from Hell, Michigan. You would have discovered that while there is a town called Hell in Michigan, no one named Peter Fletcher lives there. So it must be a pseudonym. That's why you broke in here—to find out the author's real name."

"And why would I care enough about the author to go to such lengths?"

"I'm not sure," I said. "I've got a couple of ideas, but you'll think they're outlandish. One is that you thought the story had been written by the real driver from the Great Lakes robbery, and you wanted to see to it he didn't make a nuisance of himself and interfere with Callie Spencer's run for the Senate."

"You're right," said Beckett. "That's outlandish. What's your other idea?"

"I'm not sure I want to say."

"Oh, come."

"All right, but you have to tell me something first. How old are you?"

I was echoing a question he had asked me, and it threw him. But he answered.

"Forty-three."

I didn't try to hide my surprise. "All along I've been thinking fifty," I said. "But if you're only forty-three, then it's possible."

"What's possible?"

"That you were the driver in the Great Lakes robbery. You would have been twenty-six at the time, a little older than Bell and the others, but in the ballpark."

He let out a short bark of a laugh. "You're an amusing man, Mr. Loogan."

"I'm glad you think so," I said. "If you were the driver, you might have read something in the story that bothered you, some detail that cut too close to the bone. You might have wondered if your secret was safe. That might have prompted you to break in here looking for the identity of the author."

"Amusing, as I said. But I'm not the driver from the Great Lakes robbery."

"What were you doing back then, seventeen years ago?"

"That would have been just after I lost my bid for the city council."

"You must have been disappointed."

"Yes."

"That might have made it easier for Floyd Lambeau to recruit you."

"I never met the man," Beckett said. "That autumn was when I first began working for the senator. I didn't have time to rob any banks."

"Well, it was just a thought," I said. "The bottom line is, I don't know why you broke in here this weekend, but I know you didn't learn anything about Peter Fletcher."

"No?"

"No. We don't even have a file on him. The man doesn't exist."

"Then who wrote the story I was supposed to be so interested in?"

"I wrote it. But I never publish in *Gray Streets* under my own name. I'm the editor-in-chief; it wouldn't look right. I always use the name Peter Fletcher."

Beckett rubbed his palm over his scalp. "That's fascinating. But of course I never had any interest in Peter Fletcher, and I'm not the one who broke into your office."

"If that's the way you want it, it's fine with me," I said. "As long as we understand each other. I don't want to find out later that some poor bastard named Peter Fletcher got run off the road on a dark night because I wrote a story under his name."

"You have a very active imagination, Mr. Loogan."

"Yes, I do. And as for Lucy Navarro, I can see how she might be a thorn in your side, but I confess I've grown a little fond of her. Whether she goes ahead with her investigation or not is up to her—I don't intend to advise her one way or the other. But if anything should happen to her, I'm afraid my imagination might get the better of me. I might imagine that there's an elaborate conspiracy at work, and that you're at the center of it."

"I think perhaps you've read too many stories, Mr. Loogan."

"I'm just telling you how it is. What was it you said about the senator—you feel responsible for him? It's the same with me and Lucy Navarro. As far as you're concerned, she's under my protection."

Beckett braced his hands on his knees and pushed himself up from his chair. "That's a noble sentiment," he said, "but I can assure you Ms. Navarro has nothing to fear from me. I'd like to persuade you of that, but I won't take up more of your time."

He nodded his farewell and turned to go. I got up to see him off. He had only taken a few steps when I noticed he'd left his book behind.

"You forgot something," I said.

He paused midstride and looked back. "No, I brought that for you. Think of it as one last argument to convince you to help me."

I came out from behind the desk and watched him cross the outer office. When the hallway door closed behind him I reached for the book. The cover felt dry and slightly rough. A glance at the spine told me the title—*Stakes*—and the name of the author: E. L. Navarro.

CHAPTER 27

Elena Lucia Navarro," I said.

"You got me, Loogan. You've discovered my dark secret."

We were sitting in her yellow Beetle with a view of Callie Spencer's Ford—a distant patch of silver parked beside the cottage. I had the book in my lap.

"It's really good," I said.

"Oh, go on," said Lucy.

"I've only read the first few chapters, and I usually don't go in for urban fantasy—"

"Not so many caveats, Loogan," she said. "You had me with 'It's really good.'"

I wasn't alone in my opinion. I'd done some searching online and found glowing profiles of the author in the *Los Angeles Times* and the *Chicago Tribune*. The piece in the *Tribune* had a picture of Lucy: younger, paler, with her hair dyed jet black. She looked vaguely Gothic, which must have been the point. *Stakes* was a novel about vampires.

I had picked up the essentials of the story: The protagonist dreams onc night that his wife has been abducted from their bedroom by a shadowy intruder. In the dream he finds himself paralyzed, unable to react as his wife tries to fight off her captor. The struggle grows violent—sheets torn from the bed, mirror broken on the bureau. In the morning he wakes to find that the struggle was real, his wife is gone, and all he can remember about her abductor is that he had no reflection in the mirror.

The husband gets no help from the police. They think his story is nonsense and suspect he's done away with his wife, but they can't prove it. He's left to try to find her on his own.

Some of the critics found the plot melodramatic, the twists implausible. But they all agreed that the language was gorgeous, and that E. L. Navarro was a major new talent.

"The bio note says you were writing a second book," I said to her.

"That's true. I was planning a trilogy."

"So what happened?"

"The first one didn't sell," Lucy said. "That's an achievement in itself, I think—writing a vampire novel that won't sell. In my defense, they tried to market it to twelve-year-olds. But that's not who I wrote it for."

"I know a sixteen-year-old who loves it," I said. I had talked to Sarah a short time before and learned that *Stakes* was one of her favorite books. That's why she had asked me if Lucy was any relation to E. L. Navarro. "She's waiting for the second book."

"She'll have a long wait," Lucy said.

I felt the rough cover beneath my fingers. "But that's what Beckett offered you, isn't it?"

"Beckett never offers anybody anything. I'm sure he told you so."

"But someone made the offer."

She nodded. "I got a call from my old editor this morning. She wants me to sign a contract for two more books. A nice advance. I'm supposed to drop everything and get to work."

I tapped the book. "This was Beckett's last argument. He thought it would sway me. He thought I'd read it and try to convince you to forget your investigation. He was right. You're wasting your time working for the *Current*. You should be writing another novel."

"I warned you about him, Loogan. You let him work his spell on you."

"No, this is my own judgment. I know a writer when I see one. Callie Spencer's not your problem. No matter what she's done—if she drove the getaway car at the Great Lakes robbery herself, if she killed Henry Kormoran with her bare hands—it's not your responsibility to expose her. Let it go."

"Don't tempt me, Loogan."

"I'm serious. Let someone else at the *Current* take over."

"You think I haven't thought of that?" she said. "You're assuming the publishing contract is real. But it's not. It's Beckett's creation, and if I don't do what he wants, it goes away. He wants the investigation to end."

Lucy gazed down at the backs of her hands where they rested on the steering wheel. I had an idea of what she was seeing—a different future, something that might have been.

"No," she said at last. "I wrote a book and it didn't sell. No regrets. I made a decision to move on. To try being a reporter. I'm not going to stop."

I could have stayed and tried to change her mind, but it was her decision, and I had business of my own. I'd fallen behind on my editing. I needed to get back in my car and back to *Gray Streets*.

As I opened the door beside me, she brought a pen from her bag and held her hand out for the book. She found the title page and scribbled her name.

"There," she said with a wan smile. "Now you've got a signed copy of E. L. Navarro's only novel. Hang on to it. It'll be worth something when I break this story about Callie Spencer."

CHAPTER 28

Elizabeth sat cross-legged on the floor with the sofa at her back. On the coffee table in front of her she had spread the contents of Callie Spencer's loony file—letters from constituents that had been set aside because they contained threats or seemed to have been written by people who were mentally disturbed.

Callie Spencer had promised Elizabeth the file on Sunday night; her office had delivered it on Wednesday afternoon. Now, on Wednesday evening, with a glass of wine within reach and a Mahler symphony playing on the stereo, Elizabeth sorted through it, looking for a letter that went out of its way not to use adverbs, a letter that might have been written by the man in plaid.

Earlier, Sarah had fixed dinner for the two of them: pan-fried steaks served with cauliflower that had been tossed in olive oil and baked in the oven. As the twilight deepened into dark, she joined Elizabeth on the living-room floor.

"What are you doing?"

"Police business," Elizabeth said.

Sarah plucked a letter at random from the coffee table.

"If I read this, am I going to be scarred for life?"

"I don't think so."

At one time, Elizabeth had tried to keep her home life strictly separate from her work life. She had gotten along fairly well until Sarah entered her teens and developed a strong curiosity about what her mother did for a living. Eventually, Elizabeth had given up on trying to keep the girl entirely out of police business. But she still tried to preserve some boundaries. "Scarred for life" was one of them: anything traumatic was off-limits, including things like autopsy reports and crime-scene photos. From what Elizabeth had seen, the letters from Callie Spencer's file seemed relatively harmless.

Sarah looked up from the letter she had chosen and said, "This one's about mourning doves."

Elizabeth set aside a rambling note scrawled on a page torn from a phone book.

"What about them?" she asked.

"This guy wants Callie to vote to lift the ban on hunting them."

"That's ill-advised, but not crazy. Maybe that one got misfiled."

"He wants to be able to shoot them because he thinks they're travelers from another dimension," Sarah said. "He can't get their cooing out of his head. He thinks they're trying to control his thoughts."

"Interesting. But if they could control his thoughts, would they have let him write that letter?"

"Well, they're only trying so far. They haven't succeeded."

Elizabeth reached for her wineglass. "Does he use any adverbs?"

"I don't see any," said Sarah. "No, wait. Here's one: the doves taunt him *mercilessly*. That's not our man, then."

He's not in here, Elizabeth thought. The man in plaid could pass for normal. If he was in Callie Spencer's files, he was with all the other ordinary citizens who cared about ordinary things: unemployment and taxes, green technology and better schools. But Callie had refused access to those files.

Elizabeth sipped wine and returned her glass to the table. Sarah read aloud from a letter that requested funding from the legislature for research into levitation and telekinesis. When she came to the end of that one, she found another that described a plan for fortifying Michigan's southern border against the coming invasion from Ohio.

"It has pictures," Sarah said. "Diagrams of battlements. A system of trenches." She was on her feet now, pacing around, riffling through the pages. "I want to keep this out and show it to David. Do you know when he'll be home?"

Elizabeth picked up a fresh letter. "He didn't say."

"I think the spirit of it might appeal to him. You know how he is, always checking the locks on the doors and windows." Sarah paused before one of the windows that looked out onto the porch and the street. The white slats of the blinds alternated with the dark outside.

Elizabeth heard the snick of the blinds being closed. A moment later she heard the front door opening and being pulled shut again. She didn't look up from her letter. She assumed Sarah had gone onto the porch to look at the night.

A minute or two passed before she heard the door again. Sarah came into the living room and touched a button on the stereo. The symphony cut off abruptly. She turned the switch on the floor lamp and the room went gray dark.

"What are you doing?" Elizabeth said.

Sarah knelt beside her. "There's a car parked on the street with its engine running. Two people in it—a man and a woman. There's something strange about them. The man slouched down when I walked by, like he didn't want to be recognized."

Elizabeth frowned. "You should have said something to me before you went out there."

"I was curious."

"I don't suppose you got a plate number."

"Are you trying to hurt my feelings?" said Sarah, looking wounded.

"Let's have it, then."

Sarah recited the number. "It's an Audi. Looks new."

Elizabeth got up, found her cell phone in her bag. Dialed the Investigations Division on her way to the window.

"Shan here."

"Carter. You're working late." Parting the blinds, Elizabeth spotted the car down the block, in a dark patch between two streetlamps.

"Paperwork," Shan said.

"Check a plate for me?"

"Sure."

She gave him the number. Heard him working a keyboard.

"What's this about?" he asked.

"Call it curiosity. The car's been sitting on my street."

"Hmmm. Maybe I should come over."

"Who is it, Carter?"

She heard the squeak of his chair as he sat back.

"The car's registered to Jay Casterbridge," he said.

Callie Spencer's husband. Elizabeth watched the doors of the car swing open. Two figures got out.

"Say the word," Shan said, "and I'm on my way."

Elizabeth saw Jay Casterbridge step into the light of the streetlamp. The woman with him was tall and rail thin. Not Callie Spencer.

"No. Let me see what he wants, Carter. I'll call you if I need you."

JAY CASTERBRIDGE MOVED restlessly around the kitchen, skittish as a pony in an unfamiliar stall. His tie was loose and one end of his shirt collar hung over the lapel of his jacket.

"Callie doesn't know I'm here," he said.

"Is that right?" said Elizabeth.

She had turned on the downstairs lights, and the fluorescents in the kitchen made Casterbridge blink. His companion seemed more at ease. She had long slender limbs and a delicate face. Blond hair with dark roots. She wore deep blue slacks and a matching blazer with a white blouse underneath. The blouse was open at the collar, showing freckled skin stretched over prominent clavicles. Casterbridge had introduced her as his law partner, Julia Trent.

"What Jay means," she said, "is that we'd like this conversation to remain confidential."

"That's fine," said Elizabeth.

Julia Trent braced her arms against the counter behind her. "We saw a young woman come out of the house a few minutes ago. Was that your daughter?"

Elizabeth nodded once. "She's gone upstairs. She's won't overhear us."

Jay Casterbridge wandered over by the refrigerator and stood with his arms crossed.

"I think you had a good idea the other night," he said. "About the files."

Elizabeth watched him pluck at the sleeve of his jacket. She said nothing.

"If you found someone that way," he said, "no one would need to know, would they? I mean, no one would need to know *how* you found him."

"All I need is a name," Elizabeth said. "Once I've got it, I can look into his background, determine if he's a viable suspect."

"And it wouldn't come back to Callie. That's important."

"There's no reason it should have to. Are you suggesting she might be willing to let me see her files?"

Casterbridge grimaced. "God no. She's set against it."

Elizabeth touched the glass beads of her necklace. "Are you offering to let me look at the files without her knowing?"

He glanced at Julia Trent, who stared right back at him.

"Callie's been here for the past three days," he said carefully. "I've been in Lansing. Her main office is there. All the files."

"You've found something," Elizabeth said.

He nodded. "A typical letter from a constituent. He wrote to her about an issue—violence against women. That makes sense, doesn't it? If he thinks he's protecting Callie from harm, if he's targeting the Great Lakes robbers because, in his mind, they pose a danger to her—"

"Yes, it makes sense."

"Now Callie gets a fair number of letters about violence against women," Jay Casterbridge said. "I would have passed over this one, except that it fits the pattern you described. It goes on for three pages without using a single adverb. The guy who wrote it, he talks about a friend who was beaten by her husband. He attacked her again and again—'beat her like a savage would.' That's the phrase that caught my attention. The writer doesn't say 'savagely'; he won't use the adverb. In the next paragraph he says, 'Threats are serious and should be heeded'—when anyone else would say, 'Threats should be taken seriously.' There are at least five more examples like that. Sounds like the man you're looking for, doesn't it?"

Elizabeth had been standing across the room from the other two. Now she moved closer. "It does," she said. "I need to see that letter."

Julia Trent stepped over to Casterbridge's side. "We're willing to let you see it," she said in a crisp lawyer's voice, "but we have conditions. You get one look. You don't keep the letter, or even a copy. You don't reveal that we showed it to you."

"That won't work. The letter's evidence—"

"It's not evidence," said Julia Trent. "It's not a crime to write to your state representative. You get a look, that's all. The letter's signed. You said all you needed was a name." She shrugged as if the matter were settled. A woman used to getting her way.

Elizabeth sighed. "Fine. Let me see it."

She would have bet that Julia Trent had possession of the letter, but Jay Casterbridge was the one to reach inside his jacket, draw it out, pass it over.

Elizabeth accepted it, three sheets clipped together. She saw the date: May of this year. The salutation: "Dear Ms. Spencer." Neat blocks of text. She turned to the last page and the signature had a half-familiar look. The sharp angles of the capital A and L reminded her of the man in plaid's note: LET ME HAVE BELL AND I'M DONE. Some of the letters of the signature were hard to make out, but the name was right there in type underneath. She felt a rush of heat in her fingertips, goose bumps rising on her arms. She knew it was him.

Anthony Lark.

CHAPTER 29

Lark's hand felt better every day. The swelling had gone down and a scab had formed over the cut. He could poke it without wincing. He left the bandage off now, and if he curled his fingers no one would notice the wound. He kept taking the Keflex, morning and evening. A ten-day course, Sutton Bell had told him.

He had been testing his strength, venturing out of the apartment. Working on the problem of how to get to Bell. *Slow and steady,* his father used to say. Lark had driven through Bell's neighborhood and past the clinic where he worked. He had gone at different times of day. He had seen patrol cars parked in front of the house and the clinic, but never at the same time. The police were conserving manpower. They watched the house when Bell was home, but not when he was at work.

That probably meant that Bell's wife and daughter weren't staying at the house, which was fine with Lark. When the time came, he didn't want the wife and daughter to be there.

Lark drove into his apartment complex Wednesday night with a deli sandwich and a six-pack of beer on the car seat beside him. A dim suggestion of a headache had begun to stir behind his eyes, but he thought if he went in and took a pill and laid some ice on his brow he might be able to fend it off.

He passed along a curve in the drive that led to his building and his headlights washed over the Dumpsters. He spotted a flash of movement, orange and gray, quick as lightning. An animal darting through a break in the wooden fence that framed the Dumpsters on three sides. Through the break and into the tangle of brush on the other side.

A cat, he thought.

He stopped the Chevy and left it idling. Got out before he had a chance to think about the wisdom of it. He crouched to look through the break in the fence and thought he could see eyes peering back at him.

He retreated to the car, unwrapped his sandwich, and peeled off a slice of turkey. Took it with him and left a scrap of it by the break in the fence.

More scraps at small intervals, a trail to lure the cat out. Lark knelt on the bare concrete before the Dumpsters, a last scrap of turkey dangling between his fingers. The eyes watched him.

He waited. The cat made a foray through the break, putting its nose out to sniff the air, and then a paw. It came out to the first scrap of turkey and nibbled at it. Lifted its head to stare at Lark. Nibbled some more.

It came forward, its tail raised cautiously in the air. The pattern of its fur resolved itself for Lark's eyes: faded calico. White patches on large paws.

When it came to Lark, it had lost interest in the turkey. It turned its head to the side and rubbed its neck against his wrist. He put the last scrap on the ground and the cat nosed down to smell it politely, then stretched, swaybacked. It turned sideways to rub itself on Lark's knee, and he ran his fingertips along its back.

He thought its claws would come out as soon as he tried to lift it—he remembered the scratches on his neighbor's hands—but he got a palm beneath its belly and it seemed all right: no struggle, just sober green eyes regarding him.

He hugged the cat to his chest with both arms. Left the Chevy running and walked steadily toward the apartment building's entrance. Halfway there he felt the cat begin to squirm, but he knew better than to stop and try to soothe it. He got through the glass doors and into the ground-floor hallway. The thing was whining now, the legs flailing. Lark came to his neighbor's door and kicked the gray metal—not hard, but insistently.

She took forever answering and he dropped the cat as the door swung open. It darted inside.

"Roscoe!" she cried, spinning after it. Lark watched it dash through the kitchen and duck under a recliner in the living room.

He thought it best to close the door. Wasn't sure which side of it he should be on. She made the decision for him. "Come in," she said.

He went as far as the threshold between the kitchen and the living room and watched her crouching by the recliner with her ear against the carpet.

She talked to the cat first—"Roscoe, baby, are you all right? I was so worried. Where have you been?"—but after a while she got up and talked to Lark.

"Thank you," she said. "You don't know—" She didn't finish the sentence; astoundingly, she threw her arms around him.

He patted her shoulder and tried not to focus too much on the smell of her: lavender and something else—peach shampoo, he thought.

After a moment she stepped back. "Where did you find him?"

"By the Dumpsters," Lark said.

"I've looked there every day."

"There's a hole in the fence. He was behind that, in the bushes."

He told her how it had gone. She admired his trick with the turkey. The cat's whiskers edged out from underneath the recliner, but the rest of him stayed hidden.

The conversation trailed off. "I should go," Lark said.

She followed him out through the kitchen, thanking him all the way. When he reached the door something changed. He felt her fingers on the bare skin of his arm. Something intimate in the touch. He thought she would ask him to stay.

"Listen," she said, her voice suddenly a whisper, "are you in trouble?"

He turned, found her standing close. Her expression serious.

"I don't think so," he said.

"Someone came looking for you."

He thought at once of the lady cop—the one he had seen at the hospital, and at the Spencer house. "What did she say?"

His neighbor's answer surprised him. "Not a she. A he. He told me a story—about how you'd run out on your wife and now she was raising your kids on her own. And she asked him to find you and get you to do the right thing. 'I can't say he'll be glad to see me,' he said. 'But you'll be doing his wife a kindness if you keep an eye out for him and call me if you see him.' He gave me a card, but it had no name on it, just a phone number."

"When was this?"

"About an hour ago. Was any of what he said true?"

Lark shook his head. "I don't have a wife, or kids."

"That's what I thought. Is he a private detective? He didn't act like a proper policeman."

"I don't know who he is."

"He had the look of a policeman, though, the way he carried himself. Like someone used to giving orders, and having them obeyed. . . . I'll tell you who he reminded me of—the actor who starred in that movie with Sidney Poitier. What's his name? Rod Steiger."

The description made Lark uneasy, though he couldn't say why.

"Do you think he's gone now?" he asked.

"Dunno," she said. "But I haven't seen him—and I've been looking out into the hall, watching for you. I can tell you I saw someone else at your door, after he left. A skinny man wearing a windbreaker and a ball cap. When I tried to speak to him, he hurried off. I thought about calling the police."

"I'm glad you didn't."

"Maybe we *should* call them. I got the feeling those men could be dangerous."

Lark stood with his back to the door, his mind working fast.

"No," he said. "I'm sure it's all a misunderstanding. Maybe they had the wrong address. If they come back, they'll take one look at me and realize they've got the wrong guy."

"Are you sure?"

Not at all. But it didn't matter. He wasn't going to stick around.

"Absolutely," he said. "Don't worry about me. But I should go. Maybe I'll come back tomorrow, see how Roscoe's doing. How would that be?"

"All right."

"Good night, then."

He got the door open and went out before she could think of an objection. The door closed with a metallic click and he stood looking from one end of the barren hallway to the other.

No time to dawdle. She might be watching him through the peephole. He crossed the hall in three strides, keyed open his door and went in, switching on the light in the entryway. No sign of damage to the door; he didn't think anyone had been in the apartment. But he wanted to be sure. He put on the overhead light in the kitchen and grabbed the chef's knife from the drawer.

Down the short hall at a slow walk and at the end he faced a choice: bathroom on the right, bedroom on the left. From the hall, both looked empty. But the shower curtain was thick, white, opaque—someone could be hiding there. And most of the bedroom was out of view. If you wanted to hide, the bedroom would be the obvious place. Press yourself against the wall beside the doorway and you'd be invisible from the hall.

Then again, if you were clever, you might not choose the obvious place.

Lark stepped into the bathroom, the knife held down at his side. He flipped the light switch and his own image loomed in the mirror. His heart skipped and he looked behind him at the darkened bedroom. Nothing stirred. Turning back to the shower, he stepped closer. Reached for the curtain with his free hand. Swept it back.

The shower was empty.

"Bad guess," said a voice behind him.

He spun around to see a tall solid shape in the doorway—a man dressed all in black, like someone on a secret mission in a second-rate movie. Black boots laced high, black trousers, black T-shirt stretched tight over a bulging stomach. Broad shoulders, black hair streaked with silver. Lark recognized him; he had seen him on television in Sault Sainte Marie. Walter Delacorte, the sheriff of Chippewa County.

Lark brought the knife up automatically. Delacorte raised a pistol in a thick-fingered hand.

"Don't be stupid," he said.

Lark felt a laugh burst out of him. It doubled him over. He was hearing his father's voice, another bit of wisdom: *Never bring a knife to a gunfight.*

He straightened and lunged at Delacorte, leading with the knife. At least he would have surprise on his side. But Delacorte proved nimbler than he looked. He turned sideways and his left hand caught Lark's wrist, slamming the knife into the wall beside the light switch.

The knife fell to the floor. Delacorte let go of Lark's wrist and seized his collar, shoving him into the mirror above the sink. Lark caught the impact on his shoulder, shattering the glass. One-handed, Delacorte spun Lark around and propelled him through the doorway. Momentum carried Lark into the bedroom and sent him sprawling, the air rushing out of his lungs as he hit the carpet. Before he could get up, he felt Delacorte's boot between his shoulder blades and the cool muzzle of the gun at the back of his neck.

"You got that out of your system now?" the sheriff said quietly.

CHAPTER 30

Lark gave no answer, but when Delacorte ordered him to put his hands on his head, he complied, and he didn't resist when the sheriff brought one wrist and then the other around to his back to snap on the handcuffs.

He felt Delacorte searching through his pockets, tugging out his wallet and his notebook. He heard the flick of a switch and the overhead light came on, a weak bulb that gave off a yellow glow.

"You're an odd little bird," he heard Delacorte say. Then the sound of pages being turned. The rough feeling of the carpet beneath his cheek.

"Do you mind if I sit up?" he said.

Delacorte chuckled, a rumbling, lazy sound. "Oh, I don't mind, Mr. Lark. Go right ahead."

Lark rolled onto his side, used an elbow to push himself up. He sat with one leg extended, the other bent. There was a wall two feet behind him; he slid along the carpet and leaned his back against it.

Across the room, Delacorte had dumped out the contents of a plastic crate so he could turn it over and use it as a stool. He sat reading Lark's notebook, the wallet forgotten at his feet. The pistol was out of sight.

"What is this," Delacorte said, "your diary?"

Lark looked around the room, at his clothes and books on the floor, at the mattress and the wrinkled sheets. On the far end of the mattress he saw a bar of black metal with a ninety-degree bend. A tire iron.

"Answer my question," Delacorte said.

Lark closed his eyes against the yellow light. "Could I have some ice?" he asked.

He heard an edge in Delacorte's voice. "What?"

"I have a headache."

The lazy chuckle again. "You answer my questions, maybe I'll get you some ice. Is this your diary?"

Lark shrugged as well as he could with his hands cuffed. "I like to write things down."

He inhaled deeply. The pain behind his eyes was all sharp corners, like the bend in the tire iron. *Deep breaths.* That was something Dr. Kenneally always used to say to him. As if deep breaths could solve any problem. Feeling stressed? Take deep breaths. A headache coming on? Deep breaths. Held prisoner by a sheriff dressed in black?

Lark took deep breaths. He understood now how Delacorte had gotten into the apartment. The bedroom had sliding glass windows behind white vertical blinds. The bottoms of the windows were just about level with the ground. If you had a tire iron, you could pry a window open and climb through.

Lark heard Delacorte get to his feet and cross the room. He opened his eyes, squinting against the yellow light. The sheriff was showing him a page of the notebook. Three names—*Henry Kormoran, Sutton Bell, Terry Dawtrey*—the first and the last lined through. The red letters rippled and breathed.

Deep breaths.

"You wrote these names?" Delacorte said.

"Yes."

"Did someone give them to you? Did someone hire you?"

"No."

"Then why? Why would you go after these three?"

"Don't you know who they are? What they did?"

"They tried to rob a bank."

"They shot Harlan Spencer in the spine."

"Terry Dawtrey did that. Not the other two."

"All three of them decided to rob that bank. They're responsible for what happened. They're all bad men."

Delacorte snorted. "I've seen a lot worse."

"Men like that have to be stopped. Or they'll just keep on doing bad things."

"Sutton Bell's a nurse, for Chrissake. What do you think he's gonna do?"

"He's as responsible as the others," Lark said. "If you don't stop men like that, then whatever they do, that's on you. Because you didn't stop them."

"So you stopped Terry Dawtrey and Henry Kormoran, and you crossed them off your list."

"That's right."

"But you're not the one who killed Dawtrey. One of my deputies did that."

"I wanted him dead. He's dead. Close enough."

Lark watched Delacorte page ahead in the notebook. Another name in red: *Charlie Dawtrey*.

"Was he a bad man too?" Delacorte asked.

"He was necessary."

"He didn't rob any bank. Didn't shoot anybody."

"I needed him, to get to his son," Lark said. "I couldn't think of another way."

"You beat him to death with a tire iron."

Lark glanced at the mattress, the folds of the sheets, the hard lines of Delacorte's tire iron lying there. Even if he could get to it, he wouldn't be able to make any use of it, not with his hands behind his back. He looked at the windows, covered by the blinds. No one would be able to see what was happening in this room. No help would come to him.

Delacorte backed off. He closed the notebook and tucked it under his arm.

"I didn't believe in you at first," Delacorte said. "Even when they sent me that story you wrote."

"How did you find me?"

Delacorte drew a small plastic bag from his pocket. When he held it up, Lark saw a slug and a shell casing and an intact cartridge.

"You left some things behind at Whiteleaf Cemetery," Delacorte said. "I couldn't get a decent print off the casing or the cartridge, but at least they told me you were real. So I started looking for you. Showed your sketch at hotels.

I found the one you stayed at, but it was the kind where they take cash for a room and have fuzzy memories. I had to try something else. What did I know about you? You were a fella with a rifle on a hill. I started showing the sketch at sporting-goods stores. It didn't pan out at first, but I kept going. I found a clerk in Traverse City who recognized you, said he sold you a Remington rifle. You paid with a credit card.

"Once I had your name, I could have found you in my sleep. When you rented this apartment, they ran a credit check. It's in your records." Delacorte returned the plastic bag to his pocket, along with Lark's notebook. "And now I've got you. You're not much of a killer, are you?" he said, with a gesture that encompassed the room. "Living like a bohemian. Making friends with the neighbors. That gal across the hall likes you. You should have seen her face when I came around asking questions—I think she was worried for you."

The pain behind Lark's eyes twisted around on itself.

"Let's leave her out of this," he said.

"Fine by me. You come along peaceful, she doesn't need to be involved." Delacorte stepped back and retrieved Lark's wallet from the floor, and the tire iron from the mattress. He slipped the wallet in his pocket, the tire iron through a belt loop. "I don't figure I want to climb out the window towing you behind me," he said, "so we're gonna walk out the front door. My car's not far away."

Lark breathed deep. "Where are you taking me?"

"For a long drive."

"I'm under arrest, then?"

Reaching behind his back, Delacorte came out with the pistol.

"You're under arrest. Let's move."

In the moments that followed, the pain in Lark's head found new ways to bend back on itself. He felt a series of disjointed sensations. Delacorte gripping his arm and lifting him to his feet. The floor of the hallway listing beneath him. His eyelids fluttering in the bright light of the kitchen, and the light coming through, coiling around inside his skull, pressing in at his temples like a vise.

He hesitated as he came to the line where the vinyl floor of the kitchen met the carpet of the entryway. Delacorte pressed the muzzle of the pistol into his back.

"I need ice," Lark said.

"You need to keep moving," said Delacorte. "I'll give you ice when we get where we're going."

"I can't wait."

Lark felt the sheriff's fingers on the back of his neck, felt himself falling forward toward the wall beside the entryway. His feet hurried to catch up. He landed soft, turning his face to feel the cool of the wall against his cheek.

Delacorte's voice a whisper in his ear. "You don't want to try me, son."

The fingers left his neck and he heard the door opening. The muzzle hard between his shoulder blades as Delacorte guided him out into the hall. The dim light a reprieve. The gray steel of the neighbor girl's door. She might be behind it now, watching through the peephole.

Or she might be playing with her cat.

Lark turned his head to the left and the coiled ache behind his eyes played a trick on him. He felt Delacorte's pistol against his back and at the same time, impossibly, he saw it coming toward him. A black void, smooth and round and perfect, and the foreshortened shape of the gun around it. A finger on the trigger, the white of the nail like a crescent moon. Eyes looking down the length of the barrel at him. A face shadowed by the bill of a ball cap. A skinny man in a loose windbreaker.

Lark heard Delacorte's voice soft behind him. "Jesus Christ, Paul. What the hell do you think you're doing?"

"I could ask you the same thing, Walt," said the man in the windbreaker.

LARK STOOD IN the center of the bare living room, his eyes half shut against the unforgiving light from the kitchen. Paul Rhiner was a gray silhouette rimmed in a white glare. His right arm rigid, holding his pistol level, the muzzle less than a foot away from the bridge of Lark's nose.

Paul Rhiner, one of the deputies from Whiteleaf Cemetery. The one who had shot Terry Dawtrey as he tried to escape.

Lark took deep breaths, tried to get the pain in his head to hold still. He was vaguely aware of the touch of Walter Delacorte's gun at his back. He felt the floor solid and steady beneath him. Progress. He tried to focus on minor discomforts: the bite of the handcuffs on his wrists, the stiffness of his arms.

Delacorte had pulled him backward through the doorway, through the kitchen, to the living room—a slow reverse march as if they were traveling back in time. Rhiner had followed, closing the door behind him. His pistol had never wavered.

Now they were continuing the conversation they had begun in the hall.

"You shouldn't have come here, Paul," Delacorte said. "I don't know how you managed it. Did you follow me the whole way?"

"You're not that hard to follow, Walt," said Rhiner.

"Well, what you want to do now is walk away," Delacorte said. "Get yourself home and stay there. That's where you belong."

"I like it right here," said Rhiner. "This is him, isn't it? The rifleman from the cemetery. He's not made up. He's real."

"Walk away, Paul."

"You know I can't, Walt. I need to talk to him. He killed old Charlie Dawtrey. That's how everything started. I need to know there's a reason for what happened." Rhiner's eyes shifted to Lark. "You killed Charlie so they'd let his son out of prison. Isn't that right?"

Lark nodded.

"And you meant to kill Terry Dawtrey. That was your plan."

"Yes," Lark said.

"Why?"

"He needed killing."

"That's not a reason. There must be more to it. I have to know."

Delacorte said, "There's no reason, Paul. He did it because he's a goddamn nutcase."

"No. I need to understand."

"There's nothing to understand."

Something like desperation in Rhiner's eyes. "I need this, Walt. He has to talk to me. After that, you can take him in. But he talks to me first."

Lark bent his body forward as if he were leaning into the wind. He pitched his voice low.

"Do you really think he's going to take me in?"

"What?" said Rhiner.

"He never showed me a badge," Lark said. "He hasn't read me my rights."

Rhiner's pistol dropped slightly and doubt entered his eyes.

"What's going on, Walt?"

Delacorte's voice was cold. "I'll tell you what's going on. You're putting your gun away. You're driving home and you're forgetting all about this."

"Ask him if he's called the local police," Lark said. "Shouldn't he have done that as soon as he tracked me down?"

The barrel of Rhiner's pistol traced a small circle in the air. "I don't like this, Walt. What's the plan here?"

"I told you the plan. You leave. I deal with him. Don't make me say it again."

"If you leave me alone with him, I'm dead," said Lark. "You know that, don't you?"

Suddenly Lark felt Delacorte's hand on his neck. He felt himself shoved to the side, his feet swept from under him. The floor rushed up toward his chin, but he managed to twist and catch the impact on his shoulder. With a groan he rolled onto his back. Now he could see Rhiner and Delacorte facing off like duelists.

"Come on now," Delacorte said to Rhiner. "Put the gun away."

Rhiner stood firm. "What are you going to do with him?"

"I'm trying to look out for you, Paul. You shouldn't even be here."

"Are you going to shoot him?"

"What kind of question is that? No one's getting shot tonight."

Delacorte tipped his pistol up toward the ceiling, then swept it around behind his back and slipped it into the waistband of his trousers. He showed Rhiner his empty hands.

"Come on, Paul," Delacorte said. "How long have we known each other?"

Lark watched Rhiner's profile, saw the moment when he decided. Rhiner's chin dipped toward his chest, eyes downcast. A sheepish look. He aimed his gun up as Delacorte had done, brought it slowly around to the small of his back.

Delacorte's hands descended to his sides. Lark watched them move in measured arcs. But when the right hand should have come to rest, it kept going. It crossed the big man's stomach, reaching for something.

The tire iron, Lark realized. The sheriff had it hanging from his belt loop.

Delacorte drew it like a sword. Rhiner's eyes went wide. Delacorte sprang forward, nimble. Rhiner yanked his pistol around from behind his back, too late. The tire iron slapped down hard against the barrel, the sound of it sharp like the crack of a whip. Rhiner's hand jerked away as if he'd been stung. The pistol bounced on the carpet.

The tire iron leapt up again and Rhiner had the presence of mind to duck under it, driving his shoulder into Delacorte's chest with a force that might have carried a smaller man across the room. Delacorte faded two steps back. The tire iron fell weakly across Rhiner's shoulder blades.

Anthony Lark braced an elbow against the floor and in one motion rocked himself up to a sitting position. He bent his legs and used his feet to push himself along the carpet until he had a wall at his back. Rhiner was grappling with Delacorte, the tire iron held high between them so that the tip of it scratched the ceiling. The deputy aimed a knee at Delacorte's groin, but the bigger man twisted sideways to catch it on his hip. He wrenched the iron away from Rhiner and jabbed the bent end at Rhiner's midriff.

Lark saw it connect, saw Rhiner's body fold. The deputy backpedaled, struggling to get a grip on the iron. Delacorte charged forward. Rhiner tripped over his own feet, fell back against the counter that separated the living room from the kitchen. Then the full weight of Walter Delacorte hit him.

There was a scream, a scream that belonged in a slaughterhouse. Lark turned his face away, as if that might dull the sound. When the scream ended and he turned back, he saw Paul Rhiner crumpled against the counter, a splotch of red on the front of his windbreaker. He saw Walter Delacorte's broad back, Delacorte drawn to his full height, walking backward on tiptoe. He saw Delacorte turn a half circle, his hands held up, palms facing his body, fingers curled. Head bowed. Eyes gazing down raptly at the tire iron sticking out of his chest.

CHAPTER 31

Rhiner struggled to his feet as Delacorte's knees buckled. The sheriff turned as he fell and landed on his side. Rolled onto his back. The tire iron had entered low on his chest and traveled upward. It jutted out of him now, a thin black line leaning over the bulge of his stomach, then bending down ninety degrees.

Lark saw the sheriff's blood flowing out of him, a wet sheen spreading over the man's black shirt. Rhiner knelt down beside Delacorte and laid a palm against the sheriff's chest, as if it might stop the bleeding.

Delacorte's head slumped to the side, his eyes fixed on Lark. His mouth opened and closed, but the only sound was the labor of his breathing.

Lark turned his left shoulder to the wall, rocked himself onto his knees, got to his feet.

Rhiner pointed a finger at him. Said, "Stay right there. Don't move."

Lark nodded and Rhiner turned his attention back to Delacorte, whose right leg had begun to twitch. Rhiner lifted his palm from the sheriff's chest as if he meant to move it to the leg, to hold it still. A second later he shook his head. He dug into a pocket and came out with a cell phone. Flipped it open.

Lark pushed off from the wall with his cuffed hands. Rhiner looked up from the phone, then cast around in a panic, searching for his pistol.

"No," he said. "Don't you move."

Lark kept coming. Rhiner sprawled across the floor, reaching for the pistol. Lark stepped over Delacorte's legs and drove the toe of his shoe into

Paul Rhiner's ribs. Rhiner scrambled for the gun and Lark hopped sideways, steadied himself, and kicked with everything he had at Rhiner's temple.

Rhiner groaned and tumbled onto his side, the fingers of his right hand still groping for the gun. The clear white light from the kitchen gleamed in a fine line along the barrel. Lark balanced himself on one leg, hopped twice, and came down with both heels on Rhiner's hand.

Rhiner shrieked. A sweep of Lark's foot sent the pistol gliding down the hallway. Another sent the cell phone in the opposite direction. Rhiner had curled himself into a ball. Lark couldn't see his face, could only hear the whine of his breathing.

Lark kicked him, solidly, at the base of the spine. Heard a gasp.

A smile, unbidden, tugged at the corners of Lark's mouth.

"Try to take deep breaths," he said.

He crossed to Walter Delacorte. Saw the man's eyes staring up at him. Lark pressed the sole of his right shoe against the tire iron, gave it a little push. Delacorte's eyes rolled up white. The twitching in his leg became more pronounced.

Stepping over the sheriff's body, Lark eased himself to his knees. Patiently he worked his cuffed hands around to the man's pocket, probed for his key ring. A jingle of metal. He got a finger through the ring and drew it out.

He found the handcuff key by touch and worked it in the locks, left and right. The pressure on his arms released, a magnificent feeling.

He dropped the cuffs and the keys to the floor. Kneeling by Delacorte's body, he rolled the man gently so he could search his pockets. He found his own wallet and notebook, a money clip thick with cash, the sheriff's pistol in his waistband.

He took them all, stowed them away. The gun stayed in his hand. He stood and looked at Rhiner, who had started crawling down the hallway toward his pistol. Rhiner's head was bare; he had lost his ball cap in his struggle with Delacorte. His thinning hair stuck out in tufts.

Lark strode after him, and when he caught up he kicked his heel into the deputy's side, knocked him over. He bent to press the muzzle of Delacorte's gun to Rhiner's temple.

Rhiner shut his eyelids tight. He whispered, "Don't."

Lark spoke to him calmly. "You should have waited a little, before you shot Terry Dawtrey. If you had waited, I would have done it for you. You wouldn't be here."

"Please," Rhiner whispered.

Lark trailed the muzzle along the line of the deputy's jaw. "You should give yourself a break," he said. "You were in a hard spot. Anyone else would have done the same thing. If it's any consolation, I think you're a good man. Most people are good at heart. That's something my father used to tell me."

Rhiner stretched his hand out toward the pistol that remained beyond his reach. Lark shifted Delacorte's gun from his right hand to his left, curled his fingers into Rhiner's hair, and slammed the man's face into the floor. He did it a second time to make sure the deputy's nose was broken. The carpet muffled Rhiner's cries.

Lark left him there. Picked up the pistol from the carpet, stuck it in his pocket. Pulled the tail of his shirt over it. Crossing through the living room he glanced at Walter Delacorte. The sheriff's leg had ceased its twitching.

One last look around. Lark grabbed the bottle of Keflex from the counter and headed for the door. The hallway outside was deserted. Lark turned the pill bottle over in his hand, considering. He made up his mind, put the bottle in his pocket, and rapped on the steel of his neighbor's door.

When she didn't answer right away, he began to imagine the worst. Maybe she had heard all the mayhem. Maybe she was cowering inside now, dialing 911 on her phone. Then the bolt turned and the door swung inward. At the last possible instant, Lark looked down and realized he was still holding Walter Delacorte's gun in his left hand.

He hid it behind his back as the door opened wide. There she stood, her face turned up to him. Something white and rectangular in her hand. An iPod. One of the buds still in her ear, the other held between two fingers.

She smiled at him. She had fine teeth. The smile bloomed as she stepped back to let him in. A wondrous thing, as good as Callie Spencer's.

He lingered near the door. Said, "What are you listening to?" Not what he'd planned to say. He hadn't planned anything.

As an answer she lifted up the bud for him, settled it into his ear. Her fingers brushed his cheek, withdrawing. The music was loud and energetic: crashing drums and raging guitars. He listened for a few seconds and passed the earbud back to her. She took hers out too, and pressed a button to turn the iPod off.

"You were meant to come back tomorrow," she said.

He raked the fingers of his right hand through his hair. "That's what I wanted to tell you. I won't make it tomorrow. I don't think I'll be around for a while."

Her smile vanished. "Are you okay? Did those men come back?"

"I'm fine. You shouldn't worry about me."

Urgency in her voice. "What happened? Tell me."

She had no idea, Lark thought. She hadn't heard a thing.

"It's nothing important," he said. "They came back, but I got through it all right."

"Are you sure?"

"I look all right, don't I?"

She studied his face. "The truth is, you look a little flushed."

"Well, you should see the other two."

She laughed at that, her smile blooming again.

"I'm fine," he repeated. "I'll need to go away for a while, but I didn't want to leave without saying good-bye." He glanced down at his shoes. "I don't even know your name," he said.

When he looked up she had her hand held out to him.

"It's Mira."

He took it. "I'm Anthony," he said.

WARM NIGHT WITH A MILD WIND. Lark found his car near the Dumpsters where he'd left it—the engine still running, the driver's door unlocked. No one had stolen it. Most people are good at heart.

He drove south with Rhiner's pistol out of sight in the glove box and Delacorte's on the passenger seat beside him. Before he had gone half a mile he heard sirens. Rhiner must have pulled himself together and called 911.

Lark motored on, past the entrance ramp for I-94. He found a fast-food restaurant open late and ordered a Coke at the drive-through. "Lots of ice," he said.

He kept moving, heading east, until he came to a movie theater with scores of cars in the parking lot. He poured out the Coke and with the engine idling leaned back and laid the cup of ice against his forehead.

His thoughts turned to what he had left behind. Clothes, books. His tin of Imitrex—the pills for his headaches. He could picture it on the floor of the bedroom by the mattress. He needed those pills, and he could never go back for them now.

But he had extras—a bottle from the pharmacy, the same place where he had stolen the Keflex. He remembered tossing the bottle into the backseat.

Setting the cup down, he clicked free of the seat belt. Twisted around. He found the bottle on the floor and washed a pill down with meltwater from the cup. After a while longer with the ice against his brow, the sharp corners in his head wore down a little. He realized he was hungry, thought about the sandwich he had bought earlier, and the beer.

ELIZABETH HAD LARK'S ADDRESS by 11:30—an apartment off State Street. She arranged for Carter Shan to meet her there.

On Eisenhower Boulevard she realized something was wrong. A patrol car roared past her in the left lane. She had no doubt where it was going. She didn't believe in coincidences.

TWENTY MINUTES TO MIDNIGHT. Lark drove north and west from the movie theater and parked on a quiet street. A gust of wind sent a scrap of newspaper skipping along the gutter. He got out and went to the trunk. Came back rolling a thin metal tube between his fingers—the scope from his hunting rifle.

Behind the wheel again, he laid the scope on the passenger seat. He crumpled the empty sandwich wrapper and tossed it in the back. A single bottle of beer rested inside the cardboard cup, cooling in the melting ice. He lifted it out and a drop of water fell on the grip of Walter Delacorte's pistol.

Twisting off the cap, he tipped the bottle up and drank. It wasn't cold, but the ice had taken the edge of warmth off it. He put the bottle down and picked up the scope. Adjusted the focus and the first thing that came into view was a street sign: ARLINGTON BLVD. The letters blue and still like the surface of a pond on a midsummer day.

He swung the scope up and to the right, worked the focus again, and found the roofline of the Spencer house. All the windows dark on the second floor. Most of the first floor was obscured by a looming shape. He turned the dial on the scope and the blurred lines became sharp: the eastern face of the guest cottage. Callie Spencer's Ford parked outside.

Lark felt a breeze through the open window beside him. He took another taste of beer. The pain behind his eyes had smoothed itself away. When he left his apartment and Mira, he had felt lost. Adrift. Now he felt grounded again.

Callie Spencer was inside the cottage. He was sure of it. He moved the crosshairs of the scope to a lighted window and saw a few inches of space between parted curtains. He kept the scope steady and willed her to make an appearance.

Five minutes later he caught a glimpse of her in profile. A wild strand of hair fell across her brow. She was carrying an empty glass. The glimpse was enough. He lowered the scope.

He needed a place to spend the night. Needed a plan. To stay here would be ideal. He didn't think he would have any trouble falling asleep, not with Callie Spencer so close by. But that would be reckless, sleeping in the car. He would have to think of something else.

A flash of movement on his left. Someone strolling on the sidewalk, a few dozen yards away, on the opposite side of the street from Callie Spencer's cottage. A woman. She reached a point directly across from the cottage and slowed, stepping toward the curb as if she might cross.

She was illuminated by the glow of a streetlamp. Lark had his engine off, no lights. He lifted the scope and turned the dial to bring the woman into focus. He knew her. Knew the blond highlights in her brown hair. She was the woman he had seen on the night he went after Sutton Bell—the woman from the Eightball Saloon.

He traded the scope for Delacorte's pistol on the seat beside him. He didn't know her purpose and he didn't intend to take any chances. If she crossed the street, he would get out of the car; if she approached the door of the cottage, he would put a bullet in her.

She stood at the curb, one foot hovering in the air over the street. Lark heard the whisper of leaves, the electric hum of the streetlamp. His thumb touched the safety of Delacorte's pistol.

Her foot drew back and she reached for something at her hip. A cell phone.

CHAPTER 32

The phone on my desk rang a few minutes before midnight. I had the window open and the pages of a manuscript in front of me. It was the same one I'd been editing earlier—the story of the corrupt detective and the heiress.

I picked up the receiver and said, *"Gray Streets."*

"I'm wasting my time," said Lucy Navarro.

"Where are you?"

"Where do you think? Listen, I'm getting nowhere. I need a new plan. Do you want to meet?"

"Do you know what time it is, Lucy?"

"I'll buy you a drink," she said. "The bars are still open, aren't they?"

I tapped my pencil on the edge of the desk. "The ones that are open aren't the kind where you'd want to sit and think and make plans."

"Meet me at my hotel, then," she said. "I've got a minibar in my room, and an expense account from the *National Current.*"

I had a vision of her sitting on a hotel bed. Her legs bare. A drink in her hand. Attribute it to my active imagination. "I don't think that's a good idea," I said.

"I'm serious. They'll cover it."

"That's not the problem."

"Then what—" She took a second to catch on. "You're afraid to come up to my room."

"I'm not afraid," I said.

"You are. That's sweet. And puritanical. What about meeting in the hotel lobby?"

I leafed through the pages of the manuscript. Six more and I'd be done.

"I think I'll pass," I said. "There's something I want to finish here."

"Puritanical," she said again. "All right, Loogan. I'll talk to you tomorrow."

We said our good-byes and I went back to the detective and the heiress. The pair of them had worked out a scam to swindle her father out of half a million dollars. I got through two more pages, jotting the edits in the white spaces between the lines of type. They were laughing and counting the loot. I'd read the thing before and I knew that in the next paragraph she would haul out a cute little chrome-plated twenty-two and shoot him in the gut.

I tossed my pencil onto the desk. The pair of them could wait until the morning. I was more curious about the story of Callie Spencer and Lucy Navarro.

I closed the window and locked the office. The stairs at the end of the hall took me down to the service entrance, to the alley behind the building. I got in my car and aimed it toward Lucy's hotel.

LARK WATCHED THE WOMAN close her phone and walk back the way she'd come. The fading sound of her footsteps reached him through the open car window.

He returned Delacorte's pistol to the passenger seat, re-engaging the safety with his thumb. The window of the cottage had gone dark.

The beer was colder now. He killed the bottle in three swallows. The woman reached her car. Lark heard the engine start, saw the headlights flare. The car pulled away from the curb, rolled toward him, and turned right onto Arlington Boulevard.

He cranked his key in the ignition and powered up the window. Drove past the cottage in the dark and put his lights on only after he made the turn.

FOLLOWING HER WAS EASY. A yellow Beetle has a distinctive look.

She traveled west and south, coming eventually to State Street. Familiar territory for Lark, not far from his apartment.

By the time she turned into the parking lot of the Winston Hotel, there were three cars between them. He lost sight of her for a moment, and when he spotted the Beetle again it was parked on the western edge of the lot, away from the hotel itself.

There were picnic tables there on a patch of lawn, and a line of tall evergreens intended to drown out the sound of semi trucks passing on the interstate nearby.

Lark pulled into a space closer to the hotel. From there he could watch her and make up his mind. Because he wasn't sure what he wanted to do about her. She had been loitering around Callie Spencer's house. He still wondered if a bullet might not be the best solution.

A blue minivan drove along the row in front of him—slow as if it were searching for a spot. It obscured his view of the woman, but when it passed he saw that she had gotten out of the Beetle. She had plastic water bottles and fast-food wrappers in her hands. She carried them to a trash barrel near the picnic tables and dropped them in.

She made another trip: more bottles and cardboard cups. A woman who had spent a lot of time in her car. One of the bottles got away from her and rolled along the ground.

Lark took out his notebook and his father's Waterman pen. He didn't know her name, so he found a blank page and wrote, *The woman from the Eightball Saloon.* The letters looked orange to him. A pale orange, not as bad as red, not as benign as green. They rippled and swayed, as if he were viewing them through air rising from hot asphalt.

He didn't know what that meant.

He looked up from the notebook and saw the blue minivan again. He saw it pull up next to the yellow Beetle.

Interesting.

When he glanced down at the page once more, the letters were still orange. No guidance there. Lark closed the notebook and left it on the seat. He picked up Walter Delacorte's pistol.

When he opened the door, the rumble of a diesel engine was loud in his ears. One of the semis had pulled off the interstate and into the hotel lot. He turned his head automatically to look at it. Big block letters along the length of the trailer: COLEMAN TRUCKING.

The semi's brakes squealed as it came to a stop around ten yards away from him—obstructing his view of both the yellow Beetle and the blue minivan.

Lark stepped out into the night and slipped Delacorte's pistol into his pocket. He headed toward the semi at a jog. The driver of the truck had his window cracked, a cell phone to his ear. Lark called to him, waving to tell him to move along. The driver glared at him and went back to his call.

Lark jogged between a pair of parked cars and then cut left in a long arc that took him around the front of the semi. He felt the idle of the engine in the soles of his feet. The yellow Beetle came into view. No one inside, no one nearby.

The blue minivan was gone.

The bulk of the semi obscured Lark's view of the rest of the lot. He dashed around to the back of the trailer and saw the glow of brake lights in the distance: the blue minivan slowing at the exit of the lot and turning onto State Street.

I USED TO BE AFRAID of parking lots, especially at night.

If someone comes knocking on your door and he seems a little off, if he's ill-groomed and shabbily dressed, you can refuse to let him in. If he hangs around, you can call the police. If you see the same guy in a parking lot, you're out of luck. There's nothing to be done.

People are always on the move in parking lots. That guy walking toward you, the squirrelly one, is probably just heading for his car. He probably doesn't mean you any harm. But you won't know until he's right next to you. Until he's got his gun in your ribs and he's demanding your wallet.

I could go on, but here's an experiment that should tell you everything you need to know. Turn to the police blotter in your local paper and count the number of incidents where someone was shot, stabbed, robbed, or beaten. Eliminate the ones that happened in somebody's house or on their front lawn. Of the ones that are left, how many happened in a parking lot?

It was after midnight when I drove into the lot of the Winston Hotel. It looked peaceful. Neat rows of cars and SUVs under the crisp light of arc lamps.

No sound but the clean throb of a diesel engine. An eighteen-wheeler with COLEMAN TRUCKING in block letters on the back of the trailer. There was no room to pass the truck on the left. I moved to pass it on the right and saw Lucy Navarro's yellow Beetle.

The headlights were on, the driver's door open. I couldn't see Lucy anywhere, but there was someone in the car. I almost missed him, because the only part of him I could see was one of his shoes. It stuck out beneath the open door.

I heard a change in the tone of the diesel engine and the truck began to roll forward.

I hit my brakes and stopped twenty feet short of the Beetle. Shifted into park and got out. I remember my feet hitting the pavement. The Swiss Army knife already in my hand.

I ran to Lucy's car, folding out the blade as I went. The rumble of the diesel covered my approach.

He was half sitting, half lying in the driver's seat, reaching across to the open glove compartment. His gray dress shirt was untucked and fit him loosely. He never looked my way until I got hold of his arm and started dragging him from the car.

His legs flailed and when I had him halfway out he kicked me in the thigh. It didn't hurt much but it annoyed me and I stepped back and slammed the driver's door on his shin. I grabbed his arm again and pulled him out. Threw him against the side of the car. I held him there with my hip and pressed my left forearm to his throat. The knife was in my right hand, the blade at his cheek.

I heard the diesel engine receding into the distance. The driver of the semi had made a wide U-turn and was heading for the exit. Which left no one watching.

"Where's Lucy?" I said.

He leaned back to relieve the pressure on his throat. "I don't know."

"What were you doing in her car?"

He raised his left hand, which held a wrinkled square of paper: Lucy's registration.

"I wanted to know who she was," he said. "I saw her at Callie Spencer's house."

That caught me off guard. I still hadn't placed him. His eyes were unfamiliar. But now, studying his face, I recognized his jawline and the shape of his mouth.

"You're the man in plaid."

He gave me a blank look.

"What's your name?" I asked him.

"Anthony Lark."

Simple as that.

I said, "Where's Lucy, Anthony?"

I felt his shoulders lift.

"I told you. I don't know," he said. "Did you see the van?"

"What van?"

"A blue minivan. That's all I can give you."

I grabbed a handful of his collar. "What did you do with her?"

"I'm not the one you should be angry at," he said. No emotion in his voice. "There's something going on here, bigger than you and me."

I shoved him back against the car. "You're going to tell me where she is."

"You're hurting me," he said. "There's no call for that. I've been reasonable up till now."

I held the blade where he could see it. "Reasonable?"

"I've answered your questions," he said. "I think you should take that into account."

"You do, do you?"

"Yes. I think you should let me go."

I adjusted my grip on his collar. "Why would I do that?"

"Because I haven't caused you any harm."

"Is that the best you can do?"

He exhaled through his nose, one impatient breath.

"No," he said. "There's another reason."

"What's that?"

"Because you only brought a knife."

A cryptic remark. I was slow to puzzle it out. He was fast.

In a movie there might have been more warning. I might have heard a tiny mechanical click, the sound of him releasing the safety. But in reality that single impatient breath was the only warning I got. Then the muzzle brushed my side and he pulled the trigger.

CHAPTER 33

I read somewhere once that the impact of a bullet is usually not enough to knock you down. If it doesn't stop your heart or blow out your knee, or something along those lines, there's no reason for you to fall. But people do anyway, because they think they're supposed to. They've seen too many westerns and cop shows. When the guy in the cowboy hat or the fedora gets shot, he falls over.

So over they go.

I fell when Anthony Lark shot me. In my defense, he pushed me.

I let go of the knife on the way down. Landed on the grass not far from a picnic table. I remember looking up and seeing the silhouettes of tall pine trees.

I remember Lark standing over me and dropping something that floated lazily down into the grass. Lucy Navarro's registration.

"Don't come after me," I remember him saying. "I'm not the one who took her."

The details are rough after that, like a series of underdeveloped photographs. I don't remember sitting up, but I remember being on my feet. Looking down and seeing my pocketknife on the ground. Deciding that bending over to pick it up would be a bad idea.

The smell of burning cotton—the fabric of my shirt smoldering from the heat of the muzzle blast.

Lark in the distance, taking the last few steps to his car, favoring his left leg. He stood with the door open for a moment and stared back at me.

People coming out of the hotel. Two girls in blazers who must have been desk clerks. Too young to be dealing with a bleeding man in the parking lot. An older couple came with them. I remember he wore suspenders; she had soft gray hair and a soothing voice. She sympathized when I told her Lark was getting away.

By then his car was out of sight.

When the EMTs came I was sitting on the bench of a picnic table with a hotel towel pressed against my side. Lucy Navarro's yellow Beetle idling a few yards away.

The EMTs wanted to put me on a gurney. I told them I wouldn't need it. I explained my theory about people who fall over when they get shot.

They let me ride in the ambulance sitting up.

LATER THAT NIGHT, at home, Sarah asked me how it felt, being shot. I told her it stung a little but it wasn't bad. The pain didn't last.

That was not entirely true.

If you took your thumb and index finger and pinched a fold of flesh on your side, low down on your rib cage, and if you squeezed really hard, you might get an inkling of how it felt. And if you took something metal and sharp, like a railroad spike, and heated it in a fire and rammed it through that little fold of flesh—then you'd have an even better idea.

I SAT UP IN THE AMBULANCE and felt every bump and jostle along the route like a fresh railroad spike. In the emergency room, the doctor asked me to lie down. He told me it would be easier for him to work on me that way. I went along for his sake.

He was a compact man, young, from one of those countries where they speak English in a charming, lilting accent. He told me my gunshot wound was the finest he'd ever seen. "GSW through-and-through," he said. "If you must be shot it is assuredly the best way."

He told me the bullet might have easily struck a rib, but he didn't think it had.

"Someone must have been smiling down upon you, my friend."

"He wasn't smiling," I said.

A COUPLE HOURS LATER they were ready to let me go. By then the wound had been cleaned and debrided, closed at both the entry and the exit. Bandaged. They'd given me antibiotics, and an X-ray to rule out a fractured rib. ("An abundance of caution, my friend.") Somewhere in there Elizabeth turned up. I'm not sure exactly when, because the doctor gave me something for the pain and I lost track of things. I remember him telling her about my condition. ("Very fortunate. No damage to any vital organ or structure.") I remember him asking her about a white shape on the X-ray that looked like a flattened bullet lodged behind my lung.

"Has he been shot before?"

"Just once," she said.

"Is he with the police?"

"No."

"Was he at one time a military man?"

"No."

"Ah. He's led a colorful life, then."

"You might say so."

SHE DROVE ME HOME. Sarah came out to help get me into the house and up the stairs. She asked her question about how it felt to be shot, and I told her my lie.

She left us and Elizabeth got me out of my clothes. I remember her piling things on the floor: shoes and socks, pants, the hospital gown they'd given me in lieu of my ruined shirt. She had me lie down on her side of the bed and she climbed in on my side so she could be on my right, away from the wound.

I remember waking sometime later and feeling her body against me, her right leg crossed over mine, her palm on my chest. I let my eyes adjust to the dark, focusing on the curve of her hip.

From the pattern of her breathing I knew she was awake.

"It was the man in plaid," I said. "He's the one who shot me."

"I know," she said. "You told me at the hospital."

"His name is Anthony Lark."

"I know. Go to sleep, David."

Sometime later I woke again. I found Elizabeth propped on an elbow, watching over me.

"He had a pistol," I said.

"Sleep."

"He's never had a pistol before. Where did he get it?"

She sighed and told me about Lark's apartment. She told me Walter Delacorte was dead. Paul Rhiner would recover, eventually.

"He has a concussion, a broken nose, several broken ribs," she said. "His right hand is swollen like something out of a cartoon."

She'd spoken to Rhiner at the hospital. He told her that Lark had taken his pistol, and Delacorte's. That was all he would tell her about what had happened.

"How did Lark manage to get away from them?" I asked.

"No more questions, David."

"And how did they find him in the first place?"

"No more. Go to sleep."

The night crept on toward dawn. I remember seeing Lucy Navarro in a dream; I saw her with the turtle, saw her giving water to the stray dog at Nick Dawtrey's house. I remember trying to sit up, and wishing I hadn't. Elizabeth easing me down again.

"Lucy's missing," I said.

"I know."

"Lark said he didn't take her. Said it was a blue minivan."

"You already told me."

I lay still and tried to get back to a place where it didn't hurt to breathe. Elizabeth brushed her fingertips over my brow.

I said, "I don't remember if you asked me what I was doing at Lucy's hotel."

"I didn't," she said. "But the question crossed my mind."

"She wanted to talk. She needed advice. That's all it was."

"All right."

"Lucy's been staking out the Spencer house the past two days. Parked on the street in that Beetle of hers. There's no way they didn't notice."

"Maybe they did. That doesn't mean they took her."

"They're involved—the Spencers or Alan Beckett. I don't trust Beckett."

Elizabeth bent close and kissed my mouth. "I don't want you to worry about it, David. It's not your problem to solve."

CHAPTER 34

Thursday morning. Elizabeth met Carter Shan at eight in the bullpen of the Investigations Division at City Hall. He was transferring images from his digital camera to his computer—crime-scene photos from Anthony Lark's apartment.

She handed him a cup of take-out coffee, dark roast with cream, no sugar. She kept another for herself. Standing behind his chair, she watched the images pass over his monitor.

"Did you get any sleep last night?" she said.

"Enough."

He would have had two or three hours at most, she thought. But he looked alert. He had on a fresh suit. The jacket hung over the back of his chair.

"How's . . . David?" he asked. A hesitation between the two words; he almost said *How's Loogan?* but caught himself.

"No lasting damage," Elizabeth said. "He'll have an interesting scar."

A series of photos on the monitor: Walter Delacorte's body from various angles. A close-up shot of the tire iron. Then a pair of handcuffs on the floor. A chef's knife.

"I stopped by the hospital this morning," Shan said. "Paul Rhiner's still not talking. I asked him flat out if Lark was the one who planted the tire iron in Delacorte. He wouldn't answer."

She watched him pull the plastic lid off his cup and flip it into the trash.

"You think Rhiner may have done it himself?" she asked.

"It would explain why he doesn't want to talk," Shan said. "And maybe other things too. Like how Lark went up against two men with guns and got the better of them. If Rhiner and Delacorte fought with each other, they may have done half his work for him."

He took a drink from the cup and set it down. "There are other hints that they might not have been on the same page," he said. "They drove to Lark's apartment separately—we found both their cars. And one of Lark's neighbors saw them both, but not together."

"Which neighbor?"

"Girl across the hall," he said. "Mira Talwar. An engineering student at the university. She had spoken to Lark, but had no idea who he was. Last night he knocked on her door. Her cat had been missing and he found it for her."

"Good Samaritan."

Shan nodded. "It gets better. She saw him again—it would have been after he tangled with Delacorte and Rhiner. But he seemed perfectly normal. He told her he was going away, but he didn't want to leave without saying good-bye."

"That's smooth," Elizabeth said.

"He's cool under pressure. Too cool. It makes me think he's not hooked up right." Shan spun his chair around to face her. "That apartment was eerie, even if you ignored the body on the floor. No furniture, the cupboards just about empty. It almost would have been better if he had pictures of Callie Spencer plastered to the walls. It would have given the place some personality."

"He left in a hurry though. He had to have left something personal behind."

"Just books, and clothes." Shan turned back to his computer. "And this." The photos had finished transferring, leaving rows of thumbnail images on the monitor. He reached for his mouse and clicked on one of them.

Elizabeth studied the image. It showed a small tin box of the kind that would hold breath mints, with a white label stuck to the lid.

"Where did you find this?" she asked.

"In the bedroom."

The label had a word written on it. She recognized the handwriting as Lark's.

"'Imitrex,'" Shan said. "It's used to treat headaches."

"He stole a bottle of Imitrex from the pharmacy, the same night he stole the Keflex."

"He must have done it because his own stash was running out. There were only five pills left in the tin."

"That's an odd way to carry them around," Elizabeth said. "Do you think he bought them on the street? Is there a black market for Imitrex?"

"I don't think so. But we can ask him when we find him." Shan got up from his chair. "How are you feeling?"

She gave him a noncommittal look. "What do you mean?"

"You know. After what happened—David getting shot."

"I'm fine, Carter."

"Because the chief had some concerns. He's gone home now, but I talked to him earlier. He wanted my opinion."

"About what?"

Shan lifted his shoulders a fraction of an inch. "About whether he should keep you on the case. Lark shot your—" He paused, and she could see him considering possibilities: *boyfriend, partner, lover.* He decided to start again. "Lark shot David. So there's a question about how it would look, and whether you can be objective—"

Elizabeth smiled. "Is that right?"

"I told him he was worried about nothing—that you would conduct yourself professionally, like you always do. I kept the rest of my opinion to myself."

"What's the rest?"

The same little lift of his shoulders. "That if you wanted to take revenge on Anthony Lark he wouldn't stand a chance."

She reached to straighten his tie. "That may be the nicest thing you've ever said to me, Carter. Now how are we going to find him?"

"It shouldn't be hard," Shan said, picking up his jacket from the back of the chair. "I figured we'd start with his mother."

. . .

HELEN LARK LIVED in Dearborn, in a house with peeling yellow paint on the porch. The sidewalk in front was cracked and uneven, but the grass had been cut and there were flowers growing in a garden ringed with stones.

At nine-thirty in the morning, young mothers were on the move through the neighborhood, pushing infants in strollers, with toddlers ambling along in their wake. Many of the women wore scarves to cover their hair.

"They're Lebanese," said Helen Lark. "They get married young and start having babies fast. Sometimes I want to ask them what their hurry is, but it's not my place. I wish them luck."

She sat in one of two folding chairs on the porch and offered Elizabeth the other. Carter Shan leaned against the railing nearby.

"You think I'm a terrible mother," Helen Lark said, raising a hand before Elizabeth could reply. "You don't have to deny it. I've seen the news this morning. Those two policemen you found in Anthony's apartment, one of them beaten, the other dead. The man in the parking lot. And the other one, Corrigan."

"Kormoran," Elizabeth said.

"I've been waiting for you to come, wondering what I should say. I thought about telling you you've made a mistake. It couldn't be Anthony. I know he's not capable of . . ." She let the sentence trail off.

"But you think he is," Elizabeth said gently.

The woman turned away. She had blond hair shading into white, and fine wrinkles in the skin of her face. Her clothes were unassuming: pleated slacks, a blouse with a well-worn collar and a mended tear in the sleeve. She wore glasses with tortoiseshell frames.

"I don't know anymore," she said. "He's a stranger to me now. He hasn't been the same since—I want to say since his father died, but it started before that."

"What did?" Elizabeth asked.

"His obsession with that girl. The girl with the pretty smile."

"Callie Spencer?"

Helen Lark bowed her head. "No. Not her. At least not at first."

Elizabeth exchanged a quizzical look with Shan.

To Helen Lark she said, "Maybe you could explain."

The woman rose from her chair. "It would be easier to show you."

"THIS IS MORE LIKE IT," said Shan in a low voice.

The Lark house had a basement that seemed to have been finished in the 1970s. Shag carpet, walls paneled in wood. Banks of fluorescent lights overhead.

"When he was a boy, Anthony had a bedroom upstairs," said Helen Lark. "But when he came home after college, he moved down here."

One paneled wall was covered with a patchwork of photographs and news articles. On the right the photos were of Callie Spencer, most of them clipped from magazines. The articles were printed from the Internet; they chronicled the Great Lakes Bank robbery and its aftermath. There were pictures of Floyd Lambeau, long-haired and goateed, wearing a rogue's grin. Mug shots of Terry Dawtrey, Sutton Bell, and Henry Kormoran.

But on the left the photos told a different story. They started out as snapshots of a teenaged girl: she smiled shyly and hid behind an armload of schoolbooks. She got older, went to parties and football games. Sometimes she had her arm around Anthony Lark. In small stories clipped from a newspaper, she won an art award, graduated from high school, enrolled at Michigan State University on a scholarship.

At Michigan State, she got a new wardrobe and a better haircut. She posed for the camera on the steps of a lecture hall.

At some point she and Lark took a trip out west. They stood side by side in a forest of redwood trees.

At twenty-four she got engaged, but not to Anthony Lark. She made a beautiful bride. A newspaper photo captured a wide, gorgeous smile.

There were far fewer snapshots after that. In one of them she wore a cast on her hand. In another she crouched beside the wheelchair of a man who may have been her father. She still had a pretty smile, but it was dimmed and looked forced.

At twenty-eight she died. The obituary said she had passed away suddenly at home. Her name was Susanna Marten.

CHAPTER 35

"What happened to her?" Elizabeth asked Helen Lark.

"Just what you're thinking," the woman said. "Her family tried to cover it with code words, but that never really fools anyone, does it? 'Passed away suddenly.' She killed herself. An overdose of sleeping pills."

She went quiet, standing with her hands behind her back like a patron in a museum. Carter Shan peered at the man in the engagement photo: blond hair, wide shoulders, an athletic build. A smart-aleck grin. The caption identified him as Derek Everly.

"The husband—" Shan said.

"Yes, the husband drove her to it," said Helen Lark. "They went to high school together: Anthony, Susanna, and Derek. Susanna was the sweetest thing you could imagine. Anthony was in love with her. He never had much ambition as a boy, and I thought it would be a battle to get him to go to college. But when she went to Michigan State, he went too.

"She majored in Fine Arts, and I think he would have done the same, if he'd had any talent for it. He wound up in the English department.

"They dated, Anthony and Susanna. In high school, then in college. She's the one who broke it off. I couldn't tell you why; he never wanted to talk about it. But it happened during their senior year at Michigan State, and after that she stayed on to get a master's degree. Anthony came home, because there was nothing holding him there anymore.

"He coasted along for a couple of years, working temp jobs. He spent most of his free time in this room. Then she came home one summer and he started to come alive again, but it didn't last. She took up with Derek Everly.

"Derek had never gone to college. His family owned a landscaping company here in town. He pursued Susanna; they were engaged before the year was out, and married in the spring. I don't think he started hitting her right away."

Helen Lark let out a weary breath. "You see the picture there, where she has her hand in a cast. Derek slammed her fingers in a door. That was before he got smart, before he learned how to hurt her without leaving marks that people would see. I know about it because Anthony told me. He heard it from Susanna. He heard the reasons too. The excuses. The landscaping business wasn't doing well. Derek wanted a baby, and Susanna couldn't get pregnant fast enough to suit him. Derek thought she was having an affair with Anthony. Which wasn't true, though I know there was nothing Anthony wanted more than to be with her.

"He begged her to leave Derek, but she thought the man would change. Derek promised her he would. Every time he hit her, he told her he was sorry and it would never happen again. And for a while it would look like he was sincere. For a while.

"When Anthony couldn't stand it anymore, he went to Susanna's father. That's the gentleman in the wheelchair there. He wasn't in a wheelchair at the time. He was a bear of a man who worked construction jobs all his life. He went to see Derek at the office of the landscaping company. Said he was there about his daughter. Derek told him they had nothing to talk about. 'We're not going to talk,' he said. Then he took Derek apart. Left him bruised and bleeding on the floor. Told him if he ever had to come back again he would kill him.

"You can guess what happened next. Derek acted like he'd learned his lesson. And, god help her, Susanna stayed with him.

"A month later her father drove out to meet a friend at a bar. Four men jumped him in the parking lot. They had baseball bats. They broke his legs and his arms and his ribs. The police never caught them, and no one ever connected them to Derek Everly.

"But Susanna knew he was responsible. She finally left him and took out a restraining order against him. Moved in with her father so she could take care of him. He seemed to improve, but his breathing was always a problem. Pneumonia was what got him in the end. He was too weak to fight it off. She was with him when he died.

"Anthony went to the funeral. Derek turned up at the cemetery. He waited until the reverend said the final prayer and people were heading to their cars. Then he approached Susanna. Anthony stood between them. 'You shouldn't be here,' he said. Derek ignored him and spoke directly to Susanna. 'You think a restraining order's going to stop me?'

"She stayed here that night. But the next day she went back to her father's house. She told Anthony there were things she needed to attend to. She wouldn't let him go with her. 'I'll be fine,' she told him. 'You can't be with me every minute of the day.' She promised she would come back here before it got dark. When she didn't, he went looking for her. He found her in the spare bedroom of her father's house, an empty pill bottle beside her on the bed."

HELEN LARK TURNED her back on the wall of photographs. She looked around as if she didn't know where to go, and ended up moving toward the bottom of the basement stairs. Elizabeth joined her there.

"All this," Elizabeth said, gesturing toward the wall, "when did it start?"

"A few weeks after she died," said Helen Lark. "At that point, Anthony was too depressed to work. He dug out all the pictures of Susanna he had ever taken. I tried to talk to him. His father—I don't like to say it, but his father wasn't any use. When Anthony was younger he hung on every word his father said, but over the years they grew apart."

She took off her glasses and polished the lenses with a tail of her blouse. "My husband was a reserved man. He had a boat. He liked to fish. Anthony didn't care much about fishing, so his father didn't know what to do with him."

She slipped her glasses on again. "After six months, I asked Anthony to see a therapist. He went to a few sessions. It didn't suit him. Anthony believed he was responsible for Susanna's death, because he didn't do enough to prevent it. When the therapist questioned his way of looking at things, he didn't want to hear it. I think he was really looking for someone to tell him he was right.

"When he didn't get that, he stopped going. But he started working again. I think he did it so I'd leave him alone." She nodded toward the wall. "After Susanna had been gone a year, I asked him if it might be time to take this stuff down. He just stared at me. 'I'm never going to take it down,' he said."

Elizabeth pointed toward the right-hand side of the wall, the side dominated by photos of Callie Spencer. "What about this?" she asked. "When did your son get interested in the Great Lakes robbery?"

"This spring," said Helen Lark. "I remember I was angry with him at the time, because he sold his father's boat." She stood with her eyes downcast. "My husband passed away in March. He left his boat to Anthony. I thought it should mean something to him, but all he wanted was to be rid of it. I suppose it hurt my feelings.

"Right around then he started putting pictures of Callie Spencer on the wall. I didn't like it. I could see the reason—she had a smile just like Susanna's. But it wasn't healthy, obviously. I didn't want to deal with it anymore. I told him he should think about moving out.

"Susanna had been gone three years. Anthony was thirty-one. I didn't want him to waste his life. You have to use the time you're given—that's what I always told him." She reached for the railing of the stairs, as if she needed the support. "I should have kept him here with me."

Elizabeth laid a hand on the woman's shoulder. "We need to find him, Mrs. Lark. Do you have any idea where he might be?"

"I don't."

"When did he move out of the house?"

"In May."

"He only started renting his apartment in Ann Arbor a couple weeks ago. Where was he living in the meantime?"

"He had a place here in town," Helen Lark said. "I can give you the address."

"Did he have friends he kept in touch with?"

"I can give you some names. There weren't many."

"When was the last time you spoke to him?"

"He called on my birthday, the twenty-eighth of June."

"If he calls again, or comes here, we need to know."

Helen Lark nodded slowly, as if it pained her. "All right."

"What about Susanna's family?" Elizabeth asked. "Is there anyone Anthony might contact?"

"She had no brothers or sisters, just some cousins. But Anthony didn't really know them."

Shan broke in. "And Derek Everly—what ever happened to him?"

"He's not around anymore," Helen Lark said, looking at Shan with an odd intensity. "He came to a violent end."

"A VIOLENT END? Is that what she told you?"

After leaving Helen Lark, Elizabeth and Shan had driven to the Dearborn Police Department. The watch commander had sent them to talk to a detective named Hiller whose cubicle was littered with boxes and case files.

"Derek Everly was beaten to death this spring in a storage shed at the Everly Landscaping Company," Hiller said. "Someone staved in the back of his skull with the handle of a rake. Then hacked up his body with a lawnmower blade. So yes, he came to a very violent end."

"Would it be safe to assume Anthony Lark was a suspect?" Elizabeth asked.

Hiller tipped his chair back. "Derek Everly was a prick, so it could be a lot of people wanted him dead. But Lark was at the top of the list. You know about the Marten girl."

"Yes," said Shan.

"So there's no question about motive," Hiller said. "The timing seems a little off. Lark waited three years after the girl passed."

"But this spring—" Elizabeth said. "That's when Lark's father died."

Hiller bobbed his head in agreement. "Exactly. You figure maybe once Dad was gone, he gave himself permission. Or he got to thinking about what was really important. Whatever. What I know is that Lark's father died in March and Everly was killed in April."

"But Lark was never charged?" Elizabeth said. "Did he have an alibi?"

"He said he was home with his mother that night," Hiller explained with a shrug. "She backed him up. Maybe she was covering for him, or maybe he slipped out without her knowing. The bottom line is we never found the evidence to charge him. He didn't leave prints. The first blow put Everly down, so there was no struggle. Lark didn't have so much as a bruised knuckle."

Hiller turned his chair slowly from side to side. "His mother got him a lawyer as soon as we came around, and the lawyer didn't let him talk. If he had, I think we would have gotten a confession. In a case like that, it usually doesn't take much. You sympathize with the guy, act like you understand why he did what he did. With Lark—well, I remember Susanna Marten, and I remember her father. I wouldn't have had to act."

CHAPTER 36

A few minutes after four on Thursday afternoon I walked down the steps of City Hall. I'd spent two hours with one of Elizabeth's colleagues, a young cop named Wintergreen, going over the events of the night before. I told him everything I could remember about Anthony Lark, including what Lark had said about Lucy Navarro and the blue minivan that had taken her away.

I mentioned the semi truck from the hotel parking lot. Suggested that the driver might have seen something.

Wintergreen asked me about my dealings with Lucy, and I gave him a full account. I included everything she said she had learned from Terry Dawtrey and Henry Kormoran. Wintergreen wrote it all down without comment: Dawtrey's story about Floyd Lambeau, who claimed to have been Callie Spencer's real father; Dawtrey's assertion that he knew the identity of the fifth bank robber; Kormoran's story about seeing Lambeau and Callie Spencer together at the Great Lakes Bank.

I told Wintergreen about accompanying Lucy to her meeting with Callie Spencer. About Lucy's belief that Callie knew the fifth robber and would try to contact him. "That's what Lucy was doing up until last night," I said, "watching Callie, waiting for her to make a move."

Lastly I filled him in about Alan Beckett and his attempt to get Lucy to abandon her investigation.

As I went through the details I could tell Wintergreen was trying to keep his skepticism in check. Finally he looked up from his notes. "So Beckett wanted you to help him persuade Ms. Navarro to drop her story," he said. "And he offered you funding for your magazine in exchange."

"That's right," I said.

"And he made the same kind of offer to Ms. Navarro. She used to write novels, so he tempted her with a book contract."

"Right."

"And you want me to believe that when persuasion didn't work, Beckett decided to take a more forceful approach."

I turned my head to look around at the walls of the interview room. A small movement, but it made itself known in the wound at my side.

"I haven't said that."

"No. You're just implying it," said Wintergreen, gathering up his notes. "Do you expect me to go to my boss and tell him that Alan Beckett, either on his own or at the request of Callie Spencer, arranged to make Lucy Navarro disappear last night?"

I pushed my chair back from the table, wincing at the pain in my side.

"No," I told him. "I really don't."

WHEN I DESCENDED the steps of City Hall, I took things slow. It seemed to help. I strolled along the sidewalk and the pain faded a little. The ibuprofen I'd taken seemed to be keeping it in check. I'd left the stronger stuff behind. I wanted to stay alert.

At a crosswalk waiting for the light, I got out my phone and dialed Lucy's number. I'd already done it three or four times and I knew what I'd hear. *You've reached Lucy Navarro of the National Current . . .*

I pushed the cutoff button and called Bridget Shellcross.

"I'm finished," I said.

"When I didn't hear from you, I thought you changed your mind," she said.

"No. It just took longer than I expected. Are we still on?"

"We're still on."

"Good. I'm on my way now."

The light turned to green and I closed my phone and went looking for John Casterbridge.

IT'S NOT AS HARD as you'd think, tracking down a U.S. senator.

Anyone willing to do some digging could have discovered that John Casterbridge rented an apartment in the Dupont Circle neighborhood in Washington, D.C., and another in Lansing, the capital of Michigan. He had a house in Grosse Pointe that had been in his family for generations, and a bungalow in St. Ignace on the shore of Lake Huron.

You'd need to dig deeper to learn that the senator had a condo on Liberty Street in Ann Arbor. I never knew about it, but I had seen him Sunday night at the Spencer house, and again on Monday when he had his accident, so I assumed he must be staying in town. I asked Bridget, who has lived in Ann Arbor for twenty years and knows everyone worth knowing.

She told me about the condo. It was in a pile of steel and concrete known as the Bridgewell Building, put up seven years ago by Casterbridge Realty. The units sold out quickly for a million and a half apiece, and John Casterbridge wound up with one of them. He stayed there a few weeks out of the year and took most of his meals at the Seva Restaurant next door.

I passed the restaurant and walked up to the Bridgewell Building like I belonged there. The glass doors opened into a lobby with a scattering of plush armchairs and a concierge desk. A fountain bubbled near the elevators: water murmuring over a heap of river stones.

The kid behind the desk perked up as soon as I came in. His suit looked inexpensive, but he wore it well. I thought about heading for the elevators and wondered if he would chase after me. He looked like he might.

Getting chased wasn't part of my plan.

I stopped at the desk and said, "I'm here to see Senator Casterbridge."

The kid looked at me gravely. "I'm sorry, sir. The senator doesn't wish to be disturbed."

"Why don't you call him and let him know I'm here. My name's David Loogan. He knows me."

"I'm afraid I can't call him, sir."

"Why not?"

"If I did, it might disturb him. He doesn't wish to be disturbed."

I had to smile. "You're very pedantic."

"Thank you, sir."

"That wasn't a compliment."

He smoothed his tie. "I know that, sir. But I'm expected to treat members of the public with patience and courtesy."

"That must wear you out, some days," I said. "Did you hear about the reporter who went missing from the Winston Hotel parking lot last night?"

He nodded. "I saw it on the news."

"Her name was Lucy Navarro. She was doing a story on the senator's daughter-in-law."

"I see."

"I'm curious to hear what the senator has to say about it. I've got a friend at Channel Four in Detroit who's curious too. He should be along any minute with a camera crew. We may decide to camp out here. That's how eager we are to talk to the senator."

"I understand. But the senator doesn't generally comment on news stories."

"We'll see."

I turned and crossed the lobby and settled into an armchair. I pretended to watch the traffic on Liberty Street, but kept half an eye on the kid behind the desk. He picked up a slim black phone and punched a number. Spoke quietly to someone. I couldn't make out what he said over the bubbling of the fountain.

Fifteen minutes passed. Then the glass doors opened and a young man walked in—the senator's driver from Sunday night. Alan Beckett came in behind him.

The driver went and stood by the concierge desk. Beckett plopped himself into a chair across from me.

"You don't have a friend at Channel Four," he said.

"I could make one," I said.

"I doubt it. What's the purpose of your theatrics?"

He looked relaxed in the chair, but I heard a strain in his voice.

"I called you this morning," I said. "You didn't answer. I thought this would be the easiest way to get your attention."

He rubbed a palm over his scalp. "I didn't want to talk to you. The senator doesn't either. You're presuming a great deal by coming here. You're not his pal because you've shared a drink of whiskey with him."

"If he doesn't want to see me, that's fine. My business is with you."

"What business?"

"Lucy Navarro. I told you to leave her alone."

He scowled. "I've done nothing to Lucy Navarro."

"This is the way it's going to work," I said. "If she turns up safe, then all's forgiven. You got carried away; I can understand that. There's a lot at stake. You want to get Callie Spencer elected to the Senate so you can be her adviser. I don't care. I don't care who gets elected or who the power is behind her throne. I especially don't care who robbed a bank seventeen years ago. As long as Lucy turns up alive."

Beckett tilted his head. "And if she doesn't?"

"Then you're done."

A pause while he thought it over. "So you think you can keep Callie out of the Senate?"

"I'm not talking about the Senate, Al. I'm talking about you. If Lucy's dead, you're done."

He held himself very still. "Are you threatening me, Mr. Loogan?"

I raised an eyebrow at him. "Yes. I thought that was obvious."

"You're threatening me with violence?"

"I told you she was under my protection. What did you think I meant?"

He crossed his arms over his stomach. We listened to the murmur of the fountain.

"I don't look kindly on threats, Mr. Loogan."

"I don't care how you look on it. As long as I get Lucy back. You haven't killed her, have you?"

"I've done nothing to Ms. Navarro, as I told you." He uncrossed his arms and hauled himself to his feet. "I've heard enough. I'm asking you to leave now." He glanced at the driver and the kid behind the concierge desk. "You can walk out on your own, or those two young men can escort you."

I got up and fixed my eyes on his, a nice long glowering stare. Then I walked out on my own. Through the glass doors and down the steps. I crossed Liberty Street and looked back to see Beckett leaving the building. The senator's driver stayed behind, presumably to guard against my return.

I pulled out my phone as I watched Beckett retreating through the alley between the building and the restaurant next door. There was a parking lot back there where he would have left his car. I pressed a number and listened to the phone dialing Bridget Shellcross.

"Hi, David."

"He's coming back now."

"I see him," she said.

I PICKED UP MY CAR at a garage on Washington Street and drove to Bridget's townhouse. Got out and walked up onto her stoop. The sky was full of low gray clouds getting ready to rain.

After a few minutes Bridget rolled up in her sporty little Nissan. Another car trailed after her, something compact and electric. Bridget's girlfriend got out of it: Ariel or Amber. The lute player. They came up the walk and I stepped down to meet them.

"Summit Street," Bridget said. "Number 315. He drove straight there."

"He didn't spot you?" I said.

"No way. It was a perfect tail. Amber's a natural."

Amber, then. Not Ariel. I watched the woman take hold of Bridget's hand. "Tell him about the fence, Bridge," she said.

"There's a driveway along the side of the house," Bridget said, "and a tall privacy fence that surrounds the place on three sides. You could back a van in there and get someone into the house without any of the neighbors seeing."

I nodded at that. "What about the other thing we talked about?"

She let loose Amber's hand and asked her if she wouldn't mind leaving us alone. Amber rolled her eyes and said, "The grown-ups need to talk." She brushed past me with a wink, and a moment later I heard the door of the townhouse close behind her.

Bridget said, "Are you sure you want it?"

I left the question unanswered and she reached into her handbag—a bigger one than she'd been carrying the last time I saw her. She took out a makeup case, a zippered cloth pouch with a flowery design.

I felt the weight of it when she handed it over.

"It's a revolver," she said. "I got it last year from an admirer."

"Is it registered?" I asked. "I don't want to make trouble for you if I have to use it."

"The gentleman who gave it to me doesn't believe in permits or registrations. . . . I imagine it won't do any good to tell you to be careful."

"You can try."

She didn't try. Instead, she stood on tiptoe and brushed her lips against my cheek.

CHAPTER 37

Rain speckled my windshield as I drove along Summit Street. I passed number 315 and saw Alan Beckett's Lexus in the driveway. The tall fence leaned in over it.

I parked half a block away. The house across from 315 had a FOR RENT sign on the lawn. The rental company was Casterbridge Realty.

It didn't take much of a leap to assume that number 315 might also be owned by Casterbridge Realty. It would explain a great deal. I knew Beckett lived in Lansing. But if he wanted to stick close to Callie Spencer, it would help to have a place to stay here in town. I had called the major hotels and he wasn't registered at any of them. An empty Casterbridge property would make a good place to stay.

It might also make a good place to keep Lucy Navarro.

I unzipped Bridget's makeup pouch and drew out the revolver, a silver .38 with black grips. All the chambers were empty when I cracked the cylinder. I loaded them with six rounds from the pouch. There were six left over.

I thought about waiting. If Beckett were to leave, it would make things much easier. I could go in and it would still be breaking and entering, but I wouldn't have to threaten him with the gun. There was something to be said for committing as few crimes as possible.

I sat watching the front of number 315. The seconds ticked by. A minute. Two. Beckett didn't leave.

My phone rang.

The sound startled me. I checked the display. "Hello, Nick."

"Hey, sport. I heard you got shot."

Fine flecks of rain gathered on the window beside me. "Where'd you hear that?"

"We got the Internet up here. Is it true?"

"It's true. But it's exaggerated. I only got shot a little."

"A little?"

"Hardly at all. What are you doing?"

"I've been watching Sam Tillman's house. He slept on the couch again last night. I don't think his wife's happy with him."

I looked at the front of number 315. "You shouldn't be watching people's houses, Nick."

"It's down to one house now," he said. "Used to be three, but I hear Sheriff Delacorte won't be coming back no more."

"That's right."

"Can't say I mind. And I hear Paul Rhiner got stomped on pretty hard."

"Yes."

"I figure that's a good start. So all that's left is Tillman. How much trouble can I get in, watching one house?"

"This isn't a game, Nick."

"You sound tired, sport. Did I wake you up? Maybe you should go back to sleep."

I felt a rush of annoyance. "I wasn't asleep. You need to leave Tillman alone. Stop screwing around."

"I can barely hear you, sport. You get some sleep. We'll talk again when you're awake."

He ended the call before I could respond. I snapped the phone shut and slipped it in my pocket. Picked up Bridget's revolver from the passenger seat and opened the driver's door.

My phone rang again as I stood in the rainy street wondering where to conceal the gun. I decided it could go in my right back pocket with my shirt hanging over it. I listened to two more rings before I pulled the phone out. It was Sarah.

"Are you about to do something reckless?" she asked.

I had to suppress a laugh. "Where'd you get that idea?" I said.

"Mom figured you'd go blundering around today, looking for Lucy Navarro. I thought you might be too tired, and you'd have to wait a day. Which one of us was right?"

"I haven't been blundering around."

"In that case, could you pick me up?" she said. "I'm at the library. I've got my bike here, but it's raining."

THE ANN ARBOR District Library sits on the corner of South Fifth Avenue and William Street. I got there in five minutes and found Sarah waiting in the shelter of the entryway. The front wheel of her bike had a quick-release lever; she already had it off. I popped the trunk and helped her stow the bike.

The rain had tapered off, and it had never been very strong to start with. But I knew Sarah hadn't called me for a ride because of the rain. And I hadn't come here to save her from bad weather. I'd come because her question had hit too close to the mark.

Are you about to do something reckless?

Barging into 315 Summit Street with no plan, with nothing but a loaded gun—that would have to count as reckless.

Sarah got the bike settled and shut the trunk. A few drops of rain sparkled in her hair.

"Are you all right, David?" she said. "You look worn out."

She wasn't afraid of a little rain. Her mother had probably asked her to keep an eye on me, but that wasn't why she had called me either. Not really. She was sixteen. She wanted what all sixteen-year-olds want.

"You should let me drive," she said.

SARAH GOT HER learner's permit in March, right after the last big snow melted. Since then we've practiced once or twice a week. She could pass the test for her license tomorrow, though Elizabeth would rather have her wait until the fall.

I buckled into the passenger seat and had her drive down Fifth to

Packard, then east to State Street. I'd hidden the revolver away in the glove compartment.

"I've got an idea," she said.

I let her go where she wanted. All men by nature desire to know, and the same goes for teenaged girls. She made her way through heavy traffic on State and turned into the lot of the Winston Hotel. We got out and I showed her the spot where Lark had shot me. There was nothing to mark it, not even a strip of crime-scene tape. Lucy Navarro's Beetle had been towed away.

I'd left my pocketknife behind the night before, and I didn't think I'd find it, but there it was in the grass near the picnic tables. I started to bend to pick it up, but Sarah got to it first. She folded the blade and passed it to me.

From the hotel I let her drive on the interstate for a short stretch—seventy miles an hour, seventy-five in the passing lane. We took the north exit onto Route 23 and went as far as Washtenaw Avenue.

From there we drove west toward home. After we passed through downtown, I realized we weren't very far from Summit Street—from Alan Beckett. I made an impulsive decision.

"Turn right up here."

Our early lessons always went this way, with me telling her where to go. In the very beginning I used to recite every move she should make. *Check your mirrors, put on your turn signal, foot off the gas and onto the brake.*

She turned right and we rode north to Summit.

"Left here," I said.

The rain had stopped falling, but drops of it hung from the tips of the leaves along Beckett's street. We coasted past number 315 and I saw the car in the drive, the privacy fence leaning over it protectively. I glimpsed Beckett opening the driver's door.

I had Sarah make a left at the next intersection and we circled the block. When we passed the house again, Beckett and the car were gone.

"Whose house is that?" she asked me.

"Nobody's," I said.

"Shall I go around again, to nobody's house?"

I closed my eyes. "I'm tired. Let's go home."

Five minutes later we were there. No sign of Elizabeth at the house. I helped Sarah wrestle her bike out of the trunk. She did most of the wrestling. I held my hand out for the car keys and told her I'd be back in a little while. "I need to pick some things up at *Gray Streets*."

She had leaned the bike against the elm tree on the lawn. She held the detached front wheel.

"I thought you were tired," she said.

"I plan to take a long nap when I get back."

She let the wheel fall onto the grass. "I'll go with you."

"I can manage on my own."

"I'll go with you back to Summit Street. That house—you think Lucy Navarro's there?"

I shook my head. "That's not where I'm going. You've got the wrong idea."

"I can help, David. What if that man comes back? You need someone to keep watch."

"I'm not going to Summit Street. And if I were, I wouldn't take you. I'm not that reckless."

CHAPTER 38

I went to Summit Street, of course.

Beckett's car was still gone when I got back to number 315. I drove past and went around the corner. Left my car on a street called Fountain and walked back to the house.

I ducked around the privacy fence and up the driveway. Bridget's revolver rested in my back pocket.

Drops of rain fell from the eaves of a porch at the rear of the house. I went up to the door and found it locked. But it had a window, four panes of glass in a square. I found a stone in the backyard, wrapped a handkerchief around it to muffle the sound, and smashed one of the panes.

Reaching through, I turned the dead bolt and the lock on the knob. The door opened into a kitchen that looked unused. I figured Beckett might have gone out for dinner. If he went to a restaurant he could be away for quite a while. If he went to pick up carry-out he could be back any minute.

Off the kitchen I found a small room with a washer and dryer and a set of pantry shelves. Beyond the shelves was a whitewashed door that might have been a closet, but more likely led to a basement. I decided to save the door for later.

The living room spanned the front of the house. It had a bricked-over fireplace and the kind of furniture you find in rental properties: bland, beige. The place was tidy apart from sections of a newspaper scattered over the cushions of a sofa, and a drinking glass abandoned on a side table.

From there I passed into an unfurnished space that might have been intended as a dining room. Smooth wooden floorboards underfoot. A stairway on the right, leading to the second floor.

Upstairs were three bedrooms and a single bathroom. Beckett had an electric razor on the sink, and a toothbrush balanced on the rim of a coffee mug.

I found more of his things in the largest of the three bedrooms. A robe tossed carelessly at the foot of a full-size bed. A suitcase on a chair. Three decade-old suits in the closet, along with a selection of shirts. The other two bedrooms were bare. No evidence that anyone had been held captive in them.

Down the stairs again and I looked out at the street and the driveway. No sign of Beckett's car. I moved through the kitchen to the laundry room and tried the whitewashed door. The hinges made a sound like a far-off cavalry horn. Wooden stairs led down into darkness. I flipped the switch at the top of the steps and a bulb lit up at the bottom. Wood bowed and creaked beneath my feet as I descended.

First thing I noticed: a basement window that had been boarded over. The floor was cracked concrete. A heavy punching bag, the kind boxers use to train, hung by a chain from a steel I-beam.

The back wall, farthest from the street, had a door in it.

I could see no furnace or water heater. Logically, they would be on the other side of the door. I didn't know what else might be there. The house seemed solidly built. The back wall was of the same concrete as the foundation. The door was locked.

I pounded it with the side of my fist and called Lucy's name. No answer.

No reason to think she was back there. The lock on the door didn't mean anything. It would have been put there years ago, probably by parents who wanted to keep their kids from playing near the furnace. I looked around for a key. Reached up and ran my fingers along the top of the frame. Nothing but dust.

I stepped back and kicked hard at the door with the heel of my right shoe. A bad idea. The force of the blow sent a fresh spike into the wound in my side.

I spun around and braced my back against the wall. Waited for the pain to settle down to something manageable. Battering down the door wasn't going to work. I had the revolver, but I didn't like my chances of shooting out the lock either. I needed to find the key.

Up the stairs. I checked the pantry shelves and a cabinet on the wall above the clothes dryer. In the kitchen I found a key rack by the door. Four metal hooks, all of them empty.

As I stepped over the broken glass on the floor, I got a call on my cell phone. I had turned the volume down to nothing, so I felt the phone vibrate in my shirt pocket.

Ignoring it, I started opening drawers in the kitchen. The first was empty. The second held a notepad and a lot of mismatched pens. I pushed the pens around. No key. The third drawer had a hammer in it, a set of screwdrivers. A roll of silver duct tape.

My phone had stopped vibrating, but now it started again. I drew it from my pocket and saw Sarah's name on the display.

Outside, a car pulled into the driveway.

I opened the phone. She didn't wait for me to say hello.

"You didn't answer," she said. "I tried to warn you."

I crossed to the window that overlooked the driveway. Heard the sound of an engine being cut off. Through the parted curtains I saw the door of Beckett's Lexus swing open. I leaned closer so I could look down the length of the drive. Sarah came into view, walking her bike along the sidewalk. Cell phone held to her ear.

"What do you think you're doing?" I said in a low voice.

"Helping," she said. "I'll stall him as long as I can."

She snapped her phone shut and I did the same. I watched Beckett haul himself out of the car. He was several feet away, and lower than the window. I could see his bare scalp, straw-colored hair on either side.

His left hand held a paper bag with the logo of a Mexican restaurant called Tios. He spotted Sarah and turned toward her. My first instinct was to go out there and get between them.

I looked back at the drawer I'd left open. The duct tape. I imagined Lucy Navarro on the other side of the door in the basement, lying unconscious on the floor with her wrists and ankles bound. A strip of tape over her mouth, another over her eyes.

Outside, Sarah started in on a tale of woe about her bicycle. I could hear her clearly; the window had been left open a couple of inches to let in a breeze.

"... ran over a pothole, like, a foot deep, and I think there were nails at the bottom or something ..."

Last chance to find a key. I went back to the drawers—three of them I hadn't checked. One of them empty, one with a heap of loose silverware, one with towels and pot holders.

"... lucky I didn't go over the handlebars ..."

I wasted time looking under the towels. Wasted more time sifting through the silverware.

"... front tire is totally flat. I could patch it but I've got no way to reinflate it after."

I started looking in the cupboards. Saltine crackers, a can of coffee. Dinner plates, chipped bowls.

"... on top of everything my cell flaked out on me. Dead battery. Could I maybe borrow yours? I gotta call my dad and get him to pick me up ..."

Coffee mugs. Glassware. A shotglass with a cloverleaf on it. A brass key standing up in the shotglass.

I grabbed it and headed for the laundry room. Outside, Sarah was holding an imaginary phone conversation with her dad's secretary. The secretary put her on hold. "It's after six and he's in a meeting," she said to Beckett. "He's a major workaholic. I swear, you could shoot him and he'd be back at his desk the next day."

I raced down the basement stairs, skidded on the concrete floor. The key slipped into the lock. It didn't turn. I jiggled it, eased it out a fraction of an inch and then it went. Leaned my shoulder into the door and it scraped open.

Dark in there. Another boarded window. I could see the shape of the furnace. The water heater. Nothing else. I used up seconds looking for the pull chain of an overhead light. Sixty watts lit the room. Not even a scrap of duct tape on the floor. Lucy had never been here.

I doused the light and locked the door. Used my handkerchief to wipe my prints from the key as I ran up the stairs.

Outside, Sarah was thanking Beckett for letting her use his phone.

I dropped the key into the shotglass and eased shut the door of the cupboard. Beckett offered to let Sarah come inside and wait for her father.

"No, thanks," she said. "He's going to pick me up on the corner."

I stepped on the broken glass on my way out. Used the handkerchief to turn the inside knob, and again to wipe down the one outside. I left the door ajar.

From the back porch I could hear Beckett's approaching footsteps.

I turned away from the sound, took two steps to the porch railing, and vaulted over. Landed easy apart from the stabbing pain in my side. I sprinted along the side of the house, came to a gate in the fence and thought for a frantic moment it would be locked.

I worked the latch and went through. Got to the sidewalk in front of the house and looked to my left. Saw Sarah rounding the corner, walking her bike. I could follow her, but I'd have to cross the end of Beckett's driveway. Better to take the long way around.

I ended up cutting through a neighbor's yard and passing behind number 315 on the far side of the privacy fence. Made my way to Fountain Street. Sarah was waiting beside my car.

We stashed her bike in the trunk. I drove this time. Over to Spring Street and then south. My breathing was rough and my body was sending me messages about the wisdom of jumping and running. They were being delivered to the bullet wound in my side.

"That was brave, but foolish," I said.

"I agree," said Sarah.

"Do you?"

"I assume we're talking about you breaking into that guy's house."

I glanced over and saw her looking back at me with a cool smile on her lips. It reminded me of her mother.

"I'm talking about you," I said softly. "Following me. You shouldn't have done it. What if he had taken a closer look at your bike tire?"

"He would have seen it was flat," she said. "I let the air out of it."

"When did you have time?"

"I did it as soon as I got there. Some of us plan things ahead."

We drove along under a gray sky, a few odd drops of rain falling from the trees.

"Why did you take so long?" she asked me.

I told her about the locked door in the basement.

"So, no Lucy," she said. "Where do you think she is?"

"I don't know."

"But you still think he took her—what's his name?"

"Alan Beckett," I said, slowing to make the turn onto our street. "He's Callie Spencer's adviser. I think if he didn't take Lucy himself, he's behind it. Or at least he knows about it."

"And he's keeping her somewhere," Sarah said. "Or someone is."

Her tone was even, as if she were stating a fact. But she was really asking a question. A question I'd been asking myself. If Beckett and the Spencers wanted Lucy Navarro out of the way, was there any reason to suppose she was still alive? She posed a danger to them because of what she'd learned from Terry Dawtrey and Henry Kormoran. I'd half convinced myself that they would keep her around, at least for a while. They'd have questions: How much did she really know? Did she have any hard evidence?

It seemed thin, when I thought about it. Any questions they had could have been answered by now. I had no reason to think they would keep her. But I wanted it to be true. I wanted to believe there was a door somewhere, and she was waiting behind it. Waiting for me to find her.

CHAPTER 39

On Friday morning, Lucy Navarro was still missing. Anthony Lark was on the loose.

Callie Spencer went on television.

They interviewed her live via satellite on one of the network morning shows. I slept late and missed it, but in the office that afternoon I watched it online.

The interview focused on Lark, whose story had been pieced together by reporters who had spoken to his mother and his friends. The picture that emerged was of a troubled man driven to violence by a twisted sense of justice. It helped that there was a pretty girl at the center of the story—someone had dug up videotape of Lark and Susanna Marten at their high school prom, Susanna in a blue dress with her hair up, laughing and waving at the camera.

Susanna Marten's story was all too common, Callie Spencer told the interviewer. A young woman full of promise who had fallen victim to domestic abuse. Callie had known many women like her in her years as a prosecutor. She understood the damage that domestic violence could do, to the victims and their friends and family members.

She felt sympathy for Lark, for his frustration over what had happened to Susanna—though of course she condemned his violent reaction. She was saddened that Lark had latched onto her own family's tragic history, turning his anger toward the men who robbed the Great Lakes Bank seventeen years ago. She seemed to take it for granted, too, that Lark was responsible for the death of Walter Delacorte, whom she described as a dear friend of her father.

Only at the end did the interviewer mention that Lark had shot me ("a local magazine editor") outside the Winston Hotel—and that Lucy Navarro had gone missing at around the same time. Callie expressed the wish that Lucy would be found unharmed, and viewers were left with the impression that Lark had abducted her.

Watching the interview, I had to admire Callie's performance. People who saw her wouldn't remember the details, but they would remember that Callie Spencer was thoughtful and tough-minded. They might forget Anthony Lark's name, but they would remember that the world is a dangerous place, and that Callie seemed to have a sincere desire to make it safer.

LARK WATCHED CALLIE SPENCER'S interview on a thirteen-inch TV in a dive hotel in South Bend, Indiana.

When he saw the video of Susanna Marten at the prom, he thought it would stop his heart. He had begun to lose his memory of her; he had left it behind on the wall of the basement in his mother's house. But the images on the television brought everything back to him. She had been real, and alive, and he had been with her.

It wasn't the first time he'd had that thought. The first time had been on a night three years ago, in the spare bedroom of her father's house. The bed made up with white sheets, and Susanna lying on it, legs bare and crossed at the ankles, hands folded over her stomach. Lips parted, eyes staring. An empty pill bottle beside her. He knelt by the bed and wept and thought that she had been alive just a few hours before, and he had been with her.

Now he sat in a hotel chair, feeling an ache in his chest and half listening to Callie Spencer's words. She didn't approve of him, that was the message. It disappointed him, but it didn't matter. She didn't understand the danger they represented—Dawtrey and Kormoran and Bell. Susanna hadn't seen the danger in Derek Everly either, not even when the evidence was painted on her own body, a canvas of purple bruises turning black. She only saw the truth when Everly put her father in a wheelchair, and then it turned out to be too late.

Lark had seen the danger all along, but he had been guilty of a different sin. The sin of delay, of uncertainty, of waiting too long to do the right thing.

He wasn't going to worry about Callie Spencer's approval. He got up and crossed the room, favoring his left leg—the one Loogan had slammed in the door of the yellow Beetle. The limp wasn't as bad as it had been, and the swelling had gone down.

He went into the bathroom and swallowed a tablet of Keflex, chasing it with water from a plastic cup. He studied himself in the mirror. Two days of stubble and his jaw firm and lean. Lines etched in his forehead. Not like the soft boy in the video at the prom.

He would give the leg another day to heal, but after that he would need to move. He had waited long enough. Tomorrow he would head back to Ann Arbor and deal with Sutton Bell.

PAUL RHINER WOKE to the sound of snoring.

They had him in a semi-private room, and the patient in the other bed was recovering from an operation. They must have scooped out most of the man's internal organs, Rhiner thought, because his snoring sounded deep and hollow, like wind blowing through a mine shaft far underground.

Every few hours a nurse would come in with a syringe. She'd tap the side to get rid of the air bubbles and she'd inject it into the snoring man's I.V.

Rhiner had an I.V. of his own. They were giving him drugs for the pain, strong ones that made him sleep. He didn't want to sleep. When he closed his eyes, he saw things. He saw Terry Dawtrey lying in the grass on the hillside of Whiteleaf Cemetery. Dawtrey struggling to breathe and blood staining his white shirt. Blood bubbling out of the wound in his throat.

He saw Walter Delacorte at Lark's apartment. The moment when the tire iron sank into Delacorte's flesh. His mouth opening to scream.

Whenever the nurses came in, they asked Rhiner to rate his pain on a scale from one to ten. He lied and gave them low numbers. He didn't want them to increase his dose. He wanted to stay awake.

A doctor stopped by to talk to him about his hand. The fingers wouldn't move the way they should. With surgery and physical therapy, he might be able to recover full function. He might also want to think about plastic surgery to straighten his broken nose.

Rhiner nodded his agreement and the doctor went away. As he left, Rhiner caught a glimpse of the uniformed cop in the hallway. There'd been one posted outside his door for as long as he could remember.

The detective had come to see him twice. The Asian one, Shan. Wanting to know what happened at Lark's apartment. Rhiner had come close to admitting it—that he had stabbed Walt. It was an accident. They might not even charge him, and if they did, a good lawyer could get him off. He could have the doctors fix his hand and his nose, and he could go on like nothing had happened. Except he couldn't close his eyes.

A nurse came in with a syringe for the man in the other bed. She flicked her finger against the side of it, because air bubbles are dangerous. If they get in your veins, they can kill you.

Rhiner watched her, but even now, awake, he was seeing Walter Delacorte's face. The dull fear in his eyes as he bled out on the floor.

After the nurse left, Rhiner looked at the I.V. running into his arm and wondered what would happen if he bit through the plastic tube. If he blew air into his vein.

No, he thought. *Too fancy*. Better to stick to something he knew would work.

He rolled onto his side—the one without the fractured ribs. He sat up by slow degrees, letting the pain sear through him, beads of sweat breaking out on his scalp. He opened a drawer by his bedside, ignoring the tears that ran down his face. They had left him his clothes—some of them at least. Not his shirt or his windbreaker, but his shoes, his pants.

His belt.

ON FRIDAY AFTERNOON Elizabeth stood by the row of windows near her desk in the Investigations Division. The temperature outside stood at ninety degrees. The building's air-conditioning overcompensated as usual. Inside, it felt like fifty.

She looked down at heavy traffic on Fifth Avenue—people getting an early start on the weekend. A few students were out walking in short sleeves and cutoffs. One young man stood across the street in front of the old firehouse. Dressed in black jeans and a black turtleneck. Long dark hair slicked back from a tall pale forehead.

Elizabeth listened to the rhythm of Carter Shan's fingers on his keyboard. He was typing a report on their interview the day before with Anthony Lark's mother.

Without turning she said, "What if I told you there's a kid down on the sidewalk, maybe twenty-two, dressed all in black?"

No pause in the rhythm. "I'd say we're living in a college town."

"It's awfully hot for it, though. He has to be burning up."

"Maybe the emptiness in his soul is keeping him cool."

She touched the sunlit glass. "What if I told you he's carrying a bowling bag?"

"I'd say he's probably got a severed head in it." The sound of Shan's typing broke off. "Is he really carrying a bowling bag?"

"No, but he's got a backpack. You could carry a head in a backpack."

They had spent the morning at Helen Lark's house, searching through the possessions her son had left behind and photographing his shrine to Susanna Marten and Callie Spencer. They had Mrs. Lark's permission to conduct the search, and a warrant as well, in case anyone decided to object later.

The Dearborn police had agreed to keep an eye on the house, but Elizabeth didn't think Lark would show up there. He seemed to be lying low. His description and a description of his car had gone out to law enforcement agencies throughout Michigan and the surrounding region.

At one o'clock Elizabeth and Shan had met with Chief McCaleb in his office, along with several other detectives from the division. McCaleb broke the news about Paul Rhiner's suicide. A nurse had found Rhiner's hospital bed empty, and when she checked the bathroom she found him with his belt around his neck, hanging from a hook on the back of the door.

"I just talked to the Chippewa County administrator," McCaleb said. "He's feeling a little anxious. He's now lost a sheriff and a deputy in the space of three days. He'd like to believe that Walter Delacorte was a hero who died trying to bring in a killer. That's a story that works better if Lark was the one who stabbed him. Is there any chance that's true?"

Elizabeth shook her head. "The lab found two sets of fingerprints on the tire iron, Delacorte's and Rhiner's. None from Lark. The evidence points to a quarrel between Delacorte and Rhiner."

"You think they quarreled over what to do with Lark?" McCaleb asked.

"That's really the only way it makes sense."

"We know Rhiner felt guilty about having to shoot Terry Dawtrey at Whiteleaf Cemetery," said McCaleb. "He blamed Lark for what happened. Could he have intended to kill him?"

"It would be simpler that way," Elizabeth said, "and I imagine it would make the Chippewa County administrator happy—he could still paint Delacorte as a hero."

"But you don't believe it."

"No. When I spoke to Walter Delacorte a week ago, he claimed he didn't believe Lark was ever at the cemetery. But he went to the trouble of tracking him down—without telling anyone what he was doing. I don't think he meant to arrest him."

"What was Delacorte's motive? Why go after Lark?"

"That would be one of those things we don't know yet," Elizabeth said.

Owen McCaleb planted his elbows on his desk, rubbed his hands over his face. "All right," he said. "Let's move on. I want to hear about the reporter."

Detectives Ron Wintergreen and Harvey Mitchum were leading the search for Lucy Navarro. They were a mismatched pair: Wintergreen was thirty-one, tall and slender, serious and reserved; Mitchum was twenty years older, heavyset, affable and outgoing. Wintergreen had contacted Lucy's cell phone provider, hoping to use her phone's signal to locate her, but the phone must have been switched off or damaged, or the battery dead. There was no signal.

Mitchum had tracked down Lucy's parents, a job that proved more difficult than anyone expected. Standing at ease near the chief's desk, hands clasped behind his back, he reported that they were on a cruise ship in the Mediterranean, touring the Greek isles. They had been on the ship for a week, and traveling for two weeks before that. They hadn't spoken to their daughter in all that time.

"They're worried, naturally," Mitchum said. "They plan to fly home as soon as they can make arrangements."

Lucy's editor at the *National Current* could offer no help. He told Mitchum he hadn't heard from her in a week. "Her cell phone records bear that out," Mitchum added.

The same records showed calls to Kinross Prison in the spring, presumably in regard to Terry Dawtrey, as well as calls to Henry Kormoran and Sutton Bell. David Loogan's number popped up several times in recent days—both his cell phone and his phone at *Gray Streets*. Lucy's last call on Wednesday had been to Loogan's office.

"Other than that, there were some calls to California," Mitchum said. "She kept in touch with friends from back home. But none of them have heard from her since Wednesday night."

A search of Lucy's room at the Winston Hotel had turned up nothing of use. Mitchum and Wintergreen had questioned the hotel's staff and guests, but no one there had witnessed what happened to Lucy on Wednesday night. Wintergreen had contacted a manager at Coleman Trucking, and after some wrangling was put in touch with the driver of the eighteen-wheeler Loogan had seen in the parking lot of the hotel.

"His name is Sullivan," Wintergreen said. "He was on his cell talking with his wife and he pulled off the interstate. Wound up in the hotel lot. His wife was on his case about being away from home. She was complaining about the kids and the bills. When I pressed him he said he remembered a yellow car, and a guy who waved at him to move his truck. The guy fit Lark's description. But that's all he remembered. He was preoccupied with the call. 'If you ever got chewed out by my wife you'd understand,' he told me."

Wintergreen shrugged. "I checked into him. He's got no criminal record. As far as I can tell, he has nothing to do with Lucy Navarro. He's a dead end."

. . .

THE MEETING IN McCaleb's office had broken up around two. Now, as Shan finished typing his report, Elizabeth crossed from the windows to her desk. She found the list of names Lark's mother had given her the day before. Lark's friends and acquaintances. She and Shan had already spoken to a few of them, and the plan was to head back to Dearborn and continue working through the list.

When they walked down the stairs and through the lobby and out into the heat, Elizabeth saw that the kid dressed in black was still loitering by the old firehouse. His backpack lay at his feet on the sidewalk.

She told Shan she'd meet him at the car and started across the street. The kid locked his gaze on her and ran a hand over his slicked-back hair. He stepped over his backpack as she approached. As if he wanted to block her view of it.

"Are you waiting for someone?" she asked him.

His lips parted to show her his teeth. "No."

"Is there something I can help you with?"

He looked past her at City Hall. "Are you a cop?"

She nodded.

"I've been thinking things over," he said, "trying to make up my mind."

She waited. Shan stood a few steps away. He had followed her instead of going for the car.

"Now that I'm here, I'm not sure," the kid said.

He pushed the backpack with his foot, nudging it toward the firehouse wall.

"Is there something you need to talk about?" Elizabeth asked him.

"That depends. Are you working on the E. L. Navarro case?"

Elizabeth studied the fine sheen of perspiration on the pale skin of his forehead.

"You mean Lucy Navarro?"

A strange light flashed in the kid's eyes. "You shouldn't call her Lucy," he said. "It's not respectful."

"Do you know something about her?" asked Elizabeth.

The tip of the kid's tongue ran along his front teeth.

"I know everything about her," he said. "I killed her."

CHAPTER 40

"His name is Jeremy Dechant," Elizabeth told me that night. "He's from Sylvania, Ohio, a suburb of Toledo."

She'd just come home, around eight-thirty. Sarah and I had already eaten dinner: barbecued chicken and a salad of tomatoes and cucumbers. I was loading the dishwasher.

"He read Lucy's novel," Elizabeth said. "He claimed it made him realize he was always meant to be a vampire. He thought if he kidnapped her and drank her blood, that would do the trick. Said he never meant to kill her."

It turned out that almost nothing he said was true.

"He doesn't drive a blue minivan," Elizabeth told me. "I doubt he's ever been in the parking lot of the Winston Hotel. He couldn't give us a description of the place. We asked if he could lead us to Lucy's body, and he said it turned into a mist when she died. Apparently that's what happens when you kill a vampire."

She stood by the counter, holding a glass of lemonade. "We talked to the police in Sylvania," she said. "They know about him. He was diagnosed with schizophrenia a couple years back. They've picked him up a few times, for shouting at people on the street. He has an unhealthy fascination with roadkill. Once they caught him walking along the highway near his parents' house, dragging the carcass of a deer."

She paused for a drink. "He had a backpack with him today. Two things inside—a copy of Lucy's novel, and a dead squirrel wrapped in a garbage bag. He said he's been feeling thirsty for human blood, but thought he'd better stick to squirrel."

"That's admirable," I said. "What did you do with him?"

"We sent him back to Ohio. His parents are going to have him evaluated. The Sylvania police said they'd look around his parents' property—there's a wooded area nearby. They think it's possible he's involved somehow with Lucy's disappearance. I think he made it all up. He saw a story about her on the news and spun out a fantasy about her. The only thing he's guilty of is wasting half my day."

Elizabeth fixed herself leftovers, and I finished cleaning up. Then she went off to meditate over the file on Anthony Lark, spreading the pages over the dining-room table and jotting notes on a legal pad. She was making a timeline of the events surrounding the deaths of Charlie and Terry Dawtrey and Henry Kormoran, the attack on Sutton Bell. It's something she does when she's working through a problem. When you put things in order, sometimes you can see connections you didn't see before.

Jeremy Dechant made the local news at ten o'clock. The story was thin on detail, and I got the feeling the reporter just wanted the chance to say the words "bizarre confession." He gave his pitch from the front lawn of Dechant's parents' house. An eager-looking cop from Sylvania talked about an ongoing search. No one from the Ann Arbor police made any comment.

I switched the TV off afterward and told Elizabeth I was going in to *Gray Streets*. I said the same to Sarah, who was sitting on the front porch, talking with a friend on her cell phone. She looked at me dubiously. "Really," I said.

And that's where I went. I left my car behind the building and rode the elevator to the sixth floor. Sat at my desk with the window open and the notes of a saxophone wafting up from the street. Ann Arbor on a Friday night.

I lasted twenty minutes, working on the story of the detective and the heiress. After that I closed the window and locked the door and drove north to Summit Street. The curtains of number 315 were drawn tight, but I could see some light behind them. I circled the block and dialed Alan Beckett's number. He took his time answering.

"Mr. Loogan."

"I've said it before. You're very good."

He let out a labored breath, as if he were getting up from a chair. "You'll have to speak plainer."

"Very good or very lucky," I said. "Have you seen the news?"

I came around to the front of number 315 again and pulled over to the curb.

"Not plain enough yet," he said. "I've seen a great deal of news."

"Jeremy Dechant."

"The young man who confessed to killing Ms. Navarro."

"That's the one. Where'd you find him?"

I imagined him pacing behind the curtains.

"I've no idea what you mean," he said.

"It's convenient for you," I said. "Dechant showing up. People don't want to think that Lucy's disappearance is connected with Callie Spencer. Now they don't have to. They can believe it was some misfit who read Lucy's book and got ideas. Doesn't matter if the police don't buy his confession. It's out there now."

"I had nothing to do with Mr. Dechant's confession."

I listened to the hum of the car's engine.

"Maybe not," I said. "Maybe it's just my active imagination."

"That seems likely," said Beckett. "By the way, someone broke in here yesterday. You wouldn't know anything about it, would you?"

"Why should I?"

"I've a feeling it was someone with an active imagination. Naturally I thought of you."

"It was probably kids from the neighborhood."

"It was certainly childish," he said. "And whoever did it had an accomplice. A young woman, though I don't think she was from the neighborhood."

"Is that so?"

"Charming really. She used my phone to call her father. Only her father's number turned out to belong to a shop that sells art supplies."

"That's odd."

"There was something familiar about her, but I only realized it after. She reminded me of Detective Waishkey."

"That's—"

"—odd, yes." He drew a breath. "I trust your visit eased your suspicions, and you won't need to come 'round again."

"I've no idea what you mean."

"Of course not. Good night to you, Mr. Loogan."

We disconnected. I waited a moment on the quiet street, then rolled along to the end of the block and turned south.

Fountain Street took me to Miller, and from there I drove east. A handful of minutes later I came to a stop on Bedford Road at the spot where I'd sat with Lucy in her yellow Beetle only two days before.

Light glowed in the windows of Callie Spencer's cottage. Some of it spilled out into the driveway and glinted off the hoods of two cars: Callie's Ford and another I didn't recognize.

I left the engine running but switched off the headlights. I focused on the window next to Callie's desk, hoping to catch sight of her.

After a while I shifted my attention to the front door. Dark, rough wood, unpainted. I thought of walking over and knocking on it. Tried to work out what I might say if she let me in.

The door opened. A man passed through. I recognized him from his posture as much as anything else—Callie's husband, Jay Casterbridge. He walked by the silver Ford and got into the other car, an Audi. Backed it into the street and started toward me. He came as far as the intersection with Arlington Boulevard and swung a left.

I switched on my lights and followed him.

He drove less than two miles. The house where he stopped stood in the middle of a block on a street call Fernwood, under the shelter of old oak trees. It had an American flag hanging from the front porch, and a FOR RENT sign on the lawn with a phone number and the words CASTERBRIDGE REALTY.

He pulled into a driveway that led back to a detached garage. I drove past and parked on the street. The moon shone somewhere, but not under the dark of the oaks. I walked carefully along the uneven sidewalk, slowing as I approached the end of the driveway. Casterbridge's car sat there empty. I saw a lighted window on the side of the house.

I was about to step into the driveway when I caught a flash of movement farther down the sidewalk. A shadowy figure slipping behind the trunk of a tree.

CHAPTER 41

She waited for me there, as still as if she had grown up out of the grass.

"Are you supposed to be hiding?" I said.

"I haven't decided."

"What are you wearing?"

"I don't think that's relevant."

"Levi's and sandals. Not very senatorial."

"I'm not a senator yet."

The jeans were faded. The T-shirt she wore with them had a tear in the collar and the logo of the University of Michigan. I was getting a glimpse of what Callie Spencer must have looked like as a law student in her twenties.

"You followed me," I said. A brilliant deduction. I could see her silver Ford parked behind her on the street. I'd been so preoccupied with tailing Jay Casterbridge, I hadn't noticed I had a tail of my own.

"You followed my husband here," she said. "Why?"

"I'm looking for Lucy Navarro."

Her tone had been serious up till now, so her laugh came as a surprise.

"You think Jay has her?" she said.

"I should've thought of it before. Whoever took Lucy felt threatened by her. She's been asking questions about the Great Lakes Bank robbery. What was Jay doing seventeen years ago?"

"Law school," she said, stepping close so she could study my face. "You think Jay was the fifth bank robber?"

"Why not? Floyd Lambeau recruited idealistic students. He took pleasure in the idea that he could corrupt them. I think he would have gotten a kick out of recruiting a senator's son as a getaway driver." I waited a beat. "It explains the cover-up too."

"The cover-up?"

"Your father never gave any description of the driver. Maybe that's because a United States senator asked him not to."

She reached up to touch the tear in her collar. "That's an intriguing theory. Am I in on this plot too, or do I get a pass?"

"I haven't sorted it all out yet," I said. "But you should go home."

"Why?"

I pointed at the house. "I'm going in there. You won't want to be around."

That brought another laugh. "I don't think I can stay away."

"I'm not kidding."

"Neither am I. If my husband's holding a reporter captive in there, I think I'd like to know." She stepped out of her sandals and started walking barefoot along the sidewalk toward the house. I had to hurry to catch up to her.

"Should we burst in," she said, "or should we look around a little first?"

I started to respond, but she silenced me with a finger raised to her lips. I followed her in the dark, passing the front of the house, pausing for a moment at the edge of the driveway.

There was still just one lighted window on the side of the house, near the back. The curtains were parted slightly, leaving a gap wide enough to see through, if you could get close. You'd need something to stand on though; the window was above eye level.

Callie had come to the same realization. She touched my arm. Pointed to a plastic recycling bin leaning against the side of the garage.

She waited by her husband's car while I retrieved the bin and set it top-down in the grass beneath the window. I glanced a question at her and she gestured in answer: *After you.*

A last look around. No one on the street. The house next door seemed deserted.

I took my time planting my left foot on the bin, stepped up, steadied myself.

Through the space between the curtains I saw a kitchen counter. Cabinets in dark wood, stainless-steel dishwasher. Granite countertops. A radio mounted under one of the cabinets. I could hear it faintly through the closed window: the BBC World News on NPR.

Jay Casterbridge stood near the dishwasher. Oxford shirt and gray slacks. He had a woman with him—but not Lucy Navarro. The woman was tall and thin. I could have counted her ribs if I wanted to, because Casterbridge had her blouse off and was making good progress on her bra. He slipped the last hook free and peeled it off—an insubstantial thing, white and plain—and ducked his head to kiss her breasts. His hands moved down her back and underneath the waistband of her skirt. He lifted her off her feet, spun her around, and sat her on the counter.

I'd seen enough. I stepped down soundlessly to the grass. When I looked to Callie Spencer, she wore the kind of carefully composed expression that told me she had a good idea of what I'd seen. I started to shake my head as if that might dissuade her, but she had already put one bare foot up on the bin.

I helped her up and laid a hand on the small of her back to steady her. She needed the support; she had to stand on tiptoe. I waited, listening to her breathing. She stayed up there for a few seconds, long enough to take things in. And long enough for me to realize my mistake. I wasn't the one she'd been following tonight. That should have been obvious. I'd parked on her street and watched her house, but she would've had no reason to know I was there. She had been following her husband.

She braced a hand on my shoulder getting down, said nothing, walked off barefoot along the driveway. I left the recycling bin in the grass and went after her. Back at her car she stepped into her sandals and turned to me. Too dark to read anything in her eyes. She looked away and rounded the car to the driver's side. "I'm going home," she said.

Not quite an invitation, but as close as I was likely to get.

By the time I walked to my car she had disappeared around the block. But I didn't need to follow her; I knew the way. The moon put in an appearance on Bedford Road, a sliver high over the roof of the cottage. Callie's Ford sat in the gravel drive.

I rolled east past the cottage and left my car on the street. Admired the neighbors' manicured lawns in the light of the streetlamps. The same light fell on the vines along the cottage walls, sending curled shadows over the brick. Callie had left the door ajar.

I closed it behind me, loud enough for her to hear. She stood by a leather sofa with her back to me, her head bowed. When I got close she spun around. Lips pressed together, a woman trying not to cry.

I reached for her and she came to me, hid her face against my shoulder. Her hair silky and smelling of strawberries. I touched a palm to the back of her neck and felt the heat of her skin. She got her arms around me and held on with a strength that surprised me.

I lost track of how long we stood like that. I felt the damp of tears against my shoulder. Pain where her arm squeezed against the wound in my side. I moved my palm down between her shoulder blades and rubbed her back through the thin fabric of her T-shirt.

Eventually Callie pulled away and wiped her face. I watched her transformation. She stood straight and lifted her chin. She was locking away whatever vulnerability she had shown me.

"You shouldn't have come here," she said in a dry, empty voice. "I don't know you. I can't afford to trust you. If you think I'm going to fall into bed with you, you should think again. I've got better judgment than my husband, and more self-control. I'm not some frail little thing who needs to be consoled."

She crossed her arms defensively. "You put on a good act," she said. "So very kind. I don't need your sympathy. I don't like you. You know something now that can hurt me. I'm sure that makes you very happy. I hate it. If you've got any decency at all—and I suppose I'm crazy to think you do—you'll get out of here and forget all about what just happened."

She kept her eyes on mine for most of the speech, but at the end she looked away. I wondered which thing I was supposed to forget—our embrace or her husband's infidelity.

I said, "I'm afraid I didn't hear a word of that. So if any of it was meant for me, you'll have to go through it again."

Her chin dropped a little and I thought I could see her shoulders relax. "I don't think I will," she said with a bitter twist of a smile. "Do you want a drink? I've got beer or wine. Or I could mix you something."

"Beer's fine," I said.

She took longer than she needed in the kitchen, digging around in the refrigerator, opening and closing cabinet doors. I left her to it, taking a seat on one of the two sofas. She brought my beer in a glass, and another for herself. She drank a sip of it and settled onto the other sofa. I watched her getting comfortable, tucking her right leg beneath her.

"Who is she, the woman?" I said. "Do you know?"

She frowned over the rim of her glass. "I'm not sure I want to tell you."

"Suit yourself," I said, leaning back against the cushions.

Another sip of beer and she said, "Julia Trent. She's his law partner."

"Did you know it was going on?"

"No. But something usually is, with Jay. That's why I followed him tonight. He told me he was going for a drive to clear his head." She tapped a finger against her glass. "Julia Trent. I never suspected her. I've always thought she's sort of a dried-up husk. The last one was at least younger than me, and prettier. That made it easier to take. What are you smiling at?"

"You can't expect me to let that go by," I said. "Younger and prettier. I'll believe the first, if you say so. Not the second."

"You're a charmer. But it's true. Jay's always had an eye for pretty women. And he doesn't try very hard to resist. It's his one vice."

I took a long drink of beer and set the glass on a side table.

"Are you sure he doesn't have any others?"

Her brown eyes narrowed. "You're not still thinking he's the missing bank robber."

"I haven't ruled him out. You said he was in law school at the time."

"That's right. Harvard Law. A long way from Sault Sainte Marie."

"Did you know him then?"

She shook her head. "I met him later."

"So you can't tell me where he was on the day of the Great Lakes robbery. When did you meet him?"

"A couple years after the robbery, during one of the senator's campaigns. My father turned up at a lot of political rallies at the time. He was popular with the police unions. His endorsement was worth something. So the senator asked him to speak at some of his campaign events, and I tagged along. That's where I met Jay."

I tilted my head. "And when you married him—what did your father think of that?"

"He thought I was too young. He advised me to wait."

"That's interesting."

"Just the way you would if your daughter was about to marry a bank robber," she said wryly. "Look, you're wrong about Jay. I know his faults. They're not the ones you're thinking of. He didn't drive a getaway car for Floyd Lambeau. And if he did, my father wouldn't have covered it up. Not even as a favor for a senator."

"How can you be so sure?"

"My father has integrity."

I reached for my glass and took another drink. I didn't see any point in arguing with a daughter about her father's integrity. We watched each other for a while. Her eyes looked guileless, her lips made a pleasant line.

I decided to press my luck. "Let's talk about Floyd Lambeau," I said.

Her expression darkened, but only a shade. "What about him?"

"Henry Kormoran said he saw you with Lambeau at the Great Lakes Bank."

"We've been over this—"

"I know. Kormoran claimed he recognized you by your gorgeous smile, but your teeth were crooked back then. I've been thinking about that. Memory's a funny thing. If he thought he remembered seeing you, his mind might have filled in the details. If he got that one detail wrong, well, that doesn't mean you weren't there."

Callie gave me a warm, open look. "Do you honestly think I helped Floyd Lambeau case the Great Lakes Bank?"

I waved the question away. "Alan Beckett asked me the same thing. He was spinning me just like you are."

"How am I spinning you?"

"Kormoran never claimed that you cased the bank," I said. "All he said was that he saw you there with Lambeau. Maybe it was a chance encounter. Or maybe Lambeau asked you to meet him. I think the situation would have appealed to him—having the sheriff's daughter there while he cased the bank. He would have seen the poetry in it."

She didn't deny it. Her expression didn't change. I said, "If that's the way it was, it puts you in an impossible situation. On the one hand, you did nothing wrong. On the other, you've kept quiet for seventeen years about what really happened, and that makes you look guilty. And along comes Lucy Navarro, dredging everything up. That makes her a threat to your political career."

"If you think I did something to Lucy Navarro—"

I raised a hand to cut her off. "I don't. But I think Alan Beckett might have."

"That's not something I would allow—"

"He would have done it without telling you. He would have kept you out of it."

I thought I saw a flicker of doubt in her eyes, but I could have imagined it. "No," she said. "He wouldn't do that." I waited for something more, maybe a defense of Beckett's integrity. I didn't get it. I watched her rise and knew our talk was at an end.

She led me to the door and I thanked her for the drink and told her good night. She didn't answer me. She let me get halfway down the walk before she said, "I'm sure you're mistaken."

I GOT HOME after midnight and found Elizabeth sitting on the floor with the pages of her timeline scattered around her. A Mozart concerto played softly on the stereo. I sat beside her and slipped my arm around her shoulders. She turned to me for a kiss. We took our time about it.

"You taste like beer," she said when it was done, "and you smell like strawberries."

"I had a beer with Callie Spencer," I said. "That's probably her shampoo you're smelling."

The corners of her mouth curled up. "Is that right?"

"I let her cry on my shoulder."

"Aren't you gallant. What did she have to cry about?"

"Her husband's having an affair." With Mozart in the background, I spent a few minutes going over the details of my night.

When I finished, Elizabeth said, "So now you think Jay Casterbridge is the fifth robber? And he abducted Lucy?"

"Either that or Beckett took her," I said. "I could go either way."

Elizabeth stared thoughtfully across the room. "I think you're wrong about Beckett."

"I don't see why. On Wednesday he tried to bribe Lucy to give up her investigation. She rejected his offer. That night, she went missing."

Elizabeth started collecting the pages of her timeline. "That's just it," she said. "It happened too fast. When she rejected him, he had options. He could come back with a better offer. He wouldn't jump right into a kidnapping. I think it must have been someone else."

"We're back to Jay Casterbridge, then," I said.

She looked unconvinced. "Jay Casterbridge came here Wednesday night, because he'd gone through his wife's files and found Lark's letter."

"Exactly. Lark's been going after the Great Lakes robbers. If Casterbridge was one of them, he'd have a reason to want Lark caught."

"Only if Lark knew he was one of them."

"Maybe Casterbridge wasn't sure what Lark knew," I said. "What time did he leave here Wednesday night?"

"Around eleven-fifteen."

"So he would have had time to get to the Winston Hotel."

Elizabeth rounded up the last of her pages. "I still don't buy it. Jay Casterbridge could barely bring himself to give me Lark's letter. He was afraid his wife would find out he had gone behind her back. I can't see him engineering a kidnapping."

CHAPTER 42

Anthony Lark slept late on Saturday. He drove out of South Bend just after noon.

He had his hunting rifle in the trunk of the Chevy, along with Walter Delacorte's pistol. Paul Rhiner's pistol was hidden beneath a newspaper on the seat beside him. Lark was wearing a suit bought off the rack the day before. Charcoal gray over a white dress shirt and a black silk tie.

Delacorte's money clip rested in his pocket. Even after the clothes and the hotel, it still held almost three thousand dollars.

Lark traveled east through Indiana on Route 20, turning north near Middlebury and crossing into Michigan around one o'clock. On Route 131, a few miles south of Three Rivers, he spotted flashing lights: a sheriff's cruiser had pulled over a speeder. Lark moved into the left lane and watched the lights recede in his rearview mirror.

He made himself stay on 131 for another twenty-five miles, then took Stadium Drive into Kalamazoo. He stopped at the first big discount store he came to—a Walmart Supercenter—and broke one of Delacorte's fifties to pay for a six-pack of bottled water and a set of screwdrivers.

Back in the car he opened a bottle of water and tried to decide if he felt a headache coming on. He shook a capsule of Imitrex into his palm, considered it, and then dropped it into his pocket. He keyed the ignition and cruised up and down the aisles of cars until he found one just like his own—a gray Chevy Malibu.

Parking three spaces away, he used one of the screwdrivers to remove the license plate from his rear bumper and swap it with the plate from the other Malibu.

From the Walmart he drove south looking for I-94, which would take him to Ann Arbor and Sutton Bell. He figured it would take about an hour and a half. The state police would be watching for him, but the new license plate might be enough to throw them off. The only thing better would be to have someone else driving.

He came to an intersection and eased on the brake. The red light must have mesmerized him, because the tap on his passenger window made him flinch.

He turned to see an unshaven man with wild salt-and-pepper hair and a camouflage jacket. The man held a cardboard sign that read HOMELESS VET—WILL WORK FOR FOOD.

To Lark, the letters were the color of grass in springtime.

"YOU DON'T LOOK comfortable back there."

"I'm comfortable," Lark said.

He lay curled on his side in the backseat, with a blanket from the trunk rolled up for a pillow. His suit jacket hung over the front passenger seat. Through the window he could see blue sky and the tops of trees rolling past.

"The radio bother you?" his companion asked. "I can turn it down."

They were traveling east on I-94, with a baseball game playing on an AM station.

"It's fine," Lark said.

"I don't want to keep you awake, if you're worn out."

Lark could see the back of the driver's head, a snarl of salt-and-pepper hair. He didn't believe the man was homeless, or a veteran. A genuinely homeless person would have a bedroll or a rucksack, or something. More than a camouflage jacket and a cardboard sign.

"I'm all right," Lark said. "Don't worry about me."

He didn't intend to fall asleep; he didn't trust HomeLess Vet that far. He'd given the man one of Delacorte's hundred-dollar bills, and promised him another when they reached Ann Arbor. He'd been careful not to let him see the money clip. But he'd noticed something in the man's eyes, a spark of cunning and greed. HomeLess Vet hoped to get his hands on more than two hundred dollars.

Lark had hidden Paul Rhiner's pistol under the floor mat behind the driver's seat, within easy reach.

"What kind of business did you say you were in?"

Lark hadn't said, but now he thought it over. "Advertising," he decided.

"No kidding," said HomeLess Vet. "Like commercials, on TV?"

"Billboards," Lark said.

That bought him some silence. What is there to say about billboards?

On the radio someone hit a long fly ball to center field and someone else caught it. Lark surveyed the litter of beer bottles on the floor behind the passenger seat. He'd bought a six-pack on Wednesday. Two of them were still unopened. They would be too warm to drink, though he was tempted.

Amid the bottles he saw a notebook. Not his own; this was a spiral-bound pad. It took him a moment to remember that it had come from Lucy Navarro's yellow Beetle. He had found it in her glove compartment and stuffed it in his pocket. Then tossed it back here. He reached for it now and flipped open the cover.

"There's a billboard," HomeLess Vet said. "Is that one of yours?"

There was a touch of gravel in the man's voice. Not so bad, really. But Lark didn't want to listen to it for the whole trip.

"Is it okay if we don't talk?" Lark said. "I need to catch up on some reading."

HomeLess Vet nudged up the volume of the radio. "You're the boss."

THEY STOPPED FOR GAS at a station outside of Jackson. Lark worked the pump himself. He was tired of lying in the backseat; his neck had begun to ache. He sent HomeLess Vet inside to pay, giving him a fifty-dollar bill. The same spark lit up the man's eyes when he took the money.

Lark considered driving off and leaving him there, but he'd begun to think he might be able to use him to get to Sutton Bell.

THEY MERGED ONTO the interstate again, HomeLess Vet behind the wheel. Lark sat in the front passenger seat now, with his suit jacket on. The day was too warm for it, but he switched on the air-conditioning to compensate.

He had moved Rhiner's pistol into the jacket's inside pocket.

The headache he'd been fearing since Kalamazoo began to curl itself around behind his eyes. He popped one of his Imitrex pills and washed it down with bottled water.

On the radio the baseball game ended. HomeLess Vet dialed around to a country station.

Lark had Lucy Navarro's notepad open on his lap. The pages were covered with notes on her conversations with Henry Kormoran and Terry Dawtrey. Lark was unimpressed with Kormoran's story about seeing Callie Spencer with Floyd Lambeau at the Great Lakes Bank. But Lucy's conversation with Dawtrey intrigued him.

Part of it seemed absurd—the idea that Lambeau was Callie's real father. Pure fantasy. But then, at the end, there was the suggestion that Dawtrey knew the name of the fifth robber.

You come back, we'll talk again. Maybe I give you the driver.

Lark had thought a lot about the fifth robber. He was as guilty as the others. His name belonged on Lark's list. But you do the best you can. You can't fix everything.

Something Lark's father used to say.

Maybe I give you the driver. Lucy Navarro had written the words in blue ink, but to Lark they looked red. They breathed on the page.

Well, he didn't know the name of the driver. Maybe Dawtrey knew, but Dawtrey was dead. Lark had Sutton Bell to deal with, and that would have to be enough.

You have to accept your limits.

That one came from Dr. Kenneally, though Lark's father would have agreed with the sentiment.

AROUND CHELSEA, fifteen miles shy of Ann Arbor, Lark figured out how he would kill Sutton Bell.

He would do it at Bell's house, with the rifle. He sketched a diagram of the neighborhood on a page of Lucy Navarro's notebook: Bell's street running west to east. The house a box at the end of a row of boxes. To the north, an open space. To the south, another row of houses on the other side of the street. To the east, a playground built for young children: swings and plastic slides. A street running north to south bordered the playground.

From the playground you'd have a line of sight to Bell's front yard. The playground was where Lark would need to be with his rifle.

There would be cops at the house. They would have to be distracted. Bell would have to be lured out into his yard.

Lark punched the off button on the radio and turned to HomeLess Vet.

"Do you think you could fake a seizure?"

HOMELESS VET CAME OUT of the Meijer gas station carrying an armload of newspapers. Lark watched him from behind the wheel of the Chevy. They had exited the interstate at Ann Arbor–Saline Road. Bell's house was less than three miles away.

HomeLess Vet dumped the papers on the backseat and slid in beside Lark.

"Okay, boss," the man said. "You've got your papers. Now you can fill me in about your plan."

Lark showed him the sketch of Bell's neighborhood.

"This is where we're going. Mallard Drive. I'll let you off here." He tapped his finger on the western end of Bell's street. "You'll take the papers, and you'll walk along like you're delivering them. Toss them on the porches, not on the lawns."

"Okay."

"You don't have to hit every house. Just enough to make it look good. Be sure to save one for the last house. Here." Lark tapped the box on the end. Bell's house.

"That's the target?" said HomeLess Vet. "That's where I do my act?"

"Right. You should go up to the porch. Drop the paper. Make some noise. Yell something."

"What do you want me to yell?"

"Anything. It doesn't matter."

"What about this—what if I yell 'Attica!' like Al Pacino in that movie?"

"That's perfect," Lark said. "Do that. The guy who lives there'll come out. Then you fall on the ground and have your seizure."

"Where will you be?"

By the playground with a rifle, Lark thought.

"Don't worry about me," he said. "I'll show up when the time is right."

"Screw that. Don't try to keep me in the dark. What's the con? Is it an insurance scam?"

An undercurrent of anger in HomeLess Vet's voice. Lark answered him calmly. "Yes, it's an insurance scam."

"But what's the angle? Those insurance companies don't like to part with their money. They won't pay a claim if they can find a way to weasel out of it."

"We won't need to file a claim," Lark said, improvising. "The threat of a claim'll be enough."

"How come?"

"Because the guy who lives in that house doesn't like to deal with insurance companies. He doesn't want the attention. He definitely doesn't want to go into court."

"You know him?"

"I know about him," said Lark in a sly voice. "I've done research. He'll pay."

HomeLess Vet broke into a grin. "Research. Ha. I had a feeling about you. That line about billboard advertising. I never bought that."

"No?"

"Hell no. How much do you think we'll get out of this guy?"

"I figure we ask for ten thousand."

"No way."

"I'm not saying we get that much. But that's what we ask for."

"What's the split? Fifty-fifty?"

"I was thinking seventy-thirty," Lark said, trying to seem affronted. "I did the research."

"Fifty-fifty," said HomeLess Vet. "I'm the one puttin' myself out there."

A reluctant pause. "Fine. So you're in?"

"Not so fast. I need something up front. In case it doesn't go like you planned."

While he was alone in the car, Lark had separated some bills from Delacorte's money clip. He passed two of them to HomeLess Vet.

"That's the hundred I owe you for driving me here," Lark said, "and another hundred as an advance."

"I'd be happier with five hundred."

"I bet you would. A hundred's fair."

"Split the difference. Three hundred."

Lark closed the notepad and tossed it on the dash. He drew out two more hundreds from the pocket of his jacket and handed them to HomeLess Vet.

"Are you ready to do this?"

Driving south, they passed a farmhouse with a barn painted the color of rust. A trio of crows perched on the peak of the roof. Anthony Lark powered down the Chevy's windows without thinking. The wind tossed his tie over his shoulder.

He closed his eyes, only for a second. When he opened them he focused on the bright yellow lines running into the distance. If he didn't turn his head, he could imagine Susanna Marten beside him in the car. He remembered a day in college when he had driven her out to the countryside. She needed to photograph a barn—it was for one of her art projects.

They found one with weeds growing up around it and the roof fallen in. She traipsed around it with her camera, shooting it from every angle.

Afterward they took a walk along a stream, looked for turtles sunning themselves by the water. He drove her home that day with the windows rolled down and his arm around her, her head on his shoulder.

Lark thought the memory should make him sad. He didn't feel sad. He was coming to the end of the Great Lakes Bank robbers. Bell would be the last. There might be a fifth out there somewhere, but he wasn't Lark's problem, because you have to accept your limits.

His headache had gone. The Imitrex must have done its work. He would finish Bell, and there wouldn't be any more headaches. Because the headaches were a symptom.

You'll have them until you deal with the underlying problem.

Now he was dealing with the underlying problem. He wouldn't have to lie in bed tonight with ice against his forehead. He hadn't needed ice for the past few days. He must be doing something right.

He came to the sign for Mallard Drive. The letters were the color of the weeds around that barn years ago. He turned onto Bell's street and slowed, and there was Bell's house less than three blocks away. A patrol car sitting in front. That meant Bell would be home.

Lark pulled over to the curb and held his foot on the brake.

"That's the house?" HomeLess Vet said beside him. "The one on the end?"

"That's it."

"There's a cop car in front of it."

"I know. But that doesn't change things."

"It sure as hell does."

"Take the newspapers and do it just like we said. When you get down there, make some noise. It's no good if he doesn't come out."

"I'm not going down there if there's cops. Are you crazy?"

Lark winced at the word. "I'm not crazy."

"What kind of neighborhood is this, anyway?" said HomeLess Vet. "It doesn't look like anyone here would have ten thousand dollars to burn."

Lark eased off the brake and rolled closer. "You agreed to do this," he said.

"Not with cops. No fuckin' way."

"All right, then. Get out of the car."

HomeLess Vet laughed at him. "You're not leaving me here. Take me back to the interstate. I can hitch a ride from there."

Lark bore down on the brake and drew the pistol from the inside pocket of his jacket.

"Get out of the car," he said again.

"Jesus Christ! Put that away."

"Out," Lark said, slipping off the safety. Less than two blocks away now. He didn't dare go any closer. A door of the patrol car opened and a cop stepped out.

"Jesus!" HomeLess Vet said, climbing out onto the curb. He stood there with one hand on the door of the Chevy. "You're a fuckin' psycho. You know that?"

Lark held the pistol steady. "The man in that house is a nurse," he said evenly. "He'll be able to help you."

HomeLess Vet slammed the door and backed away, looking confused.

"He's a nurse," Lark repeated. Then he lined up the sights with HomeLess Vet's shoulder and fired through the open window.

CHAPTER 43

Lark dropped the pistol onto the seat beside him and slammed the Chevy into reverse. At the end of the block he jerked the wheel to the left, pointing the car south. HomeLess Vet had gone down on one knee, but he was struggling to his feet again, clutching his shoulder.

There were two cops in front of Bell's house now, one talking into a radio handset, the other starting to jog toward HomeLess Vet.

Lark sped away south on a street called Cottonwood, out of sight of the cops. He came to an intersection with Aspen and turned east. He was already rehearsing things in his mind: popping the trunk, taking out the rifle, setting the crosshairs on Sutton Bell.

He raised the windows and looked for a sign for Heather Drive. Found it and turned north. Heather Drive bordered the playground.

The last house on the left before the playground was a two-story place with white vinyl siding. He parked the car in front of it. Got the rifle from the trunk.

Farther down the street, a shirtless man rode a lawn mower in a circle around a magnolia tree. A woman poured seeds into a bird feeder.

At the playground a young mother in a summer dress pushed a boy on a swing.

Anthony Lark, in his suit and tie, with the rifle held at his side, walked unhurriedly past the swings toward an empty wooden bench.

He could see Sutton Bell's house. The patrol car in front. HomeLess Vet half sitting on the hood of the car, with one of the cops looking at his shoulder. A dark oval of blood on the camouflage jacket.

HomeLess Vet shaking his salt-and-pepper head from side to side, yelling something Lark couldn't hear—not from this distance, not over the sound of the lawn mower.

The second cop hurrying toward Bell's house. The front door opening. Sutton Bell himself coming down the steps, holding something white—Lark thought first of gauze, of bandages, but it looked like plain white towels.

The second cop trying to stop Bell, trying to hustle him back inside.

Bell brushing past the cop.

Lark sat sideways on the bench, resting his arm on the back of it, aiming the rifle. Out of the corner of his eye, he saw the young mother pull her boy off the swing and hustle him away.

Looking through the scope, Lark saw one of the cops toss the camouflage jacket onto the ground. He saw the gray T-shirt HomeLess Vet had on underneath, the crimson stain at the shoulder.

Sutton Bell with his white towels. He pressed one of them against the wound.

Lark moved the crosshairs to Bell's neck, to his face in profile. He fixed them on a spot just behind Bell's ear.

The crosshairs swayed. The buzz of the lawn mower was loud, but it didn't bother Lark. He took a breath. Laid his finger on the trigger. The crosshairs held still.

His vision was clear. His brow felt cool. Nothing twisted behind his eyes.

The headaches are a symptom.

He didn't have a headache. He'd felt one coming on, and he'd taken a pill, and it had gone away. The pill worked.

The sound of the lawn mower faded from his mind. The crosshairs drifted along Sutton Bell's cheek.

The headaches are a symptom. You'll have them until you deal with the underlying problem.

Lark didn't have a headache. Not now. And not in the past few days.

Because the pills were working.

The crosshairs drifted into empty space.

Now or never, Lark thought.

He moved them back to the spot behind Bell's ear.

Do it now, or lose your chance.

His finger tensed on the trigger.

The pills—

"DID YOU HEAR what I said about the pills?"

On Saturday afternoon Elizabeth and Shan cruised along a pitted street in a neighborhood of bland brick houses. They had driven back to Dearborn to work their way through Helen Lark's list of her son's friends.

They'd already spoken to half a dozen men in their late twenties or early thirties, unambitious and underemployed, living in ratty apartments. None seemed to have been very close to Anthony Lark. They didn't strike Elizabeth as the kind of men who would take you in if you were on the run. She didn't expect to find Lark hiding out with one of them.

But there were more names on the list. She still hoped that one of them might tell her something useful. From behind the wheel of the Crown Victoria she looked out at houses of dull red brick. Shan was in the passenger seat beside her. He'd been texting back and forth with his son, who was pitching in a Little League game today.

Elizabeth had been listening to a classical station on the radio, her mind wandering along with the melody of a Bach sonata. She noticed when Shan's cell phone rang, but she didn't pay attention to his conversation.

"Lizzie," he said in a raised voice. "Did you hear me—about the pills?"

She touched the power button on the radio. "What pills?"

"The pills I found in Lark's apartment," he said. "They were in a metal tin with a handwritten label that said 'Imitrex.' But the lab says they're not Imitrex. They're vitamin D."

She could still hear Bach's music in her head.

"What do you think that means? Lark got his pills mixed up?"

"I don't know," said Shan. "But if he's taking vitamin D for headaches, he's probably not getting much relief."

. . .

At twenty after four I heard a siren, distant but coming closer. I saw a chaos of lights in my side mirror and pulled over to the side of the road. The ambulance filled up the mirror until it sped past me heading south.

That morning I had returned to the house on Fernwood, the one Callie Spencer and I had visited the night before. I didn't really believe I'd find Lucy Navarro there, but I couldn't shake the image of her lying in a basement somewhere. My dreams had been filled with stairs running down into darkness.

At the house on Fernwood I walked up the driveway scanning the ground for stones. I found one and was about to break a window when I remembered the FOR RENT sign on the lawn. I used my cell to dial the number for Casterbridge Realty.

A rental agent showed up half an hour later, a cheery woman in a red blazer with a lot of platinum blond hair. She took me through the place room by room, showed me the attic, the basement, and the garage. I saw nothing to suggest that Lucy had been there.

I spent the early afternoon at my desk at *Gray Streets*, pretending to work on the story about the detective and the heiress. But I couldn't get my mind off Lucy. I had nothing but hunches about what might have happened to her and no ideas about where to look for her. About all I could say was that her disappearance had something to do with the Great Lakes Bank robbery. I knew of two people who had been at the bank and were still around to tell the tale: Sutton Bell and Harlan Spencer.

The coin I tossed came up heads, so at twenty after four when the ambulance roared past me, I was driving south on Ann Arbor–Saline Road, bound for Sutton Bell's house.

When I reached Bell's neighborhood I saw people gathered on the sidewalks in small groups. I saw the ambulance at the end of the street, and as I drove closer I watched the EMTs lift a gurney into the back. They slammed the doors and drove off, leaving two patrol cars behind, and four uniformed cops on the lawn of Bell's house.

I parked a block away and walked over. One of the cops was a kid named Fielder—Elizabeth and I had seen him Monday night, when the senator had his car accident. Fielder stood talking to a woman in a summer dress who kept pointing at a playground in the distance.

She held fast to the hand of a young boy who acted like he wanted to drag her away. "Push me," I heard him say. "I want you to push me on the swing." She managed to quiet him down, and after a time the two of them walked off, but not toward the swings.

Fielder gave me a neutral stare when I approached, but then he remembered me.

"What happened here?" I asked him. "Was it Lark?"

He hesitated, making up his mind about whether he should answer.

"It must have been," he said at last. "He shot a vagrant, a guy he had picked up on the road. And while we were dealing with that, he drove around to the playground there and got his rifle out. Not a bad plan, and Bell walked right into it."

Fielder glanced at the house. "Bell comes out to help. Florence goddamn Nightingale. Brings *towels*. I tell him to get back inside, but naturally he won't. Stupid son of a bitch."

His tone made me fear the worst. "Is Bell dead?"

"He's fine," said Fielder gruffly. "Turns out he's a lucky son of a bitch too."

"What happened? Lark missed?"

"He never took the shot."

CHAPTER 44

They had changed the lock on the door of his old apartment.

Lark expected to find something more, some kind of official seal from the police department or bands of yellow crime-scene tape. There was nothing like that, but his key wouldn't turn in the lock.

He got his tire iron from the Chevy and went around to the bedroom window. This was the way Walter Delacorte had broken in. When Lark tried the window it slid open easily; the latch hadn't been repaired.

He climbed down into the room and stood by his mattress for a moment. His clothes were gone from the closet, his books and magazines no longer littered the floor.

He looked down at the tire iron in his hand and remembered Charlie Dawtrey's cabin in the woods. He had used the iron to beat the old man to death. Lifting it up, he stared at the bend in the metal. He could see streaks of dried blood.

He dropped the iron, feeling queasy. Bowed his head and breathed through his nose until the feeling passed.

He looked around. His old pills should have been on the floor by the mattress, but he didn't see the tin there. The police must have taken it.

He checked the bathroom and the kitchen, just to be sure. No pills. An odd smell in the air, slightly metallic. It might have been from the blood that stained the carpet: Delacorte's blood in the living room, Rhiner's in the hall.

The stains didn't bother Lark, not like the streaks on the tire iron.

He ran the water cold in the kitchen sink and drank some from the palm of his hand.

You don't need to find the pills, he thought. *You know what happened with the pills.*

As he shook his hand dry, his glance fell on a yellow sheet of paper. His neighbor's flyer: LOST CAT. The letters a cool blue-green, the color Lark associated with calm, with peace.

He left by the door, found the hallway outside deserted. No reason to think she'd be home on a Saturday afternoon, less reason to think she'd let him in. He fiddled with the cuffs of his shirt until half an inch of white showed at the ends of the charcoal gray sleeves of his jacket. He smoothed his tie.

Should have brought flowers, he thought.

Ten seconds from his knock until the metal door drew inward. She was listening to her iPod, just like the last time. She wore a tank top and shorts, as if she'd been exercising. She was slow to recognize him in the suit, but then her eyes went wide.

Surprise, he thought. *Not fear.* She started to shut the door, but her heart wasn't in it. He could have stopped it. He let it close. Waited for the sound of the dead bolt.

When he didn't hear it, he called her name.

The click of a chain lock sliding into place, and the door opened again, just a few inches.

"Mira," he said.

"Anthony." She held the earbuds of the iPod in her fingers.

"What were you listening to?" he asked.

She frowned at the question. "Anthony, the police are looking for you."

"I know."

"They're saying—"

"I know what they're saying. Do you have a car?"

She had a worry line between her eyebrows. He watched it deepen.

"I can't help you get away," she said, "if that's what you're asking."

"Doesn't matter," he said. "A plane is better anyway."

"A plane?"

"Have you seen the redwood trees?"

"Anthony, you sound—"

"Crazy, I know." He raised his hands in a gesture of surrender. "Story of my life. If you fly into Eureka, California, and rent a car there, you can drive north to Prairie Creek State Park. They have redwoods. You've got to see them. I went there once with a girl I used to know. It's as far away from home as I've ever been."

He watched her try to make sense of him. Her eyes a deeper brown than the color of her skin. He thought he could see flecks of gold in them, like the gold of the chain that stretched across the opening between the door and the frame.

"Anthony, I can help you," she said. "We can find you a lawyer."

He moved closer to her. "I don't know if it's possible to make a new start," he said, almost in a whisper. "For a long time I didn't think so. But if it's possible, then that's the place to do it. Prairie Creek State Park. Remember that. I won't be able to fly, so it'll take me a few days. I'll look for you there."

"Anthony—"

"You should see them, the redwoods. We tried to take pictures, but they're so big they won't fit inside the frame." He let out a breath. "Look, I know how I sound, and I know what you must think of me. I've killed three people. I wish I could tell you it's not true. I killed a man named Derek Everly, because he took away someone I loved. I don't regret that one. The others—I'm not sure anymore."

He watched her close the door, heard the chain slip free, saw the door open again.

"Anthony," she said gently, "you need help."

He shut his eyes. "I'm done with all that. I want a new start. Prairie Creek. I'll understand if you're not there."

"I can't—"

"Don't say yes or no right now." He opened his eyes and stepped back. "You should close the door. You don't want the cat to get out."

She glanced back into the apartment. "He's hiding under a chair."

"You can't be too careful," Lark said. "And I can't stay. So there's nothing to do but close the door."

"I'LL TELL YOU what I'm looking forward to," Sutton Bell said. "The day I can open the curtains again."

We were sitting at a maplewood table in his dining room. The police were still outside, keeping watch in case Lark should come back. Bell had agreed to see me when I told him I wanted to talk about Lucy Navarro.

At the other end of the table lay a pad of newsprint open to a crayon drawing of horses in a field. The only light in the room came from a hanging lamp. Heavy curtains were drawn tight over the windows.

"You must think I'm foolish for staying here," Bell said. He had turned his chair to face me. His left arm rested on the table, the hand in a brace.

Before I could answer, he went on. "I probably am. I convinced my wife to take time off from her job. She's staying with a friend out of state. She's got our daughter with her."

"You could have gone with them," I said.

"I almost did, but then I thought it over. If someone wanted to kill you, would you want to be with your wife and daughter, or as far away from them as possible?"

"I see your point."

He used his good hand to brush his long hair out of his eyes. "Apart from that, I have obligations here. The clinic where I work is short-staffed as it is. They can't afford to give me an indefinite leave. And they don't mind having the police watch the place. The patients there can be a little rough around the edges, especially late at night." After a pause, he added, "The way I look at it, the clinic took a chance, hiring me. I don't want to let them down."

I nodded and watched him turn to stare at the wall opposite the windows, at a cluster of photographs hanging there. The largest was of his daughter, a tow-headed girl with blue eyes.

"The police suggested I stay at a hotel," he said. "But this house has an alarm system, and there's a car out front whenever I'm here. The truth is, I feel like I need to be here. Otherwise it's like I'm abandoning the place. Does that make sense?"

"It does to me."

Bell studied the photographs and seemed to search for something more to say. I thought he looked at ease in his surroundings—a decent man living out a plain, middle-class life, a man who cared for his family and didn't want to abandon his house. Then I remembered what he had been once, and a question occurred to me. I found myself asking it out loud.

"How did you get mixed up in the Great Lakes robbery?"

He turned back to me, shifting uneasily in his chair. "I was twenty. I was an idiot."

"Most twenty-year-olds don't try to rob a bank," I said. "There must have been more to it. I know Floyd Lambeau recruited you. How did he convince you?"

His head moved side to side. "You wouldn't understand."

"Try me."

I watched him thinking about it. After a time he said, "The thing about Floyd . . . he never tried to convince me to do anything. He had a way of sitting back and listening. And he had kind eyes." Bell hesitated. "I'm not expressing this well."

"Go on."

He thought about it some more. Then: "Everyone knows now that Floyd Lambeau was nothing but a con artist. Of course I didn't know that when I met him. I was in college. He was a guest lecturer in one of my classes—a course on Native American culture. He was only there for three or four weeks, talking about living conditions on Indian reservations. A lot of them are plagued by high unemployment. Alcoholism. The kind of poverty you usually find in Third World countries. The class met in the evening, and a few people would get together afterward, and Floyd would take us out to a coffeehouse or a restaurant. The first time I went, I did it to impress a girl I liked. But later she dropped out, and I kept going. I liked to listen to Floyd talk. I had no experience of the things he talked about, but he was obviously very intelligent. And he was soft-spoken. He seemed humble."

Bell scratched the side of his face with his good hand. "One night the others in the group had left and it was just me and Floyd. I remember sitting across from him with a lot of empty glasses spread over the table between us. I remember him looking at me as if he were seeing me for the first time, as if he regretted not paying more attention to me sooner. I remember him asking me a question: 'What do you want out of life, Mr. Bell?'

"I had to think about it. What did I want? I was a kid from the Midwest with an accountant for a father. My mother had raised four kids and never worked outside the home. They had struggled to save money to send me to college—the same college my father had gone to. I was a member of his old fraternity. No one had ever asked me what I wanted out of life, and the best answer I could give was that I wanted to be like my father. I wanted to get a degree and work in a profession. Maybe I'd be an accountant. Maybe a doctor. I wanted to meet a girl in college like my father did, and I wanted to marry her and have a family.

"That's what I told Floyd, and he listened, and at the end he said, 'That sounds like a very respectable life, Mr. Bell.' And as far as I could tell, he meant it. He wasn't mocking me. He wasn't questioning the worth of what I wanted. But I was.

" 'It sounds like a very ordinary life,' I said.

"His smile was slow and gentle. 'There's nothing wrong with an ordinary life.'

"And then he had me, though I didn't know it yet. I said, 'I want something more.'

"He laughed, but the laugh was gentle too. 'You must be careful, Mr. Bell,' he said. 'It's not something to be done lightly—wishing for an extraordinary life.'

"He didn't say anything more that night. It was only later that he told me about the Rosebears—two brothers falsely accused of murdering a woman in Ohio. It was only later that I found out what he meant by 'an extraordinary life'—that he wanted me to help him rob a bank so we could use the money to make sure those brothers got a good legal defense—so they weren't at the mercy of some overworked, court-appointed lawyer. When Floyd told me that, I thought he was nuts, and I let him know it.

"He gave me that same smile. 'I'm sure you're right, Mr. Bell. I shouldn't have asked you. Don't give it another thought.'"

Bell moved his left hand back and forth over the maplewood table. "Floyd didn't mention it again," he said, "and not long after that, he was gone, on to a different college. But he left me a phone number so we wouldn't lose touch. *Don't give it another thought,* he'd said, but of course I did. One night I called him and we ended up talking about it—just hypothetically. About the morality of it. We figured that since the money people deposit in banks is insured, no one would really lose anything. And no one would get hurt—we agreed on that. We would bring guns to scare the tellers, but at the most we might fire a shot in the air. We wouldn't actually harm anyone. And it could mean the difference between life and death for the Rosebear brothers—that's what Floyd kept saying. I'm sure now that he never meant a word of it; he always intended to keep the money for himself. But I wanted to believe. And somewhere along the line it changed from something Floyd and I were just talking about to something we were going to do."

Bell shrugged his shoulders and closed his eyes to let me know that he'd given me all the explanation he could. "I was twenty," he said again, "and I wanted something more than an ordinary life. Which is just another way of saying I was an idiot."

His eyes opened and settled on mine. "This isn't what you came here for."

No, it wasn't. I realized I'd been stalling because I didn't know where to begin. I regarded him across the corner of the table and said, "We need to talk about Lucy Navarro."

"I'm not sure what I can tell you," he said. "I don't really know her."

"She saved your life last week," I reminded him, "outside the Eightball Saloon."

He focused on his left hand in its brace, as if he were remembering. "That's true, but I didn't talk to her that night. I've never really talked to her."

"I know she tried to interview you—about what happened at the Great Lakes Bank."

"She tried. But I don't do interviews."

"She spoke to Terry Dawtrey and Henry Kormoran," I said. "She was working on a story about the Great Lakes robbery. And three nights ago she disappeared. Somebody didn't want her to write that story. I think it might have been the fifth robber. The getaway driver."

Bell shook his head. "I can't help you there."

"Dawtrey claimed to know who the fifth robber was. But you don't know."

"I don't."

"I want you to look at a picture for me."

He started to protest. "It's been seventeen years—"

I took a sheet of paper from my pocket, a page torn from a copy of *Newsweek*. I unfolded it on the table.

"That's Callie Spencer," Bell said, "and her husband—the senator's son."

"Jay Casterbridge," I said, nodding. "Could he have been the fifth robber?"

A pained expression passed over Bell's face. "I can't help you."

"Imagine him younger."

He pushed the page away. "I just don't know. Do you think I'm lying?"

I studied his eyes. No answer there. I refolded the page and returned it to my pocket.

Looking at his hand resting on the table, I realized I wanted to bring the heel of my palm down hard on his broken fingers. I wanted to shout at him. Instead I made my voice quiet.

"I think Lucy may be dead soon, if she isn't dead already," I said. "She saved your life. You owe her. I think you know something about the Great Lakes robbery—maybe not the identity of the getaway driver, but something that could help me."

"I don't—"

I went on in the same voice, empty of hope. "It's something you don't want to tell me, because you've put it all behind you. You think it's in the past, but it's not. Not for Lucy."

"I'm sorry. You're asking the wrong person."

"No, I don't think so. Dawtrey got thirty years for what happened at the Great Lakes Bank, and Kormoran served six years. But you served two and a half."

"Dawtrey's the one who shot Harlan Spencer—"

"Kormoran didn't shoot anybody, but you made out better than he did." I leaned closer to him. "You're a lucky man. But I don't think it was luck. I think you knew something, and you used it to get a better deal."

Bell's head bowed and his eyes went into shadow. "I wish you'd let it lie."

"I can't."

"What I know won't help you."

"Maybe not," I said. "But you're going to tell me."

CHAPTER 45

Elizabeth learned about Lark's aborted attack on Sutton Bell a little before five o'clock. She heard the details from Shan, who heard them over the phone from Owen McCaleb. Her first instinct was to head back to Ann Arbor, and Shan agreed, but McCaleb told them to keep plugging away at Helen Lark's list of names.

"I've already got everyone looking for Lark here," McCaleb said. "I want you to stay there and find us a lead."

Their next stop was a duplex with a pair of dead ash trees in the front yard. This was where Lark had lived after he left his mother's house and before he rented his apartment in Ann Arbor. Elizabeth and Shan had driven by earlier in the day but had found no one home. Now they found a beat-up Firebird in the driveway.

The owner of the Firebird was a guy Lark had gone to school with. Glen Gough answered the door wearing a T-shirt and sweatpants and smoking a cigarette. He got a guilty look on his face when Elizabeth showed him her badge—as if cigarettes weren't the only thing he ever smoked. He seemed relieved when he found out they were there to talk about Lark.

"Is it true what I'm hearing on the news?" Gough asked, leading them inside. "He's some kind of serial killer?"

Elizabeth pretended she hadn't heard the question. "What sort of person was he in school?"

Gough plopped himself down on a ragged sofa. "Honestly? He was always a little weird. Kept to himself."

"So you weren't friends?"

"I don't know if he wanted friends. He was never one of the guys. For a long time, I thought he was a fag."

"Is that right?"

Gough nodded, brushing at the cigarette ash that had fallen on the cushion beside him. "I guess he wasn't though, because of the way he fawned over Susanna Marten. You know about her, right?"

"Yes," Shan said.

"He used to follow her around in high school. Even signed up to work on the yearbook because she was one of the photographers."

"What about after high school?" asked Elizabeth. "Did you see him much?"

"We worked some temp jobs together. Then back in May he was on the outs with his mom—she was mad at him for selling his dad's boat. I told him he could stay here. I needed help with the rent."

"What was he like to live with?"

Gough dropped his spent cigarette into a mug on the coffee table. "Honestly? He was kind of a slacker."

Elizabeth looked around at the shabby furniture and the giant flat-screen television. At Gough's uncombed hair and slouching form. "Is that right?"

"Yeah, he never really went anywhere. Except to work."

"Did he ever talk about Susanna Marten?"

Gough shook his head. "I tried once, because I knew they'd been close right up until she died. But he turned cold on me, like I didn't have any right to say anything about her."

"What about Callie Spencer?" Elizabeth asked. "Did he ever talk about her?"

"The chick who's running for Senate? No. But if he saw her on the news he'd always watch. And if he got one of his headaches he'd go looking for her, flipping through the channels as if seeing her would help."

Shan broke in. "Did he get a lot of headaches?"

"He got 'em all the time."

"Did he take anything for them?"

"Sometimes he'd fill a towel full of ice and put it on his forehead."

"But you didn't see him take pills?"

"Sure, he took pills, but I couldn't tell you what they were. You should ask his doctor."

That got Elizabeth's attention. "He was seeing a doctor?"

"A shrink. Sometimes Anthony would pass along his psychobabble—about how we all want to be known for who we really are. Stuff like that."

"Anthony's mother told us she tried to get him to see a therapist," Elizabeth said, "but he only went a few times."

Gough shrugged. "Would you go see some shrink your mother picked out?"

"What was his doctor's name?"

"I'm not sure. It might've started with a K."

"We need more than that. It's important."

"I don't remember," Gough said. "But what about the boat?"

Elizabeth tilted her head curiously. "What about it?"

"Anthony sold it. There must be a record. His shrink's the one who bought it."

THE BOAT SAT on a trailer in the driveway. Sunlight threw the shadows of birch leaves onto the hull and the wind set the shadows in motion. Anthony Lark trailed his fingers along the hull as he went by; he had parked his Chevy on a side street out of sight.

A stone path led around the garage to the back of Dr. Matthew Kenneally's house. Moss grew in the cracks between the stones. The path widened out into a patio. Four metal chairs surrounded a table topped with glass. A wheelbarrow held gardening tools. A soccer ball and a set of Rollerblades lay abandoned in the grass.

At the far end of the patio, wooden steps led up onto a deck. Lark mounted the steps and saw himself reflected in the mirror of sliding glass doors. The wind opened his suit jacket and he could see Paul Rhiner's pistol tucked into his waistband on the left side.

He stepped close to the glass and brought both hands up to block the sunlight so he could see inside. A big, high-ceilinged room. Red pillows on a sofa of black leather. A bowl of fruit on the tiled surface of a coffee table. No movement. There might be no one home, Lark thought.

He climbed down from the deck and walked back across the stone patio until he came to an unassuming door painted white. It was locked, but it rattled loose in the frame. All he needed was a lever to pry it open. A pair of hedge trimmers from the wheelbarrow did the job.

There was hardly any sound, just the splintering of wood.

The book-lined room on the other side was Dr. Kenneally's study. Lark had been here before. His first session with the doctor had been held in his office near the north campus of the university. But their later sessions had been here. Lark would come in through the white door and they would sit in low-slung chairs in the middle of the room, Lark with his feet on an ottoman, the doctor with his fingers interlaced beneath his chin. They would talk about Susanna Marten.

Once, Kenneally had left Lark waiting while he made a phone call in another part of the house. Lark drifted around the study, scanning the books on the shelves. He came back to his chair and noticed a magazine lying on the ottoman—a copy of *Time* open to a profile of Callie Spencer. The story detailed the injuries her father had suffered during the Great Lakes robbery and the role she played in his recovery. A sidebar showed pictures of Terry Dawtrey, Henry Kormoran, and Sutton Bell.

Lark became so engrossed in the story that he didn't notice when Kenneally returned to the study. He got to the end and looked up to find the doctor sitting across from him, gray eyes kind and patient.

"What are you reading?" Kenneally asked him.

Lark held up the magazine in answer. He tapped a picture of Callie Spencer talking with a group of her supporters, wearing a brilliant smile. "She reminds me of Susanna," he said.

"Does she?" Kenneally said. "Why do you think that is?"

FROM KENNEALLY'S STUDY Lark walked down a short hall to the living room he had glimpsed through the glass doors. He picked out an apple from the bowl on the coffee table and ate it as he wandered through the house. In the hallway on the second floor, he found a collection of framed black-and-white photographs. In one of them Kenneally had his arms around his wife, a woman with dark wavy hair and a plump face. Other photos featured their children—two boys, one girl—all of them wavy-haired like their mother.

In the most recent pictures the older boy seemed to be around twelve, the younger ten, the girl seven or eight. Lark moved down the hall, glancing through open doors. A room for each of the children: clothes on the floor, beds unmade. And a master suite where Kenneally and his wife would sleep. The light from the south-facing windows would wake them early in the morning. Lark ate the last bites of his apple standing by the windows, looking down at the yard. He tossed the core into the wastebasket in the master bath.

Down the hall again to the stairs, and he made it halfway to the bottom before turning back. There was something familiar in one of the photographs; he had seen it without really seeing it. He found it right away: an image of the older boy posing in a uniform with a soccer ball under his arm. Posing in the driveway with a minivan in the background. Lark couldn't tell the color from the black-and-white photograph, but if he had to guess he would have guessed blue. Like the minivan that had taken Lucy Navarro.

THERE WAS NO MINIVAN in the Kenneallys' garage.

There was certainly room for one. It was a cavernous space, lit by fluorescent lights hung from the rafters. It had two doors, a double and a single, and room for three vehicles. When Lark switched on the lights he saw two: a Dodge pickup truck and a BMW. He had seen the pickup before. Kenneally had driven it when he came to buy Lark's father's boat.

One spot left over for the minivan. The Kenneallys must be using it now. That's what you would take, if you were going for a drive with the family.

Lark wondered if Lucy Navarro had ever been here. If Kenneally took her that night from the parking lot of the Winston Hotel, it seemed unlikely he would have brought her here. It would make more sense to kill her somewhere faraway and dump the body.

But the police hadn't found the body.

Lark stood in the still air of the garage and heard the hum of the fluorescent lights overhead, a pleasing, steady sound. Mingled with it was a second hum, deeper and rougher. He looked around to find the source. A tool bench ran along the back wall, with lines of screwdrivers and socket wrenches hanging above it from hooks on a pegboard.

Beside the bench was a white metal box, long as a coffin and twice as deep. A freezer. Lark rested a hand on the lid and felt the hum. He knew before he tried that it wouldn't open. It needed a key. He was scanning the hooks of the pegboard when he heard the squeal of a garage door beginning to rise behind him.

ELIZABETH AND SHAN left Glen Gough slouching on his sofa in the late afternoon. They got onto I-94 heading west, Elizabeth behind the wheel, Shan making phone calls. Anthony Lark had sold his father's boat at the end of March. Helen Lark told Shan she had met the man who bought it, but couldn't remember his name. Shan called in to the department and asked a dispatcher to run a vehicle registration search, which turned up a record of a twenty-four-foot runabout that had once been registered to Thomas Lark of Dearborn. The same boat was currently registered to Matthew Kenneally of Ann Arbor.

Shan took down Kenneally's address and asked the dispatcher to run another computer search, which revealed that Matthew Kenneally was a licensed psychiatrist.

Elizabeth heard the snap of Shan's phone closing. Heard him say, "Do you think Kenneally went down into Lark's room in the basement? Do you think he saw the shrine to Susanna Marten on the wall?"

She had been wondering the same thing. "I think he did."

As the Crown Vic shot along the interstate, she visualized Lark's wall: images of Susanna Marten on the left, images of Callie Spencer on the right.

"Do you remember what Lark's mother told us?" Shan said.

Elizabeth remembered. *When did your son get interested in the Great Lakes robbery?* she had asked Helen Lark. *In the spring,* the woman answered. *I was angry with him at the time, because he sold his father's boat. Right around then he started putting pictures of Callie Spencer on the wall.*

THE KENNEALLYS WERE a lively bunch. The sons kept up a stream of banter about the soccer game they'd just played in. The daughter fired up the television and found a channel showing cartoons. Mrs. Kenneally teased her husband about leaving the lights on in the garage and asked him what he wanted for dinner and what were the chances he would help cook it.

Lark listened to them from behind the closed door of Dr. Kenneally's study. He had run into the house at the first sound of the garage door. Now he heard footsteps tromping upstairs—probably the two boys. If he waited a few minutes, he could slip back into the garage. The key might be out there, and if not, he could find some other way to open the freezer.

Or he could forget about the freezer. Because really he was here for Dr. Kenneally, wasn't he? No accident that he had Paul Rhiner's pistol tucked in his waistband. The doctor would be in the kitchen now with his wife. Lark could get to him. Nothing stood in his way.

Lark realized he had backed away from the door. He had Rhiner's pistol in his hand, though he didn't remember drawing it. *Mixed messages,* he thought. *You want to do it and you want to back away from it at the same time.*

He sat in one of the low-slung chairs and returned the gun to his waistband. Covered it with his jacket. He could afford to wait, to think things through.

He had his notebook and his father's pen out when the door opened.

Matthew Kenneally was in his middle thirties. Medium height, medium build. His dark hair had begun to recede at the temples. He wore glasses with silver frames.

There was the barest break in his stride when he saw Lark, but he recovered and came into the room, tossing some letters onto a table just inside the door.

It was typical, Lark thought. Maybe it was something they taught therapists in school: never to react. Kenneally's face had always seemed to Lark like a mask. The man's eyebrows were straight lines with no arch at all, as if he were incapable of expressing surprise.

"How long have you been here?" Kenneally said.

"Not long," said Lark.

"I knew I didn't leave those lights on in the garage. How did you get in?"

Lark glanced at the white door that opened onto the patio. "I had to break in," he said.

Kenneally frowned, the first real reaction he had shown. "That's bad form."

"It's not the worst thing I've done."

"Trespassing is a violation of trust. We've talked about the importance of trust, Anthony." Kenneally took off his glasses and rubbed the bridge of his nose. "Let's leave that aside," he said. "It's a good thing, your coming here. I've been worried about you. You need help."

"You're the second person to tell me that today."

"Who was the first?"

"Someone who actually wanted to help me."

Kenneally frowned again and slipped his glasses on. From the hall a voice said, "Where'd you go, Matt? Are you talking to someone in there?" A woman's voice. Kenneally's wife.

The doctor stepped out into the hall. "I'm with a patient, darling."

"Now? I didn't know you had an appointment."

"I'm sorry. It slipped my mind. It shouldn't take long."

She told him she would go ahead with dinner, and Kenneally came back in and closed the door. He sat opposite Lark and crossed one leg over the other. He brushed lint from his slacks. He didn't say anything. That was one of his tricks: not saying anything.

Lark spoke into the silence. "I've got the headaches under control."

"Have you?" Kenneally said. "That's good."

"Do you really think so?"

Kenneally laced his fingers. "Do you see what you're doing, Anthony? You've already suggested that I don't really want to help you, and now you're implying that I secretly want you to have headaches. Why would I want that?"

"That's what I've been wondering," Lark said, sliding his pen into his jacket pocket. "Can I show you something?"

Without waiting for an answer he held his notebook out, open to the page where he had first written down the names of Terry Dawtrey, Sutton Bell, and Henry Kormoran. Now he had added another.

Kenneally reached for the notebook. "What's this?"

"Those are the men who robbed the Great Lakes Bank."

The doctor studied the page. "You've got my name on this list."

"It belongs there, doesn't it?" Lark said, sitting back in his chair. "Do you see how the names move, how they breathe on the page?"

"We've been over this, Anthony."

"Can you see how red they are?"

Kenneally shook his head sadly. "You suffer from synesthesia, Anthony. The words aren't really red. They're not really moving."

"Can you see how your name is different? The others are red, but yours is pitch-black. It's broken into a million pieces, and the pieces are crawling over one another."

Kenneally sighed. "And what do you think that means?"

"It means you're worse than the other three," Lark said. "Can't you see it?"

"It's not there to see, Anthony. There's nothing here but names you wrote on a page. The rest is in your mind."

"Is it? Where's the key to the freezer in your garage?"

The question seemed to give Kenneally pause. He closed the notebook and tapped it against his chin.

"Why?" he asked.

"I'd like to see what's in there."

"What do you think is in there?"

"A body," Lark said. "Lucy Navarro's."

He watched Kenneally's straight brows knit together.

"The missing reporter? Why would her body be in my freezer?"

"I was there that night," Lark said. "I saw. She got taken by someone in a blue minivan. Just like yours."

Kenneally leaned forward. "We can go out there right now, Anthony. I'll show you. There's no body in the freezer. If I show you, will you admit that you're not thinking clearly and you need help?"

His voice fell until it was just loud enough to span the distance between them. He sounded sincere. Lark almost believed him.

Almost. "You might have buried the body."

"You just said it's in the freezer. Which is it?"

"I said I wanted to see. You're twisting what I said."

In the same quiet voice Kenneally asked, "What if we went out into the garage and I showed you that my minivan isn't blue at all? It's gray."

Lark felt a moment of doubt, but he shrugged it away. "You could have had it repainted."

"I'm not going to play this game, Anthony," the doctor said, rising slowly to his feet. "I can't help you if you won't listen to reason."

Across the room, the ruined white door opened on a gust of wind.

Lark stood up and drew the gun from under his jacket. "I don't want your help."

He snatched his notebook from Kenneally and returned it to his pocket.

Kenneally spread his arms. "You're going to kill me? How many people have you killed, Anthony? What good has it done you?"

The gun felt heavy. "You wanted them dead."

"Do you hear what you're saying? You can't escape responsibility. You need to own your actions."

Lark took a step back and raised the gun between them. "I'm tired of listening to you."

He tugged at the trigger, but it felt solid and leaden, as if the metal had fused together.

Somewhere off in the depths of the house, a bell rang.

Kenneally turned his palms out. "See? You don't really want to kill me."

"Yes, I do," Lark said, releasing the safety with his thumb.

ELIZABETH REMEMBERED IT this way. The sun warm on the back of her neck. Shan beside her with his badge out. He reaches to ring the bell a second time, but the door swings inward before he touches the button.

The smell of cooking. Burgers sizzling in a pan. A woman with wavy brown hair wiping her hands on a paper towel. Shan making introductions, asking if Matthew Kenneally lives here.

"Matt's with a patient," the woman says.

Then the shot. You could almost believe it's the sound of grease snapping in the pan. The woman looks back over her shoulder, confused. Then she's running and Elizabeth calls for her to wait. She doesn't stop. Elizabeth draws her nine-millimeter. Shan already has his drawn; he's close on the woman's heels.

Cartoon penguins on TV. A young girl rising from the sofa. Elizabeth tells her to get down, down on the floor. The woman with the wavy hair dashes along a hallway, throws her shoulder against a closed door. Shan follows her through. Her scream is like another gunshot.

Elizabeth pauses in the doorway, takes in the scene. Two chairs in the middle of the room and a man sitting in one of them. Blood soaking his shirt. Eyeglasses askew on his face.

Shan on one side of him. The woman with the wavy hair on the other. She reaches for his right hand; the index finger is bent at an impossible angle. Shan tears open the man's shirt. Pale chest, pale stomach. No wound.

"He tried to shoot me," Kenneally says in a dazed voice.

Crossing the room, Elizabeth spots the gun on the floor. She sees the white door half-open. A smear of blood on the knob.

"I shot him," Kenneally says.

You're leaving a trail, Lark thought.

He rounded the hull of his father's boat at a run, throwing out a hand to steady himself. A bloody handprint hung there amid the shadow-leaves on the white fiberglass.

Drops of blood on the sidewalk too. He didn't stop to look at them, but he knew they would be there—tiny circles on the ground.

Strange how alive he felt, the air filling his lungs, his heart racing. The sidewalk pounded beneath him. He didn't feel any pain, not in any part of him.

Kenneally had surprised him, grabbing for the gun—the most decisive thing he had ever seen the doctor do. *You don't really want to kill me.* Lark wondered, as they struggled, whether it might be true.

Maybe it was. There had been a moment, after the gunshot, when Lark needed to make a choice. Kenneally dropped the gun and stared at his bent finger—it had been caught somehow in the trigger guard and broken. He fell back into the chair. Lark was still standing; he might have reclaimed the gun. He chose to run instead. Maybe he wanted to live more than he wanted to kill Matthew Kenneally.

At the corner Lark stumbled a little on the turn. He saw the Chevy parked in the shade on the opposite side of the street. Twenty yards away. He could run twenty yards.

He tripped down from the curb and into the street, scrambled to get up again. The beat of footsteps sounded behind him. Fifteen yards now. Up ahead, a girl with a collie on a leash crossed into the street. Ten yards. Lark had his keys in his hand. Five yards. The girl spotted him and reined in the collie. Behind him, a clear voice called out his name. Told him to stop.

The push of a button and the Chevy's door is unlocked. The twist of a key and the engine surges to life. The collie barks in answer. Lark punches the Chevy out into the street. In his rearview mirror he sees the lady cop standing with her gun raised. The gun dips a little, a mark of hesitation. She doesn't want to risk hitting the girl, or the driver of the coupe gliding north in the opposite lane. Lark sees her growing smaller in the mirror, sees the gun coming up again, steady, before finally dropping down to her side.

CHAPTER 46

I parked in the horseshoe drive of the Spencer house and Ruth Spencer met me at the door. I had called ahead and her husband had agreed to meet with me. She led me through the house to the backyard and we walked along the flagstone path to the gazebo.

Harlan Spencer waited there in an open-collared shirt and linen trousers. His motorized chair faced southeast, so he could look across his lawn at the guest cottage and Bedford Road.

Ruth Spencer left us there alone. A patio chair had been drawn up into the gazebo for me, and a tray with a pitcher of iced tea and two glasses occupied a small table between us.

Harlan Spencer gestured toward it. "I told Ruth you weren't coming to drink tea, but she wouldn't dream of having a guest and not offering him something. Help yourself if you like." His voice was deep and courteous.

"Not just now," I said. I was about to ask if I could pour him some, but he saw the question in my eyes and answered it with a shake of his head.

"You're here about Lucy Navarro," he said. "I've already talked to the police about her. A detective named Wintergreen came and asked me if I'd seen her this past week, parked down the street in her yellow Beetle."

"What did you tell him?"

"I told him it's my legs that don't work. My eyes are fine. Of course I saw her."

A breeze came up and Spencer put his head back to feel it on his shaved scalp.

I said, "Did he ask if you could shed any light on what happened to Lucy Wednesday night?"

"He didn't want to. He thought the question was rude. But he asked. I told him I couldn't help him."

"I'm hoping you can help me."

"I thought as much," Spencer said. "What have you got to bludgeon me with?"

One corner of his mouth turned up, but his eyes watched me intently. "You must have something," he said. "I understand you threatened Alan Beckett with violence, if he didn't return the girl unharmed."

"I'm not going to threaten you," I said.

"Not with violence. But you have something. What is it?"

"I talked to Sutton Bell today."

"Did you now?"

"About the Great Lakes robbery."

His nod was slow and thoughtful. "He knows a thing or two about that."

"He told me his big secret," I said. "The one that got him a deal. Only two and a half years in prison."

"What did you think of it—his secret?"

"At first I thought it was a disappointment."

"Most secrets are."

"He told me he saw you in a diner with Floyd Lambeau two days before the robbery."

Spencer gazed off across the lawn. "So he did."

"The sheriff and the bank robber having coffee together," I said. "Bell knew it was scandalous. He wasn't sure exactly how. He thought maybe you were in on the robbery. That you had agreed to look the other way."

"That's not a very credible theory," Spencer said, "given the way things turned out."

"No. I think I can do better. I know things Bell doesn't know. For instance, Floyd Lambeau claimed to be Callie's real father. That's what he told Terry Dawtrey."

Spencer turned his head toward me sharply. "That's nonsense."

"I know," I said. "Callie explained why it's impossible—the business about the blood types. But Lambeau made the claim. Maybe it was an empty boast. Or maybe he believed it was true, or could have been true. Do you have a gun?"

The sudden transition made him laugh. A deep laugh, like his voice. "Why do you ask?"

I shrugged. "The other day the senator told me you always keep one handy. If you've got a gun, I should be careful about suggesting your wife might have had an affair with Floyd Lambeau."

His right hand rubbed his chin. "You should be. But let's suppose the suggestion doesn't shock me."

"If they had an affair, that could explain some things," I said. "Lambeau might have seen you as a rival. So when he decided to rob a bank, he picked one in Sault Sainte Marie. Right in your backyard. It was a demonstration of his contempt for you. And if you found out he was in town—if you ran into him in a diner, for instance—I think you'd want to have a talk with him."

Something flashed in Spencer's eyes. "You'd be right about that."

"So that explains what Bell saw," I said. "It explains another thing too. I've read about the Great Lakes robbery, and I never bought the idea that you just happened to turn up at the bank that day. The story was, you went there to open an account."

"You think that's too much of a coincidence, Mr. Loogan?"

"I think you were watching Lambeau's hotel that morning. Once you knew he was in town, you would want to keep an eye on him. I think you saw him get into the black SUV—him and the other four. I think you followed them to the Great Lakes Bank."

Spencer nodded. "That's a plausible story."

"I could embroider it a little, if I were cynical," I said. "Suppose you knew in advance what they had planned—"

"How would I know that?"

"The Great Lakes robbers were all amateurs. Maybe one of them talked to somebody, maybe somebody passed the word along to you—"

"And if I knew about the robbery in advance, why wouldn't I have stopped it sooner? Why wait till they were inside the bank?"

I raised an eyebrow. "It would be awfully tempting, wouldn't it? Floyd Lambeau slept with your wife. If you just let the robbery happen, you could shoot him. And get away with it."

Spencer laughed again, deep like before. "Alan Beckett told me you had a wild imagination." He gave me a candid look. "I admit it would have been tempting. But that's not the way it happened."

"Fair enough," I said. "It doesn't really matter. Bell saw you with Lambeau. That's embarrassing enough on its own. If it came to light, you would need to explain how you knew him, what you talked about that day in the diner. Maybe you could come up with a convincing lie—or maybe people would find out that the man who slept with your wife also planned a bank robbery right under your nose."

The wind stirred the vines around the pillars of the gazebo. "So you would want to make a deal with Bell, to keep him quiet," I continued. "But only the prosecutor could make a deal. You would need to influence him—or someone would. Someone with the power to influence a prosecutor. Like Senator Casterbridge. And I think the senator had a good reason to do you a favor."

"You're letting your imagination get away from you again," Spencer said. "Callie told me about your theory: that Jay was the fifth robber, and I kept quiet about it because the senator asked me to."

I leaned forward in my chair. "When I talked to Callie, she said you would never take part in a cover-up. You had too much integrity. But she didn't know about Sutton Bell. She didn't know you had a reason to make a deal. You'd forget you saw Jay at the Great Lakes Bank, and the senator would make sure Bell forgot he saw you and Lambeau together."

"You tell a good story, Mr. Loogan. But it's only a story. Jay Casterbridge wasn't the fifth robber."

I shrugged and sat back again in the chair. "I'll tell you what I told Alan Beckett: I don't care who robbed a bank seventeen years ago. I care about what happened to Lucy Navarro. I haven't been able to find out. Maybe you can."

Spencer showed me the palm of his right hand. "How am I supposed to do that?"

"Ask around," I said. "I figure whoever took her was someone you know. Maybe Beckett. Do you think he's capable of it?"

He mulled the question over. "I think he might entertain the idea. I don't know if he'd follow through."

"If not him, maybe Jay Casterbridge."

"I told you, Jay's not the fifth robber—"

I waved away his impatience. "Fine. But whoever was the fifth robber might be worth a look. And don't tell me you don't know who it was. I never bought that part of your story either."

He didn't react to that, unless the lines on his forehead grew deeper. We were both silent for a moment, there in the shade of the gazebo, in the warmth of the late afternoon.

"Suppose I agree to ask around," he said at last, "and suppose I come up empty."

"Then I'll have to spill Sutton Bell's secret."

"The press won't believe you, unless you can get Bell to talk to them."

I nodded over my shoulder in the direction of the guest cottage.

"I'll start by telling Callie," I said.

Harlan Spencer scowled at that, his eyes darkening, his mouth forming an ugly line, and it occurred to me that despite all appearances I was dealing with a dangerous man. I'd come here thinking I had nothing to lose. Knowing his secret gave me the upper hand. He was almost twice my age and he literally couldn't touch me, couldn't rise from his chair. Maybe he carried a gun—if the senator was right—but even that would do him no good unless he was willing to shoot me in broad daylight.

All this went through my mind as I waited for his answer. When I look back on it I think he probably would have agreed to do what I asked, to make inquiries about Lucy Navarro. But he would have hated it, and hated me.

I think he would have agreed, but he never answered me. I watched him carefully, waiting. But he was looking past me at the street in the distance. When he spoke, I didn't understand at first what he had said.

He said it again. "Take the gun."

He must have had it in the chair. A nine-millimeter. I could have sworn I never took my eyes off him, but I didn't see him draw it out. Now he offered it to me, grip first.

Behind me, in the distance, the brakes of a car were squealing.

I got to my feet, spun around. Saw a car jump the curb of Bedford Road and come to a stop on the lawn. I knew it from the parking lot of the Winston Hotel. Lark's Chevrolet.

"Callie's in the cottage?" I said.

"Yes, god damn it," said Harlan Spencer. "Take the gun."

I took it and leapt over the railing of the gazebo, landing on my feet in the grass, the impact traveling up like a current to the wound in my side. Running full out, I watched Lark open the door of his car. I didn't know which one of us would reach the cottage first.

CHAPTER 47

Lark meant to go to Mira's apartment, but somewhere along the way he realized he wouldn't make it.

The blood had made his white shirt red. He buttoned his suit jacket to hide it before he got out of the car. His shoes touched the grass and it yielded beneath him, as though he might sink into it. He braced a hand on the car seat to lever himself out, and his palm came away slick and dark.

The air on his face revived him, though he might have liked it cooler. He might have liked to have more feeling in his legs, but they moved him onto the path that led to the cottage door. He fiddled with his sleeves as he went, and the gesture made him smile.

Maybe you should have brought flowers.

THE SUIT MADE Lark look young, like a boy on his first date. He moved stiffly in it. I thought he might be drunk.

The lawn sloped downhill and I gained speed as I approached him. I called to him and he seemed to notice me for the first time. He grinned. I remember that. Like you would if you saw an old friend unexpectedly.

By then I knew something must be wrong, but it was too late to stop. Momentum carried me into him, carried us both into the side of Callie Spencer's silver Ford.

His head jerked with the impact and his eyes closed. A ragged breath escaped him. The grin had gone from his face but now it returned. "I really wish you hadn't done that," he said.

I stepped back from him and saw the blood on his hands. "What happened to you?"

No answer. His breathing shallow. I worked the buttons of his jacket and saw his blood-drenched shirt. A small hole in the fabric, an inch or two above his navel. "Who did this?" I asked him.

His eyes opened then, and the palm of his right hand moved to cover the hole. He looked me up and down, his gaze coming to rest on Spencer's nine-millimeter.

"You brought a gun this time," he said, half amused. "Too late."

I reached behind him and set the gun on the hood of Callie's Ford.

"Who shot you?" I said.

He opened his mouth to answer and his expression darkened. He looked around helplessly. "What was his name?" He patted the pockets of his jacket. "I wrote it down."

He fished a notebook from one of the pockets, opened it. Turned it around to me.

I scanned the list. Three familiar names: Kormoran, Bell, Dawtrey. And a fourth.

"Matthew Kenneally," I said.

"That's him."

"He's one of them?" I said. "One of the robbers?"

Lark nodded distractedly. "It's cooler now," he said, "the wind."

The wind wasn't any cooler. I dug my cell phone out and punched 911.

"You don't have to," Lark said. "She already called."

He nodded toward the door of the cottage and I turned to see Callie Spencer. She snapped her phone shut and came down the steps.

"Ambulance on the way," she said in a quiet voice. "How bad is he?"

As if to answer, Lark slid down the side of the car, sat heavily on the ground.

I knelt beside him, returning my phone to my pocket. He had both hands over his wound. I pressed my hands against them.

"Cooler," he said. "No. That's not right."

Callie was down with us now too. She smoothed his hair back from his forehead.

"Not a cooler. A freezer," Lark said. "He's got a freezer in his garage."

"Who does?" I asked. "Kenneally?"

The smallest fraction of a nod. "He's got a minivan too. He says it's gray, but I don't trust him. I think it's blue."

I leaned in closer to him. "Kenneally has a blue minivan?"

"And a freezer. I couldn't open it. I'm sorry."

Lark's notebook lay on the gravel beside him. The pages fluttered in the wind.

I heard the low sound of a motor behind me. Harlan Spencer's chair. He would have had to take the long way around.

Far off, I heard the first note of sirens.

Lark tipped his head back against the car and smiled at Callie Spencer. "I don't think I'll make it to the redwoods," he said. "But you should go."

She glanced at me, confused. I shrugged. She turned back to him and brushed her thumb along his forehead. "All right."

"They're really something," he said. "Promise me."

Her smile started in her eyes before it went to her mouth. It moved slow and it didn't dazzle. It was heartbreaking and fine, and if it was false then she's the smoothest liar I've ever seen. "I promise," she said.

Lark never looked away from her, but his last words were for me. "He's got a freezer," he said. "Remember."

"I'll remember," I told him.

"I tried to open it. I couldn't."

"It's all right."

The sirens were closer now. Lark's voice faded, but I could still make out the words.

"I'm sorry about the girl," he said.

ON A SATURDAY NIGHT in Ann Arbor you can eat *ropa vieja* at the Café Habana or an Ethiopian feast at the Blue Nile. You can find dance clubs and martini bars and shops that sell chocolate truffles for thirty-two dollars a pound. You can hear a poetry reading or a symphony. You can see stand-up comics in a crowded bar in what used to be the basement of the VFW hall. You can attend the premiere of a new work by a local playwright, or the latest independent film.

I spent my Saturday night in the break room of the Investigations Division at City Hall. A windowless room with a scarred table and six mismatched chairs. A sofa with tattered cushions. The smell of strong coffee.

I saw Elizabeth early on. She came in to look me over, to make sure there was no fresh damage. She brought me pills—ibuprofen. I needed them. The pain in my side was a jagged, grinding ache.

Sarah came by sometime later, after the pills had smoothed over the worst of the jagged edges. She rode her bike and brought take-out from a Middle Eastern place. We ate hummus and fattoush, chicken shwarma sandwiches. She hung around for an hour or so.

After she left, I stretched out on the sofa and closed my eyes, but I couldn't sleep. I suppose I could have gone home. No one would have stopped me. But Ron Wintergreen, the first detective on the scene at the Spencer cottage, had asked me to wait here: I would need to give a statement. He had asked the Spencers to come in too, Harlan and Callie. Both were somewhere in the building. And I gathered, from the chatter among the cops who came by to fill their coffee mugs, that Matthew Kenneally had been brought in as well. I was a minor player; I would have to wait my turn.

I never did see Wintergreen again that night. Owen McCaleb turned up instead, looking harried, his shirt wrinkled, his tie loose. By then it was nearly eleven. I'd scrounged up a pen and a legal pad and had written an account of the last minutes of Anthony Lark's life. McCaleb read it through, tossed it back across the table at me, and told me to sign and date it. When I'd done that, he told me to go home.

"You don't want to ask me anything?" I said.

"No, I don't," he said, scraping his chair back from the table. "I figure I'd better not."

He began to rise, then reconsidered. Crossed his arms over his chest and let me have a long stare. "If I did want to question you," he said, "I'd start by asking what you discussed with Sutton Bell this afternoon."

I tapped my fingers softly on the tabletop. "I talked to him about the Great Lakes Bank robbery," I said. "I'd rather not get into specifics."

"No. Bell didn't want to either. As for Harlan Spencer, he admitted you came to ask him about the missing reporter, Lucy Navarro. But of course he doesn't know anything about her, so apparently the two of you sat around drinking iced tea and talking about how green the grass was and how blue the sky. Does that about cover it?"

"We didn't actually drink the iced tea," I said.

He smiled without any humor. "I'm glad to have that detail straightened out. But I think we'd better leave it there. Because if I were to inquire too closely, I might discover you've been conducting your own private half-assed investigation of Lucy Navarro's disappearance. And since you're living with one of my detectives, that discovery might reflect poorly on her."

"Lizzie hasn't done anything wrong—"

"I trust she hasn't. But she's chosen to associate with a man who can't keep his nose out of trouble, and if I thought too much about that, I might begin to question her judgment." He stood up and collected my statement from the table. "So, no, I don't want to ask you any questions. I don't want to hear whatever line you'd try to feed me. I'd rather you just went away."

I WENT AWAY—out of the break room and down the hall to the stairs. I ran into Elizabeth there; she had come from questioning Matthew Kenneally. She walked with me down to the lobby and out into the night.

It had cooled into the low seventies and the streetlights lent everything a crisp, unreal appearance. The cracks in the sidewalks were sharply defined, and looked as if they had been put there on purpose. Away south we could hear hints of music and voices—nightlife on Liberty Street. We turned our backs on it and walked north.

"Did you find anything in Kenneally's freezer?" I asked her.

"We haven't looked," she said.

"Are you waiting for a warrant?"

She took my arm. "There's not going to be a warrant, David. Lark saw a freezer in a garage. It's a huge leap to say there's a body inside. No judge is going to make that leap."

"And Kenneally won't consent to a search?"

"Kenneally doesn't have to consent to anything. He's got a lawyer telling him so. The whole notion that he's the fifth man from the Great Lakes robbery—he claims it's nothing more than a wild allegation Lark made."

"Do you believe him?"

"It doesn't matter what I believe," she said. "What matters is what I can prove."

CHAPTER 48

Elizabeth and Shan had accompanied Kenneally to the University Hospital, where an ER doctor had checked him over and put a brace on his broken finger.

Kenneally's wife had contacted the law firm of Harris and Chatterjee, and Rex Chatterjee himself had been cooling his heels in an interview room when Elizabeth and Shan brought Kenneally in to City Hall. After consulting with his client privately, Chatterjee announced that Kenneally would be willing to make a statement.

Kenneally then led them through the events of the late afternoon, beginning with his discovery that Anthony Lark had broken into his study. In a flat, detached tone, he described Lark's erratic behavior, and his bizarre claims about the Great Lakes Bank robbery and the abduction of Lucy Navarro. When Lark drew a gun, Kenneally said, he had feared for his life and the lives of his wife and children. He had grabbed for the gun on instinct, and in the ensuing struggle it had gone off.

Rex Chatterjee sat impassively all the while, a pudgy man in a tailored suit. When Kenneally finished, Chatterjee swept his fingers through his gray hair and said, "Surely you won't be charging my client with any crime? I can't imagine a clearer case of self-defense."

"We have a few questions all the same," Elizabeth said, "if your client will indulge us."

Chatterjee waved a hand. "If you must."

"Do you keep up with the news, Doctor?" Elizabeth asked.

"Yes," said Kenneally.

"So a week and a half ago, when Henry Kormoran was found dead in his apartment, you were aware of that?"

"I heard about it."

"And you didn't think Lark might be responsible? You knew he had an unhealthy obsession with Kormoran, didn't you?"

Chatterjee interrupted. "You can't expect my client to discuss what obsessions Anthony Lark may or may not have had. That information is confidential."

Elizabeth arched her eyebrows. "Dr. Kenneally just told us that Lark accused him of being one of the Great Lakes robbers. Are we supposed to believe he wasn't aware of Lark's attitude toward Kormoran and the others?"

"I was aware of it," Kenneally said.

"But when Kormoran was murdered, you didn't think to contact the police?"

"I didn't know anything about Anthony's involvement in that."

Kenneally's trigger finger touched the table, the metal brace clicking against the wood.

"All right," Elizabeth said. "This Thursday, when we released a photograph of Lark and a statement that he was wanted for questioning in connection with Kormoran's death, and the death of Walter Delacorte, you still didn't feel the need to contact us?"

"I didn't have any useful information to give you," Kenneally said. "I didn't know where Anthony was. I hadn't spoken to him since he stopped coming to our sessions."

Shan had been sitting quietly, but now he said, "This afternoon, when you walked in on Lark in your study—did you know he had a gun?"

Kenneally turned to him. "No. Not right away."

"So what prevented you from calling the police the moment you saw him? He was an intruder in your house, wanted for murder."

Kenneally adjusted his glasses on the bridge of his nose. "I didn't know he was armed, but I considered him dangerous. I wasn't about to call the police in front of him, and I didn't dare leave him alone. I wanted to keep him calm, and keep him away from my family. And I thought I might be able to help him."

Chatterjee let out a sigh. "I don't understand the point of these questions."

He understood perfectly well, Elizabeth thought. Lark had gone on a crime spree and Kenneally had done nothing to stop it. So maybe he didn't want it to stop. But she knew if she made the accusation out loud, Chatterjee would shut the interview down.

"We're just trying to get a complete picture of what happened today," she said. Then, to Kenneally: "Could you tell me what medications you prescribed for Anthony Lark?"

"You can't expect my client to discuss the details of a patient's treatment," Chatterjee insisted.

Elizabeth kept her eyes on Kenneally. "Sorry," she said to him, smiling. "Confidentiality covers a lot of ground, doesn't it? I'd like to ask you about your diagnosis of Mr. Lark's condition, but I suppose you couldn't tell me. That would be a no-no, wouldn't it?"

A little life came into Kenneally's eyes, and into his voice. "That's one of the biggest no-no's there is," he said.

"Right," said Elizabeth. "Let's try this another way. Maybe I could ask you some questions and you could answer them in general terms. For instance, Lark's mother thought he was depressed over the death of Susanna Marten. I assume he would have been taking antidepressants, but we never found any—not in his apartment or in his car or on his body. Does that seem as strange to you as it does to me?"

Kenneally smiled faintly. "I won't talk about Anthony's diagnosis," he said. "But in general I can tell you that drugs aren't the only way of treating a patient with symptoms of depression. Some respond well to talk therapy. Even if antidepressants are called for, some patients aren't willing to take them. Or if they are, they may stop taking them because of the side effects. Does that make sense?"

"It does. Thank you. Now, we understand Lark suffered from headaches. Talk therapy wouldn't help with those, would it?"

The same faint smile. "No. There are a number of prescription medications to treat headaches, if over-the-counter remedies don't work."

"We found a bottle of Imitrex in Lark's car. Is that something you might prescribe?"

"It's something a patient would normally get from his primary physician."

"But if he didn't, you could give it to him, right?"

"I could," Kenneally said. "I'm not going to say if I did, in Anthony's case. But if you've got the bottle, the label should tell you who prescribed it."

"I'm afraid not. Anthony stole it from a pharmacy." Elizabeth opened a folder and brought out a photograph of the tin Shan had found in Lark's apartment. "Have you ever seen this?" she asked Kenneally.

"Not that I remember," he said.

"Anthony kept pills in it. The label says 'Imitrex,' but the pills inside were vitamin D. Do you have any thoughts on that?"

Chatterjee slapped an open palm on the table. "Enough," he said. "I don't know what thoughts you expect the doctor to have on Mr. Lark's vitamins—"

Kenneally ignored him. "Actually, a deficiency of vitamin D has been linked to mood disorders," he said, "so it's not surprising that someone suffering from depression would be taking it. Speaking in general, of course."

ANTHONY LARK'S NOTEBOOK lay on the blotter of Chief Owen McCaleb's desk. McCaleb himself perched on a corner of the desk and listened as Elizabeth summarized her interview with Matthew Kenneally. Shan sat by the window, tossing in a comment now and then. They had left Kenneally in the interview room to write out his statement, with Rex Chatterjee looking over his shoulder.

When Elizabeth finished, McCaleb asked, "What do we think of Kenneally?"

"He could be just what he seems," she said. "A doctor forced to defend himself against his patient. But I doubt it. For one thing, I'd expect him to be more broken up about it."

"On the other hand," Shan said, "he didn't try to lie to us. He could have held back the accusations Lark made against him when they were alone—the stuff about the Great Lakes robbery and Lucy Navarro. But he didn't. So either the accusations are false and Kenneally sees no reason to hide them, or they're true and he's smart enough not to get caught hiding them."

McCaleb bumped his heels against the pinewood front of the desk. "I haven't talked to the prosecutor yet, but I don't see him bringing charges. The evidence supports Kenneally's story. The gun that shot Lark was Paul Rhiner's, so Lark had to have brought it with him. I've had a preliminary report from the medical examiner: she found gunshot residue on Lark's hands and clothes, which supports Kenneally's statement that they were fighting over the gun when he pulled the trigger."

"Classic self-defense," Shan said, "just like Chatterjee claimed."

"What about the other stuff?" McCaleb asked. "Do we believe Kenneally is the fifth man from the Great Lakes robbery? Do we think he manipulated Lark—wound him up and sent him after Dawtrey, Kormoran, and Bell?"

"It's possible," Elizabeth said. "Lark met Kenneally in March. That's when Kenneally bought Lark's boat. At the time, Lark had been in mourning for years over Susanna Marten. He'd been afflicted with headaches. He had a shrine to the girl on the wall of his room."

"Kenneally could have seen the shrine when he picked up the boat," added Shan.

Elizabeth touched the glass beads of her necklace. "Lark's mother told us he had resisted seeing a therapist. He felt responsible for Susanna's death, because he hadn't done enough to prevent it. She told us something else too. She thought Lark didn't want a therapist who would tell him to go easy on himself. He was looking for someone who would agree with him. Someone to tell him he really was responsible."

"So Kenneally came along and agreed with him?" McCaleb said.

Shan stepped away from the window and paced across the carpet. "If Kenneally was the fifth robber, then he's been living with the secret for seventeen years. He managed to get away from the Great Lakes Bank, but he did it by ramming a patrol car and killing a Sault Sainte Marie cop—Scott White. So Kenneally knows he's got a murder charge hanging over him. After all this time he ought to be safe—but then Callie Spencer decides to run for the Senate and suddenly people are talking about the robbery again. Dawtrey, Kormoran, and Bell saw him back then. He can't be sure what they remember."

McCaleb nodded. "So he has a motive for wanting them dead."

"Right," said Elizabeth. "And then he meets Lark, a man who's tormented because he didn't do enough to save a girl with a pretty smile—a smile like Callie Spencer's."

"Kenneally gets Lark to come to him for therapy," Shan said. "Lark talks to him about feeling responsible for Susanna's death. Kenneally tells Lark what he wants to hear: he *is* responsible."

"Then Kenneally steers him toward Callie Spencer," said Elizabeth. "He plants the idea that Dawtrey and the others are a threat to her, just like Susanna's abusive husband was a threat. No rational person would believe that the Great Lakes robbers posed a threat to Callie after all these years, but Lark wasn't rational. And Kenneally knew it. I think Kenneally played up the similarities between Susanna and Callie. There was the physical resemblance—the smile—but just as importantly there was the similarity between their fathers: both ended up in wheelchairs. Susanna's husband, Derek Everly, was responsible for putting her father in a wheelchair, and Lark did nothing about it. If only he had done the right thing—if he had killed Derek—then Susanna wouldn't have been driven to suicide. Lark would have saved her. Likewise for Callie. The Great Lakes robbers put her father in a wheelchair. And in Lark's mind, there was still time to do something about it. To save her."

McCaleb looked skeptical. "This sounds like an awful lot of speculation."

"It's not all speculation," Elizabeth said, pointing to Lark's notebook on the desk. "I've only had time to skim through what Lark wrote in there, but I can tell you that he wrote pages and pages about how he failed Susanna, and how he wasn't going to fail Callie. And the entries in there are dated. The first reference to Callie comes after Lark met Kenneally."

McCaleb glanced at the notebook. "I don't suppose there's anything explicit. Lark doesn't actually say that Kenneally told him to kill anyone."

"No," Elizabeth said. "I didn't see anything like that. I think Kenneally was much more subtle about it. But Lark got the message. The Great Lakes robbers were his chance to redeem himself."

Shan had stopped his pacing and gone back to the window. "If we assume Kenneally manipulated Lark," he said, "then some other things fall into place. Lark's depression worked in Kenneally's favor, so he didn't prescribe drugs to treat it. When Lark complained about headaches, Kenneally gave him some pills and told him they were Imitrex. But they weren't."

"It still sounds far-fetched," McCaleb said. "If Kenneally wanted Dawtrey and the others dead, why didn't he just hire someone to do it? Why go through all this trouble with Lark? And what made him think he could turn Lark into a killer?"

"He's a psychiatrist," said Shan. "It's not like he knows any professional hitmen."

McCaleb looked to Elizabeth for her opinion, but she was still considering his question. What made Kenneally think he could turn Lark into a killer?

The answer came to her. "He did a trial run," she said.

McCaleb's mouth made a puzzled frown.

"Derek Everly," she said. "Lark blamed him for Susanna's suicide. But he didn't do anything about it for three years. Then Lark met Kenneally, and a month later Everly was murdered."

"But Lark was never charged in that case," said McCaleb.

"No. The detective we talked to in Dearborn thought Lark did it, but he couldn't prove it."

"Then we're not likely to prove Kenneally persuaded him to do it," said McCaleb. "Look, let's assume Kenneally had some kind of influence over Lark. So he sent Lark after Dawtrey, Kormoran, and Bell. And we think he did that because he, Kenneally, was the getaway driver in the Great Lakes robbery. Can we prove that?"

Shan lifted his shoulders. "We walked Kenneally past Harlan Spencer. Spencer said he didn't recognize him."

"We can try Sutton Bell," said Elizabeth. "But he only met the getaway driver briefly."

McCaleb got down from his perch on the desk. "That doesn't sound promising," he said. "So do we have anything at all on Kenneally? Any actual proof of a crime he committed?"

Shan smiled grimly. "We do if we find Lucy Navarro in cold storage in his garage."

"Right. The freezer. Is there any reason to believe she's in there?"

"Lark thought so," said Elizabeth.

"I can't get a search warrant based on a dead man's hunch," said McCaleb. "Can we link Kenneally with Navarro?"

"Lark saw a blue minivan the night Lucy Navarro disappeared," Shan said. "Kenneally owns a minivan."

"Please tell me it's blue."

"It's gray," said Elizabeth. "His wife drove it to the hospital this afternoon."

"Could it have been painted in the last three days?"

"Didn't look like it, but we can check."

"Maybe Lark made a mistake that night," Shan offered. "He confused gray for blue."

"Maybe Lark was mistaken about a lot of things," McCaleb said. "I think the only way we're going to get a look inside Kenneally's freezer or his minivan is if he gives us permission. How likely is that?"

ELIZABETH AND I circled around and ended our walk where it began, in front of City Hall.

"We asked Kenneally to consent to a search," she said to me, "but his lawyer jumped in and dismissed the whole idea. I don't know if he did it on principle, or if he thinks Kenneally's guilty."

"So that's the end of it?" I said.

She turned to face me. "No, David. The reason I'm telling you about this is to let you know it's not the end. We're going to look into Kenneally's background, try to connect him with Floyd Lambeau and the Great Lakes robbery. I'm not giving up on this. But I don't want you to do anything. I know your first instinct when you leave here will be to head to Kenneally's house. But you won't help Lucy that way. If she's there, she's beyond your help. And if you go there, you'll make things harder for me."

We parted there, at the steps of City Hall. She had to stay behind to wrap things up with Kenneally. I walked west as far as Main Street, which was the right idea, if I wanted to go home. Then I turned south toward the *Gray Streets* building.

The air in the office felt stale. I switched on my desk lamp and touched the necklace that hung there—Elizabeth's glass beads. They glowed blue in the light. I put up the window and heard the same saxophone I'd heard the night before, the winding notes of a Charlie Parker tune coming up from the street. I thought about Lucy Navarro. On Monday night, less than a week ago, she had called to thank me for setting up a meeting with Callie Spencer. We'd joked about what might happen if she asked the wrong questions. *If I disappear, maybe you can find me,* she'd said. *If you can't find me, I wouldn't mind being avenged.*

I had her book on the corner of my desk, her vampire novel, right next to the bottle of Macallan that Alan Beckett had given me. I wanted a drink, because I didn't like the thoughts going through my head.

I didn't know where Matthew Kenneally lived, but I could find out. I didn't have my car; I'd left it at the Spencer house. But I could get it.

Maybe you can find me.

I stood listening to the music from the street and tried to think of a way around it.

If you go there, you'll make things harder for me, Elizabeth had said.

That was true. If I went there, that made me the kind of man who couldn't keep his nose out of trouble, the kind who broke into people's garages and looked in their freezers. It would be bad for me if I got caught, and worse for Elizabeth.

She hadn't made me promise her. I took some comfort in that.

I picked up the bottle from the desk and carried it with me through the outer office to the washroom. I poured it in the sink, watched it spiral down the drain. A token gesture, really. Because I had a fifth of Glenfiddich in the deep drawer of the desk.

When I dialed Alan Beckett's number, I had my feet up on the windowsill and a glass balanced on my knee.

"I'm planning to commit a crime," I said to him when he answered.

A grumble of annoyance came over the line. "I'd like to hear about it, I'm sure. But you've reached me at a bad time."

"I thought you might like to come along," I said. "You could bring your glass cutter. You might be useful."

"Have you been drinking, Mr. Loogan?"

"Not so you'd notice. The crime I'm planning—it's a break-in. At Matthew Kenneally's house."

The sound of his breathing. Then: "Is that supposed to mean something to me?"

"I'd like to have you there," I said. "To see the look on your face when I find what I think I'm going to find."

"I'm hanging up now. It would be lovely if you didn't call me again."

"She asked me to avenge her, Al. You don't think I can walk away from that, do you?"

"Good night, Mr. Loogan."

The line went dead and I dropped the receiver into the cradle. I raised the glass and studied the Scotch in the light of the desk lamp. A minute later I got up and went to pour it in the sink. When I got back the phone was ringing. I answered it.

"Did you change your mind, Al?"

After a moment of pure silence on the line, I heard a voice that didn't belong to Alan Beckett.

"Loogan, it's me."

I regretted the waste of the Scotch then. My mouth was very dry. It couldn't seem to form words.

"I'm right outside," she said. "Shall I come up?"

I moved to the window and looked down. Scanned the street and found a patch of blue: the roof of a minivan.

There's one possibility I left off the list of things to do in Ann Arbor on a Saturday night. Sometimes you can see magic.

Down on the street the front passenger door of the minivan opened and Lucy Navarro stepped out.

CHAPTER 49

In the days that followed I slept late. I spent long afternoons watching television, flipping around through old movies. Once, I found *In the Heat of the Night* and stayed with it all the way through. Rod Steiger playing the police chief, Bill Gillespie. The way he inhabited his uniform, the way he walked when he carried Sidney Poitier's suitcase at the train station—he made me think of Walter Delacorte.

Around the time I watched the movie, they were burying Delacorte in Sault Sainte Marie. The turnout was small: one ex-wife out of three, a daughter from somewhere out west, a few deputies and their families. I heard about it from Nick Dawtrey, who attended with his mother.

When I tired of television I went for walks. One ambitious evening I got out the lawn mower to cut the grass. Halfway through, Sarah came out and insisted on taking over. I let her. I was supposed to be mending.

During the daytime, I had the house mostly to myself. There was always something in the refrigerator for me to eat. There was nowhere I needed to go, no one tied up in a basement waiting for me to find her. Lucy Navarro had left town. I didn't know where she'd gone and it was none of my concern.

The Ann Arbor police weren't pleased with her. She went to see them that Saturday night, after turning up at *Gray Streets*. She told them that on Wednesday around midnight a former boyfriend had appeared unexpectedly in the parking lot of her hotel. On an impulse she had driven off with him, and they had spent three days together in his apartment in Chicago, reigniting their old romance, cut off from the rest of the world. No television, no Internet. Only on Saturday had she bothered to charge her cell phone and check her messages; only then had she learned that people were looking for her.

She told the police she was sorry. She hoped she hadn't caused too much trouble.

Some of the elements of the story—the ones that could be readily checked—were true. The putative boyfriend, an architect named Railton, lived alone in an apartment in Chicago; he owned a blue Honda Odyssey minivan. The rest of the story was barely plausible, and Elizabeth didn't believe a word of it. Owen McCaleb listened to it silently, waited for Lucy to leave his office, and kicked a wastebasket across the room—the closest he's ever come, I'm told, to throwing a tantrum.

I knew Lucy was lying.

I'd like to say she told me the truth about what had happened, but when she came up to my office Saturday night she gave me the same version the police would soon hear. I watched her across the desk: her hair in a limp ponytail; dark circles under her eyes, as if she hadn't slept in three days. Her face seemed thin and drawn, and I thought she had lost weight. She wore blue jeans and a turtleneck with long sleeves.

She tried to inject some life into her story, but it seemed like an act. Her usual energy was gone. When she got to the end, I did nothing to fill the silence. I'd brought the bottle out of the drawer again and filled two glasses; they rested on the desk between us. I sat with one foot propped on the open drawer and watched her reach for her glass.

"I'm sorry, Loogan," she said. "You must have been worried."

"Me?" I said, looking up at the shadows on the ceiling. "Why?"

"You must have wondered what happened to me. I feel terrible."

I shook my head at the shadows. "I figured there must be an explanation, and if I just sat tight, everything would work itself out." I looked down and saw her holding the glass. "And what do you know—I was right."

She didn't seem convinced, but I wasn't trying to be convincing.

"Well," she said, "I hope it wasn't too bad."

"I hardly noticed. I've had my own troubles. I got stabbed, you know."

She took a sip and returned the glass to the desktop. "I'm still catching up on the news," she said. "But I heard you got shot."

"No. Stabbed. With a bayonet."

"The report I read said you were shot by Anthony Lark."

"Goes to show you can't trust what you read. It wasn't Lark. It was an unidentified assailant. In a clown suit." I stared at her soberly across the desk. "But you had no way of knowing that. You were in a love nest with an architect."

A little life crept into her pale green eyes. She smiled. "My architect is downstairs, waiting in the van."

I shrugged. "I could find a clown, if I needed one. What really happened to you?"

"Just what I said."

"No. You didn't run off with an old boyfriend and leave the engine of your Beetle running. You didn't spend the last three days in his bed. I don't care how much lust you had to catch up on, you wouldn't have gone all that time without turning on the news. You wouldn't have forgotten that you were writing a story about Callie Spencer."

Her smile receded. "I'm done with all that, Loogan."

"You're not a reporter anymore?"

"I'm quitting the *National Current*."

"To do what?"

"I've got a book contract."

"You told me you were through writing novels."

"I've reconsidered."

I laid a hand on the blotter of the desk, a feeble attempt to close some of the distance between us. "What did they do to you?"

"No one did anything."

She was lying. Someone had done something. Maybe Alan Beckett, or Jay Casterbridge, or Matthew Kenneally. Or all three of them, for all I knew. One of them could have grabbed her on Wednesday night. They could have stashed her somewhere—maybe in a house owned by Casterbridge Realty. They would have kept her bound, maybe drugged. Kenneally was a psychiatrist; he would have access to sedatives.

As for how the scenario had played out, I had only my wayward imagination to guide me. Maybe they had threatened her. Or the ordeal had worn her down. I imagined Alan Beckett leaning over her in some dark place, telling her this could all be over if she would just accept the offer he had made her. If she would drop the story about Callie and go back to writing vampire books.

And now she sat in my office, her arms crossed protectively. I tried to remember if I had ever seen her in long sleeves before.

"Show me your arms," I said.

She uncrossed them, twining her fingers together in her lap. "Why?"

There would be needle tracks if they had drugged her. Marks on her wrists from the rope or the duct tape, or whatever they had used. I wanted to see.

"Show me," I said.

It would be easy to walk around the desk, take hold of a wrist, push the sleeve up her arm. I thought about doing it. Brought my foot down off the drawer. Lucy flinched at the movement, as if she was afraid of me, and I knew then that I wouldn't make her show me anything.

I went around to her slowly and she got to her feet. I put my hand out and after the smallest hesitation she put hers into it, warm slim fingers gliding over mine. She stepped close to me and I rested my chin on the top of her head.

"You can tell me," I said, whispering the words to her hair. "I'll protect you." A ridiculous promise, considering the job I'd done of protecting her so far.

Her head moved side to side.

"Was it Beckett?" I asked her.

She wouldn't answer me. We didn't say anything else, not in the elevator down to the lobby or between the lobby and the street. I opened the door of the van for her, and her architect nodded to me in a gentlemanly way. Closing the door, I stepped back and watched the van drive to the end of the block and around the corner.

The saxophonist was still at work in front of Café Felix. I walked over and dropped a couple dollars into the open case at his feet. I didn't recognize the tune he was playing, but it was something mournful.

CHAPTER 50

The story of Lucy Navarro's reappearance was a pale, dull thing, and no one spent much energy reporting it. The *National Current* ran a paragraph on its website and nothing at all in its print edition. The tabloid had been more enamored of the story when it looked as if Lucy might have been murdered by an obsessed fan—a kid from Ohio who wanted to be a vampire.

The writers at the *Current* got a bit more mileage out of the news that Lark had died on Callie Spencer's doorstep—but even then I thought their hearts weren't quite in it. Members of the respectable press covered the story reluctantly. Most of them decided it didn't really have much to do with Callie: Lark was a lost soul who might have latched onto anyone. The pundits on the news shows all agreed that Callie had handled an unfortunate situation with grace. If anyone had asked me, I would have said the same.

By Monday evening the news of Lark's death had faded into insignificance. Because on Monday afternoon Senator John Casterbridge held a press conference to announce that he had been diagnosed with Alzheimer's disease.

I WATCHED IT ON CNN. The senator had his son and Callie with him. He had doctors from the University of Michigan Hospital on hand to answer questions. He stood at a podium in an auditorium on campus and read a statement thanking his constituents for their support over the years. He talked about the things they had accomplished together, and the bright future he saw for the state. He assured them he felt fine, the disease was still in its early stages. So far, his symptoms were mild—small problems with his memory, nothing more.

It wasn't hard to believe. He handled himself well, spoke smoothly. I knew he was lying about the severity of his symptoms—because a week earlier he had gone on a mission to find his dead wife. But I didn't begrudge him the lie. It was nobody's business.

As he came to the conclusion of his statement he paused and brushed back a lock of silver hair. "This is not the end for me," he said. "But it is the end of my service to this great state. I would have liked to serve out the remaining months of my term, but that no longer seems possible. So it is with sadness that I'm resigning my office, effective today."

There were shouted questions, but the senator didn't answer them. He waved solemnly for the cameras and walked away from the podium, with Jay and Callie falling in beside him. The shot widened out, and you could see one of his doctors stepping up to the microphone. But the senator managed to dominate the frame, striding with his head high, until finally he passed through a door and out of sight.

Alan Beckett was missing from the scene, but I had no doubt he'd coordinated everything. The timing of the announcement was perfect. It shifted attention away from Lark and back onto the Senate race. The next few days were rife with speculation about who would fill the senator's vacant seat. By the end of the week the governor had chosen a well-respected former congressman. Everyone understood he was just a placeholder who would serve until Callie Spencer could be elected and sworn in. The polls were running solidly in her favor.

THE LAST DAYS of July gave way to August. With Lark dead, Sutton Bell brought his wife and daughter back home. Elizabeth showed him a picture of Matthew Kenneally from his college days. Bell said he didn't recognize him. Maybe he was telling the truth, but I think he would have said the same thing either way. Sutton Bell wanted to keep the Great Lakes robbery in the past.

The county prosecutor declined to bring an indictment against Matthew Kenneally for shooting Lark, on the sound theory that no jury would convict him.

ON THURSDAY NIGHT, the sixth of August, I looked in the bathroom mirror and realized I hadn't shaved in more than a week. I put a fresh cartridge in my razor and went to work. When I got into bed a few minutes later, Elizabeth glanced up from the papers she had spread across the sheets and ran a palm over my cheek. "Better," she declared.

"You might have said something," I told her.

She smiled down at her papers. "I like it when you figure things out on your own."

I picked up a random page and she slapped gently at the back of my hand. "I've got these just the way I want them."

The papers were copies of old files from the original investigation of the Great Lakes robbery. A lot of them had to do with Floyd Lambeau. I knew Elizabeth was trying to find a connection between Lambeau and Matthew Kenneally.

I reached for another page. "Does McCaleb know you have these?" I asked.

"Never mind what McCaleb knows," she said.

Owen McCaleb had decided there wasn't much point in trying to connect Matthew Kenneally to a seventeen-year-old crime from another jurisdiction. He had discouraged Elizabeth from digging around, but he hadn't forbidden it.

So she was digging. The page I'd picked up held notes on Kenneally's background. He'd been born in Steven's Point, Wisconsin. His parents were Richard J. Kenneally and Mary M. LaFleur. Elizabeth had noted the date of his birth and the date of his parents' marriage. In the margin was a scribbled note: *Significant?*

"What does this mean?" I asked her.

She glanced over. "It means you're being lazy."

I looked at the dates again and worked it out on my own. "Kenneally was born seven months after his parents got married. So he was conceived out of wedlock."

Elizabeth nodded. "Or he was premature."

"And that's important?"

"I don't know what's important yet."

Kenneally had earned his graduate degree at Johns Hopkins. But at the time of the Great Lakes robbery, he had been an undergraduate at the University of Wisconsin in Madison.

"Did Floyd Lambeau ever teach at the University of Wisconsin?" I asked.

Elizabeth passed me a folder that held a list of Lambeau's lectures and teaching appointments spanning two decades. A yellow tab marked one of the pages.

"He was there for a weeklong seminar on Native American history," she said.

I turned to the tabbed page. The seminar had been held a few months before the robbery. "It's him," I said. "Kenneally was the getaway driver."

She gave me an indulgent look. "Not long ago you thought it was Jay Casterbridge."

"That was a guess. This is evidence."

"It's not enough. Not yet."

On Friday I woke at noon. I went downstairs and found Elizabeth and Sarah gone, all the curtains thrown wide, a whole lot of bright daylight streaming in.

Forty-five minutes later I drove in to *Gray Streets*. The mailbox in the lobby was stuffed tight, and I pried the envelopes loose and took them up to the sixth floor. While I was sorting through them the phone rang.

The voice on the line said, "I've been reading more of your magazine, Mr. Loogan."

A woman's voice. It took me a moment to realize it belonged to Amelia Copeland. It sounded as if she might be driving—I thought I could hear wind rushing by. I imagined her tooling along in a roadster from a 1940s movie.

"I just finished a story called 'Blood Over Jade,'" she said. "It's beguiling. And the dialogue—just gorgeous."

"Gorgeous?" I said.

"Effervescent. You're an intriguing man, Mr. Loogan."

"I don't mean to be."

"Most people, when I offer them money, trip over themselves to collect it. But not you."

I remembered now: She had asked me to call and set up a meeting.

"I'm sorry," I said. "I've been out of the office. Recovering from"—what was I recovering from?—"a disappointment."

"A disappointment?"

"And a gunshot wound."

She laughed. "That's grand. You can tell me about it over dinner. Are you free?"

"Today?"

"Say five o'clock. At Gratzi. Do you know it?"

"I know it."

"Delightful. See you then."

I hung up the phone and said "Delightful" to the empty office. I spun my chair in a slow circle, trying to work out what had just happened. Amelia Copeland's money was supposed to buy my cooperation. The last time she called, it was because Alan Beckett wanted me to convince Lucy to drop her story about Callie Spencer. But that couldn't be what he wanted now. Lucy had already dropped her story.

The chair came to a stop. Maybe I was overanalyzing this. Maybe Amelia Copeland simply liked *Gray Streets*. Sometimes things are just as they seem.

I SPENT THE AFTERNOON sorting mail and editing manuscripts, and at five I walked over to Gratzi and found Amelia Copeland waiting for me at a table on the mezzanine, wearing men's trousers with a silk blouse and pearls. She ordered the *orecchiette alla rustica;* I had the *penne con pollo*.

Our conversation hopped from subject to subject. She quizzed me on my knowledge of the classics: Arthur Conan Doyle, Dashiell Hammett, Dorothy Sayers. She showed me pictures of her grandchildren: good-looking kids who rode horses and played hockey and softball. She wanted to know what it was like to be shot, and I told her about Anthony Lark. She'd heard of him but hadn't followed his story.

"I don't keep up with the news these days," she said. "Too dreary."

When the waiter cleared our plates away she ordered espresso and tiramisu for both of us and got down to business. She asked me if *Gray Streets* had a foundation.

"I didn't know it needed one," I said.

We lingered for another thirty minutes and I heard all about the tax advantages of nonprofit foundations. When we got up from the table I had the name of a lawyer who could set one up for me. Then her foundation would make a grant to my foundation, and we'd be off and running.

A few high clouds had drifted in over Main Street when we left the restaurant. She told me she had parked in a garage nearby. We walked there together, making companionable conversation. In the elevator of the garage I finally got around to asking her the question that had been nagging at me. "Ms. Copeland," I began.

"Amelia," she said.

"I've been wondering, Amelia, how you found out about *Gray Streets*. Did someone ask you to contact me?"

People look away from each other in elevators, but Amelia Copeland met my eyes. "If you know enough to pose the question," she said, "you must have an idea of the answer."

"Alan Beckett."

"Alan Beckett, naturally. Now there's something I've been wondering too. What did you do to offend him?"

The doors slid open and we stepped out. "Did I do something to offend him?" I said.

"Something made him change his opinion of you. Two weeks ago he had nothing but good things to say, but now he thinks you're a very disagreeable man."

I had some ideas about his change of opinion, but I kept them to myself.

"He must have his reasons," I said. "But if that's the case, why did you call me today?"

I watched her scowl. "Alan Beckett is a glorified errand boy," she said. "I don't take orders from him." Her expression brightened. "Besides, he's wrong about you."

We'd been walking up a ramp along a row of cars, but now she stopped and said, "Here I am." Over her shoulder I could see a bright red Mazda convertible, an updated version of the roadster I had imagined her driving. I pictured her tooling along with the wind ruffling her gray hair and the ends of a long scarf flapping behind her.

She smiled and said it had been a pleasure to finally get together, and I agreed.

"You'll be in touch?" she asked. I told her I would.

Then with a little nod she turned away and walked past the convertible and climbed into the vehicle parked next to it.

A blue minivan.

CHAPTER 51

When I got home I found Elizabeth waiting on the porch for me, sitting at ease in a patio chair with her bare feet on the railing. She had on jeans torn at the knees and one of my white dress shirts with the sleeves rolled to her elbows. She seemed still and calm, but her eyes were alive, the way they get when she has news to tell.

When I sat next to her she said, "All this time, we've been asking the wrong questions."

A butterfly landed on the railing by her feet. I waited.

"All you have to do is look at the timeline," she said. "The Great Lakes robbery, seventeen years ago. Floyd Lambeau died. Matthew Kenneally got away. The other three were arrested—Terry Dawtrey, Sutton Bell, and Henry Kormoran. Flash forward almost a year: Terry Dawtrey went on trial at the courthouse in Sault Sainte Marie. His father, Charlie Dawtrey, was there every day. During the breaks, he spent time in a park nearby."

"That's where he met Madelyn Turner—Nick's mother," I said.

"Exactly. Madelyn was forty years old. Charlie Dawtrey was pushing sixty. He'd spent his whole life going from one menial job to another. But a few weeks after the trial, they were married. Why? That's the question I should have been asking all along. Even Walter Delacorte saw it. Do you remember?"

I remembered. Walter Delacorte sitting across from us in a diner in Sault Sainte Marie. Elizabeth had asked him why Madelyn's marriage to Charlie Dawtrey ended. *You'd be better off asking why it started,* he'd said.

"She married him because she felt sorry for him," I said. "That's what she told us."

Strands of raven hair fell across Elizabeth's cheek. "If you feel sorry for a man, you let him cry on your shoulder. Maybe you even take him to bed. You don't usually marry him and have his baby. Madelyn Turner lied about Charlie Dawtrey. She didn't meet him by chance. She went looking for him. She couldn't help it. They had something in common."

Elizabeth took a folder from a little glass-top table beside her chair. She handed me the page I'd looked at the night before, the one with the names of Matthew Kenneally's parents. Richard J. Kenneally and Mary M. LaFleur.

"The M stands for Madelyn," she said. "LaFleur was her maiden name."

She rose and went to lean against the railing. "Madelyn grew up in Sault Sainte Marie," she said. "Moved away when she was nineteen and pregnant with Matthew. Richard Kenneally took her to Steven's Point, Wisconsin; he had an administrative job at the university there. He passed away when Matthew was in his teens. Eventually Matthew went off to college and Madelyn moved back home to Sault Sainte Marie.

"She was living there at the time of the Great Lakes robbery. Matthew sped away from the bank that day, heading for the interstate. That's where he crashed into the patrol car and killed Scott White. He would have panicked then; he would have gone to his mother. We know he got help from someone, because the police found the black SUV abandoned, but they never found him. So when Terry Dawtrey's trial came along, it must have weighed on Madelyn's mind. Terry shot a cop. Everyone understood he was going to prison. Charlie Dawtrey was going to lose his son. But Madelyn's son had been spared. She couldn't stay away from Charlie. She felt sorry for him, but more than that—she felt guilty."

Madelyn had told us part of the truth, that day we went to see her in her farmhouse up north. *When they sent Terry to prison, it broke Charlie's heart,* she'd said. *I thought I could change things by giving him another child.* She had given him Nick, a new son to replace the one he'd lost.

"There's more to the story," I said to Elizabeth.

"Of course there is."

I tapped the page I was holding. "Matthew Kenneally was conceived out of wedlock."

"That's right."

"I have my doubts about whether Richard Kenneally was the father."

"So do I," Elizabeth said. "It's been staring us in the face. Madelyn Turner was a beauty in her day. And she was attracted to older men, the kind of men who had something more to offer."

I had some fine times when I was young, she'd said to us. *If I had a mind to, I could tell you stories.*

"Men like John Casterbridge," I said.

Elizabeth nodded. "Madelyn was twenty when she gave birth to Matthew Kenneally. That was thirty-seven years ago. Back then, John Casterbridge was a congressman with ambitions to run for the Senate. He traveled to cities all over the state—including Sault Sainte Marie. He was married and had a young son already, but that wouldn't have stopped him. And if he was Matthew Kenneally's father, that goes a long way toward explaining why Kenneally was never linked to the Great Lakes robbery. I think you were right: the senator's son was the fifth robber, and the senator used his influence to cover it up. You just had the wrong son."

Something more than guesswork had led Elizabeth to connect Madelyn Turner to John Casterbridge.

"I think they've kept in touch all these years," she said, picking up the folder again. "Two and a half weeks ago, Kyle Scudder was still being held in the murder of Charlie Dawtrey. Scudder is Madelyn Turner's current beau. On Monday the twentieth, Madelyn was calling everyone she knew to try to get him released. Remember?"

I remembered. Nick had told me so, and I had told Elizabeth, and she had recorded it on her timeline. Now she passed me the relevant page.

"That was Monday," she said. "On Tuesday night, Scudder was released. The charges against him were dropped. Look what happened in between."

It was right there. *Monday night, July 20: Senator John Casterbridge in auto accident.* He'd said he was on a mission; his wife needed his help.

We'd assumed he was talking about his dead wife. He'd been talking about Madelyn Turner, the mother of his son.

The place I need to go is a long way off, he'd said to me. It was true. Madelyn lived in Brimley near Sault Sainte Marie.

He didn't get there that night. But the next day he must have come to his senses and realized he didn't need to go north to have Scudder set free. All he needed to do was make a phone call and ask a favor of a prosecutor.

"It's far from conclusive," Elizabeth said. "It doesn't prove that John Casterbridge had an affair with Madelyn Turner, or that he's Matthew Kenneally's father."

"He is," I said. "I'm sure of it."

Her eyes studied me. "How can you be sure?"

"Because Amelia Copeland drives a blue minivan."

I HAD ALMOST LET her drive away, because the sight of the van caught me off guard. But when she pulled out of the parking space, I rushed to the driver's window and rapped my knuckles on the glass. I thought she should have been startled. My movements felt wild. My mind was racing. But she powered down the window and looked at me calmly.

"Who's been driving this van?" I asked her.

Deep lines etched themselves into her brow. She didn't answer.

I tried again. "Did Alan Beckett borrow it the week before last?" Beckett. That's the way my mind was working. That's the rut I had fallen into.

"No," said Amelia Copeland. "Not him."

"IT WAS THE SENATOR," I said to Elizabeth. "He borrowed her minivan on the twenty-second, two days after his accident. His own car was in the shop. And Lucy Navarro disappeared that night." I got up and joined Elizabeth by the railing. "The senator looked after Kenneally seventeen years ago. Cut a deal with Harlan Spencer, so Spencer would forget what the getaway driver from the Great Lakes robbery looked like. And the senator's still looking after Kenneally. He found out Lucy was asking too many questions about the robbery, and he did something about it."

Elizabeth brushed her fingertips across my brow. "I assume you're not telling me the senator drove to the parking lot of the Winston Hotel on the twenty-second and dragged Lucy into a van."

"No," I said. "I don't think he had to drag her."

ON SATURDAY MORNING we packed for a short trip, one suitcase for both of us. We left Ann Arbor around nine o'clock. My car, Elizabeth behind the wheel. The heat seared the road ahead of us. We figured it would cool down as we went north.

Two hours in, we traded places. The radio station we'd been listening to began to fade, and I scanned through the dial looking for something else. I found Bruce Springsteen, "Born to Run." When it ended, a commercial came on and Elizabeth reached over to turn down the volume.

"You know," she said, "she'll probably refuse to talk to us."

She meant Madelyn Turner. And I knew she was right. But if we wanted to establish that the senator was Matthew Kenneally's father, Madelyn seemed like the person to talk to.

I would have tried talking to the senator himself, but I didn't know where to find him. His condo in the Bridgewell Building was empty. It was the first place I'd gone after my conversation with Amelia Copeland.

The kid behind the concierge desk spotted me as soon as I walked into the lobby.

"Good evening, sir," he said. "You can go right up." He wore a more expensive suit than last time.

I stopped at the desk. "You're supposed to say the senator doesn't want to be disturbed."

"Things change."

"So he wants to be disturbed now?"

"Hardly. But you won't disturb him, I'm sure."

I stood listening to the murmur of the fountain. "He's not here, is he?"

"No, sir."

"What if I told you I don't believe a word you say?"

"It would cut me to the quick."

"I bet it would," I said. "I'll need to see for myself if he's here."

He waved me toward the elevators. "Go right up."

I went up, all the way to the top. The door to the senator's condo stood half open. Inside, a woman in a maid's uniform pushed a vacuum over the carpet. She switched it off long enough to tell me that the senator was gone and she didn't know when he'd be back.

"Do you know where he went?" I asked her.

She looked me over and came away unimpressed. "That's not my business," she said. "Or yours."

A FEW MINUTES AFTER ONE, Elizabeth and I pulled off I-75 and crossed over the Au Sable River into a town called Grayling. We passed a canoe livery and a tavern called Spike's and found a café with a carving of a moose above the door. We bought sandwiches and apples and ate them in a shaded spot by the river, on a blanket spread on the grass.

Elizabeth strolled down to the water and I sat cross-legged on the ground, studying a road map. A white moth flitted over the grass. After a while I folded the map and gathered the sandwich wrappers and the blanket. Elizabeth met me at the car.

"Have you got the route worked out?"

She said it playfully, because we both knew the route. North on I-75 for another hundred and thirty miles, then west toward Brimley. No need to look at a map.

"What are you thinking?" she asked.

I looked off at the sunlight on the river. "The senator," I said. "He's got a house in Grosse Pointe and an apartment in Lansing—"

"Those are both a bit out of our way."

"—and a bungalow in Saint Ignace. We'll be passing right by it."

"You think he's there?"

"He could be."

She touched my shoulder. "What will you say to him if you find him?"

"I'll figure that out when we get there," I said. "The problem is finding the place. It's supposed to be by the lake, but I don't have a street address."

I watched her smile. That was something she could remedy. She got her cell phone out and flipped it open.

"Stick with me," she said.

SAINT IGNACE WAS ninety miles north of Grayling, on the far side of the Mackinac Bridge. When we took the exit it was going on four o'clock. We drove east with the windows down, cool air coming in off Lake Huron, the sky a washed-out blue. When the road gave out, we swung north onto State Street, catching glimpses of the water beyond the houses and the trees.

The senator's bungalow had a dark-shingled roof over white clapboard siding. A mailbox on a post at the end of the driveway. No name or number on the mailbox. We might have driven by if we hadn't spotted a familiar car parked alongside the house, half in the shade of a white oak. Not the senator's Mercury. Lucy Navarro's yellow Beetle.

CHAPTER 52

We left our car in the drive and walked along a path to the back of the house. From there Elizabeth picked her way along a rocky patch of ground that sloped down to the lake, and I climbed a set of wooden steps to a screened-in porch where I found Lucy at a mission table with a laptop in front of her and the pages of a manuscript spread all around.

She grinned like a child caught at some mischief. "Hello, Loogan."

The door clapped shut behind me and I sat in a chair across from her. I tossed a small object onto the table. Smooth and cool, almost the color of gold. It was one of the spare bullets from the revolver Bridget had given me. The gun itself was where I'd left it in the glove compartment of the car.

The bullet landed on a stack of printed pages and rolled in a little half-circle.

"I found that outside on the steps," I said.

Lucy picked it up and closed her fingers around it. Her eyes were bright and she looked well rested. She wore no makeup, nothing to hide the freckles on the bridge of her nose.

Her blouse was a wispy thing that bared her arms. There were no marks on her wrists. There never had been.

She grinned again and opened her fingers, letting the bullet roll onto the table.

"I don't believe you," she said.

"That's the difference between you and me. That night at the hotel in Sault Sainte Marie, when you told me you found a bullet outside my door, and another outside yours, I believed you. It was clever. It put us on the same side, aligned against unknown forces. It made me want to look out for you."

Her grin faded. "You can't hold that against me, Loogan. I didn't know you then."

"No. You were just fumbling around. Trying anything that might work. What was it you said? You were trying to cultivate me as a source."

"Loogan—"

"I don't think I did you any good as a source. But you did cultivate me."

"You make it sound worse than it is. I didn't plan this."

"No. You fell into it. You did pretty well for someone without a plan." I picked up a stack of pages from the table and scanned a few lines. "This doesn't read like a vampire novel," I said.

Her voice went soft. "I'm sorry I lied, Loogan. You have to look at it from my point of view." She brushed at a speck of dust on the laptop keyboard. She didn't want to meet my eyes.

"Let's have it, then," I said.

"Have what?"

"Your point of view. I'd like to hear it."

She looked past me, through the screened windows of the porch. I turned to follow her gaze. Down on the beach, Elizabeth had taken off her shoes. She was wading in the shallows.

"This has nothing to do with the Ann Arbor police," I said, turning back to Lucy. "This is between you and me."

Lucy thought it over, brushing her fingers over the keyboard some more.

"Whose idea was it?" I prompted. "Yours or the senator's?"

She left the keyboard alone and got up to walk around the room. "He came to me. He showed up out of nowhere in the parking lot of the hotel that night and asked me to take a ride with him. He wanted to talk. How could I refuse?"

"No reporter could," I said. "But why leave your car running in the lot?"

She shrugged. "I wasn't thinking. It's a wonder I remembered to grab my purse."

She told me the senator had driven her away from the hotel and down a series of random streets. "He knew about my story," she said. "Knew that I was looking into the Great Lakes robbery. He told me I should think bigger. Sure, maybe I could find something that would embarrass Callie, maybe even keep her from getting elected. But he thought it was beneath me. 'If you want scandals,' he said, 'I can give you scandals.'"

And he had kept his word. The evidence was spread across the table. Stacks of printed pages—some of them outlines, some of them rough drafts of chapters. The one I'd been looking at had a title that read "Intelligence Failures—The Iraq War."

John Casterbridge had served five terms as a congressman and another five as a senator. He was giving her an insider's view of forty years' worth of scandals, everything from Watergate to weapons of mass destruction.

"He offered me an exclusive," Lucy said. "As much access as I needed, starting that night. The plan was for me to check out of my room. We would go off somewhere and get to work. But when we drove back to the hotel we saw police cars. We kept on driving."

"Was that your decision or his?" I asked.

"It was mutual. You have to understand, I didn't know you'd been shot. I didn't realize what a big deal it would turn into. And the senator didn't want to be seen by the police. He didn't want to explain himself to anyone. His family, Alan Beckett—none of them knew he planned to talk to me. And if they knew, they wouldn't have approved. As for me—"

"You didn't want to break the spell. Here's John Casterbridge willing to talk to you—a man who never talks to reporters. You were afraid something might change his mind."

"That's true." She was standing still now, looking out at the lake. A distant patch of white was the sail of a catamaran.

"You know about his condition, don't you?" I said. "Some people might say he shouldn't be making important decisions—like whether to talk to reporters about intelligence failures."

"I didn't know about that at the time. Honestly, he seems fine to me. Sometimes he'll get tired in the evenings and go off on tangents, but other than that . . ." She let the thought trail off.

I prompted her again. "For those three days—Wednesday night to Saturday night—where did you go?"

"We started to drive here, but the senator decided against it. He thought they might look for him here—his son, or Beckett. He didn't want anyone interfering. So we found a hotel. He paid cash and used a fake name."

"No one recognized him?"

"He wore khakis and a polo shirt. Slicked back his hair. He looked like somebody's grandfather. I think he enjoyed that part of it. Putting one over on everyone."

I could believe it. He would have liked thumbing his nose at Alan Beckett. But Beckett had handled himself well. All the while, when I was searching for Lucy, he must have been searching for John Casterbridge. He must have suspected that Casterbridge and Lucy had gone off together, but when I talked to him he never let on. How could he? He couldn't admit he had misplaced a U.S. senator.

And that day at the Bridgewell Building, he had made a show of wanting to keep me away from the senator. I never suspected that the senator wasn't there.

"What did you do for those three days?" I asked Lucy.

"I set up a tape recorder and listened to him talk. We stayed in the room, except when one of us went out to get food. When he got tired, we'd take a break and he'd sleep. I'd nap for a couple of hours and then go over my notes, figuring out what questions I needed to ask him."

She came back to the table and sat across from me. "We watched a little news," she said. "Enough to know I was being thought of as a missing person. But he was still talking. So I wasn't about to stop. On Saturday things heated up: the news was full of reports about Lark getting shot, and a lot of them mentioned my disappearance. We decided we'd stretched our luck as far as it would go. It was time to head back."

"What about your cover story—the architect from Chicago?"

"He's a friend who happens to own a blue minivan. I called him and he came through for me."

She reached for the bullet and rolled it along the table with her fingertips.

"That night at *Gray Streets,*" I said, "you could have told me the truth."

Her brows knitted together. "I wanted to, Loogan. But you might have decided you had to tell the police. You with your ethics. I couldn't let it get out that the senator had spent those three days with me while everyone thought I was missing. How would that look? And he didn't want our arrangement made public. Not yet."

"What is your arrangement, exactly?" I asked. "He feeds you material for a book, and in return you leave the Great Lakes robbery alone—is that it?"

"That's it."

"And that doesn't bother you? As a journalist?"

A bit of mischief returned to her expression. "You don't know what he's been giving me. In a few years no one will remember the Great Lakes robbery. But this," she said, pointing to the stacks of pages, "this is history."

I tipped back in my chair. A breeze came through the screen behind me.

"Have you thought about the senator's motives, about why he agreed to give you all this?"

She shrugged. "There must be some truth in something Terry Dawtrey or Henry Kormoran told me. Something that would reflect badly on Callie Spencer."

"So he just wants to make sure his daughter-in-law gets elected?"

"What else could it be?" she said. "Do you know something?"

I let the chair fall forward. "I don't know anything."

"What about Lark's doctor—Kenneally? Is there a story there?"

I drummed my fingers carelessly along the edge of the table. "If there is, I'm sure it's nothing big. It's not *history*. What do the senator's people think of your arrangement?"

"Alan Beckett isn't happy. He thinks I can't be trusted to hold up my end." She waved the matter away. "There's not much he can do."

"You don't think he'll try to stop you?" I said. "Beckett likes to be in control."

"Let him try."

"I'd say he's already trying. The senator's resignation last week—don't you think Beckett was behind that? It's his way of reasserting his authority."

"That's not the way I saw it. I think it was more the senator's idea. He's been playing a role for a long time. He's tired of it."

I nodded toward the interior of the house. "Where is he now? Is he here?"

She shook her head. "He was here most of last week. Working with me. This week he's been coming and going. I haven't seen him for two days."

"Where did he go?"

"Down your way, I imagine."

I didn't feel the need to correct her.

"He's letting me stay here to work on the book," she said. "I don't expect him to tell me where he goes." She was quiet for a moment, reaching across the table to put her hand over mine. "It's good to see you, Loogan. How did you know where to find me?"

"I didn't."

The wind picked up. The leaves of the white oak whispered. Lucy drew her hand back. "You didn't come here to find me. You were looking for the senator. He's not in Ann Arbor?"

"I don't know where he is."

Her eyes narrowed. "What are you up to, Loogan?"

"I'm not up to anything. Lizzie and I are on vacation."

She looked uncertain. "You're not mad at me, are you? You're not holding out on me?"

"I'm not mad."

"I really am sorry about what happened. You understand why I did it, don't you?"

I patted her hand gently. Picked up the bullet.

"Sure," I said.

CHAPTER 53

Elizabeth drove us back to I-75 and out of Saint Ignace. I sat beside her and recounted everything Lucy had told me. I was restless, turning the bullet end over end with my fingers. Elizabeth saw it, but she didn't say anything about it. She'd glimpsed the revolver in the glove compartment earlier, but she hadn't said anything about that either.

"What do you think of this deal Lucy made with the senator?" she asked when I finished my story. "Does she really believe he would agree to give away national secrets just to save Callie Spencer some embarrassment?"

I worried my thumb over the surface of the bullet. "I think in her eyes he's an old man whose judgment is failing him. And she's willing to take advantage."

"Does she intend to honor her part of the deal? To forget about the Great Lakes robbery?"

"I don't know," I said. "I'm not sure she knows. But if she found out Matthew Kenneally was the senator's son and the fifth robber—I think she might decide that belongs in her book."

We reached Brimley around quarter to six and checked into a hotel with a view of Lake Superior. Forty minutes later, after a shower and a change of clothes, we drove to Madelyn Turner's converted farmhouse. The sunlight spread the shadow of the house over the side yard. The tire swing hung perfectly still from the bough of the elm.

There was a rusted pickup truck in the driveway, but no other car and no sign of Nick's bike. No one answered our knock.

We rode back through the center of Brimley and found the Cozy Inn. A waitress seated us at a table in a corner of the dining room, away from the noise of the bar. She brought us sweet tea and we let her talk us into ordering the shrimp cocktail. We followed that with beer-battered perch, seasoned fries, coleslaw. We were thinking about apple pie when Madelyn Turner came in.

I had my back to the wall, so I saw her entrance. "Don't look now," I said to Elizabeth.

She kept her eyes on me. "Madelyn?" she asked.

I nodded.

"Is she alone?"

"She's alone," I said. "She's heading for the bar. How should we handle this?"

"We don't want to talk to her here. Let her be."

I watched the bartender put a drink in front of her. "Could be a long night," I said.

"I don't think so. What's she wearing? A skirt?"

"Slacks."

"Tight blouse, or something loose?"

"Loose," I said. Her clothes were casual. She had her hair pinned up. She wasn't trying to impress anyone or to hide her age.

"She'll have one drink," Elizabeth said. "And dinner to go."

We passed on the pie and asked the waitress for the bill. Ten minutes later, Madelyn Turner left carrying two Styrofoam take-out boxes. We followed her.

Out in the parking lot the day had begun to fade. Madelyn's car stirred up dust when she drove out. We tailed her east to an intersection and waited behind her at the light. From here she would need to turn south to go home.

"She's not going home," Elizabeth said.

She went straight for half a mile and then turned north. She got off the main road and onto a lane that wound through the shade of tall birches and pines. We lost sight of her, and when we came around a bend we saw her pulling onto a patch of grass in front of a cabin. She parked beside a long car covered with a canvas tarp.

I pressed the brake reflexively, but Elizabeth told me to go on past. "Eyes ahead. Act natural."

I acted natural and rolled on another hundred feet. Beyond that, the lane curved and the cabin would have been out of sight. I shifted into park and watched the scene unfold in the rearview mirror. Madelyn got out of her car with the take-out and walked toward the porch. The door of the cabin opened and a man came out to meet her. If I hadn't been expecting to see him I might not have recognized him. He wore khakis and a linen shirt, and his silver hair had been cropped short like a Roman emperor's. John Casterbridge.

He collected the take-out boxes from Madelyn and they went inside. I turned to Elizabeth, who had been watching over her shoulder.

"What are they doing out here?" I asked her.

She touched the glass beads at her throat absently. "That's Charlie Dawtrey's cabin. It's been empty since he died."

I gave her an appraising look. "Did you know Madelyn would come here?"

"I thought she might. It's not ideal for a rendezvous, but at least it's out of the way. She can't parade him around town. And she can't bring him home, or she'd have to explain him to Nick."

I looked in the mirror again at the cabin and thought of the two of them sharing dinner. A simple act, but the senator had come a long way for it. I thought about what Lucy had said—that she thought the resignation was the senator's idea. Was this why he'd done it? Was being with Madelyn Turner what he wanted?

A subtle change in the idle of the engine broke my reverie. I switched it off, popped the door, and climbed out. Elizabeth did the same.

"We're going in?" she said.

"Sure. I thought that was the point."

She looked across the roof of the car at me. "We came here to confirm that the senator had a relationship with Madelyn Turner, that he's the father of Matthew Kenneally." She tipped her head in the direction of the cabin. "I think this more or less confirms it. But it's another thing to get them to admit it."

I laid a hand on the warm metal of the roof. "But if they know we've caught them here together—that'll make it harder for them to deny it. Won't it?"

"Maybe. But even if they admit that Kenneally is the senator's son, we can't prove any wrongdoing. Not yet. We can't prove that Kenneally was involved in the Great Lakes robbery or that the senator covered it up."

"Are you saying we should walk away?"

She stared off toward the cabin. "I'm saying we should think about what we hope to accomplish. I'm saying—"

She didn't finish, and I could tell something had caught her eye. I turned and saw a figure crouched by the side of Madelyn's car. Even from a distance I knew it was Nick Dawtrey.

"Where did he come from?" I said in a quiet voice.

Elizabeth answered in kind. "The woods on the other side of the cabin."

We watched him creep toward the second car, the one covered with a tarp—the senator's Mercury. He circled it, reaching beneath the canvas to try each of the doors. They must have been locked. He straightened, peering toward the cabin, then glancing in our direction. He did a double take and in the next moment moved swiftly around the car and into the woods.

Elizabeth and I stood motionless, straining to catch sight of him again. Somewhere in the trees above us a bird sang out. Elizabeth took a step toward the cabin, as if she intended to go looking for Nick. As I made up my mind to join her I heard sounds behind me: the snap of a twig, the stirring of old leaves. I spun around to see Nick stepping out of the woods.

"What're you doing here, sport?"

Elizabeth answered before I could. "Let's go for a ride."

"YOU'RE GONNA THINK this is crazy," Nick said.

We were driving south through Brimley. His bike was in the trunk; we had stopped to pick it up from a hollow by the roadside. Nick sat in the backseat, leaning forward to talk to us.

"That guy with my mom, I think he's somebody."

Elizabeth and I exchanged a look.

"Is that why you were sneaking around his car?" she asked.

Nick shrugged. "I thought there might be something in there with his name on it, but it was locked. You know who he is, don't you?"

I looked in the rearview mirror and saw his dark eyes staring back at me.

"Put your seat belt on," I said.

"You're killing me, sport."

Elizabeth gestured for him to sit back. After a moment I heard the click of the belt.

"How long has that man been involved with your mother?" she asked him.

"They been talking the last two weeks. Maybe longer. I answered the phone once or twice when he called."

"What has your mother told you about him?"

"She says he's an old friend. His name is Johnny."

"And she's been seeing him?"

"She doesn't admit it—she just tells me she's going out." In the mirror I saw him sneer. "'Going out' used to mean the Cozy Inn," he said. "That's where she used to meet up with Kyle Scudder. But she broke it off with him."

"When?" I asked.

"Two weeks ago, same time she started going out with Johnny. I been trying to figure out where she meets him. Not at the Cozy, I checked there. Today's the first time I thought of the cabin." He looked from me to Elizabeth. "You didn't answer me. Do you know who he is?"

"He's exactly who you think he is," I said. "John Casterbridge, the senator."

Nick scrunched his face into a frown. "What's he doing in Brimley?"

An excellent question. I wasn't about to tell him the truth: that Casterbridge had come here to see the woman who had given him a son thirty-seven years ago. I tried to think of an answer that wouldn't be a lie, but Elizabeth saved me the trouble.

"It's like your mother said," she told him. "They're old friends."

. . .

When we reached the farmhouse, the sky was darkening into evening. I parked beside the rusted pickup and helped Nick haul his bike out of the trunk.

We went inside and Elizabeth asked him if he'd eaten dinner. He hadn't, so we retreated to the kitchen and fixed him a sandwich and a bowl of soup. I kept him company while he ate, and Elizabeth wandered into the living room. We found her there a short while later, standing by the fireplace. A collection of framed photographs lined the mantel—most of them of Nick, one of old Charlie Dawtrey, and one that looked like a high school portrait of Matthew Kenneally.

Kenneally's name had been in the news, and one or two stations had carried footage of him leaving City Hall on the night he was questioned about shooting Anthony Lark. I knew Nick had followed the news about Lark's death, so I wondered why he hadn't made a connection between Lark's doctor and the boy in the picture on his mother's mantel.

Elizabeth must have wondered too. She reached the picture down and showed it to Nick.

"Who's this?"

He frowned. "That's supposed to be my brother."

"Supposed to be?"

"I've never met him. He's way older than me and lives down south."

"In southern Michigan?"

"Farther south than that," Nick said. "I think he moved to get away from my mom. They don't get along. He's got some big important job—he never has time to visit."

"What's his name?" Elizabeth asked, returning the picture to the mantel.

Nick had to search his memory. "Chip," he said at last.

"What's that short for?"

He shrugged impatiently. "Whatever it's usually short for. Are you gonna tell me what you're doing up here?"

The question was as much for me as for her, but I stood silently with my hands in my pockets, feeling the smooth metal of the bullet against the fingertips of my right hand. Elizabeth stared at the fieldstones of the fireplace. I knew she didn't want to answer him.

She couldn't tell him the truth: that his mother had married his father at least partly out of guilt, because her son had escaped punishment for the Great Lakes robbery and his son had gone to prison. That he, Nick, was an act of penance, a replacement for his lost brother, Terry. She couldn't tell him that his other brother, Matthew Kenneally, had manipulated Anthony Lark, sending him after Terry—an act that had led directly to Nick's father's death.

She settled on an answer that didn't really tell him anything.

"We came to talk to some people up here. To ask some questions."

"What questions?" he said.

"Just police business. Nothing you should worry about."

It was the wrong thing to say. The corners of Nick's mouth tightened with contempt. He turned his back on Elizabeth and said to me, "You lied about her, sport."

"What do you mean?"

"You said she wanted to find out the truth about what happened to my father. And Terry."

"She did. And she has."

"She's just a cop," he said, his voice rising. "Cops look out for other cops."

I answered him calmly. "We've talked about this, Nick. Anthony Lark killed your father. The cops had nothing to do with it."

"Paul Rhiner shot Terry. He was a cop."

"He was doing his job. Terry tried to run."

"They didn't have to kill him."

The words tore out of him, his voice nearly a scream. I could see the tension in his shoulders, in his clenched hands. I thought he was close to tears.

"Hey," I said softly. "Take it easy."

Elizabeth came around so she could see him face to face. "It's all right," she said. "I know this is hard. You loved Terry. You shouldn't have to deal with this alone. Have you talked to your mother? Does she know about . . . everything that happened?"

Nick turned to me, bewildered. "What's she trying to say?"

I didn't answer him right away. I was fiddling with the bullet, turning it over with my fingers. I thought I knew exactly what Elizabeth was trying to say. I should have seen it much sooner. Nick acted like an adult, but he was fifteen years old. He'd had a brother in prison, and had loved him enough to help him try to escape. But the attempt had failed. His brother had died.

I watched the bullet turning between my fingers. Without realizing it, I had taken it out of my pocket. When I looked up I saw Nick staring at me. I slipped my hand back in my pocket and let the bullet drop.

"What she's saying," I told him, "is that you shouldn't blame yourself for what happened to Terry. It's not your fault. And if you want to talk about it—"

I watched his lips tremble, his anger barely controlled. His dark eyes glared at me. "You a social worker now, sport? You want me to talk about my feelings? I'm not sorry about what I did for Terry. You don't know anything. You want to help me? Find out why they killed him."

I shook my head sadly. "They killed him because he ran."

"That's what you keep saying." He whirled around toward Elizabeth. "You said you came up here to ask questions. You talk to Sam Tillman yet?"

I had almost forgotten about Tillman. He was the other deputy who'd been guarding Terry Dawtrey. Paul Rhiner's partner.

Elizabeth shook her head. "I haven't talked to him."

"I've been watching his house," Nick said. Pointing at me, he added, "Did he tell you?"

"I told her," I said. "But I thought you stopped. I asked you to stop."

Nick ignored me. "Sam Tillman spent the last two weeks sleeping on his couch. Then on Thursday his wife left him. She took the kids and the dog. Packed a lot of stuff in her car."

Elizabeth was watching him intently. "Is that right?"

"Yesterday his priest came to see him," Nick said. "They went inside and talked for an hour. I couldn't hear what they said."

"If Tillman's marriage is in trouble," she said, "they might have been talking about that."

Nick closed his eyes in frustration. "They might have been praying for rain. But I figure if a priest comes to your house, maybe he's there to hear your confession." His eyes came open again. "Paul Rhiner's the one who shot Terry. So what does Sam Tillman have to confess?"

Elizabeth said nothing at first. She lifted her necklace from her throat, touched the beads to her chin thoughtfully.

Then she said to Nick, "I need you to stay away from Sam Tillman's house."

"Yeah," he said, "I heard that line before."

"You're right to be angry," she told him. "I haven't looked closely enough at Terry's death. But I will now, I promise you. Starting with Tillman. I'll talk to him."

"It's about time."

"That's why I need you to stay away from him. And there's something else."

"Yeah?"

"I need to know about the plan for Terry's escape," she said. "Whose idea it was, how you worked it out, all the details."

He looked at her warily. "I'll tell you, but I want to go with you to see Tillman."

I expected her to say no, but she nodded. "You can go," she said. "But you have to do as I say. We'll drive out there tomorrow. Until then, you stay away from him."

"Why can't we go right now?"

"I need time to prepare. It has to be tomorrow."

A skeptical silence. Then: "All right."

CHAPTER 54

Elizabeth and I left the farmhouse around twenty after nine. By then Nick's mother had called to let him know she'd be home soon. I listened to the snap of gravel under the tires as we coasted down the driveway and onto the road. I had my window down.

"I was surprised when you told Nick he could come with us tomorrow," I said.

Elizabeth steered through a slow curve. "Are you scandalized, David?"

"A little. It was such a brazen lie."

She smiled, but the smile held no pleasure. "Do you think he believed it?"

"I think so."

I knew she didn't like deceiving him, but she couldn't take him when she went to interview Tillman. And it made no sense to argue with him.

"So we're not waiting till tomorrow?" I said, reaching over to touch her hair.

She leaned her head back. "I thought we'd go now."

She drove us north and east on two-lane county roads. When the speed limit went up to fifty-five I raised my window. A dark line of trees swept by us on either side.

"What do we think of Madelyn Turner?" I said.

Elizabeth answered without taking her eyes from the road. "She's a careful woman. She's been walking a tightrope for the last seventeen years."

"She kept a lot of secrets," I said. "She kept Nick from knowing much of anything at all about Matthew Kenneally."

"She had to. Once she got involved with Charlie Dawtrey, she was on a dangerous path. The secrecy had to have started then, before Nick was born. She must have been afraid of Terry Dawtrey. She knew he had seen Kenneally on the day of the Great Lakes robbery, and probably before. She might have assumed he didn't know Kenneally's name—Floyd Lambeau had the robbers call each other by code names—but she couldn't be sure. Anything she revealed about her son to Charlie—and later to Nick—could get passed along to Terry."

So Matthew Kenneally became "Chip," the estranged son who lived down south and had a job that kept him from visiting. Not much more than a photograph on the mantel.

"She must have kept in touch with him though," I said, "even if she had to do it without letting Nick know."

Elizabeth nodded. "I wouldn't be surprised if Kenneally has visited her up here. She could have arranged to meet up with him while Nick was at school. And Kenneally has three children of his own—Madelyn's grandchildren. She'd want to be part of their lives."

It must have made for a lot of sneaking around, I thought. A lot of worrying. All because she couldn't be sure how much Terry Dawtrey knew about her son.

And as it turned out, she had been right to worry. Before we left the farmhouse, I had asked Nick the question I should have asked him long ago. The obvious question. Did Terry know the identity of the fifth robber, the getaway driver?

The answer he gave me was frustrating. Terry knew. Floyd Lambeau had told him things. Lambeau had trusted him more than the others; after all, Lambeau was Ojibwa and Terry was Ojibwa too. From the hints Terry dropped, Nick believed that Terry knew the driver's name—his first name at least—as well as other details. Where he had gone to school, what he had studied. Enough to expose him. Terry could have turned the driver in any time he wanted.

But if that was true, I asked, why didn't he do it?

Nick gave me an answer to that too.

. . .

SAM TILLMAN'S HOUSE sat fifty yards back from the road on a level plot of land surrounded by woods on three sides. His nearest neighbors were a quarter mile away.

Elizabeth cut the engine and we stepped out into a breeze and the song of crickets. The full moon shone silver on the grass. The woods grew close to the house, especially on the north side. That's where Nick would have hidden, I thought, when he came here to spy on Tillman.

I crossed around the front of the car and Elizabeth slipped her hand into mine. As we walked toward the house, a man came out onto the porch to meet us. He leaned against a wooden post at the top of the steps. "Pretty night," he said.

Elizabeth brought her badge out of her handbag and held it up. "Elizabeth Waishkey," she said. "I'm with the Ann Arbor police."

"I figured you'd come, sooner or later."

He shuffled down the steps and offered a hand for her to shake, then offered it to me. He had a strong grip.

"David Loogan," I said.

"Sam Tillman. Nice to know you."

THE NIGHT AIR came into the house through screened windows in the long front room. On the north side a sofa and two wingback chairs were grouped around a coffee table. On the south a grandfather clock stood beside an archway that opened into the kitchen. Beside the clock was a writing desk with a carved wooden chair, and over the back of the chair hung a belt with a holstered nine-millimeter pistol.

Tillman led us in and cleared a few small items from the sofa so we could sit—toys and stuffed animals, a woman's scarf. Things his wife and children must have left behind. He moved them to one of the wingback chairs and then eased himself into the other.

He sat with his right elbow on the arm of the chair, his cheek resting on his fingertips. Waiting. For all I knew he might have been sitting like that for hours before we arrived. There was no clue to what he had been doing, no stereo or television playing, no book set aside. An unopened bottle of beer stood on the coffee table, but it might have been there a while. There was no condensation on it.

Tillman saw me looking at it and said, "I haven't been drinking."

"No?"

"I used to drink," he said. "Gave it up when I got married. Darlene didn't like it—that's my wife." The words rolled out of him slow and even. "She had her reasons. Her dad was a mean drunk. The smallest thing could set him off. He yanked her arm out of the socket once when she was ten. She was making him breakfast and she burned his toast."

He sat straight and dropped his hands into his lap. His wedding ring glinted in the light of the floor lamp beside his chair.

"That's why she liked me," he said. "I was always even-tempered. Reliable. 'If you didn't drink, you'd be perfect,' she used to say. So I quit." He gestured toward the bottle. "I found that in the refrigerator the day she left. It must've been there since the last time we had company. I thought it might do me some good."

"What changed your mind?" Elizabeth asked him.

"I figured it's only one bottle. It's not enough to drown out what happened at Whiteleaf Cemetery." He turned the ring around his finger. "That's what you're here about, isn't it?"

"Tell me what happened at Whiteleaf Cemetery," she said.

"Isn't it obvious?" Tillman said, rubbing the gold band. "I murdered Terry Dawtrey."

THE PENDULUM of the grandfather clock marked off the seconds. A breeze stirred the sheer curtains that hung before the windows behind Tillman's chair.

"Paul Rhiner shot Dawtrey," Elizabeth said.

Tillman shook his head. The lamplight made his curly hair the color of bronze. "Paul's the one who happened to pull the trigger."

"Are you saying the two of you conspired to kill him?"

"There was a conspiracy," Tillman said. "But Paul wasn't part of it. He was a straight arrow. I don't think he would have gone along. I know Walt didn't think so."

"Walter Delacorte? Was it his idea to kill Dawtrey?"

Tillman looked down at his hands. "He asked me if I would do it. I've thought about it since—wondered why he picked me. I've been with the sheriff's office for twelve years. Some guys are attracted to the violence of the job, but I'm not one of them. If I have to slam someone into the hood of a cruiser to get the cuffs on him, I'll do it. But I don't take pleasure in it. There are guys I work with who do. Walt didn't pick one of them."

He looked up again. "I'll tell you what I think it was. He wanted someone steady, predictable. Not that he knew I would say yes. But he knew he could ask me and I wouldn't get worked up about it. You have to have strong convictions to get worked up about things. He knew that even if I said no, he could trust me not to make trouble for him."

Elizabeth leaned forward on the sofa. "Tell me what he said to you."

"He called me into his office. He'd been talking to the warden at Kinross Prison. They were letting Dawtrey out for his father's funeral. Walt offered me a spot on the escort detail, and I agreed. He reminded me that Dawtrey had shot Harlan Spencer. Paralyzed him.

" 'There's no room for mistakes,' Walt said to me.

" 'There won't be any,' I told him.

" 'If Dawtrey tries to run, you shoot him. Do you have a problem with that?'

" 'Nope. That sounds about right.'

" 'You ask me, he should've been shot a long time ago,' Walt said. 'He doesn't deserve to breathe the same air as civilized people.'

" 'He tries anything while I'm watching him, he'll regret it.'

"Walt looked me over, like he was making up his mind. When he spoke, his voice was softer. 'Good. I hoped you'd say that. Because what I'm hearing is, he plans to try something.'

"He waited for me to catch on, a strange little smile on his face.

" 'What are you saying, Walt?'

"The smile went away. 'I'm saying that Terry Dawtrey is going to attempt to escape from custody. When he does, you should shoot him—and you should shoot to kill.'

"I looked for some sign that he was kidding. Didn't find it. 'How do you know this?'

" 'It doesn't matter,' he said. 'It's going to happen. And there's someone who wants it to happen, someone who's willing to pay to be sure Dawtrey dies.' "

Elizabeth interrupted. "That's all he said—'someone'? He didn't tell you who?"

"He said it would be best if I didn't know." Tillman let out a long breath. "Part of me wanted to tell him to go to hell, and another part wanted to know how big a payment he was talking about. He answered the question before I could make up my mind to ask it.

" 'Fifty thousand,' he said. 'Half in advance, half when it's done.'

"It sounded unreal, but I could tell he was serious. I stood there staring at him for a long time. 'Jesus, Walt,' I said finally. 'What do you expect me to do here?'

" 'Go home and think it over,' he said, mild as mild. 'Let me know in the morning.'

"That night I felt strange. Off-kilter. I thought about the money. Darlene and I have always done all right, but this house has gotten crowded over the years—we've got three daughters. We've talked about a bigger place, but could never afford it. Fifty thousand dollars would change that. On the other hand, I'd have to make up a story about where it came from. I didn't think she could live with me if she knew the truth.

"I lay awake all night and by the morning I decided fifty thousand wasn't enough, not for what I'd have to do to earn it. At nine o'clock I went into Walt's office and told him I would need a hundred thousand. I figured whoever was paying would refuse and that would be the end of it. But late that afternoon Walt told me we were on.

"For the next few days I had that same off-kilter feeling. I kept stumbling back and forth between two ideas. First, it would never happen, I wasn't really going to shoot Terry Dawtrey. And second, why not? He was far from innocent. If he tried to run, he deserved whatever he got.

"On the morning of the funeral I met up with Paul Rhiner and we drove down to the prison. They had Dawtrey ready. We put the shackles on him and headed out. He was quiet in the car and when we got to the church he walked with his head bowed. He shuffled like a broken man, the way they do after they've been in Kinross long enough.

"We sat through the mass and escorted him back to the car. On the drive to the cemetery I decided Walt had been misinformed. Dawtrey didn't plan to run. That was fine by me.

"Except I didn't really believe it. Walt had warned me that it would happen at the cemetery. 'Give Dawtrey a little slack, let him wander away from you, and that's when he'll try to make a break.' Paul and I brought him to his father's grave and listened while the priest went through his routine. Afterward Dawtrey asked us if he could visit his grandmother's gravestone. Paul looked to me and I said it was all right. I started to take Dawtrey's arm but changed my mind, because if I went with him I knew I'd have to shoot him—and I didn't want to, not for any money. And then I did something unforgivable."

Tillman paused, and his pause stretched out until Elizabeth prompted him.

"You told Paul to take him."

CHAPTER 55

Sam Tillman seemed to sink into his wingback chair. "Yes," he said. "But worse than that. I knew Paul would do his job conscientiously. He'd be right on top of Dawtrey the whole time. So I told him to relax, to give Dawtrey some space. 'He's not going anywhere,' I said.

"I stopped to have a word with the priest, because whatever happened, I didn't want to see it. I guess you know how it went from there. Suddenly there was a sound like machine-gun fire. Just a couple kids lighting off firecrackers, but I didn't know that. I thought the whole thing had gone to hell. Thought I'd got Paul killed. When I finally saw what was happening, Dawtrey had the shackles off. Paul was chasing him. Dawtrey made it over the cemetery fence, and for a second it looked like he might really get away. I was thinking about what Walt would do when he found out. Then Dawtrey collapsed. Paul had shot him.

"I felt my heart pounding when I reached the fence, and not just because I'd been running. Paul had climbed over to check on Dawtrey. 'Where's he hit?' I shouted, because from a distance I couldn't see. I didn't have to worry. The bullet went through Dawtrey's throat. The paramedics got there and told us he was dead, and my heart settled down."

"What did Delacorte say about what happened?" Elizabeth asked.

Tillman smiled ruefully. "I thought he'd be angry, but he slapped me on the back and told me I'd done a fine job. It was almost as if he thought I'd planned to trick Paul into doing it from the beginning. I think he was impressed. Dawtrey was dead and I'd managed to keep my hands clean."

"What about the money?"

"It's in a cardboard box in the attic. I haven't touched it. I had the crazy idea of giving it to Paul, but Walt convinced me I couldn't—because Paul took it hard, shooting Dawtrey, and if he learned the truth it would only make things worse."

Tillman's voice dropped almost to a whisper. "Paul never suspected me, never blamed me," he said, looking at Elizabeth with sad eyes. "Instead, he got obsessed with your mysterious man on the cemetery hill. Lark, the one who killed old Charlie Dawtrey and started everything. You know where that led."

I watched Elizabeth nodding. She knew. Paul Rhiner's obsession led to Walter Delacorte's death, and to Rhiner's suicide.

Half a minute passed with only the ticking of the grandfather clock. Then in a gentle voice Elizabeth asked, "What do you want to do, Sam? Where do you want to go from here?"

"Me with my clean hands?" he said, looking off across the room. "Do you know they reinstated me? With Walt and Paul dead, they figured my suspension had gone on long enough. The county administrator told me he would have liked to make me acting sheriff, but in light of the Dawtrey incident it wouldn't look right. That's what it is now, an incident." He turned to Elizabeth and the rueful smile appeared again. "Where do I want to go? I want to go back in time. I want to get my wife and kids back."

"What made them leave?" she said. "Did you tell your wife the truth?"

"I couldn't. But she knew something was wrong these past few weeks. She kept wanting me to talk. She wouldn't let it drop. The other day I raised my voice to her, told her I just wanted some peace and quiet. When she didn't back down I pushed her away. She tripped and fell." He turned the gold ring around his finger. "She's at her sister's now. She says I'd better get right or she's not coming back."

"That sounds bad," said Elizabeth. "But not so bad that you can't recover from it."

"I talked to my priest. He said I need to confess everything. I've confessed twice now, to him and to you. I don't feel any better." Tillman sighed. "What do you think I should do?"

"Things might go easier for you if we could prove who hired you," Elizabeth said. "You might be able to make a deal with the prosecutor."

"Walt never gave me a clue about that," Tillman said, frowning. "It had to have been someone with connections, if they knew Dawtrey was going to try to escape."

"I think you're right about that."

I thought so too. It must have been someone with connections, someone who could afford to spend a hundred thousand dollars. Someone who had a reason to want Dawtrey dead. Someone like John Casterbridge.

From the look Elizabeth sent my way, I knew she had reached the same conclusion.

Tillman glanced at me and then back at her. His brow furrowed beneath his curly hair. "You know who it was, don't you?"

"I have an idea," she said. "But it's someone we can't accuse without proof."

The furrows deepened. "Now that Walt's gone, I don't see much hope of finding proof." Tillman rubbed a hand across his mouth. "It's frustrating, because he was a careful man. I can't help thinking he would have covered himself."

"What do you mean?" Elizabeth asked.

"I mean if somewhere down the road someone had to take a fall for Dawtrey's death, it wouldn't have been Walter Delacorte. He would've made sure of that." He stared across the room again. "I went to his funeral. He looked peaceful. I didn't expect it, the way he died. Stabbed with a tire iron. That must've been a sight."

Elizabeth nodded silently.

"I wonder," Tillman said, "did you find a pen on his body?"

"A pen?"

"A black aluminum ballpoint. He usually kept it in his shirt pocket."

"I don't remember a pen. Not on the body. There could have been one in his car."

"You should check," Tillman said. "It wasn't an ordinary pen. It had a voice recorder built in. Walt used it in meetings, instead of taking notes. I looked for it after he died. I didn't find it."

"You think he used it—"

"When he talked to the client. Whoever it was. If Walt met with him, or even if they just talked on the phone, I think Walt would've had a recorder running. That pen—you could download a recording from it as a computer file. You'll want to check his computer at the sheriff's office."

Tillman took a breath before continuing. "He didn't have a computer at home, but you should check there too—see if you can find the pen. I don't think you will. I went there after he died, got in with a spare key he kept in his office. I looked everywhere I could think of, but I didn't find the pen, or anything else."

"What else did you expect to find?" Elizabeth asked.

"Money, naturally. I don't know what the going rate is for setting up a hit, but I'm sure Walt didn't do it for free." His tone turned thoughtful. "Still, if there's cash in that house I couldn't find it, and I tried. I did everything but tear out the walls."

"You shouldn't have gone there."

Tillman laughed softly. "That's the least of the things I shouldn't have done."

THE SHEER CURTAINS on the northern windows billowed into the room and then retreated until they were flat against the screens. Tillman sat without speaking while Elizabeth made a call to Carter Shan and confirmed that Delacorte's pen had not been found on his body or in his car. When she got off the phone she started to relay her plans to Tillman: she mentioned getting a search warrant for Delacorte's house, but I was only half listening. I was thinking about something Nick Dawtrey had told me.

Nick had spied on Delacorte, had followed him once on a shopping trip. It hadn't seemed important at the time, but I remembered Nick telling me what Delacorte had brought home with him. "Paint," I said aloud.

They both turned to me.

"When you searched the house," I said to Tillman, "did you find paint cans?"

His eyes narrowed. "There were some in the cellar."

"What about drywall tape or joint compound?"

"Maybe. . . . I think so."

Elizabeth smiled, understanding. "We'll need to tear out the walls."

CHAPTER 56

I thought things would move slowly; it was getting late on a Saturday night. But while I stayed with Tillman, Elizabeth went out in the yard and made a couple of calls on her cell phone. She talked to Owen McCaleb and let him know what she wanted to do. From McCaleb she got the number of someone he had once served with in the army, a man named Brian Hannagan who lived in Sault Sainte Marie and was now an inspector in the Michigan State Police. She needed someone with jurisdiction, and she didn't want to involve the sheriff's office.

I'm not sure how much she told Hannagan. It must have been a hard sell, convincing him to take seriously the idea that a U.S. senator might have paid to have Terry Dawtrey killed. The story was a tangled one, and as I sat watching Tillman I tried to work through it myself. If I'd had a notebook like Lark, I might have written it down.

Lucy Navarro had unknowingly set things in motion when she went to see Dawtrey in prison. He hinted that he would tell her the name of the fifth robber. I knew there were people who could have overheard their conversation: guards, other inmates. Word could have gotten around. An inmate tells a guard, a guard tells the warden. Maybe the warden told Harlan Spencer, because Spencer had an interest in keeping tabs on Dawtrey, the man who shot him. And Spencer would have told John Casterbridge. Spencer had been protecting the senator's secret for years.

Casterbridge had a good reason to want to keep Dawtrey quiet, because the fifth robber was his son, Matthew Kenneally.

When Casterbridge heard that Dawtrey had been talking to a reporter, what would he have done? He wouldn't have ordered a hit on Dawtrey—that wouldn't have been his first reaction. But he would have warned his son.

Once, Matthew Kenneally might have thought the Great Lakes robbery was behind him, but now people were talking about it again, because Callie Spencer was running for Senate. Kenneally had been under his father's protection for seventeen years, but he must have known that John Casterbridge wouldn't be around forever. So Kenneally would have been worried, even before he heard that Dawtrey was talking to a reporter.

And by then Kenneally had already found Anthony Lark, a man who was obsessed with a dead girl. A girl who'd had a beautiful smile, like Callie Spencer's.

Kenneally lacked the courage to go after Dawtrey himself. Instead, he aimed Lark toward the Great Lakes robbers. He convinced Lark that they were a danger to Callie, and that he needed to save her.

It worked. Lark couldn't get to Terry Dawtrey in prison, but he did the next best thing: He killed Dawtrey's father so they'd let him out for the funeral. Then something happened that no one expected. Nick came up with a plan to help Terry escape.

Back at the farmhouse, Elizabeth and I had talked to Nick about the plan. He told us how he arranged things with Terry. Between the day their father died and the day of the funeral, they had only one chance to communicate. A single note passed between them in the visitation room at Kinross Prison.

Someone must have seen that note: maybe an inmate, maybe a guard. Somehow John Casterbridge got word of it—maybe the same way he got word about Terry Dawtrey talking to Lucy Navarro.

The senator might not have thought seriously about killing Dawtrey before, but now he saw an opportunity. He made a deal with Walter Delacorte to ensure that Dawtrey would die trying to escape. Casterbridge didn't tell his son about the deal, and Kenneally didn't tell his father about Anthony Lark. So on the morning of the funeral at Whiteleaf Cemetery, Terry Dawtrey was doomed twice over: Delacorte and Tillman were conspiring to kill him, and Lark was waiting with his rifle on the hill.

Delacorte and Tillman won out, but Paul Rhiner was the one who fired the fatal shot.

It didn't end there. Lark didn't stop; he went after Henry Kormoran and Sutton Bell. That might have been Kenneally's intention all along, if he felt threatened by Kormoran and Bell. Or it could be that Lark, once unleashed, was impossible to control.

There was one final twist. At some point John Casterbridge found out about Lark. It wasn't hard to see how. Elizabeth had discussed Lark's manuscript with Alan Beckett, the Spencers, and the senator's son, Jay. Any of them could have told Casterbridge about Lark. Or Kenneally might have realized that Lark was a loose cannon, and might have turned to his father for help.

One way or another, the senator had decided that Lark had to be dealt with. His solution must have been to set Walter Delacorte on Lark's trail—a decision that worked out badly for Delacorte, and for Paul Rhiner.

If I'd had a notebook with me I might have made a list of all the men who had died because of the choices John Casterbridge had made. Instead, I got up and wandered across the room to the front door. Sam Tillman was still in his chair. The light of the floor lamp made a shadowed mask of his face.

Something about him made me uneasy.

I stood listening to the ticking clock and realized that something had been nagging at me all the while as he told his story. I couldn't put a name to it. Alan Beckett would have called it my active imagination. I expect things to go wrong.

Even now, as I watched Tillman sitting passively, I found it reassuring that his pistol was on the other side of the room. I didn't expect him to try to shoot me, or even to try to shoot himself. I expected him to do whatever Elizabeth told him to do. But I knew one thing for certain: I didn't intend to let him get anywhere near that pistol.

I kept my eyes on him as I opened the front door. Outside, Elizabeth was still on the phone with Hannagan, but I could make out enough of the conversation to know that they were winding down.

Tillman must have sensed we would soon be on the move. He rose and went around behind the chair to the window, drawing aside the sheer curtain and lowering the sash. I knew his silhouette would be visible to anyone lurking outside in the dark woods, and for an instant I felt sure there was someone there. I braced myself for the sound of a gunshot and focused on the center of Tillman's back, expecting a bloom of crimson.

Nothing happened. Tillman let the curtain fall back into place. I heard Elizabeth's footsteps on the porch, stepped aside to let her through the door, and listened as she filled us in on the plans she'd made with Hannagan.

TEN MINUTES LATER we were driving south and east along the outskirts of Sault Sainte Marie. Tillman had closed the remaining windows and locked up, and now he rode silently in the backseat of the car. Elizabeth watched him from the passenger seat as I drove.

My active imagination would have liked it better if she'd been back there with him, holding a gun against his ribs. But it turned out my imagination had gone off on the wrong track. It wasn't Tillman I should have been worried about.

We found Walter Delacorte's house on a cul-de-sac off Ashmun Street. Low hedges grew along the sidewalk in front. I parked beneath a streetlight and the three of us stepped out into the night air. The neighbors on Delacorte's left had a stereo cranked loud, pounding out something by the White Stripes. Delacorte's windows were dark except for one beside the front door, where a faint glow came through the curtains.

I pointed it out to Elizabeth. "There's a light."

"It's a lamp on a timer," said Tillman. "I noticed it the other day when I was here."

I kept my eyes on the window, waiting for some movement, for a shadow to pass along the curtains. Nothing. Brian Hannagan arrived a few minutes later, along with one of his colleagues from the state police, a lieutenant named Redlake. They pulled up in a long black Dodge, in plainclothes—both of them tall and lean, with square jaws and brush-cut hair. Hannagan in his fifties, the lieutenant ten years younger.

Hannagan and Elizabeth made introductions, low-key, businesslike. I got a clipped nod from each of the newcomers and then they ignored me and focused on the important people. Hannagan explained to Elizabeth that he'd been in contact with his captain, who was even now working on an application for a warrant. They had identified a judge who lived in town, a woman who had known Delacorte and never much cared for him.

"We think she'll cooperate," Hannagan said. "She's not a pushover, though. We may have a long wait ahead of us."

We had the White Stripes to listen to while we waited. Hannagan took Tillman aside to question him about his dealings with Delacorte. The lieutenant went along to take notes, and soon the three of them were huddled in conversation beside the black sedan.

That left Elizabeth and me by our car. I leaned against the fender to watch the glow in Delacorte's window.

"Something's not right," I said.

She slipped her hand into mine. "It's nothing. A lamp on a timer."

That wasn't what I meant. "We need a flashlight."

"What for?"

"There's one in the trunk, isn't there? You may want your gun too."

"David—"

I gave her hand a squeeze and dug the key out of my pocket to open the trunk. There was a flashlight in the tire well. I closed the trunk without alerting the trio by the black sedan and walked casually through a gap in the hedges toward Delacorte's house.

Elizabeth caught up to me. She had her pistol in its holster clipped to her belt. "We can't go in," she said. "We're waiting—"

"I know we're waiting," I said, clicking on the flash and aiming it at the front door. "What I'm wondering is if everybody else is waiting."

The light fell on the seam between the door and the frame. The seam was wider than it should have been—the door hadn't been pulled all the way shut.

Behind us a voice called out. "Hey! Get back away from there!" Lieutenant Redlake.

I played the flash low along the front of the house. Behind a trampled flower bed I found a basement window with a few bits of glass remaining in the frame.

Both of them were jogging toward us now, Hannagan and the lieutenant.

Tillman followed them uncertainly. When Hannagan got close, Elizabeth gestured at the broken window. "Someone's been here," she said.

THEY WENT IN through the front door, Hannagan and the lieutenant. Elizabeth and I stood just outside and listened to them calling to each other, clearing the rooms one by one. Tillman waited farther back on the lawn.

Five minutes later, every light in the house was on. Lieutenant Redlake came out to tell us they'd found no one inside. "But there's something you'll want to see," he said to Elizabeth, waving her in. "Straight back through the kitchen."

Redlake stayed with Tillman. I followed Elizabeth and we found Hannagan in a small dining room at the back of the house. The walls were recently painted, what was left of them. Someone had taken a claw hammer to the drywall, tearing out chunks of it. Scraps and dust littered the floor.

He had found what he wanted: It was all laid out on the dining-room table. A black aluminum pen, a few printed pages, a CD, a bundle of hundred-dollar bills. A plastic freezer bag that had held everything inside the wall.

"There's your magic pen," Hannagan said. "The battery's run down."

"It would have been hidden away for a few weeks," Elizabeth said.

"So whoever pulled it out of the wall didn't listen to what's recorded on it."

"He didn't need to," I said. I was looking at the CD, which Delacorte would have used to burn a copy of the recording from the pen. It was labeled in black marker: *John Casterbridge.*

Hannagan pointed to the sheaf of printed pages. "This is a record of Delacorte's dealings with the senator. It makes it clear that the senator paid to have Terry Dawtrey killed."

"We have to go, Lizzie," I said in a soft voice.

"What I don't understand," Hannagan said, "is why someone would go to the trouble of ripping all this out of the wall and then just leave it here. Especially the money."

Elizabeth stepped back from the table. "He doesn't care about the money," she said.

I USED MY CELL to call Nick Dawtrey from the car, waiting for him to pick up as Elizabeth sped down Delacorte's street and made a sharp turn onto Ashmun. Hannagan followed us in his black Dodge. Redlake and Tillman stayed behind at the house.

Nick's voice came on the line, far off. *Leave a message and maybe I call you.*

"Nick," I said. "Call me back. Don't do anything until you talk to me."

Elizabeth swung into the northbound lane to pass a slow-moving RV.

"How much of a head start do you think he's got?" I asked her.

"I don't know."

"I suppose it's too much to hope he's on his bike."

She slipped back into the southbound lane and said nothing.

I wanted to think he was on his bike, and that we would overtake him on the road. It was fifteen miles from Sault Sainte Marie to Brimley. But it didn't matter what I wanted. Nick had a will of his own. We'd been wrong about him, wrong to assume he would trust us and stay away from Tillman's house. He must have gone there tonight. He must have crept through the woods and listened at the window. He would have been out there all the while in the dark. He would have heard Tillman's confession. He would have heard about Delacorte's pen, and from there he would have gone to the sheriff's house.

The money wouldn't matter to him. He only wanted the name of the man responsible for his brother's death.

Elizabeth touched the brake, made the turn onto Six Mile Road.

"I don't have Madelyn Turner's number," I said.

She passed me her phone and I found it in her call log.

When Madelyn answered she sounded groggy. It took some effort to explain who I was, but finally she remembered me.

"What's this about, Mr. Loogan?"

I thumbed a button to put her on speaker. "Detective Waishkey's here with me," I said. "We're trying to reach Nick. Is he home?"

"He's gone to a movie with his friends—Kevin and J.T."

"In Brimley?"

"In Sault Sainte Marie."

"How would he get there? It's a long way to ride a bike at night."

"They took the truck. Kevin has a license."

"What truck?" I asked her. Then I remembered the rusted pickup at the farmhouse.

"Nick's father's truck," she said. "I've let them take it to Sault Sainte Marie before. Kevin's responsible. Is something wrong?"

"I hope not. Are you sure the three of them are together? Did you see them leave?"

A flutter of static on the line. Then: "No. Nick called to tell me they were leaving. They were gone when I got home. You're starting to scare me, Mr. Loogan. What's going on?"

I turned to Elizabeth, unsure how to answer.

She said, "We think Nick may have gotten the idea that the senator is to blame for Terry getting shot. We're worried about what he might do."

Madelyn took a few seconds to absorb the news. I wondered how she would react to the mention of the senator—if she would pretend to be puzzled. In the end she simply said, "Where would Nick get that idea?"

"It's not important," Elizabeth said. "Is the senator still at the cabin?"

A few more seconds passed. Then: "Yes."

"Nick knows he's there," Elizabeth said. "The best thing would be to call the senator and tell him to get out. We're on our way there now."

The line went silent and I realized Madelyn had hung up. Three minutes later she called back. "I couldn't get through to John. If he's sleeping he may have his cell turned off."

"There's no landline at the cabin?" I said.

"Not since Charlie died. Nick's not answering his phone either. And there's something else—Kevin and J.T. aren't with him. I just talked to their mother."

I thought of Sarah—how eager she was to learn to drive. Nick would feel the same way. And up here, in the country, they would start early.

"Could he be driving the truck himself?" I asked Madelyn.

"He knows he's not supposed to," she said. "But he could be. Charlie was teaching him."

I glanced at Elizabeth, at her profile in the dashboard light, her easy grip on the wheel. We sped west, the straight gray line of Six Mile Road rushing to meet us.

The fields on either side of us ran out into the empty dark. Beside me I heard Elizabeth say calmly, "Mrs. Turner, I need to know if you keep a gun in the house, or if there's one in the cabin."

Madelyn answered in a hollow voice. "No. Do you really think—? No, no guns. I have to go now. I'm heading to the cabin."

"That's fine," said Elizabeth. "We'll be there in a few minutes."

As I snapped the phone shut I thought about guns and felt a ripple of dread run through me. Nick had seen me fiddling with a bullet earlier in the day. Where there's a bullet, there's a gun. We had left the car unlocked in Tillman's driveway, with my borrowed revolver in the glove compartment. If Nick had been there—

I popped the latch of the glove compartment and it fell open. I unzipped the cloth pouch and saw the barrel of the revolver.

"It's still here," I said, half to myself. "I was afraid he might have taken it."

Elizabeth lifted a hand from the wheel and brushed her fingers through her hair.

"You're forgetting about Tillman's pistol," she said.

CHAPTER 57

The truck had one headlight to pierce the dark under the trees. The light jittered over the unpaved lane and the tires sent pebbles bouncing into the undercarriage. Nick Dawtrey drove with the seat racked forward. Sam Tillman's gun belt lay on the passenger seat beside him, the nine-millimeter in its holster.

He had doubled back and discovered Tillman's house empty. Had broken a window to get in, just like at Delacorte's.

In places the trees grew so close to the lane that the branches scraped along the side of the truck. Nick liked to hear the swish of the leaves. It reminded him of driving with his father.

He doused the headlight well before he reached the cabin, lifting his foot off the gas at the same time. The truck crept to a stop. He killed the engine and let his eyes adjust to the dark before he climbed out. He left the belt and the holster on the seat. Took the pistol.

His father had always kept a spare key under a bucket on the porch. Nick found it and let himself in, slow and easy so the hinges of the door wouldn't squeak. Inside, a lamp was burning with a shade like parchment. It gave off enough light to show him John Casterbridge lying on the sofa, mouth open, snoring softly. The senator had fallen asleep in his clothes.

On the floor by the sofa were playing cards laid out in columns—a game of solitaire. What Casterbridge had been doing before he fell asleep. Nick knelt and set the pistol on the carpet and gathered the cards. He didn't like to see them there, because they belonged to his father. And because he used to play cards with Terry.

He had met his brother for the first time when he was five years old, in the visitation room at Kinross Prison. He had been afraid that day; at least that's what his father told him later. He might have been afraid of all the people and the noise, but not of Terry, who had a wide smile and a gentle laugh, who wanted to hear about his friends and about school.

He remembered other visits. Terry telling jokes. Silly ones. *Why do cows wear bells? Because their horns don't work.* Sometimes they played checkers. Sometimes Terry would have a deck of cards. The three of them would sit at a table with a white plastic top—Nick and his father on one side, Terry on the other—and they would play fish.

It took a while for Nick to realize that Terry was a prisoner—and what it meant. At the end of those early visits, his father would take his hand and tell him to say good-bye. "Can Terry come with us?" he would say. "Not this time, kiddo," Terry would tell him. Once, on the drive home, he asked his father about it—why Terry never came home with them. "He can't," his father said. "They won't let him out." "Why not?" Nick asked. "He did something wrong," his father told him, "and now he has to stay there." "Couldn't he say he's sorry?" "Sometimes sorry's not enough."

His father sounded very sad, and Nick didn't ask him any more about it. But from then on he was more aware of the gray walls of the visitation room, of the guards who wouldn't let his brother leave. The next time he said good-bye to Terry, he leaned close to him and whispered, *"Someday I get you outta here."*

Terry smiled, but he didn't laugh, and Nick was glad of that. When the next visit rolled around, he said it again, and Terry only nodded. "I bet you will, kiddo."

The visits continued. Nick got older and the card games he played with Terry evolved, from fish to hearts to crazy eights to poker. By the time he turned fifteen he had long ago stopped saying, *"Someday I get you outta here."* He had stopped because he didn't want the guards to overhear. Because it was a promise he intended to keep.

. . .

Nick squared off the cards and tucked them in his pocket. He retrieved the pistol from the carpet and flicked the little lever on the side. That would be the safety. He worked the slide the way he had seen it done in movies. Now there would be a bullet in the chamber.

He stood over the sofa and listened to John Casterbridge snoring. The man's hands, wrinkled and spotted, lay folded over his stomach. There were deep creases in the loose flesh of his neck. A patch of white stubble showed along his jaw where he had missed shaving.

Nick aimed the pistol at the center of the old man's chest. He felt a tightness in his own chest, a fluttering like a current running through him. He held his arm straight, but the gun trembled. He looked up and closed his eyes, willing his arm to hold still.

When he opened his eyes he saw his father's sparrow calendar on the wall behind the sofa. He saw his own portrait in a frame beside it.

Not here, he thought.

John Casterbridge shifted in his sleep. Nick stepped closer and jabbed the muzzle of the gun into the old man's shoulder.

"Wake up," he said.

I brought the revolver with me into the woods, when we went looking for Nick and the senator. It wasn't a conscious decision. I had the thing in front of me in the open glove compartment when Elizabeth swung onto the lane that led to Charlie Dawtrey's cabin. It was there when we passed the rusted pickup, when Elizabeth pulled over onto the grass. And when we got out of the car I took it from the cloth pouch and tucked it under my waistband at the small of my back. Sometimes I wish I'd left it behind.

The roadside near the cabin was thick with cars: the senator's under the canvas tarp, Madelyn Turner's, a cruiser from the Michigan State Police. The last was Hannagan's doing, the best he could muster by phone on short notice. Brimley didn't have its own police department.

Hannagan drove in just behind us. We joined him near the porch of the cabin, where a sergeant from the state police was waiting—a young guy with ginger hair. His name was Cooper. He had arrived only five minutes before us.

"I found the door open and the Turner woman inside," he said. "There was no one else here."

"Where is she now?" Hannagan asked him.

He pointed vaguely eastward. "She went to talk to some neighbors. See what she could find out. There's no sign of a struggle," he added, glancing into the cabin. "You'd hardly know anyone was living here at all. Is it true—John Casterbridge has been staying here?"

Hannagan looked to Elizabeth. "It's true," she said.

"And the truck down the road," Sergeant Cooper said. "That's the one the Turner woman's son was driving?"

Elizabeth nodded.

"I think you were right to be worried, then," said Cooper. "I found this in the truck." He stepped into the house to retrieve something just inside the doorway. I recognized it as Sam Tillman's gun belt. The holster was empty.

We heard footsteps on the lane—Madelyn Turner coming back from the neighbors'. She hurried up the stone walk to the cabin and told us that the couple she'd talked to hadn't seen or heard anything unusual. "It's been a quiet night," she said. "No shouting, no loud noises—they would have heard."

She was breathless and talking fast. Her eyes were a little too wide.

"They would have heard," she said again. "No loud noises. That has to be good."

Loud noises. She couldn't bring herself to say "gunshots."

Hannagan took charge, speaking to her in a reassuring voice. "That's fine. Now, do you have any idea where your son might be? Is there someplace nearby where he likes to go?"

"I'm not sure. He's been wandering around these woods almost since he could walk. He knows all the paths."

"Can you give me a direction, anything at all?"

She looked around as if there might be a trail of footsteps to follow. The only light came from inside the cabin and from the full moon high above. The ground was a carpet of pine needles and low grass. It was dry. It didn't give up any secrets.

She looked up and faced south, her back to the cabin's door. "You go that way, you'll hit the main road before long." She made a slow turn to the north. "The woods are deeper in back of the cabin. That's where most of the paths are. Go far enough north and you come to the lake."

"You think he might have gone to the lake?"

"I don't know." Madelyn's head moved side to side. "I can't—I need to look for him."

Hannagan touched her shoulder. "Ma'am, you should stay here, in case he comes back. We're going to search for him. I'll make some calls, get more people out here. We'll find him."

Madelyn answered him, but I didn't wait to hear. I slipped back to the car and found the flashlight I'd used at Delacorte's. Rooting around in the trunk, I found another.

Elizabeth joined me and I passed her the second flashlight. I nodded toward Hannagan. "We're not going to wait around until he organizes his search, are we?"

"No," she said.

Madelyn didn't wait either. She vanished into the woods, shouting Nick's name. The sergeant went to look after her. Hannagan stayed behind to make his phone calls.

Elizabeth and I walked around to the back of the cabin and picked our way north through the trees. Soon we stumbled onto a path that bent northeast—a narrow track of hard-packed earth.

We followed it down into a gully, and when it rose again it sent off a spur to the left—roughly northwest. We followed the spur through a small clearing rich with wild fern. Climbed over the rotting trunk of a fallen birch. Soon after, the path divided once more.

We halted there. Madelyn's calls to Nick had faded into the distance.

"There's too much ground to cover," Elizabeth said.

"I know."

She aimed her flashlight down the right-hand path. "I don't like the idea of splitting up."

"I don't like it either."

The trees stood quiet around us, waiting.

She kissed me once, and fast. "Don't get shot again."

"What are the odds?" I said.

I took the left-hand way, which ran west for a while before angling north. It crossed an unpaved road and ran past a dark cabin, bigger than Charlie Dawtrey's. I aimed my flashlight at the windows and doors and found nothing broken.

After the cabin, the path widened out and the woods began to thin. The land sloped down, the exposed roots of trees forming a series of natural steps. When I got onto level ground again I pulled my phone from my pocket and dialed Nick's number, listened to his careless fifteen-year-old's voice telling me to leave a message and maybe he'd call.

Farther on, the air got cooler. Somewhere a wood fire burned. The path bent a little to the east and the packed earth gave way to sand. Lake Superior came into view, green-black beneath a blue-black sky. Moonlight glinted on the foam near the shore.

I found him huddled on the sand, his arms wrapped around his knees, his head bowed. Strands of his black hair obscured his face.

I knelt in front of him. "Nick, are you all right?"

He lifted his head and wiped his face with the heels of his hands. "What do you want?"

"I've been looking for you."

"Why don't you leave me alone."

"Your mother's worried. We thought we'd find you at the cabin."

He stared out at the darkness of the lake. "I couldn't do it at the cabin."

I felt a twist in the pit of my stomach. "Do what?"

"What do you think?"

"Nick, where's the senator?"

He waved his right hand over his shoulder. "Look for him down the beach. That's where I left him."

I saw a black sheen on his fingers. The beam of the flashlight turned the black to red.

"Are you hurt?" I said.

He shook his head and wouldn't meet my eyes.

"You're bleeding."

He held his hand up to study it. "Not mine, sport."

I tried to make sense of the blood. There'd been no shot. I would have heard it.

"Where's the gun, Nick?"

"I don't know."

"What happened?"

He clutched his knees again and bent his head over them. He didn't answer me.

"I want to help you," I said gently, "but I need to know what happened."

"I don't want your help."

"What am I going to find down the beach, Nick?"

"See for yourself. Nobody's stopping you."

I reached to brush his hair out of his face. "Tell me what happened to the gun."

He slapped my hand away. "Get away from me."

"Tell me."

I saw him shudder, and then the words struggled out of him. "What do you want me to say? I made him kneel in the sand and I put that gun against his head. And he admitted it—he told me he had Terry killed."

Nick buried his face in his arms and I reached again to touch his hair. This time he let me. He rocked himself forward and back, and his voice was raw as a wound. "He admitted it, and I still couldn't do it. I couldn't pull the trigger. Why couldn't I do it?"

I sat beside him on the ground, got an arm around his shoulders. I watched the waves come in to the shore as the pace of his rocking gradually slowed to nothing. I helped him up when he was ready and took him down to the water, where he rinsed his hands and washed his face.

"I want you to wait here for me," I said. "We'll go back to the cabin together."

He answered with a distracted nod.

"I won't be long," I said, and leaving him the flashlight I set off down the beach.

The shore curved to the south and before long I came to a grassy hill that ran down from the woods almost to the water's edge. Once I navigated around that, the moonlight showed me a seated form on the sand. The senator's legs stretched out before him and as I drew closer I could see that his feet were bare, the cuffs of his pants turned up. His shoes and socks were nearby. He leaned back on his arms, taking in the sky full of stars.

He didn't see me until I was almost on top of him, and then he only sat up slowly and folded his legs. His soft laugh was barely audible. "You get around, don't you?"

I dropped down onto the sand, facing him. "I could say the same about you."

"What do you think of Brimley?"

"It's a nice little town, what I've seen of it."

He nodded, gazing past my shoulder at the lake. "I always liked it. I spent some time here when I was younger. Camping. Hiking. Before they opened the casino. If you wanted excitement you drove to Sault Sainte Marie. You crossed the bridge to Canada." He shook sand from his pant leg. "Back then you could cross without a passport. That was a more innocent time. Do you have one?"

I took a second to realize he meant a passport. "Not with me," I said.

"But you have one. Is it current?"

"I think so."

"You should keep it current," he said. "You never know when you'll need it, and it takes weeks to renew one. That's something I never got around to."

"Renewing your passport?"

"No. Fixing the system. Streamlining it. I always meant to. But that's the State Department, and it's a slog to get them to make any kind of change."

I regarded him silently for a moment. Then: "Is this the way it's going to be?"

He frowned, confused. "Beg your pardon?"

"Lucy Navarro told me you get tired. You go off on tangents."

The frown went away and he laughed. "Well, what do you expect, son? I'm losing my mind. Didn't you see my press conference?"

"I saw it," I said. "I believed it, then. Now I'm not sure."

"Oh, you can believe it. My affliction's real. All the best doctors have told me so."

"You seem to be getting around all right. You're still driving."

The senator's right hand rested on the ground at his side. His fingers dug into the sand. "They'll take that away from me in time," he said softly. "But not yet. Wait long enough and I won't be able to dress myself. I'll have nurses to do it for me, and to wipe the drool off my chin. That's what they've got planned for me. But I don't think I'll stick around for that."

His voice dropped down to nothing on the final words.

"You're not expecting me to feel sorry for you," I said.

"No. I suppose not."

I'd been studying him as well as I could in the moonlight and I could see what looked like a smear of blood at his temple, and a cut there, just below the hairline. A rag of white linen lay in the sand to his left—a piece torn from his shirttail. There were dark smudges on it, as if he had used it to stanch the bleeding.

I pointed at his temple. "How bad is the damage?"

He touched the cut with a fingertip. "It's nothing. A scratch."

"How did it happen?"

"I tripped in the woods."

"And landed on your head? That's bad luck."

He didn't say anything.

"Are you sure Nick didn't hit you with the gun?" I asked him.

"Why would you think that?"

"It's what I would've done, if I couldn't bring myself to shoot you."

CHAPTER 58

John Casterbridge looked away from me. He moved his hands restlessly until they found half a cigar and a box of matches in his shirt pocket. I watched a match flare and listened to him puffing smoke. He shook out the match, held the cigar in his right hand resting on his knee.

He let the smoke run out between his lips and said, "Is the boy all right?"

"That's a hell of a question," I said. "I guess he is, for now."

"He's under the impression I paid to have his brother killed."

"There's a lot of people under that impression. Walter Delacorte kept notes. Made a recording too."

He nodded slowly. "I should have known. Delacorte was shrewd."

"You knew him through Harlan Spencer?"

He puffed on the cigar again, taking his time.

"Harlan Spencer had nothing to do with this."

"I'm surprised you arranged things with Delacorte directly," I said. "It would have been smarter to use an intermediary."

"It's hard to find someone to trust."

"What about Alan Beckett?"

He turned the cigar sideways so he could ponder it. "You've got the wrong idea about Al. He draws lines, even if they're not in the same places where other people draw them." An idea occurred to him. "You don't have a bottle with you, do you?"

I showed him my palms. "I'm afraid not."

"It'd be a nice night for a drink," he said on a sigh.

"A drink's not going to do your head any good."

"I told you, it's nothing."

"What happened to the gun, after Nick hit you with it?"

"He threw it. Off that way, down by the water."

I looked where he was pointing. In the loose sand around us, it was difficult to make out footprints. But it appeared as if someone might have walked down to the water and back.

As I turned to face the senator again, my cell phone rang. Elizabeth.

"Nick's here with me," she said. "I found him walking on the beach."

"It figures," I said. "I asked him to stay put."

"Did you find the senator?"

"I'm with him now."

"Is everything all right? I'm on my way."

"Everything's fine. You should take Nick back to the cabin."

She answered after a pause. "Are you sure?"

"We're just sitting and talking here. Does Nick's mother know you've got him?"

"I called her on her cell."

"Drop him at the cabin, then. The senator and I will be here when you get back."

Another pause. "You're sure everything's under control?"

"Trust me."

"Okay. I'll be back as soon as I can."

I closed the phone and returned it to my pocket. The senator was watching me through a haze of smoke.

"Elizabeth's taking Nick to his mother," I said.

"Good."

"It's been a rough night for the kid. What did you tell him?"

He tapped the ash from his cigar. "What do you mean?"

I shrugged. "He said you admitted having his brother killed. He must have wanted to know why. You didn't tell him the truth, did you? About Matthew Kenneally?"

If he was surprised I knew about Kenneally, he covered it well.

"I told him it was revenge," he said. "For what Dawtrey did to Harlan Spencer."

I nodded. It made a certain sense.

"I think he was convinced," the senator added.

"Maybe," I said. "But give him some time to think about it. How did you explain how you knew that Terry Dawtrey would try to escape?"

He drew on the cigar before he answered. "I told him the truth. I have a source at Kinross Prison."

"I wonder if he believed you," I said, picking up a shell from the sand. "Elizabeth and I talked to him this afternoon about the escape plan. It was his idea—did you know that? He handled it cleverly. He couldn't have a conversation with Terry about it, because someone might overhear. So he wrote everything down: about the handcuff key beside the vase of roses at the cemetery, the getaway car that would be waiting. He fit it all on a playing card, the ace of diamonds. Then he got his mother to take him to visit Terry at Kinross.

"He snuck the card into the visitation room, hidden in his shirt. He and Terry used to play poker during their visits, so all he had to do was make sure Terry got the ace of diamonds."

I rubbed the shell between my fingers. "At the end of the visit, Nick took the card back out with him. He still has it in a dresser drawer at home—he showed it to us this afternoon. So I guess someone in the visitation room must have seen it. A guard or an inmate."

"Right," the senator said.

"Someone who happened to be looking over Terry Dawtrey's shoulder."

He waved his cigar in the air. "There are other ways it could have happened. Suppose Dawtrey talked to a friend or a cell mate. Someone he thought he could trust."

"Sure," I said. "That makes a lot more sense. And I really wouldn't want to consider the alternative—that it wasn't a guard or an inmate. That it was someone else in the visitation room, someone who sat next to Nick the whole time. Someone who caught a glimpse of the ace of diamonds—and then, later on, dug it out of Nick's dresser drawer."

The senator made a pained face. "I don't care for that idea. I wouldn't want the boy to hear it. I don't think it would be good for him."

"It's late in the game for you to be worried about what's good for him."

He found a speck of ash on his sleeve and flicked it away, saying nothing.

"I guess it was a simple calculation for Madelyn to make," I said. "Terry Dawtrey wasn't her son. Matthew Kenneally was. Dawtrey posed a threat to Kenneally. It would be rough on Nick, losing his brother. But in the end, Dawtrey was expendable."

"I think you should leave Madelyn out of this."

"Sure. I'm more interested in you anyway. You never struck me as a callous man. But you were willing to condemn Terry Dawtrey to death."

He flicked again at his sleeve, even though there was no more ash. "That's not something I care to talk about."

"How did you justify it?" I asked him. "Did you tell yourself that Dawtrey could have been shot trying to escape anyway, whether you paid to make it happen or not?"

I waited for his answer, but just then he discovered that his cigar had gone out. He took his time relighting it. The spent match went into the sand. He started to return the matchbox to his pocket, reconsidered, and flipped it into the sand as well.

"Did you ever wonder why Dawtrey decided to run?" I said. "He must have known he was risking his life. How bad must it have been in that prison, for him to take the chance?"

"Don't ask me to feel sorry for a convict," the senator said, through an angry cloud of smoke. "Terry Dawtrey was in prison for a reason."

"Sure he was. He tried to rob a bank. Just like your son."

"Don't pretend they're the same. My son made a mistake. He got drawn in by Floyd Lambeau."

"So did Dawtrey."

"Dawtrey shot Harlan Spencer."

"Your son killed Scott White."

"He didn't mean to. He shouldn't have to suffer for that."

I looked down at the shell on my palm. The surface glowed like a pearl in the moonlight. "I was thinking earlier about all the people who've died because of you and your son," I said, tossing it away. "The two Dawtreys, Charlie and Terry. Henry Kormoran. Walter Delacorte and Paul Rhiner. And Anthony Lark. A tall price to pay to keep Matthew Kenneally from having to suffer for what he did seventeen years ago. How much taller is it going to get?"

The senator's shoulders lifted and fell. "I don't know what you mean."

"What kind of game are you playing with Lucy Navarro?"

"It's no game. I didn't like the story she was writing, so I offered her another one."

"She says you're feeding her national secrets."

He smiled at the notion. "She's a bright girl, but she doesn't have much experience."

"So you're lying to her."

"Some of the things I've told her are true. They're also unclassified and available from published sources."

"And the rest?"

"I made up."

"She's going to figure it out in the long run. When she starts checking her facts."

He shook his head dismissively. "I've already told you about the long run. In the long run I won't remember my own name."

"Right. And you'll have nurses to dress you and wipe your chin. If you decide to stick around. Where's the gun, Senator?"

At first I thought he wouldn't answer me. He considered the stub of his cigar. Tossed it in the sand between us.

"I told you," he said. "The boy threw it away. Down by the water."

I glanced at the footprints around us. "I'm not asking what he did with it. I'm asking where it is right now."

"You worry far too much for a young man," the senator said, dropping his left hand over the scrap of linen by his side. "I think you should go on now and leave me be. It's a fine night for a walk on the beach."

"Let me have the gun."

He drew the linen aside and picked up Sam Tillman's pistol. Shifted it from his left hand to his right. "Go on," he said. "Take off your shoes, feel the sand between your toes. Walk down to the water and look around you. Really look. Even in the moonlight you can see the pebbles under the surface along the shore. See how clear their edges are. Put your feet in the water and feel how cold it is. It'll make you gasp. It'll hurt at first, it's so cold. That's to remind you you're alive."

He gestured with the barrel of the gun. "Go on now. Leave me here to do what I need to do."

"I can't," I said.

"Why not? It'll be justice, won't it? For Terry Dawtrey and all those others."

"I can't let you. Not with that gun."

I leaned forward, fixing my eyes on his. "That gun belongs to Sam Tillman," I said. "I don't care much about him, but if you shoot yourself with his gun, there'll be questions. He lives in Sault Sainte Marie. How did his gun get here? How did you get hold of it? The truth'll come out. Nick stole the gun from Tillman's house. He marched you through the woods with it, and when he got you down here he assaulted you with it, gave you that cut on your temple. You want to kill yourself, I'm all for it. But don't drag the kid into it. He deserves better."

The senator rested the pistol on his knee and said, "I agree with you. But I don't have many options. I'm afraid we're at an impasse."

"We don't have to be," I said. I reached behind me and wrapped my fingers around the grip of the revolver. I brought it around where he could see it, taking care to aim it at the ground.

"I got this from a friend a while back," I told him. "I thought there might be some point in carrying it around, but the truth is I haven't done a damn thing with it. It's been in my glove compartment most of the time. But maybe there's a point after all."

I lifted the revolver, holding it sideways between us. "It's not registered," I said. "It won't be connected to me or my friend or anyone I know. I'm pretty sure it was stolen somewhere along the line. It's got my prints on it, and on the bullets too, but I can fix that." I aimed it at the ground again. "So what do you think?"

His face was hard to read, but then a smile came to him slowly. There was sadness in it, and affection. He said, "I think you're a good man to have around."

"We'll trade, then?"

He nodded. I broke open the cylinder of the revolver and emptied the bullets into my left hand. They didn't glint; the moonlight seemed to make them darker. I slipped five of them into the pocket of my shirt. Held the sixth between my finger and thumb.

"I imagine one will be enough."

"I don't expect to miss," he said.

I pulled a handkerchief from my hip pocket and used it to polish the bullet, wiping away my fingerprints. Still using the handkerchief, I slid the bullet into a chamber of the cylinder. I closed the cylinder and wiped it down, then wiped the grip and the hammer. Then the trigger guard. Then the trigger—gently. I wiped the barrel last and bent forward, offering the gun to the senator grip-first. He held out Sam Tillman's pistol and we made our trade.

Around us, the world went about its business. The water lapped at the shore. Grass swayed on a breeze. Tall pines reached into the sky. The senator held the revolver loosely. He straightened his back and looked up at the stars.

"Shame to do it on a night like this," he said. "Right now my mind is as clear as it's ever been. Clear as that sky. But it's all going to slip away. Does that seem right to you?"

I tucked the handkerchief in my pocket and didn't answer him.

"When it slips away, that's when I'd like to end it," he said. "But then I won't be able to. So I have to do it now."

"You can hold off a little," I said, Tillman's pistol warm in my left hand. "You've got some time left, before anyone else gets here."

The senator didn't pay much attention when I stood up. He was still looking at the sky.

I said, "Here's something to think about, while your mind is clear. Terry Dawtrey knew enough about your son to turn him in, but he never told anyone. I don't think he would have told Lucy Navarro either. He said he might, but I think that was just because he liked talking to a pretty girl. He wanted her to visit him again. But he wouldn't have told her."

The senator looked at me with narrowed eyes. "You can't know that."

"Maybe not," I said. "But Dawtrey spent sixteen years in Kinross Prison. He kept quiet, even though giving up the fifth man in the Great Lakes robbery might have done him some good. I didn't understand why, until I asked Nick about it. Do you know what he told me?"

"What?"

"He told me Terry wasn't a rat."

I stood over him and watched it sink in. It wasn't easy to tell in the moonlight, but I thought he understood: that everything he'd done was for nothing, that none of this had to happen, that no one had to die.

When I'd seen enough of him I turned away. I didn't say good-bye.

PICTURE IT THIS WAY if you like—the final scene. Nighttime on the shore of Lake Superior. A man walks along the beach, making slow progress through the sand. That's me, the hero of the piece. The senator's there in the murky background, a small figure getting smaller with distance. There are hushed noises of water and wind and then a crack like sudden thunder—the sound of a gunshot.

Maybe it makes me flinch. I'm only human.

Maybe I pause, but it's a tiny pause, barely a hitch in my stride.

CHAPTER 59

There was no shot, of course.

Picture it this way instead. After a couple minutes I stopped at the water's edge. I looked down at Tillman's pistol in my left hand, at the blood on the barrel where Nick used it to lash out at the senator. Grains of sand clung to the blood. I rinsed the gun clean in the water.

The fingers of my right hand were clenched around something hard as stone. I drew my arm back and whipped it forward again, and something flew out over the lake. It was lost in the blackness of the sky and when it fell to the water it made no sound. It was the bullet I slid into the chamber of the revolver and then slid back out again, under the cover of the handkerchief.

When I resumed my walk, I saw Elizabeth approaching. She had Hannagan with her, and Sergeant Cooper too. When we were still a dozen feet apart, Hannagan started asking questions.

"It looked like you threw something in the lake just now. What was it?"

There was nothing wrong with his tone, but I wasn't in the mood to answer. When I got close enough I handed him the pistol. "That's Tillman's," I said.

He held it with his fingertips. "Why is it wet?"

I didn't answer that one either. "You'll find the senator down there," I said, glancing back along the beach. "He's fine, apart from a cut on his temple."

"How did that happen?"

There was an edge in Hannagan's voice now, and I had a fleeting desire to punch his square-jawed face. But he wasn't really the one I was angry with.

"He tripped in the woods," I said. "You should go get him. He's thinking about killing himself. He's got a revolver, but it's not loaded."

Hannagan frowned at me. "Jesus. Where did he get a revolver?"

"Let's stand here and discuss it. Maybe he'll drown himself in the lake while we're at it."

Hannagan had heard enough from me. He went scowling down the beach. Cooper followed him.

When they were gone Elizabeth brushed a hand along my cheek. "What I like about you," she said, "is how well you get along with people."

THEY FOUND JOHN CASTERBRIDGE where I'd left him, the revolver lying in the sand at his feet. He came back with them without any fuss, strolling barefoot along the shore with Hannagan at his side. Cooper trailed behind, carrying the senator's shoes.

Elizabeth spoke to Hannagan before he took the senator away. I watched them from a distance, lingering by a fire pit in the sand, a circle of rocks surrounding a few charred sticks of wood. The senator held his head high, seemingly untroubled and undefeated. He didn't look in my direction. He said something to Elizabeth before Hannagan and Cooper led him up the beach and into the woods.

She came back to me and we sat together on the shore.

"Tell me they're arresting him," I said.

She gave me the answer I expected to hear. "They're taking him to a hospital to have someone tend to the cut on his head. They won't arrest him. Not tonight."

"He more or less confessed to me."

Elizabeth dug her heels into the sand. "It would have been better if he waited and confessed to Hannagan. Whatever he said to you, he can always deny later. Your word against his. But don't count Hannagan out. He's going to build a case. It'll take time. He's got Delacorte's notes and the recording, but it may be difficult for a prosecutor to use them as evidence in a trial. Delacorte's not around to authenticate them."

"I don't like the sound of that."

"Give Hannagan a chance. Let's see what he can do."

She tipped her head back to feel the breeze off the lake. I studied her profile.

"What did the senator say to you?" I asked.

"Just nonsense. He wanted to know if my passport was in order."

I nodded absently at that. "He talked to me about passports too."

We watched the water lap the dark sand and I told her everything I could remember about my conversation with the senator. I described my trick with the bullet too. But the thing that got her attention was what he had said about Lucy Navarro.

"It doesn't make sense," she told me. "He made a deal with her in order to get her to drop her investigation, so she wouldn't find out the truth about Matthew Kenneally."

"That's right," I said.

"But he didn't hold up his end. The stories he fed her were invented. So what did he hope to gain? He had to know she would figure it out eventually. And there would be nothing to stop her from picking up her investigation where she left off."

"He was just buying time," I said. "In the long run it wouldn't matter—because in the long run he wouldn't be around." But even as I said it, I realized it didn't add up. The senator wouldn't be around, but Kenneally would.

Elizabeth was way ahead of me. "He wasn't stalling Lucy for his own sake," she said. "He was doing it for Kenneally. So it must have been Kenneally who needed time."

She didn't say anything more. She was waiting for me to catch up.

Finally I worked it out. "Kenneally needed time to get his passport in order."

WHILE ELIZABETH WAS on the phone with Carter Shan, I walked up to the woods and gathered fallen branches that seemed dry enough to burn. I brought them back and piled them inside the ring of stones.

She closed her phone and knelt beside me. "How are you going to light that?"

"I've got my pocketknife," I said. "I could carve a trench in one of the thicker branches and rub a sharpened stick back and forth along it."

"Really?"

"Or I could go down the beach and see if the senator left his matches behind."

We went together, with a flashlight. It took us half the matches in the box to get the fire going. As we sat watching the flames, Elizabeth's phone chirped—Shan calling back.

She listened to what he had to say and then gave me the news. "The Kenneally house is empty. Carter drove there himself. He found a neighbor up late, and she told him the Kenneallys left for Europe this morning. He already checked with the airlines. They flew from Detroit Metro to Amsterdam, with a connection to Geneva."

Another reason Kenneally needed time, I thought. He had to convince his wife to uproot their family and move to Switzerland.

"It's smart," Elizabeth said. "It puts him effectively out of reach. If he were indicted for murder, the Swiss could extradite him—in theory. But in practice it could take years. Only a prosecutor with a very strong case would go to the trouble."

I focused on a tendril of rising smoke. "And after all this time, there's not likely to be a very strong case."

We stayed by the fire long into the night, sometimes silent, sometimes talking. I wanted to know what would happen to Nick, and Elizabeth told me she thought he would come through all right. "He'll have to answer for the break-ins at Delacorte's and Tillman's—there's no getting around it—but I'll make sure Hannagan watches out for him." I told her I didn't like the idea of Madelyn hauling him around tonight, following the senator to the hospital. "They didn't go to the hospital," she said. "When I brought Nick to the cabin, she drove him home. As far as I know, that's where they are now."

It was a small thing, but it raised my opinion of Madelyn Turner. I watched a branch in the fire crack and throw off sparks, and I let myself hope that I'd been wrong about her, that she hadn't really sold out Terry Dawtrey.

Later on, I stretched out on the sand, resting my head on Elizabeth's lap. She answered a call from Hannagan and learned that Jay Casterbridge and Callie Spencer were driving up from Ann Arbor to collect the senator. An ER doctor in Sault Sainte Marie had stitched up his cut, and Hannagan had him hiding out in the office of one of the hospital administrators. Word of his injury had leaked somehow, and a stringer for the CBS affiliate in Traverse City was lurking outside the hospital with a video camera. A reporter from the local paper had been asking questions—oddly detailed ones. She wanted to know if it was true that the senator had been staying in a cabin in Brimley that once belonged to Terry Dawtrey's father.

"Hannagan's a little ticked off," Elizabeth said. "He asked me if you'd been calling reporters. I told him you're as innocent as a lamb."

"Maybe it was Sergeant Cooper," I suggested.

"Maybe," she said, but there was something enigmatic in her tone, and it occurred to me that she'd been on her phone a long time while I gathered wood for the fire.

I smiled up at her and she traced her fingers along the line of my jaw.

The news about the senator must have spread quickly, because before long my phone started to buzz. I fished it from my pocket and saw Lucy Navarro's name on the display. I could imagine what she'd say: *What's going on up there, Loogan? Why are you holding out on me?*

I let the call go to voice mail.

When the fire faded, Elizabeth asked me if I thought it was time to make our way back through the woods to the car. Before we left, I took off my shoes and socks and waded a little in the lake. The cold made me gasp, just like the senator said it would.

Acknowledgments

I'm tempted to say that working with Amy Einhorn is like being edited by a basket of kittens—but those would have to be some very smart, insightful, generous kittens. For my literary agent, Victoria Skurnick, a different metaphor is in order: She changed my pumpkin into a carriage, and my mice into horses. Amy and Victoria are two women you want to have on your side, and I'm grateful to both of them.

Thanks also to Ivan Held, Leslie Gelbman, Tom Colgan, Heather Connor, Matthew Venzon, Halli Melnitsky, Lancc Fitzgerald, Melissa Rowland, Lindsay Edgecombe, and Miek Coccia.

Finally, I want to express my gratitude to my family: to my mother and father, Carolyn and Michael Dolan, who waited a long time to have a book dedicated to them; to my brother, Terry, and my sister, Michelle, who are still waiting. And to Linda: Stick with me, kid.

Author's Note

The *National Current* is a tabloid of my own invention. The *Ann Arbor News* is a real paper—or it was, until it ceased publication in 2009. I've kept it alive in this novel, for purposes of my own.

The Great Lakes Bank and Whiteleaf Cemetery are, likewise, inventions. You won't find them in Sault Sainte Marie. What's more, I've occasionally taken liberties with the geography of the state of Michigan and the street map of Ann Arbor, all for the sake of advancing the story. To cite just a couple of examples: I've borrowed a bit of Brimley State Park in Michigan's Upper Peninsula and used it as the setting for Charlie Dawtrey's cabin, and I've made the woods around the cabin deeper and more extensive than the woods you'd find in the park. In Ann Arbor, I've placed the Bridgewell Building next to the Seva Restaurant on Liberty Street, where it has no business being, since there's already a perfectly good building there.

Last, I should mention that in chapter 23, when Senator John Casterbridge refers to his constituents' "black, flabby little hearts," he's quoting the late Robert Heinlein.

Author's Note

The *Michigan Chronicle* is a product of my own invention. The *Ann Arbor News* was a real paper—or it was, until it ceased publication in 2009. [illegible] for instance, for purposes of my own.

[illegible] are [illegible]. You won't find them in [illegible], Maine. [illegible] the geography of [illegible] Michigan and the [illegible] [illegible] Park in [illegible] [illegible] Dorothy's cabin [illegible] around the [illegible] than [illegible] Ann Arbor [illegible] placed the [illegible] [illegible] [illegible] good [illegible] there.

[illegible] in Chapter 23 [illegible] [illegible] the late Richard [illegible].

Read on for a sneak peak at Harry Dolan's *Bad Things Happen*:

Chapter 1

The shovel has to meet certain requirements. A pointed blade. A short handle, to make it maneuverable in a confined space. He finds what he needs in the gardening section of a vast department store.

He stows the shovel in his cart and moves unhurriedly through the wide aisles, gathering a few more items: D-cell batteries, a bag of potting soil, a can of weed-killer. Leather work gloves, two pairs. In the grocery section he picks up four deli sandwiches wrapped in plastic and a case of bottled water.

The checkout lanes are crowded. He chooses a line and the fluorescent lights flicker overhead as he considers how he's going to pay. His wallet holds a credit card in the name of David Loogan. It's not the name he was born with, but it's what he calls himself now. He's not going to use the credit card.

He does some calculations in his head and decides he has enough cash.

The line moves and he thinks he'll get out quick and clean, but he's wrong. The cashier wants to talk.

"I think I've seen you before," she says to him.

"I doubt it."

She's tall, broad in the hips, attractive, though the stark light accentuates the lines under her eyes and around her mouth.

"You look familiar," she says.

The man who calls himself David Loogan doesn't want to be familiar. He wants to be nondescript. Unmemorable.

"Maybe I've seen you here in the store," the cashier suggests.

He offers her a lukewarm smile. "That must be it."

He busies himself loading things onto the counter. The cashier takes the shovel and holds it with the blade pointing skyward so she can scan the bar code on the handle.

"You must be a gardener," she says.

He ought to agree and leave it at that, but he gets flustered. He starts to say, "I'm an editor," but stops himself. The truth won't do. He goes with the first lie that comes into his mind.

"I'm a juggler," he says.

It's a mistake. She decides to find him charming. She smiles and sets the shovel on the end of the counter and reaches for the potting soil in a leisurely way.

"You must be very good," she says lightly. "I've never heard of anyone juggling shovels. But one's not enough, is it? You ought to have three."

Go with charming then. "I've already got three," he says. "Anyone can juggle three. The real trick is juggling four."

"It must be dazzling," she says. "Where do you work? Kids' birthdays?"

He waits a beat and answers in his most serious tone. "Garden parties."

"Ha. Are you sure we haven't met before?"

She's flirting, Loogan decides. He looks at her fingers as she scans the sandwiches. She's wearing a wedding ring.

"I could swear I know you," she says. "Maybe we went to school together."

"I never went," he says. "Everything I know about juggling is self-taught."

"I'm serious. I think we went to high school together."

"I didn't go to high school around here."

"Well, hell, neither did I," she says. "And it's been quite a while. But you remind me of a boy in my class. I'll think of your name in a second."

She bags the gloves and the batteries together, the weed-killer separately.

"Dennis," she says suddenly, looking up at him. "Or Daniel?"

David Loogan picks up the shovel from the counter and is troubled by a momentary vision. He sees himself stabbing the blade into the base of the cashier's neck.

"Ted," he tells her. "My name is Ted Carmady."

She smiles and shakes her head. "Are you sure?"

"I'm sure."

She lets it go with a shrug. "Well, then I was way off, wasn't I?"

He puts the shovel in his cart, and she reads off his total and takes his money. He thinks she has turned shy on him, but she scribbles something on his receipt before she hands it over. He scans it on the way out, sees her name (*Allison*) and a phone number, and crumples the paper discreetly.

Out in the parking lot, Loogan adjusts the collar of his black leather coat and checks his watch. Nine-thirty on a Wednesday night in October. A mist of rain is falling and the cars in the lot glow in the yellow light of tall arc lamps.

The lamps reassure him. He is not exactly afraid of the dark, but he often feels uneasy going out after sunset. And parking lots unnerve him. The echo of footsteps in a parking lot at night can set his pulse racing.

Loogan moves steadily along a row of cars, pushing the shopping cart before him. He has an uncomfortable moment when he sees a figure coming toward him. A thin man with a weathered face, hollowed eyes. A hooded sweatshirt, pants torn at the knee. Right hand resting in a pocket of the sweatshirt.

Loogan is suddenly aware of the humming of the arc lamps, the turning wheels of the cart.

You're fine, he tells himself. Nothing's going to happen.

As the thin man gets close, his hand comes out of the pocket of his sweatshirt. Loogan sees a glint of silver. Metal, he thinks. Blade. Knife.

Reflexively he reaches out to grab the thin man's wrist, but he stops himself in time. The thin man flinches away from him and hurries past, clutching a silver-gray cell phone to the front of his sweatshirt. He mumbles something Loogan doesn't catch.

Then he's gone and it's over and Loogan comes to his car. He loads the shovel in the trunk, and the potting soil, and all the rest. He shuts the trunk and pushes the cart into an empty parking space.

The hum of the arc lamps has receded into silence. Everything is normal. David Loogan is an ordinary shopper. No one would think otherwise. He opens his car door and slides in behind the wheel. He looks nothing at all like a man heading off to dig a grave.

The man who called himself David Loogan had been living in Ann Arbor since March. He rented a small furnished house on the west side: a sharp-roofed wood-frame place with a porch in the front and a little yard in back wound about with chain-link fence.

He spent his days in the vicinity of Liberty and State streets, reading newspapers in cafés, watching movies at the Michigan Theater. He observed the comings and goings of university students, listened in on their conversations. He was not out of place in a university crowd: he might have passed for an older graduate student, or a young professor. He was thirty-eight.

The house he rented stood on the corner of a tree-lined street and belonged to a professor of history who was on sabbatical, doing research at a think tank somewhere overseas. He had left a neglected garden in the backyard, and for a few days in April Loogan tried his hand at planting flowers. He bought seeds and poked them into the dirt. He watered, he waited. The flowers showed no sign of growing.

On an afternoon in May, he found a short-story magazine that someone had abandoned in a coffee shop. The title was *Gray Streets.* He ordered a cappuccino and found an overstuffed chair and read a story about an innocent man framed for murder by a beautiful and enigmatic woman.

The next day he set up camp in the professor's home office, clearing books and papers from the desk. He turned on the computer and started to compose a story about a killer with a fear of parking lots. It took him three days to finish a draft, which he printed and read through once before tearing it in half and burying it in the wastebasket.

The second version took him four days, and he considered it barely passable. He let the pages sit on the desk for a week, until one evening he put them away in a drawer and began to click away at a third version. He kept at it for several more nights until he had worked out a plot that satisfied him. The killer turned out to be the hero of the piece, and there was a twisted villain, and a woman the killer saved from the villain. The climax took place on the top level of a parking garage. Loogan went back and forth on whether the woman would stay with the killer after he saved her, but he decided it would be better if she left.

When he had the ending the way he wanted it, he printed a clean copy with a title on the first page and no byline or contact information, and then consulted his copy of *Gray Streets* for the magazine's editorial address. The address was a dozen blocks away, on the sixth floor of a building downtown. He walked there on a Saturday and the lobby doors were locked, but in the back he found a service entrance – a steel door propped open with a brick. A dingy stairway brought him to the sixth floor. He passed the offices of an accountant and a documentary production company, and there it was. Neat black letters on the pebbled glass of the door: GRAY STREETS.

He had the manuscript in an unmarked envelope. It was too thick to slide under the door but there was an open transom above, and he slipped the envelope over and heard it drop to the floor on the other side.

In the days that followed he returned to his routine, going to movies and lingering in coffee shops. Then, on a night when he couldn't sleep, he went down to the professor's office and sat before the computer screen, reading the story again line by line, tinkering with it as he went along. Trimming words and phrases and finding that the sentences were stronger without them. The next day he printed a new copy and after business hours he walked downtown and climbed the narrow stairs and slipped another envelope over the transom.

He was sure that would be the end of it. He made himself busy, branching out in his wanderings: to museums, to art galleries, to public parks. But it wasn't the end. His memory was sharp; he could recall sentences and paragraphs; he could rewrite them as he walked along a path or stood before a painting. On another sleepless night he descended to the professor's office, intending to delete the file from the computer; he stayed there for an hour, for three, mulling every word choice, fussing over every bit of punctuation.

He thought he would leave it there, a file on a hard drive. What would it matter if he printed it again? At twilight two days later he found himself in the hallway once more, holding the manuscript in an envelope under his arm. He stood before the door with the transom and tried to see beyond the pebbled glass. There might be nothing on the other side, he thought. Maybe just an empty room with two envelopes on the floor, gathering dust. And now a third to join them.

The door opened.

The man who opened it wore a dark blue suit with a

powder blue shirt and a silk tie. He paused in the motion of putting on his hat – a black fedora with a band that matched the suit. He saw Loogan and his eyes went to the envelope and the hat came down, the door swung open wide.

"It's you," he said. "Come in."

He retreated into the dimness of the room and after a few seconds a light came on in an inner office. From the lighted doorway he beckoned to Loogan with his hat.

Loogan took a few tentative steps. "I can't stay," he said.

"Why not?"

There was no answer for that. The answer that occurred to him – *Because it's going to be dark soon* – would sound ridiculous.

"You're not going to make me drag you in," said the man in the blue suit.

His voice had an oddly formal quality, the voice of an actor running lines. He directed Loogan to a chair and went around behind the desk. Among the papers on the desktop, Loogan saw his own two envelopes, each one sliced open along the edge.

"I've been waiting for you to come by," said the man in the blue suit. "That was clever, leaving your name off. It sparked my interest."

He tossed his hat onto a filing cabinet. Loogan said nothing.

"Is this the same one again, or a new one?"

Looking down at the envelope in his lap, Loogan said, "It's the same one. I've made some improvements."

"You ought to be careful. If it gets much better, I won't be able to publish it." The man took a seat at the desk.

"The reason I've been waiting for you – I wanted to make you an offer. I want you to work for me."

This was unexpected. Loogan frowned.

"I'm not really a writer."

"I don't need another writer. I've got writers scrabbling between the walls here, gnawing on the wiring. What I need is an editor."

Loogan shifted in his chair. "I don't think I'm qualified. I don't have the training."

"Nobody does," the man said. "It's not like people go to school for it. No one sets out to be an editor. It's something that happens to you, like jaundice or falling down a well." He pointed at Loogan's envelopes. "I like what you've done here," he said. "There's a clear improvement from one draft to the next. The question is, could you do the same thing with someone else's story?"

Loogan looked to the window, where the twilight was deepening. This isn't a problem, he thought. You can always refuse.

"I suppose I could," he heard himself saying, "but I'm not looking for a job. I don't know how I feel about coming into an office every morning."

The man in the blue suit leaned back. "You won't have to come in. You can work from home. You won't have to follow a schedule. You'll only have to do one thing."

"What's that?"

"You'll have to tell me what your name is."

A moment's hesitation. Then: "David Loogan."

"Tom Kristoll."

"The reason I've been [illegible] for you — I wanted to ask you [illegible] before you [illegible] for me."